Praise for *New York Times*
and *USA Today* bestselling author
AMELIA GREY
and her acclaimed novels

"Grey's unconventional meet-cute, compelling series backbone, and authentic characters move an interesting plot forward. . . . An engaging series start."

—*Kirkus Reviews*

"Grey's prose is strong and her characters are fun."

—*Publishers Weekly*

"Grey launches her First Comes Love series with a perfectly matched pair of protagonists, a vividly etched supporting cast, and plenty of potent sexual chemistry and breathtaking sensuality." —*Booklist*

"Each new Amelia Grey tale is a diamond. . . . A master storyteller." —*Affaire de Coeur*

"Devilishly charming . . . A touching tale of love."

—*Library Journal*

"Sensual . . . witty and clever . . . Another great story of forbidden love." —*Fresh Fiction*

"Grey neatly matched up a sharp-witted heroine with an irresistible sexy hero and lets the romantic sparks fly."

—*Booklist*

YOURS TRULY,
THE DUKE

AMELIA GREY

St. Martin's Paperbacks

This is a work of fiction. All of the characters, organizations, and events portrayed in this novel are either products of the author's imagination or are used fictitiously.

First published in the United States by St. Martin's Paperbacks, an imprint of St. Martin's Publishing Group.

YOURS TRULY, THE DUKE

For information, address St. Martin's Publishing Group, 120 Broadway, New York, NY 10271.

www.stmartins.com

ISBN: 978-1-250-85041-6

Our books may be purchased in bulk for promotional, educational, or business use. Please contact your local bookseller or the Macmillan Corporate and Premium Sales Department at 1-800-221-7945, ext. 5442, or by email at MacmillanSpecialMarkets@macmillan.com.

Printed in the United States of America

St. Martin's Paperbacks edition / April 2023

10 9 8 7 6 5 4 3 2 1

CHAPTER 1

FLOWERS

—MRS. SIGOURNEY

I'll tell thee a story, sweet,
Here, under this shady tree,
If thou'lt keep it safe in thy faithful breast,
I'll whisper the whole to thee.

Bold lettering on the stiff paper in his hand blurred as the Duke of Wyatthaven tried to concentrate on the infuriating matter before him. Proposing marriage.

To a lady he'd never met.

That prospect, and sharing an overindulgence of brandy throughout the evening with his two friends, had him inwardly shuddering with indecision. A feeling that was new to him. In his defense, he had more than adequate reason for the hesitancy. After all, tying himself to a woman for the rest of his life was something he hadn't expected to do for many years to come.

Flames from the recently tended fire had the finely appointed library of his London town house teeming with excessive heat, making the back of his neck damp. With its tall ceiling, packed tight with thousands of books, old family treasures of porcelains and silver, and some of his father's cherished inscribed marble tablets scattered about, the large chamber had always been a sanctuary for him. Until tonight.

But he'd get on with reading the letter to them.

"Dear Miss Fredericka Hale," he read aloud.

"It has not been my pleasure to be acquainted with you as of this writing; nonetheless, I am compelled to contact you. I am in need of a wife. Posthaste. You come with high recommendations from your esteemed solicitor to fill that position. I am assured you'd be agreeable to an offer of marriage from me and—"

"Wait, stop." Rick shook his head in earnest while holding up his hand. "That won't do at all."

"It's bloody awful, Wyatt," Hurst mumbled in agreement while shifting his weight to rest an elbow on the arm of his black velvet chair. "That's no way to start a proposal to the lady you want to marry."

That was the problem. He wasn't ready to marry. Wyatt let the sheet of his official engraved stationery drop from his hand and fall soundlessly to the leather mat on top of the Louis XIV desk. His temples throbbed, and the room dimmed for an instant when he looked away from the thick parchment.

Muttering a curse, he cast a long glance from one friend to the other. Their dour expressions said it all, making him glad he hadn't mentioned he'd already spent hours on the letter.

Wyatt leaned away from the grand heirloom his grandfather and father once sat behind, picked up his glass, and gave the amber liquid a swirl before throwing down a swallow. Proposing marriage was no easy task.

He looked at Rick and Hurst and listened as early

spring rain fell against the windowpanes. The fire crack-led. He didn't like being pushed into a corner, as was the case this night. Which was why he'd summoned his long-time friends to come to his town house for an ur-gent matter. Sequestered in his library, he'd hoped the two dukes, along with an expensive bottle of fortified wine that was now nearing empty, would help ease his mind concerning the dreaded task of how to ask a lady for her hand. So far, neither was working.

It wasn't so much Wyatt minded marrying or be-ing married. He had to take a wife one day. It was the thought of being a husband that had him twitching like a fly-bitten horse in the height of summer. By his father's own admission, the man had never been any good at be-ing a husband. Wyatt had no reason to think he would be either, given that everyone always said he was just like his father in many ways. Wyatt accepted that assessment and lived by it.

The Duke of Stonerick, called Rick by only a handful of people, was the first to break the silence. "Staring us down isn't going to make drivel better."

A muscle in Wyatt's cheek twitched. Rick had always known how to rile him. Or anyone else for that matter.

He reached over and slowly pushed the letter toward his friend. "What would you say?"

"That you bloody well leave out 'posthaste' and 'high recommendations.' Women are looking for . . . some-thing more."

"Exactly." Hurst cleared his throat and frowned. "They want to hear things that make them swoon. Start with a gentler nature, as in calling her *My dearest*, Miss Hale."

Wyatt grunted ruefully and grimaced in earnest. "She's not my dearest," he stated impatiently, and then proceeded to drain the last sip of his drink before plunking the heavy crystal back onto his desk.

"And she'll never be if you send that rubbish." Rick pointed to the paper with the hand that held his glass. "That's no way to ask for a lady's hand. It sounds like a blasted demand."

Hurst shrugged and brushed his pale-blond hair away from his forehead. "To be fair, it reads more like a business correspondence."

"It is," Wyatt said, dismissing the comments. Perhaps they were too deep in their cups to be of much help. He wasn't going to pretend he liked this intrusion of marriage into his life. "I'm trying to enter a contract with her, not a romance."

"You best think twice about romance," Hurst encouraged in his usual patient tone. "No doubt you'll need to consider it one day if you plan on having an heir to carry on the title."

An heir. That would mean being a father.

And that scared the hell out of him too.

Wyatt settled deeper into the back of his soft leather chair. This entire process was a damned nuisance. He didn't want to think about having a son. That was like marriage. Something he always thought he'd prepare for much later.

His father hadn't married until he was near forty and had managed to produce a healthy heir. Wyatt was living proof of that, so why had his grandmother taken it upon herself to rush him to the altar by leaving the codicil in her will?

Damnation, he was only twenty-eight. He'd want a son—an heir—one day. Maybe even three or four of them for good measure. And a daughter or two, as well.

Wyatt scoffed and pressed the bridge of his nose

between his thumb and middle finger, trying to ward off the throbbing ache that was beginning to pound at the back of his head. He knew better than to drink too much brandy and seldom did anymore, but it had been a difficult day.

His solicitor, who had been his father's solicitor, had blindsided him with news the codicil had to be read today. Twenty years after his grandmother's death. When Wyatt questioned why he wasn't notified earlier, Epworth replied that he'd been duty bound to do everything per the instructions of her last will and testament. She'd made these peculiar changes shortly before her death. In the addendum, she'd stipulated that if Wyatt wasn't married by that date, he'd have to marry within seven days or lose his inheritance from her.

Which was considerable. But it wouldn't matter, if only it were going to a worthy cause.

It wasn't the possibility of losing the property that had spurred his need to marry—it was the fact that his forfeiture would mean the four square blocks of land and buildings in London's fashionable downtown would go to The London Society of Poetry.

Poetry!

The most useless of skills he'd ever been taught. He would rather rot in Newgate than see the valuable assets fall into the hands of those stuffy old snoots. And worse, watch it be mismanaged and gutted by men who had eagerly accepted into their elite society and lavished praise on Wyatt's old professor from Eton, Mr. Percival Buslingthorpe. The man who'd given him his only failing marks in all his studies.

That wasn't the main reason Wyatt detested the man. He'd force shy, nervous boys to stand up and recite a selected amount of lyrics day after day. If he didn't like the way they performed he'd ridicule them without mercy in front of everyone. Should one dare make a stutter, he'd cruelly rap the boy's knuckles until they bled as he muttered, *"Discipline, son, discipline."*

Writing verse had never come easy to Wyatt—nor did it for most lads. But being a duke's son gave Wyatt privileges others didn't receive. Buslingthorpe would never have dared lay his thick stick to the son of a duke. But he'd certainly put the strength of his beefy arm onto the hands of many students, causing them to whimper from pain for days, and sometimes longer.

Wyatt stared into the glow of lamplight on the edge of his desk as memories swirled before him. He would never forget the sound of the crack of wood on bone or the sniffle of agony in the cold dark of night when boys thought no one would hear. Discipline should never make anyone cry in pain.

Brushing the haunting memories aside, Wyatt murmured lowly, "This whole idea of forcing a man into marriage is archaic." Wyatt sent a sidelong glance to both men. "Especially when it comes from the grave."

"Your grandmother isn't forcing you to do anything—from the grave or otherwise," Hurst assured him. "It's your choice to remain a bachelor for as long as you want—even unto death."

"Just forfeit your grandmother's fortune, and the high-nose poetry gents get to spend its rich rewards any way they choose," Rick added under his breath before sipping his drink.

Hurst grunted and seemed to study on that before saying, "It would be easier than trying to find a bride in a few days."

"Good point," Rick admitted candidly as he rose and leaned a hip against the desk.

Wyatt would marry the devil himself before he'd allow *poets* to gain control of his grandmother's fortune.

"No," he said emphatically, once more giving in to the inevitability of what had to be done. "You both know how I feel about poetry. I'd rather take a wife." The words rang hollow in his roaring ears as he grabbed hold of the brass caps at the ends of his chair. "And there's little time to do it. I must dispatch a messenger to Miss Hale with an offer by morning."

"Why Miss Hale?" Hurst asked, extending his long legs out and making himself comfortable by crossing his booted feet at the ankles. "Why not ask Miss Delamere? Her voice is so soft she makes everything sound heavenly. Or Lady Betina? There's a wildness about her that might keep you interested in her long after nuptials are said. Both are lovely and in London now. I daresay either of them would marry you before sunup."

"With a host of others waiting by the garden wall should either one be stricken with a fit of the vapors and not be able to say, '*I do,*'" Rick offered with a laugh as he picked up the decanter and added another splash to Wyatt's glass.

"Both ladies are enticing to be sure," Wyatt answered with all honesty. "As are most suitable misses, but they would be expecting a long wedding journey after the ceremony which would cause me to miss our upcoming Brass Deck tournaments. Upon return, they'd want to stay in London with me and be escorted to parties, Vauxhall, parks, and the like during the week and no doubt church on Sunday morning."

Rick nodded in agreement as he added brandy to Hurst's glass and then his own. "I'm told wives do expect a lot from husbands."

The thought of a lady depending on him for a

commitment that would last longer than an afternoon ride in the park or an evening enjoying the theatre or opera made his head pound all the harder. His father had drilled that into him about his mother often enough, declaring he could never do enough to please her. She always wanted more from him than he was capable of giving. More of his time. More appreciation for her feelings. More of his love.

She insisted her happiness depended on her husband. Wyatt couldn't refute anything his father had said. His mother died in her sleep before he took his first step. All Wyatt knew was that he didn't want to shoulder that kind of responsibility for another person.

"I need a duchess who will be little, if any, bother to me," he explained further. "Epworth swears Miss Hale is not only suitable but ideal in every aspect that would be of importance. Her family lineage is good. She's lovely in countenance, intelligence, and disposition."

Rick cleared his throat rather loudly and left a long pause before saying, "So, you think she'll be manageable, grateful, and dutiful because you chose her?"

Wyatt hadn't thought of it that way. "I do. More so, though, I'm told she prefers country life to London, which suits me perfectly as I have no plans to be a doting husband."

Nodding in agreement, his friends continued to enjoy their drink.

"Epworth says the letter will be a mere formality," Wyatt added after a few moments of silence among the three.

Rick gave a knowing chuckle as he poured the last of the brandy into his own glass and set the empty container on the table between his and Hurst's chair before retaking his seat. "I'm sure that's true. What lady declines an offer of marriage from a duke?"

"Indeed," Hurst agreed. "Country girl or city lass, she'd be insane to do so."

The throb at the back of Wyatt's head and neck continued. "Apparently, Miss Hale is in need of a husband quickly too."

Rick and Hurst looked questioningly at each other.

"Not for indiscreet reasons, I've been assured," Wyatt hastened to add.

"Glad you clarified that for us," Rick added as he threw another glance Hurst's way.

Wyatt could always count on Rick to jump to conclusions. He was usually fast acting in any situation and reckless to a fault.

"She has a young nephew and two nieces she's in charge of. Apparently, she's quite attached to the children. An older relative who has remained childless in her marriage recently went to Chancery Court with an appeal to take the children from Miss Hale. With only a modest allowance, she has little chance of winning her petition to keep them from her wealthier cousin unless she marries."

"The two of you should suit adequately then," Rick offered in a tone that seemed to suggest the matter was settled. "Since she's well-appointed with beauty, a pliant disposition, and has children to occupy her in the country, what more could either of you want?"

Hurst drummed his fingers on the arm of the chair in a thoughtful manner. "I agree. As much as you loathe the thought, I think you've found the ideal wife."

"Does Miss Hale have others seeking her hand?" Rick suddenly asked.

"Not that Epworth mentioned. Her reason for needing to marry isn't as pressing as mine. Courts aren't usually in a hurry to settle these matters unless a child's welfare is at stake. They'd rather see families have time to work them out if possible. I, on the other hand, only have a few days."

"Which brings us back to—" Hurst rose and thumped the letter with his middle finger.

The men were silent for a moment as they looked at one another.

"You can't win a lady's hand with simple persuasion of the facts," Hurst stated as if no other argument were necessary. "Ladies aren't sensible when it comes to matters such as marriage, romance, and the rest of it. They want to be wooed, even if they know false intentions are behind the excitement of it all. Swallow your distaste for such things and say them in your letter to her."

"He's right. Working on borrowed time as you are, you must romanticize your proposal with things a lady wants to hear."

"Please." Wyatt puffed out a laugh and sipped from his newly refreshed drink. "This will be an arrangement of convenience for both of us. You can't be serious about romancing."

"We are." Hurst leaned forward, resting both hands down on the desk. "We'll put our heads together and write a proper proposal asking for her hand. Ladies are fond of moonlight, flowers, flowing brooks—that sort of thing. Between the three of us, we should be able to come up with something romantic."

Stifling a groan of frustration, Wyatt picked up his glass again and downed a hefty swallow while he shoved aside the letter he'd written. "I can't babble on about moonlight and roses. She doesn't have long to make up her mind. She'll have to send a response immediately. I need to wed by Friday."

Rick shook his head. "Impossible. The Brass Deck is scheduled for a card tournament Friday evening. We'll have no chance of winning without you. We've already committed. Other groups have too."

"Let's think about this." Hurst rubbed his forehead as if it were pounding as hard as Wyatt's. "You could marry by noon, have the afternoon to accept congratulations, and still be at Lord Tartanville's for the tournament Friday evening."

"And no reason you can't make the fencing match on Saturday, as it isn't until two in the afternoon."

"Both of you are forgetting that I must first get her to accept my offer." Now that he'd decided to go through with this, he wanted to get the job done.

Hurst held up his hand. "In the letter, say you'll be arriving late on the morrow to hear her answer."

"Excellent idea," Rick praised. "All ladies want to think a man can't wait to marry them."

"Epworth can take care of posting banns, getting necessary documents ready to sign, and speaking to her trustee," Hurst added, brushing his too-long hair from his forehead again.

"Did you get more details about her?" Rick asked. "The color of her eyes? Are they icy blue, summer green, or golden brown?"

Wyatt's sight blurred again. His head had begun to spin and his ears were ringing louder than church bells on Christmas morning. He felt like a wolf caught in a hidden snare.

"Brown, I think," Wyatt answered in an offhand manner. "Dark-blond hair."

"That's a start." Hurst walked behind the desk. Patting

Wyatt on the shoulder, he plunked down his glass. "Let me have your chair. I'll do the honors. My hand is better than yours."

Wyatt willingly gave up his seat and Hurst grabbed a clean sheet of fine parchment and dipped the quill into ink. Hurst was the clear, levelheaded one of the trio of dukes. He'd kept them from participating in outright foolish endeavors that would have surely gotten them killed during the daring days of their youth.

"*My dearest and lovely Miss Hale,*" he wrote quickly as he said the words aloud. "*The thought of meeting you brings fondest remembrances of starlit spring evenings in London when night birds chirp from their nests in the budding trees and velvety flowers, newly opened, bow their blossoms to await morning's first ray of light.*" Hurst stopped and looked up at them. His green eyes narrowed as if he were looking into the sun. "Is that poetic enough?"

"Damned good." Rick inclined his head and tipped his glass toward his friend before taking a swallow. "How about adding '*the scent of lilacs danced on the air*'?"

"Excellent." Hurst hastily plunged the quill into the inkpot again and continued to write. "I've never met a lady who didn't adore the smell of lilacs. And we should add something about a rose among the thistles."

"And moonlight sparkling in her blue eyes."

"They are brown," Wyatt corrected.

"Even better. And she must have enchantingly dewy lips with blushing cheeks."

"Wait." Hurst held up the quill and blinked quickly several times as if trying to clear his muddled thoughts. "Best we don't mention the color of her eyes or hair. We can't afford to get the particulars wrong."

Did Wyatt really need to put all this frippery into the

letter? It sounded much like the poetic verse he'd been forced to recite while at Eton. He rubbed the back of his neck and rolled his shoulders restlessly, trying to loosen the tight knot of tension that had gathered at the top of his spine.

"You best have another bottle of your finest opened for us, Wyatt," Hurst said without looking up from his writing. "This might take all night."

And it almost did. There were many starts, stops, and arguing about the use of words and the true way to actually romance a lady into saying yes until the entire process of writing a proposal of marriage felt wrong and ridiculous.

The next morning, Wyatt woke seated at his desk. He blinked dry, grainy eyes and tried to ignore the fierce headache his overindulgence had gifted him. Regardless of his condition, he was thinking a little clearer. He read the pages of garbled words and winced.

How the hell had they come up with such blather in their drunken state? It was pure rubbish!

Without questioning himself, he tore up the final draft his friends had proclaimed as the perfect letter to woo a lady and plucked the quill from its cradle. On a fresh sheet of paper, he wrote:

Dear Miss Hale,
    I will arrive late in the afternoon with an offer of marriage.

Yours truly,
The Duke

CHAPTER 2

A CLUMP OF DAISIES
—RICHARD DANA

For in thy play,
I hear them say,
Here, man, thy wisdom borrow,
In heart be a child,
In word, true and mild,
Hold by faith, come joy, or come sorrow.

Fredericka Hale had always prided herself on her sensible behavior, tolerance of others, and quiet disposition. But of course, that was before she became mother to her sister's three young children. Since then, her patience always seemed to be at the snapping point, and she never felt as if she was in complete control of anything.

"Charles! Bella! Elise! Calm down!" Fredericka called from the dressing area of her bedchamber doorway while adding an amethyst-studded comb to her upswept hair. Her door was open, but she didn't know if the children could hear her above their own laughing and squealing as they tried to yell louder at one another.

If not for her plans, she might not have minded the noise so much. The children knew if they were going to be in the drawing room they should be either reading poetry or writing it. Today was too important for them to misbehave. It was nearly time for Mr. Maywaring to call on her. If he heard such screeching and carrying on, he'd never consider allowing the children to remain with her if they married.

With nervous fingers, she picked up one of the tear-drop earrings that matched her necklace and started fastening it to her ear. Mr. Maywaring was the last gentleman on her carefully detailed list of possible husbands. If she couldn't bring herself to welcome a proposal from him, she'd have to make another list.

The thought was almost as daunting as the idea of marriage.

Fredericka had already met with, considered, and decided against the other three gentlemen. An elderly earl had been her first choice, but after the second visit with him she concluded he was simply too much her senior and they would never suit. Sir Michael Salter was only fifteen years older than her twenty years and had children of his own. She'd been hopeful he'd be acceptable when she learned of his fondness of writing poetry. She imagined the two of them reading their verse to each other in the evenings. Those thoughts fled her mind quickly. As soon as she'd dismissed the children from the room, he was chasing her around the settee trying to kiss her. Such behavior would be expected after marriage, she supposed, but certainly not before. She wanted nothing more than to show him the door.

And then there was the very proper bachelor, Mr. Calvin Coppinger. He had immediately turned his nose up at the children when he entered the drawing room and later gave Bella a disdainful look when she started coughing. He made it quite clear he'd never be tolerant of her nieces and nephew or any children who were allowed to be in the presence of adults for an extended length of time.

Fredericka had no choice but to decide against him too. And counted it as no loss.

Now she was down to Mr. Maywaring. Most ladies would think him handsome enough with straight ash-brown hair and deep-set brown eyes, but he was a stiff fellow to say the least. He kept his collar and neckcloth so high and tight he could hardly move his head without turning his whole body. However, she supposed she could manage to live with that. When she'd engaged in conversation with him at the Christmas ball, and later at a spring dance, he'd kept sniffing. It was appropriate for a man to enjoy a pinch of snuff once in a while, but he seemed to take the indulgence to the extreme. The habit was most annoying.

Nonetheless, there were good things about him to consider as well. He had a delightful sister, whom Fredericka was quite fond of, and he was closer to her age than the other men.

She would have no choice but to start over and make another list if she didn't find Mr. Maywaring more acceptable than she had during her previous meetings with him. The problem was that she was running out of time. If her cousin, Jane, hadn't decided she wanted to take the children from Fredericka's care, a husband wouldn't be necessary.

Fredericka would have been content to remain unmarried and dedicate her life to taking care of Elise, Charles, and Bella. It was not only her duty but an honor. A husband had not been in her plans until her cousin challenged her rights. Shame that it was, a lady couldn't be a legal guardian for children who had property and must defer that position to her husband. Which meant Fredericka now had to find one.

Her barrister had made it clear that as a young miss

she would have little to no possibility of winning official guardianship of children. She had to marry if she wanted a chance of keeping them out of Jane's clutches. Even then it wasn't certain she would win custody.

Not only did Jane have a doting husband of eight years to promenade in front of the court, she and her husband had substantial allowances and an expensive barrister to represent them in court. Fredericka was an accepted member of Polite Society by birthright, but unfortunately, her finances had limitations.

She couldn't dare use any of the children's inheritance to keep them even if their trustee would allow it. The girls would need the money for their dowries when they made a match and Charles for his education and allowance until the time came when he could take over the Paddleton estate. The only things of theirs Fredericka made use of were the house and staff already working for her sister when she and her husband died.

Jane was nowhere to be found after that dreadful event and was happy for Fredericka to handle everything. She didn't offer to move in and help comfort the broken-hearted children with the terrible loss that made them orphans. They had never been invited to visit with Jane at her impressive estate in Kent. Not even for Christmastide. When Elise was ill with fever, Jane merely sent a note of mild concern, and that was just a few months ago. No, her interest only started when she finally accepted, after years of marriage, she must be barren and would never have a babe of her own.

At first Fredericka's heart ached for Jane's devastating news, but that was before she realized Jane wanted to separate the children and take only Charles into her home. She was going to kindly allow Fredericka to keep the girls.

She would never allow that to happen to her sister's children. Losing their parents was hard enough. They couldn't be separated from one another. To lose their brother would be far too upsetting for them.

Besides, she loved Charles and the girls equally. How could she give up any of them?

Fredericka clasped her hands together for a moment to regain her composure before picking up her necklace. Though it had been over a year, she still felt tightness in her chest, a catch in her throat, and the hollow sinking pull of guilt in the pit of her stomach whenever she thought of the passing of her sister. She'd often tried to erase those feelings of pain and sorrow from her mind but finally decided they were ghosts that would never go away.

She would have to learn to live with them. Every time they were brought to mind, it hurt deeply that she felt responsible for her sister's death. If Fredericka hadn't insisted Angela go with her husband to London that day they wouldn't have stopped at the tavern and eaten the spoiled food that had poisoned their stomachs so severely recovery wasn't possible. Angela hadn't wanted to go, but Fredericka had insisted a short visit to London with her husband would be good for their troubled marriage. Instead, it had ended their lives.

A shrill peal of laughter from Bella shuddered through Fredericka. She swallowed the lump that had lodged in her throat. This wasn't the time to think about things she couldn't change or bury. She had to move forward and hope this would be a joyous day.

After connecting the two ends of the necklace, she pressed her hands down the front of her pale-amethyst day dress and looked into the mirror one more time. She didn't want a strand of hair to be out of place when she greeted Mr. Maywaring. He was a dandy of the highest order and fashion was of upmost importance to him. Pushing one of the combs deeper into her hair, she made a hasty exit from her bedchamber.

Her efforts to halt the noise below from the top of the stairs fell on deaf ears. The squealing continued as she made it to the bottom and called the children's names again in an effort to get them under control. She had no idea how only two small girls and a boy could sound as if a group of thirty youngsters were playing on the back lawn.

Fredericka rounded the doorway and almost lost her breath.

"Sweet gooseberries!" she managed to whisper when shock left her immobile.

The drawing room was in shambles. Bella was pounding seven-year-old Charles in the chest with a cluster of long-stemmed peonies. Pink petals from the blooms fluttered everywhere. Elise was bouncing a pillow off the top of his head. His laughter was loud enough to raise the rafters and caused the freckles across his nose to brighten.

Newsprint and other pillows were strewn around the floor, along with several blooms from the destroyed bouquet. A gray woolen shawl that should have been neatly draped across the end of the settee was wadded in a ball. The expensive silk tapestry that Fredericka had finished embroidering just a week ago was being trampled beneath Charles' big feet. At the claw-footed legs of a side table, a blue velvet cushion lay in a puddle of water from the overturned vase of flowers.

"Stop immediately!" Fredericka exclaimed, though it didn't appear they heard her above their gaiety. "Quiet this instant!" she called in a louder, more defiant tone as she stomped toward them. "Or I shall send you to bed this evening without the sweet confections Mrs. Dryden is making for you at this very moment."

The siblings seemed to freeze in their steps and stared at her with their big blue, innocent eyes. It always amazed her how guiltless they could look whenever she caught them doing something they shouldn't be doing.

Which, fortunately, wasn't too often.

Charles held his spindly arms limp at his sides as if he hadn't moved a muscle in years. Elise clasped her hands behind her back and delicately swung her bony shoulders from side to side. Bella looked down at the destroyed peonies in her little hands as if to wonder what had happened to the blossoms.

Fredericka tried to be patient with the children. She and their mother, Angela, had been orphaned at a young age too. Their deep hurts and heartaches were emotional, but they wouldn't have dreamed of participating in some of the things that Bella, Charles, and Elise had done. While Fredericka did her best to keep the children in line, she readily admitted to herself she had a problem with them misbehaving and indulging in youthful folly. She wanted them to be perfect.

"I can't believe this." Fredericka's voice was tinged with fatigue and irritation as she surveyed the jumble of mess once again. "It's almost time for Mr. Maywaring to arrive. Can you imagine what he would think if he walked up to the door and heard the way you were carrying on? Or if he saw this disarray? He'd turn on his heels and march off without a word. I've explained to you that you mustn't misbehave when I'm expecting a visitor." Realizing what she'd said, she amended, "Well, you should never misbehave, but certainly not when guests are due."

Fredericka shook her head in frustration. She was constantly overwhelmed by all she didn't know about caring for children. Keeping up with a five-, seven-, and nine-year-old wasn't easy. And she had very little help from their governess.

"Where is Miss Litchfield?"

Elise and Charles only stared at her and blinked.

"She's in the garden resting her eyes," Bella said calmly. "She gets sleepy when she sits in sunshine."

Fredericka could always count on the youngest to answer first.

"We didn't want to disturb her, so we came inside to play," Elise admitted quietly, brushing her golden-colored tresses to the back of her shoulders.

"Th-the s-sun was hot anyway," Charles added, his head bobbing to underscore his comment. "B-but she likes to rest in the f-fresh afternoon air."

If only the children wanted to nap every afternoon, Fredericka thought crossly.

She took in a deep breath, hoping to settle the annoyance she was feeling for Miss Litchfield, who could sleep through anything. The governess was too old to care for three rambunctious children, but she had been working for Angela when Fredericka took responsibility for them. After much thought, Fredericka decided it was best to keep everything as normal as possible, and that included retaining Miss Litchfield and all the other staff employed.

In the midst of all the other challenges, each child had issues that had arisen since their parents' deaths. Bella was having accidents in the bed several times a week. Charles had developed a stutter that seemed to be getting worse, not better, and Elise had an uncommon fear of not wanting to be left alone. Even during the daytime.

Being a mother was far more than Fredericka could have imagined. She never dreamed she'd have this responsibility, but now, more than a year later, she knew she could never give them up without a fierce fight. She loved them as if they were her own. Which was why she had to marry and give herself every advantage possible to keep them with her. Right now, Mr. Maywaring was her best chance.

"I'll help you clean up," Bella said with a chubby-cheek smile that always delighted Fredericka.

But then, her heart usually melted whenever one of the children looked at her so happily. "All of us will help," Fredericka said, softening her tone. "Bella, pick up every blossom and throw them on the fire. Don't miss a one. Elise, gather the newsprint, wad it tight, and do the same. Put the usable flowers back in the vase, and then pluck the petals from your sister's hair and retie the ribbon on her dress. Charles, take up that tapestry you're standing on, fold it properly, and place it on the window seat. When finished, I want to see each of you sitting down and quiet as a mouse." She pointed to the three straight-back chairs lined up near the fireplace. "I don't want to hear one peep out of you while Mr. Maywaring is here. We need to show him that you know how to conduct yourselves properly when we have guests."

Quietly, the children started working and so did Fredericka. She had to remain formidable with the children or they would completely take over the household.

It was an odd thing to do, and most inappropriate, but she needed the children to be in the room when she invited prospective husbands to call on her. Whomever she married had to understand they came with her. The girls would not be sent to stay with Jane. And at seven, Charles was still too young to attend Eton or any other boarding school.

They were hers to love and care for as long as they needed her. Not Jane's or anyone else's.

Fredericka resettled the throw and picked up a book she hadn't seen lying under one of the chairs and placed it on top of the secretary in the corner. While trying to decide what to do with the drenched pillow that had soaked up the flower water, she heard a forceful knock on the front door.

Dread filled her chest. Her hands tightened on the soft cushion.

Marriage had been something she'd considered years ago but not now. At the time, thoughts of a handsome gentleman to make her swoon and sweep her off her feet with sweet smiles, romantic words, and brief touches on her arm or hands were welcomed dreams. She enjoyed putting her contemplations about romantic love in verse and poetry and had been working on her own book. Now such things were visions of the past. Most of her poetic writings were about flowers—not fanciful ideas of love. She wanted a man who would help make sure her sister's children stayed in her care and flourished.

Fredericka turned to them. "That will be Mr. Maywaring. Hop onto your chairs and keep your hands folded in your laps as you've done before. Don't say anything other than a greeting and only if he should speak to you first. Otherwise—" She put her forefinger to her lips, pursed them, and whispered, "Shh."

"W-what if I have to s-scratch my nose or c-chin?" Charles asked, twisting his fingers together nervously in front of him.

"Of course you may do that. Your elbow or anywhere else. Well, almost anywhere. You know what I mean, Charles. This is not the first time we've been through this. If you remember your manners, everything will be fine. Your evening dessert depends on how well you conduct yourselves."

And, most likely, where they would live for the rest of their childhood also hinged on their behavior. But she couldn't tell them that. Not yet anyway. There was no need to alarm them by letting them know how close they were to having to live with Jane.

"I'm thirsty," Bella whimpered as she crawled onto her chair.

"M-me too," Charles whined.

Fredericka cleared her throat, feeling wretched she'd been so terse with them earlier. But what was she to do? She was never supposed to be the disciplinarian, but she had to be since Miss Litchfield hadn't stepped up to the responsibilities of her job to do it.

It wasn't surprising they wanted a drink after all the playing. But there wasn't time. "If all goes well with Mr. Maywaring, I'll see to it you get milk and a cranberry tart after he leaves. How does that sound?"

Bella smiled. Charles clapped his hands, and Elise hesitated, but slowly nodded in appreciation.

Fredericka hurriedly stuffed the wet pillow into the corner of the settee as the housekeeper stepped into the doorway.

"Excuse me, Miss Hale. The Duke of Wyatthaven is here to see you."

A duke? To see her?

CHAPTER 3

TO A YELLOW VIOLET
—ANON.

Oft in the sunless April day,
Thy early smile has stay'd my walk;
But 'midst the gorgeous bloom of May,
I pass'd thee on thy humble stalk.

Puzzlement wove through Fredericka as the shadowed outline of a powerfully built man appeared behind her housekeeper, causing Fredericka's heartbeat to skip with apprehension. She'd never met the Duke of Wyatthaven, but she'd certainly read about him many times in the scandal sheets and Society pages. And from the little she could see of him, what she'd read was true. He was quite tall, handsome to a fault, and simply magnificent to look at.

"Thank you, Mrs. Dryden," Fredericka said.

Her housekeeper hesitated before turning away. The duke stepped forward, staring straight at Fredericka.

It took a moment or two for her eyes to adjust from the bright sunlight streaming into the drawing room to the darker corridor. Blinking so she could focus on his intimidating form, she noticed the way he watched her. Intensely. As if he was demanding her attention without saying a word. When their eyes met, there was a strange and immediate connection. An odd tingle raced through her and settled low. She didn't know what it was or why it happened, but she'd felt it and sensed he had too. She wasn't experienced in such matters but knew it was a sensation unlike the usual passing interest between a lady and a gentleman.

Seconds later, his eyes narrowed as if he wanted to conceal his gaze. That didn't stop their penetrating observation of each other from continuing.

The thought that he didn't want her regarding him too closely pricked her interest even more. His gaze skimmed over her from head to toe with candid concentration, then strayed to the children behind her, a curious expression on his face.

The duke was dressed in expertly tailored black trousers and coat, gleaming white linen shirt, and moderately starched neckcloth—elegantly knotted. His blue-striped waistcoat, seamed with burnished brass buttons, fit his wide chest and slim waist to perfection. Thick chestnut-colored hair with an attractive wave swept evenly but naturally across his forehead. Highly polished, expensive boots added to his impressive appeal.

Not surprisingly, there was a touch of arrogance to his stance that caused a change in her breaths. She detected a prevailing inner strength within him that most ladies would find attractive.

So did she.

It was no wonder he was written about so often. He looked every inch the commanding and dashing rake the pink pages swore he was.

"Miss Hale," he said, striding into the room with a casual confidence few men had mastered. "It's a pleasure to meet you."

His voice, deep and smooth, washed over her like heated cider splashed with a heaping spoonful of brandy.

She wasn't the type to be drawn to exceptionally fine-looking men, but with this one, her senses obviously made an exception. All of them seemed intentionally concentrated on him and delighted by what they saw, felt, and heard. Her heart thudded loudly, her stomach felt jumpy, and a prickling of something stimulating skipped wildly and deliciously across the tips of her breasts.

Still, Fredericka managed a perfunctory curtsey and slight smile. "My pleasure as well, Your Grace."

She'd always heard dukes were above reproach. This proved it. They could make up new rules for themselves and Society and receive no backlash for breaking the ones the elite of the ton held most dear. Obviously, that included the highly inappropriate act of introducing himself to someone.

He stopped a step or two in front of her. Up close, he was even more imposing. That caused another catch in her breath. They looked into each other's eyes for a long moment. If she wasn't careful she could find herself mesmerized by the light blueish-gray color. There was a strong aristocratic quality to his features—high cheekbones, slender-bridged nose, wide, attractive mouth, and determined set to his square chin.

His gaze swept slowly down her face and lingered on her lips. A tingling sensation raced over her. That made her look at his mouth again and an unexpected surge of womanly desire held her spellbound for a few seconds. She'd never been so profoundly aware of a man before.

Pushing aside the newfound and heady feelings, she lightly cleared her throat before asking, "Would you like to sit down?"

He shook his head. "Not now, thank you."

Good. Whyever he was there, he apparently didn't intend to stay long.

Confident he'd soon be gone, she asked, "Then may I offer you refreshment?"

He didn't move an inch from his uncompromising stance. "Thank you, no," he answered in an even tone.

Wonderful. That was even better. Much as she hated for it to be true, his physical presence was making her uneasy. On this day, when she was waiting to meet another man to consider the possibility of marrying him, she didn't need these improper sensations erupting inside her for such a fine-looking man who exuded power and lived a devil-may-care life.

The duke looked past her to the children again. The corners of his eyes tightened, but this time seeming with more concern rather than curious expression. That was understandable, she supposed. Children were not usually seen in drawing rooms. Nevertheless, she saw no reason to explain their presence, since his arrival was unexpected. For now, she simply needed to find out what he wanted and send him on his way before Mr. Maywaring arrived.

Which could be any minute.

Fredericka exhaled a steadying breath. "Then please tell me how I may help you."

Cocking his head back, centering his concentration solidly on her once more, he offered, "Perhaps we could take a walk in the garden."

That was a devilishly brash invitation so quickly after introducing himself to her. What nerve. Yet uncommonly, her pulse thumped erratically. Her stomach tumbled over at the thought of strolling elbow-to-elbow alongside this powerful-looking man.

For a fleeting moment she wanted to accept that invitation, but before she had time to seriously consider such a bad idea, her sensible self returned and took over.

She remembered Miss Litchfield snoozing in the sun and immediately answered, "It's rather sunny out, Your Grace. I would need time to properly prepare for an outing—put on my bonnet and cape. Fetch my parasol."

Fredericka didn't know His Grace at all, and not any man really well, but the duke's countenance seemed un-usual. It was as if he expected her to somehow know why he was there. She gave him an inquisitive stare.

"Is your driver lost and in need of directions?"

His brows knitted together in a frustrated frown. "No. Why do you ask?"

Was he deliberately being evasive with his answers? They'd all been so short. Perhaps he was simply a man of few words.

"I don't know," she answered, beginning to feel a little flustered. "I thought perhaps, well—it doesn't matter."

The duke acknowledged her pitiful answer with a nod and asked, "What's wrong with the children?"

Alarmed, Fredericka recoiled and looked back at them, thinking Charles had made a rude or funny face or maybe Bella had stuck out her tongue to the duke.

A brush of pride rushed through Fredericka and her spine straightened as she let out a satisfied breath. They were behaving beautifully. Not twitching or stirring about at all. The girls had their hands neatly folded in their laps and Charles had made a perfect little steeple with his fingers, keeping them still. They weren't even staring at the duke with youthful interest.

His bold and unwarranted question irritated her, and she faced him defiantly. "Nothing's wrong with them," she answered more tersely than would be considered an appropriate tone to take with a duke. But he deserved no quarter for his somewhat rude comment. They weren't doing anything that could disturb him. "They are all sweet natured. . . ." She paused and swallowed hard as memories of peonies flying through the air and water puddling on the floor flashed before her. "Most of the time. They're healthy, bright, and obeying mannerly rules admirably well."

"Rules," he muttered as if he had great distaste for the word. "They look like wooden soldiers."

Fredericka gasped in outrage. "What did you say?" She lifted her shoulders so high she rolled onto the tips of her toes to make herself almost face-to-face with the duke. She gave him what she hoped was a withering glare. "Whatever would make you say such a thing about a child?"

His brows rose and his lips parted ever so slightly. "It's an observation," he argued.

"A critical observation," she said impulsively, not caring at the moment how she spoke to the duke.

"No," he said without backing down. "I don't criticize children."

"You could have fooled me," she shot back, and then set her lips in a resolute line.

"It's a fact," he stated with no ambiguity. "They aren't moving."

Determined not to let him rile her further before sending him on his unmerry way, she settled flat on her feet once more. The last thing she needed was to be in an agitated state when Mr. Maywaring arrived, but the duke was testing her limits. "What do you mean?"

"Children are supposed to be squirming about as if they have ants in the seats of their unmentionables. They should be swinging their legs, moving their arms, snickering, or elbowing each other. They've hardly blinked since I walked into the room."

"Of course they aren't fidgeting," she remarked quite proudly, thinking the boorish duke should have offered an apology for his insult, not an explanation. She clasped her hands together tightly, lest she seriously consider attacking him before asking him to leave. He truly was beyond the pale with his *observation*! "They are being polite and mannerly in your presence. As they should be."

His expression looked more suspicious than persuaded with her answer.

Really, she thought vengefully, it would probably be best if they were frolicking with abandon and screaming to the high heavens as they were only minutes ago. That would send the insolent, commanding man on his way in a hurry. Perhaps she'd give them liberty to do so. That way she could see how fast he could run.

However, self-important as the duke thought he was, he might merely be upset they hadn't stood and given him proper courtesy when he entered the room. Fine. Maybe then she could find out why he was there. If he wanted a bow and two curtseys, she'd indulge his whim. She quickly turned to the children and made a motion with her hand for them to stand, which they obeyed.

"Your Grace, may I present the Misses Elise and Bella Baldwin and their brother, Master Charles."

He nodded to them and, after giving the duke the recognition his title deserved, they quietly hopped back onto their chairs with hardly a rustle of sound. That showed him. They had been exemplary and flawless. She wanted to rush over and give them hugs. Her sister would have been proud of them. And of Fredericka for teaching them so well.

Satisfied, she turned to the duke and smiled quite splendidly. "Now, I believe it's time you told me why you're here."

He looked at her as if wondering why she asked him that question. "I'm here concerning the letter I had delivered to you."

Letter?

Instantly thinking it might have something to do with the children, since he had just mentioned them, Fredericka visibly tensed. "I'm sorry, Your Grace. I don't recall receiving correspondence from you."

He lifted his brows in doubt. "My courier didn't arrive with it earlier today?"

"Today?" She glanced at the clock on the secretary. In another couple of minutes Mr. Maywaring would be late. That worried her. Best she hurry the duke along. She didn't need a discussion going on about the children when Mr. Maywaring arrived. That would be disastrous no matter the duke's reason for being there.

"Oh," she said as politely as she could muster. "It's quite possible it came while we were out for a walk. If so, it was placed on my desk. I don't usually look through my mail until evenings after the children have gone to bed."

The duke lifted his chin a notch without taking his gaze off hers and scoffed ruefully. She didn't know what that sound was for, but he certainly wasn't happy to hear her answer. That was all right with her. She wasn't happy he was lingering.

She had things to do and getting rid of him was at the top of her list.

He relaxed his arms and stepped closer to Fredericka as another breath of sound passed his lips. There was something unsettling about the intensity of his expression. It gave the feeling he was trying to see inside her and know her thoughts, which made her more determined to stay in control of the situation.

"Why did you do that?" she asked, beginning to feel more unease at his seeming reluctance to leave.

"What?"

"You made a sound as if you were filled with disbelief."

For a moment, his eyes seemed clouded with confusion as he continued to take in every detail of her face. "More on the order of frustration."

She was feeling that as well.

"It had to do with the letter you haven't opened. A lot of . . ." He paused briefly and then offered a smile so devilishly sweet she sensed a warm fluttering swirling in her lower stomach. "A lot of thought and time went into it. Now I find you haven't even read it."

Wanting to fortify her position and get on with this, she asked, "Should I go get it?"

A short, attractive laugh tumbled from his throat and caused a shiver of excitement to race up her spine.

"It's not important now that I'm here."

"Good," she said, as if to let him know that settled the matter.

For all his bluster about the children earlier, there was a rakish hint of mystery surrounding him that drew her and made her want to know more about him. But she was intelligent enough to know that wasn't a good idea. She needed to spend her time, womanly interests, and charms on men who were matrimonial candidates.

The duke made no comment or movement to indicate he was about to leave. She looked at the clock again. Perhaps he was waiting on her to make the first move.

"Well, in that case, Your Grace, may I show you to the door?"

Fredericka moved to pass the duke, but with more speed than she would have thought possible he appeared in front of her, blocking the way. Her heart thumped with trepidation at his lightning-fast reaction, yet somehow she managed not to flinch. Her chest heaved, but not from fear. Taking care of the children had taught her not to give in to any type of panic. She must always be strong and courageous for them no matter what was happening.

The duke leaned in so close she felt as if his forehead was going to touch hers. She caught the enticing, familiar scents of fine woolen fabric, iron-pressed linen, and woodsy shaving soap. A shiver of anticipation peppered her skin.

Fredericka didn't think she'd ever been so close to a man. Not even when dancing. His proximity to her wasn't threatening in any way. It was quite stimulating. Impossible as that was to believe, for a moment or two she wanted to forget about the responsibility of the children, the pressure from Jane to give them up, Mr. Maywaring's sniffing, and everything else that had occupied her mind for the past few days and just enjoy the sudden romantic feelings that cloaked her like a warm blanket in the bleakest of winter.

But those were foolish and fanciful notions she didn't need to dwell on when such important matters were at stake.

Her gaze dropped to his mouth. There was a serious set to his full lips and strong, square jaw. An intense gleam brightened his eyes. "I'm not leaving, yet. Perhaps we should have a private conversation."

His words did nothing to alleviate her worry, irritation, and impatience to have him gone, but they did bring her sanity crashing back. Whether or not he meant to intimidate her, he had.

But that only strengthened her resolve not to recoil or budge an inch from his powerful body.

She searched his tight brow. "It's not necessary nor appropriate for us to be alone, Your Grace," she reminded him, once again wanting only to be rid of this man who infuriated her but also reminded her of suppressed womanly desires. "Tell me what you want, and I'll be happy to oblige so you can be on your way."

His brows rose in anticipation briefly, but then he lowered his lids slightly over those expressive blueish-gray eyes as they suddenly filled with amusement. A trace of a grin curved the corners of his mouth. Without warning or reason as far as she could tell, he moved his face even closer to hers and placed his lips just above her ear.

In a husky and almost sensual voice, he said, "That's good to hear, Miss Hale. I know you are looking for a husband, and I'm here to ask you to marry me."

CHAPTER 4

THE EVERLASTING ROSE
—ANSTER

Thine is, methinks, a pleasing dream,
Lone lingerer in the icy vale,
Of smiles that hail'd the morning beam,
And sighs more sweet for evening's gale.

Fredericka felt as if she'd swallowed an apple. Whole.
While a tingle ran through her limbs.

His words couldn't have startled her more if he'd declared he was her long-lost twin. She couldn't speak or
blink. Staggering heat blazed up her neck and into her
cheeks like fire sweeping through dry brush. Sheer will,
summoned from deep inside herself, kept her legs from
wobbling out from under her. Only when she realized the
children had gasped and stirred behind her did she spin
and see a bug-eyed expression on each innocent little
face.

A tidal wave of emotions too tumultuous to discern
washed over her.

Though his words were clear to her as a resounding
bell, she whirled back to him and asked, "Did you say
what I think you said?"

Locked in her stare, he nodded slowly, seeming not to
have noticed the astonishment that had to be evident in

her expression and voice. Typically, she was fairly good at concealing her emotions, no matter the circumstances. However, right now she was astounded.

Seconds ticked by. A sense of inadequacy filled her, threatened to overwhelm her, but pulling up her outrage like a shield, she forced her voice to remain steady and said, "You can't be serious."

He seemed to reflect on that for a moment. "Proposing to a lady isn't something a man would joke about. Not even a scoundrel like me."

"You can't just come in here and say an incredible thing like that to me," she challenged, keeping her voice low. "And in front of the children! What were you thinking?"

Fredericka rushed over and helped Bella off the chair. "Elise, go with Charles and Bella out to the garden and find Miss Litchfield. Tell her I said to take you to the schoolroom by the back stairway."

Bella gave Fredericka a wide girlish grin and asked, "Are you getting married?"

"No, no, of course not," she mumbled nervously, and immediately realized what a blatant untruth that was and hastened to add, "not today, anyway."

"I want a wedding when I get married," Bella announced innocently.

"Is that why you've been receiving gentlemen guests?" Elise asked, looking confused and almost grief-stricken by the thought. "Are you going to leave us?"

"Leave you?" Fredericka's heart squeezed at the pain in Elise's voice. She glanced over to the duke and gave him what she hoped was a stern expression that said, *Look at what you've done*, and then turned a softer countenance to Elise. "I would never do that, my darling. What would I do without you three in my life?"

Fredericka felt the sharp prick of guilt as she realized she'd waited too long to explain what she was being forced to do. She had wondered if, at the age of nine, Elise would know what Fredericka must do. Certainly, Bella at five and Charles at seven were much too young to comprehend Fredericka needed to marry so she would have a better chance of keeping them under her guardianship.

Elise remembered more about her parents than the other two and it had taken her longer to accept the fact that her mother was never coming home. She still had real fears of being left alone again. Because of that, Fredericka had always considered her more fragile than the other two.

There were times in life when things had a way of getting out of hand. Sometimes things happened that you had no way of preparing yourself for. This was one of them. No doubt, it would have been better to break the news of a possible marriage to Elise in a gentler fashion. And Fredericka would have, after she'd settled on a husband.

She laid a comforting hand on Elise's shoulder and, with the other, she gently took hold of her chin and looked sweetly into the young girl's eyes. "I'm not going anywhere. I promise to tell you everything later tonight after the little ones have gone to sleep. All right?"

The doubt didn't leave her face, but Elise nodded and then suddenly grabbed Fredericka around the waist and held tightly.

"Don't leave me," the little girl whispered.

Fredericka returned the hug with an affectionate squeeze and then gently pulled Elise's arms from around her waist. "You have my word. Now, please do as I say. Come on. All of you out into the garden to find Miss Litchfield and let me talk to the duke."

"W-w-what about our f-fruit t-tart for b-being good?"

"Yes, of course," she said, brushing Charles' sandy-blond hair away from his forehead in a gesture to calm him. It was so like a boy to think of his tummy while little girls thought of their hearts. "Thank you for reminding me. I'll have Mrs. Dryden take them up to the schoolroom for you and tell her to add cups of warm chocolate. Would you like that?"

Satisfied, Charles whooped and quickly covered his mouth. Elise grabbed hold of Bella's hand as they walked out of the room.

Now it was time to deal with the duke. He stood quietly, regarding her with daring interest that sent a shiver of expectancy down her spine. She feared he wouldn't be as easy to handle as the children. But handle him she would.

After taking in a deep breath, Fredericka regained her composure and strode over to the towering man. She didn't stop until she stood toe-to-toe with him. All her hard-earned lessons in decorous behavior failed her. "Look what you have done! What kind of man introduces himself with a proposal of marriage? Forget 'How do you do, Miss Hale.' And in front of delicate children! You should be ashamed of yourself. Though based on your rumored reputation, I'm sure you aren't."

He crossed his arms casually on his chest and looked as if he didn't have a care in the world. "How is a proposal something to be ashamed of? You need to get married. I need a wife. Seems simple to me."

"To a simpleton, maybe."

"Fine, my apologies." His jaw ticked, but to his credit he seemed sincere. "I didn't know it would upset the little girl. But tell me what is so horrible about something as common as marriage, Miss Hale?"

"It's a delicate matter and not something to be talked about in front of little ones," she asserted. He was unbelievable. Fredericka moved her face closer to his, not caring whether she kept her voice low. Before the children became her responsibility, she was always calm, always reasonable, always in control. She never raised her voice to anyone. Certainly not a guest.

And a duke at that!

"It's an adult subject," she finished firmly, still not ready to forgive or accept his rational, purely masculine thought process.

He dropped his arms to his sides and pinned his intruding gaze on her eyes. "I sent you a letter stating my intentions," he assured her in a tone almost as severe as her own, and then grimaced. "Shortly after I arrived, I asked if we could take a walk in the garden. Speak in private. You refused. Twice. I assumed it was all right to talk in front of the children."

She expelled a surprised sound. Her chest heaved as her nose edged closer to his. Despite his statement being true, she couldn't believe he was suggesting this debacle with the children was somehow her fault.

"I refused because I had no idea what you wanted to say. You could have given me a hint."

He looked incredulously at her and folded his arms across his chest once again, seeming unperturbed by the censure in her glare. "Tell me, how does one hint at a marriage proposal, Miss Hale?"

Fredericka had no idea. Proposals were a man's responsibility. Still, she said, "You could have simply stated you had a delicate matter to discuss with me."

"Ah," he whispered softly, giving her another one of his charming grins as he nodded slowly. His voice lowered again. "You like the word 'delicate.' I'll be sure to remember."

In that moment, she realized they were standing so close they could have touched. Kissed. And it was all her doing. She had advanced on him without realizing it. She was the one on her toes, lifting her face to his, staring into his dreamy-colored eyes, and making the inappropriate advances. That's when her heart tripped, and when she should have moved away from him.

But she couldn't. Not yet.

She once again felt that intangible connection between them that seemed to cause her world to shift and change. She couldn't help but think he must have felt it too. His expression was suddenly unreadable and his body still as his gaze drifted over her face like a caress.

It was exhilarating to be so near him she could feel the heat of his body, hear his erratic breaths, inhale the scent of his fresh-shaved face. She didn't want to deny herself the immense pleasure of enjoying these titillating sensations arousing her senses to new heights. If only for a few seconds. Surely that would be long enough for her to remember and study at a later time.

"You intrigue me, Miss Hale," he said in a soft tone as his lips moved closer to hers.

Yes. He had felt the attraction between them too. She drew in a steady breath and fought the impulse to stay exactly where she was and continue to drink in all the sensations surrounding him.

The man she was experiencing right now must be the captivating man some of the scandal sheets swore he was even though others swore he was a permanent rake who would never be tamed. Whichever the case, she had to gain control of herself and not get caught up in the things about him she found appealing and inviting, or wondering why her heart was pounding.

They were too close. But she couldn't complain when she hadn't bothered to step away. Keeping a man in his proper place was a lady's responsibility. She couldn't allow him to make her forget that.

She slowly backed up a step and asked, "How did you hear I was considering marriage?"

"Nothing is private or even sacred in London, Miss Hale. Not the streets, the parks, the drawing rooms, nor the bedchambers."

From what she read in the scandal sheets, she believed that to be true. But here in the country where social standards were more relaxed and houses were much farther apart, she thought she could entertain a gentleman or two with afternoon tea and polite conversation and no one would notice.

"It had to be my barrister," she mused. "No one else knew. I wanted it kept quiet because of the children."

He pursed his lips and remained silent, letting her know he wasn't going to admit to anyone telling him.

"I didn't realize it had gotten out that I—" She looked away, unable to finish her sentence. It really didn't matter how he found out. She was determined to manage this as she had everything else since she became the children's unofficial guardian.

The significance of her situation suddenly felt heavier than it ever had. It was one thing for her to be privately considering gentlemen as prospects for the position of husband; to have one actually offer for her hand was most unexpected. What was she going to do?

"It's not public knowledge from what I understand," he added in a soft tone.

A swift measure of relief shivered through her. It was

good to know she wasn't being talked about in polite circles.

His expression gentled. "I know you have a cousin who wants to take guardianship of the children from you and, because of circumstances, her chances of winning in Chancery Court are good."

Fredericka's heart pounded at hearing him speak the cold, hard truth of her situation even though he did so with a measure of understanding. Only natural instinct kept her calm on the outside while inside she felt the turmoil of what losing the children would do to her.

"You will be in a better position to keep them if you are wed," he continued. "Especially to me."

"You?" She exhaled unevenly, feeling overcome by the unfairness of it all. No, she would be better with Mr. Maywaring, who was obviously now late for their afternoon visit. "How can *you* benefit me, Your Grace? You have the worst reputation in London. You've renounced two engagements already and had to pay enormous sums of money because of them."

"It was only one broken betrothal, and it was the young lady who rescinded her acceptance." The wrinkle returned to his brow, but his tone remained level. "Believe me, the lady was far better off without me, and I did the right thing and made a settlement with her father even though it wasn't necessary or expected. In the end, everything turned out for the best and she is now happily married."

"The broken engagement isn't even the half of it," she added, as more of the things she'd read about him through the years came to her mind. "You shot a man in a duel, and he almost died. You were forced to leave London for a while because of it."

"I can't refute that. . . ." He paused and cursed softly

under his breath. "Not that it matters now, but he challenged me. I had no choice in the matter if I was going
to save his honor and my own. He's damned lucky I'm a
good marksman and didn't kill him."

She huffed at his brusque language. "You've been
seen throughout London with all manner of disreputable
people. Men and women. And just recently you and your
equally wild friends, the Duke of Stonerick and Duke of
Hurstbourne, had a mad, reckless curricle race through
town that caused several accidents before you finally
stopped your rigs. Everyone was surprised no one was seriously injured in the incident. Not to mention the string of
broken hearts you've left behind at the end of every Season. If a man could be ruined, you'd be ruined! How could
you possibly make a good husband?"

"Perhaps much of what is written about me is true,
but not all." A small muscle worked in his jaw. "Surely
you know that the gossipmongers excel at making up stories about the people whose names help sell their news-
prints. Hurst and Rick included. I won't answer every
ridiculous charge, Miss Hale."

"Why would the scandal sheets make up something
when you give them fresh stories every week?"

"I admit my reputation is far from exemplary and
I have been ungovernable and reckless for most of my
life. . . ." He paused and suddenly a touch of an attractive
grin settled softly around his mouth, making her unbear-
ably aware of her interest in him. "I'm glad to hear you
do read the scandal sheets. You seem rather decorous
about all things; I was beginning to wonder if you ever
did anything that would be considered even slightly improper."

His inviting demeanor and casual comment, which
she felt was meant to take some of the steam off her ex-

asperation, had done exactly that. She relaxed a little. Her muscles were beginning to cramp from holding herself so rigid.

"I would think everyone reads them from time to time," she answered, hoping that would absolve her of any seemingly wrongdoing. "And it's certainly not inappropriate to read tittle-tattle. The gossip sheets are very informative. That's how I know you've been a rakish, boisterous man-about-town given to drinking bouts, excessive gambling, and—" Her mind struggled to find more offenses.

Far from being upset by her charges, he smiled and nodded again. His face eased into an expression of amusement and his look caused her to feel those decidedly feminine sensations once more.

"I don't think you missed one of my faults. You covered them all."

"No, there are others," she said before she could stop herself.

"What can I say?" He held up his hands in a gesture of surrender and chuckled attractively, making it clear he wasn't taking umbrage. "I am without excuse. Please continue with more. I've forgotten a lot of the things I've done." He shrugged good-naturedly. "Too many bad things to remember."

Fredericka almost smiled at the charming remark. She took a deep, solid breath, bound and determined not to let this man get the best of her, though she felt she was failing miserably. It was difficult to be upset with someone who agreed with you. Along with how he made her feel, he had an answer for every accusation put forth. What would be the use in adding to the list?

"As it happens, I do need a husband," she admitted with more than a little grudging sound to her voice, as she wondered whether Mr. Maywaring was going to show. Until recently she'd shunned thoughts of marriage, thinking it would be an impediment to taking care of the children.

The duke relaxed his arms and shoulders. "I'm glad you finally admitted that. You had me worried for a moment or two."

"But not a duke," she added with quiet resolve. "Especially one with your reputation."

"Even with my faults, you are still better off in your court pursuits married to me. A certain amount of power and privilege comes with my title and, because of my questionable character, I have no misgivings about using it to aid you if it becomes necessary."

That reminder gave her pause. What he said was undeniable. She wavered and quickly tried to bolster her weakening feelings by saying, "I was looking to marry someone more suited to me and the kind of life I want for myself and the children. Why would you even want to marry me? We're strangers. Surely there are many ladies who would be more suited to your life and the way you live it."

"That's probably true," he said without a trace of arrogance. "But you have exactly what I want, Miss Hale."

His quiet statement shortened her breaths and made her stomach quiver. A comfortable edge to his voice sent a shivery feeling up her spine that chilled her and then washed over her like warm, soapy water filled with bubbles.

Instead of giving in to the wonderful feeling, she pushed it aside and asked, "How can you say that? You don't know me."

"I know enough," he continued with his bid to win

over an affirmative answer from her. "We will suit perfectly."

"Perfectly?" she admonished with more angst than she wanted to convey to him.

He shrugged. "It's true." His tone was matter-of-fact.

"We won't suit at all," she insisted, refusing to surrender to the unexpected feelings going on inside her or even the possibility what he just declared might be true. "Your arrogance is proof. No matter your title, you are still an undisciplined, restless, and irresponsible bachelor who spends all his time gambling, fencing, and doing other things for a group called the Brass Deck."

"My sporting club is active and important to all of us. Many wagers are placed on each game and we always play to win. I make no apologies for it."

"Obviously not. I've heard card parties go on for days at your house and your dinner parties are quite loud, lavish, and last until sunup. I am an uncomplicated, modest miss who has no desire to put up with your foolish behavior."

An endearing smile spread his masculine lips and she sensed a sudden change in him; a softness that intrigued and frustrated her. He was far more competitive than she and it showed in every word and movement.

"And a very prim and proper miss you are, Miss Hale, but you are far from simple. You have taken me to task at every turn."

She accepted what he said as a compliment and appreciated it. If only she could find joy in it. "Your sudden entrance into my life distresses me," she admitted honestly, as it made her realize the true sharp point of her dilemma. How realistic, really, was it that she would find a suitable man to marry her when she would insist three children come with her into the marriage?

"For what reason?" he asked, evidently not understanding her continued reservations. "I'm offering you
exactly what you need. A husband."

"But I never expected a duke," she answered defiantly, as she was forced to consider the possibility that
Mr. Maywaring was not going to be a possibility since he
hadn't bothered to keep their appointment. "I don't even
want a duke. An unassuming poet would do."

His brow tightened. "I doubt that, Miss Hale, but who
I am doesn't matter. What I'm prepared to do does. I'm
told you are happy living here on Paddleton with the
children, which I know is held in trust for Charles. I am
most at home in London, where I have my own pursuits.
There's no need for either of us to change our lives for the
other in any way except for the fact we'll be married. I
have no reason to rush to have a son, and you have plenty
of children to occupy you for years to come. There's no
cause why we can't continue to live our lives separately
well into the foreseeable future."

Separate lives?

Was he serious?

"You mean we wouldn't have to live together? As
husband and wife?"

A hint of amusement laced his tone. "Not even a wedding night, unless you'd rather we—"

"No, no," she interrupted him while trying to quell her
jumping stomach and racing heartbeat. He was making
it clear he didn't want her. A wave of old, stinging hurts
of not being wanted flushed through her. She would be in
his way if she were in London with him. That was simple
enough to understand. Fredericka thought she was past
those childhood fears of rejection and being in the way.
The duke had revived them. She quickly banished the un-

wanted feelings from her mind. "I'm only trying to make sure I understand your intentions."

He indicated he understood by a slight nod. "Eventually we would have to live together, but not for some time."

"And my sister's children?"

"Will stay here with you in their home as they do now. I see no reason to upset any of you by moving into one of my homes unless that's what you prefer. If this is where they are happy, this is where they belong. But of course, I would insist on assuming all of your financial obligations."

She felt another apple trying to go down her throat. "All of them?"

"It's only right I do. On that, there could be no persuasion otherwise. That includes all the responsibilities for this house, as it would be considered your home for now."

To be taken care of in such an elaborate way as a duchess would be, yet free to live her own life? She had to give this more serious consideration, but she needed time. Her breaths came shorter as her mind whirled with possibilities. With no monetary worries she could get a tutor to help Charles with his speech and hire another, younger governess to assist Miss Litchfield, and they all needed new clothing.

Fredericka's mind churned with all the things she could do for the children if she didn't have financial restrictions. Things that Jane had declared only she could do because Fredericka couldn't afford the extras that came with giving the children a proper childhood.

Until now, if . . .

She mentally shook herself. Marriage to a duke had

never entered her mind. It was still preposterous to even consider. "I don't know," she said, feeling she couldn't make a snap decision, no matter how tempting it was. "You've obviously had time to think about this and consider all the possibilities that might arise."

"Not much longer than you," he admitted. "I had hoped you would have some time to think on this today as well, but—"

Puzzled, she asked, "But what?"

He shrugged. "The letter I sent."

Yes. She supposed that was neither his fault nor hers. But she wasn't sure a few hours would have made much difference. The answer to his proposal would take a great deal of serious thought.

"Everything you've said so far is to my benefit. What are you expecting from me in return?"

"The only thing I ask of you is fidelity."

"*Fidelity?*" she challenged, outrage spreading all the way to her core. How dare he! Not caring to hide her indignation, she contested, "I beg your pardon, sir. You do me an injustice."

He seemed to weigh what she said, before answering, "My apologies, but you asked."

She wouldn't have if she'd had any inkling what his answer might be.

On the other hand, his words held a ring of sincerity. She searched his eyes and saw no hidden meaning or accusation in his words, so she gave him a brief nod of acceptance. What he was offering was more than she was expecting from anyone on her list. Most especially not having to live with him as his wife. For some time to come. That offer seemed too good to be true, but indeed, if it was, she'd be foolish not to say yes immediately. Especially since it appeared she could now mark Mr. Maywaring off her list.

Still, she hesitated, not yet wanting to give in to any of his arguments until she could further study the matter. She was marrying because of necessity and always thought she'd have more time. Not only that, it was also a huge decision to marry someone of such great title and wealth. She had never been schooled to be a duchess. Only a handful of young ladies would be each Season.

Ladies whose pedigrees and dowries far exceeded hers.

"What you offer is substantial. It would be desirable to stay here where the children are familiar with their surroundings. How much time do I have to think about this arrangement with you?"

"Not long. I will admit that you are in a more favorable position than I am."

"You jest, Your Grace." She puffed out a short laugh. "How can you say that with a straight face?"

"It's true. You have the liberty of time. I do not. Yesterday a codicil to my grandmother's will was read. If I'm not wed by Friday, I will lose my inheritance from her."

"Friday? I don't believe you. That's preposterous."

"As we speak, my solicitor is making all the necessary arrangements for me to marry you. I've no time to waste and will be cutting it close to the clock with timing of the banns as it is."

Fredericka wasn't the kind of person who made rash decisions. She wanted all the facts, the little details, and plenty of time to think over whatever she was facing.

Would no husband at all give her a better chance at keeping the children than a wild duke who lived only for his own pleasures? Would a very attractive duke be a better husband than a man prone to sniff every other breath? Of that she was sure.

In reality, the duke's proposal sounded cold. An impersonal business arrangement. Not even the pretense that it was anything more. Nothing like she'd imagined it would be should she ever have anyone offer for her hand. But really, what had she ever imagined about courting, romance, and marriage other than a young girl's fancy to think about a young man who loved poetry as much as she did? There was a time that would have been a heavenly match. She had often imagined sitting in the garden under a shady tree with a handsome poet, his head in her lap while he read his latest verse to her.

But memories of those wistful thoughts were not helpful right now. Those possibilities had remained far from her thoughts for a long time and the past is where they needed to stay. She had to be as pragmatic concerning the duke as she'd been about the gentlemen on her now useless list of possible husbands.

She couldn't think about herself and the kind of life she once dreamed about. That ended with her sister's death. She now had to live for Angela's beautiful children. Fredericka had to put aside a young girl's dreams and consider what was best for her chances to win in Chancery. She'd be a fool to refuse a duke under ordinary circumstances, but the man standing before her was no *ordinary* duke.

"May I at least have the time it takes to drink a cup of tea to think this through?" she asked on a sigh of resignation.

As if sensing her conflict, he gave her an understanding smile. He moved closer to her and lifted his hand as if he were going to brush the backs of his fingers down her cheek. Her skin tingled at the mere possibility of his touch. Something halted him, and he dropped his hand to his side.

His action was unsettling but fascinating too. What would she have done if he had carried through and touched her?

"Perhaps I could wait that long," he offered in a sincere tone.

"Excuse my interruption, Miss Hale."

Fredericka turned toward the doorway and saw her housekeeper. "Yes, Mrs. Dryden."

"Mr. Maywaring is here to see you. Should I ask him to wait in the music room?"

Fredericka looked back to the duke.

"Maywaring?" he asked with questioning eyes that seemed to want to delve too deeply into her soul.

"A prospective husband," she admitted with no small amount of sudden dread, and surprisingly feeling a little guilty that she hadn't told the duke about him right away.

The duke's mouth thinned. A deeper frown returned to his face. He muttered a near-silent oath. "I don't think you have time for a cup of tea, Miss Hale."

CHAPTER 5

LINES TO A BELLE
FOR THE ORCHIS
——O. W. HOLMES

Yes, lady! I can ne'er forget
That once in other years we met;
Thy memory may perchance recall
A festal eve—a rose-wreathed hall.

He had unexpected competition.

Slightly bemused, Wyatt studied Miss Hale with heightened concentration. She was everything Epworth said she was and 100 percent more. His interest in her was acute and stimulating beyond anything he could have imagined. He'd caught the scent of wildflowers drifting from her skin when she'd moved in so close to him he could have pressed her lips beneath his before she had a chance to blink.

And he had been tempted to do just that.

He didn't know how he'd stopped and held himself in check. Perhaps it was an inner sense warning that he needed much more from her than a single kiss. Surely that's all he would have ever gotten from this miss had he followed his primal urge.

The fragrance of field flowers had surprised him. He would have guessed, and been wrong, that she would use rose water. Perhaps lavender. Seldom was he fooled when it came to a lady. Or a woman. Miss Hale looked so prim and sedate in her pale-amethyst dress with its modest neckline and long, sheer sleeves. The fine silk of her skirts swished and fluttered invitingly around her legs every time she moved. A large gemstone nestled sweetly in the hollow of her throat.

Despite their less than desirable beginning, because of his misstep with the children, she was approachable and as beautiful as a cool, starry night. Yet her true beauty wasn't just in the fetching shade of her golden-brown eyes, the slight tilt to her small nose, or the bow shape of her rosebud lips. Not even the scowls she'd given him, and there had been plenty, could obscure the natural pink tint of her cheeks or the stirring beauty of her delicate-looking, parchment-pale skin and arched brows.

His attraction to her was due more to the way she presented herself with confident ease and took him to task without an ounce of reservation. Surprising as it was, he liked the manner in which she talked to him, having no fear to say what she was feeling no matter what the consequences might be. That let him know she was the right lady for him. He had a feeling she wouldn't be easily tamed—if he ever had the desire to do so.

Her spirit and strength were evident in everything she'd said and how she'd reacted from the moment their eyes met. She was not the shrinking violet he'd envisioned. Far from it. That pleased him.

Miss Hale appeared a little strict with her nieces and nephew. Maybe more than a little. But once he had a son with her, he would be in charge. They would have a talk about her thinking children should be proper at all times and march around like little soldiers. There was nothing wrong with a little bad behavior, his father always said, and Wyatt agreed.

For now, he'd keep that bit of information to himself.

He hadn't won her over even though attraction flowed between them as easily as a fine silk thread through the eye of a needle every time their eyes met. Attraction he felt certain she sensed as well.

He stood quietly and listened as Miss Hale spoke in soft tones to Mrs. Dryden about fruit tarts and chocolate for the children and where she should have Mr. Maywaring wait. After the housekeeper left, Miss Hale turned and gave her attention back to Wyatt.

Apprehension swept across her features and she swallowed hard as her lashes fluttered. She didn't immediately say anything and suddenly appeared uncertain. Wyatt had the feeling she struggled with how to best proceed now that she was actually faced with the prospect of two marriage proposals.

On the same day. At the same time.

Clasping her hands together in front of her waist, she cautiously glanced around the room as if hoping she might find an answer to her dilemma hidden behind the blue velvet draperies or lurking somewhere in the room. He wasn't thrilled to be in this position either—vying to win her hand from another. What he'd expected to be a simple matter he could finish quickly and be on his way was turning into an ordeal.

Wyatt couldn't say he minded the extended reprieve from continuing their conversation. He was still trying to put aside his masculine instincts of wanting to pull her close and smell the bouquet of her fresh-washed hair, nuzzle the warmth at the curve of her neck, and kiss the slight swell of breasts showing so pillowy soft from above the neckline of her dress.

Urges he hadn't expected—but should have. He was a man after all.

Miss Hale cleared her throat. "I'm afraid I'm not the kind of person who can make rash decisions easily, Your Grace. I study through everything quite carefully before coming to a suitable conclusion about any big decision."

There was something innocently alluring about her courage and the directness with which she approached him on every matter. On another day, for a different reason, he might have welcomed her challenge to proceed. But not this day. And really, who in their right mind would refuse an offer of marriage from a duke and marry another man?

He cleared his throat too. Showing his impatience wouldn't help. Other than to make him feel better.

"I agree that ordinarily a lady shouldn't be called upon to make such a hasty judgment. Especially about something as important as marriage. However, in this instance, there is nothing else to be done. You have me standing in front of you and another man down the corridor waiting for your answer."

With a worried frown and a lingering glance, she offered, "Yes, well, not exactly."

His eyes narrowed and a throb of tension started at his temples. It flashed through his thoughts that he might have been misinformed by Epworth in some way. "What exactly are you saying, Miss Hale?"

There was a skip in her breaths, and her hands tightened in front of her.

He didn't like where his thoughts were going. This needed to be settled. "Have you already promised yourself to another?"

"No," she answered with conviction. "I have not. You see, I don't actually have an offer of marriage from Mr. Maywaring or anyone else. He's on the list of gentlemen I've been considering for that possibility."

"You have a list?" She certainly knew how to keep him on his toes.

"Yes, of course," she stated as if making a list of prospective husbands was a normal thing to do. "What responsible lady wouldn't have? I couldn't possibly entertain the idea of marrying just anyone. I have to be selective because of the children. I need to make a match that will be good for them as well as for me."

No, he thought rather firmly. She needed to make a match with *him*.

A lady had never spoken so honestly to him. Women and mistresses would sometimes be plainspoken in conversations. If they were confident in their position. But it was rare for a young lady to do so. He found that most of the time they could be exasperating by only saying what they thought he wanted to hear.

Miss Hale frustrated him by being forthright in the things she said. Things he didn't want to hear and her seeming not to mind that he didn't.

All ladies were beautiful to look at dressed in their wispy silk gowns trimmed in delicate laces and flounces, jewels in their hair and pearls around their necks. They were delightful to converse with. Their voices, soft and flowing, were filled with a cadence he enjoyed. He appreciated, accepted, and followed the intricate dance of manners and standards they had to abide by. His mistresses were professional, enjoyable, and satisfying. He had always cherished the fairer sex.

However, the thought of having a wife to honor, protect, and be responsible for her happiness scared the hell out of him. Marrying by the end of the week hadn't been part of the plans for his life.

Still, he was certain the one standing before him fit

all his current and future needs. It was settled as far as he was concerned. She was the one he wanted. The problem was that he hadn't expected her to put up any resistance. Nor had he considered she might be so strong-willed he'd have to work at talking her into marrying him.

Damnation, he was a duke and in need of nothing from anyone. Except of course, right now he needed a wife. And Epworth had, without any doubt, picked the most pertinent young lady in all of England. Once married, they wouldn't be living under the same roof, nor would there often be need to have contact.

Not for quite some time anyway, he mused. He had his tournaments for his charities that took most of his time. A wife in London would interfere with that. There were still many men suffering from wounds received during the wars with Napoleon. Wyatt, Rick, and Hurst considered it an honor to play and win money for the hospitals and infirmaries to help treat and care for those who'd risked their lives to fight for king and country. His father had built a similar institution for soldiers coming home after the war with the colonies. And like his father, he would deal with the future when it arrived.

Right now, irritated that Miss Hale didn't seem to be comprehending the ramifications of his predicament, he took a couple of steps toward her, stopped, and crossed his arms over his chest, feeling a bit resolute himself.

Keeping his gaze tightly on her vivid golden-brown eyes, he said, "It's not that I would mind vying for your hand and winning you over with all the usual accoutrements a young lady would expect for such an occasion in her life. I don't have the time to romance you and fall dutifully in line with all the other men on your list. I need an answer."

Unclasping her hands, she let her arms drop to her sides. Her frown assured him she wasn't happy with what he'd said.

After a long breath, her features suddenly seemed filled with fortitude. Her shoulders moved back, and she took a more relaxed stance. "Romance is the farthest thing from my mind, Your Grace. I will forget you said that. I have the children to consider. However, if I *were* to consent to a union with you . . ." She hesitated for another moment or two. "There would be certain conditions you would have to agree to first."

The seriousness of her expression and tone intrigued him, and her words gave him reason to hope she would acquiesce to his appeal. It was best she not know that, at this point, he would agree to anything to get this marriage behind him.

"Go on," he encouraged, as he watched conflicting emotions shift across her face.

"I would want you to have papers drawn up in which you disavow any claim to properties, trusts, allowances, or anything else that is currently held in trust for the children on their parents' behalf."

Already disgruntled by what he was forced to do, Wyatt stiffened. His jaw clenched tight, and he felt his eyebrows pinch and rise. "Wait just a—" Wyatt quickly bit back the oath that hovered on his lips and what he really wanted to say, muttering the curse only to himself.

Did she truly think he might want to claim a child's inheritance? If so, she really thought he was as bad as the scandal sheets said he was. By law, of course, he could take control of everything she owned or might ever own. Some men would relish the thought. He never would do that to her or the children, and he didn't like her thinking he might. But he'd swallow what he wanted to say to her about that assumption and give an answer more appropriate for a lady.

"I'll start working on the documents as soon as I get settled at the village inn."

Her eyes softened and her shoulders relaxed. "I'd like for my barrister, Mr. Franwipple, to be here to represent the children's interest and make sure all necessary papers are in order and to authenticate them. He's been kind enough to handle everything a solicitor would as well as his duties as barrister before Chancery."

More tension settled in the back of his neck and between his shoulders. She was making it clear she didn't trust him an inch to keep his word.

"I think that's wise," Wyatt offered pliantly. "We'll handle legal matters when we arrive in London tomorrow, and then we can be set for the ceremony on Friday. I'll send a message to Mr. Franwipple asking that he make himself available to you for the entire day."

Her hands clasped in front of her again. A little line formed in her brow and she pursed her lips in concern. He already knew her well enough that the gesture worried him. What else did she have in mind?

"I assumed if we were to wed, it would be here."

"At Paddleton?"

"Yes." Her eyes remained calm and steady. "Or we could go to the church in the village if you'd prefer. I would hate to upset the children with a long journey into London and for such a short time. Is there any reason we couldn't call on the vicar to come to the house?"

"No. None at all. In fact, I agree with you that it would be best we marry here." That way he wouldn't have to explain to anyone why they weren't invited to attend the happy occasion. "I'll dispatch an urgent request for Franwipple to come to Paddleton without delay."

"There's one more thing."

"Only one?" he asked with a comfortable smile, and was rewarded with a faint smile of amusement from her. It caused a tightening in his lower stomach.

"I will require an allowance, as there are things I'd need in order to—"

"Please, Miss Hale," he said, interrupting her. "You needn't make that a condition to accepting my proposal. You will be my wife, my duchess, and receive all the rewards the title entails. Which will include a generous allowance you can draw from anytime you wish, for whatever you wish. I will also have an irrevocable trust arranged for you. If anything unfortunate should ever happen to me, you will be provided for. I wouldn't trust my cousin, who would be the next duke, to do so fairly. I'll have accounts set up for you at every shop in the village and wherever you would like in London."

Expectancy lit in her face. It made him feel good to know he'd finally said something she approved of.

"That would be kind of you."

The corners of Wyatt's mouth tightened again, and he bit back a grimace. He would demand it for her or anyone he married. Providing for her wasn't a favor. It was expected of him to give her everything she wanted. Whether or not that made her happy was up to her. Damnation, her happiness couldn't depend on him. He would fail miserably at it just as his father had.

She could get under his skin faster than anyone he'd ever known. But he would continue to be patient. Being irritable wasn't the way to win her hand. Now that he had decided she *was* the one he wanted, he didn't intend to let her slip through his fingers because he couldn't behave as properly as she was.

"I'll do better than just what would be expected of me as your husband, if you agree to marry me."

Her eyes narrowed perceptibly, giving him more optimism for a good outcome. She quirked her head to the side and looked at him with suspicious interest.

"I'll set up irrevocable trusts for the children as well. They'll never lack for anything the rest of their lives."

Her faint gasp gave him a thrill of satisfaction. It was downright exciting that he was getting through to her. Even if it were by way of the children. Whatever worked was fine.

"Are you serious, Your Grace?" She took a couple of hesitant steps toward him.

He welcomed the eagerness in her voice and felt her weakening to the idea of his proposal. Bantering with her had been as strenuous as a fencing match. Some of her jabs were just as sharp as the tips of the many swords he'd felt over the years. But the battle hadn't been won yet.

"You have read many objectionable things about me and have no doubts about my distasteful reputation. Given I explained the broken betrothal, have you ever read anything that indicated I am not a man of my word?"

She stood very still with only her gaze moving from one corner of the room to the other in indecision before it settled on his once again. She was considering what he said, and he had no idea what her answer would be.

His breathing kicked up. He'd never had a man or woman make him feel as if he were sitting on a pincushion. Would she trust him?

"I've never heard you aren't true to your word," she answered without equivocating. "What you offer is far more generous than I could have ever imagined from a husband."

Wyatt let out a deep soundless sigh. He didn't want her continuing to look for logic or sound reasoning. Time was passing. "You have my word on everything I say. I appreciate your reluctance to tie yourself to a man such as I, but I need an answer, Miss Hale. Will you marry me?"

CHAPTER 6

'Tis not thine, with flaunting beauty
To attract the roving sight;
Nature, from her varied wardrobe,
Chose thy vest of purest white.

Perhaps Wyatt should have had more than a nip or two of brandy with his toast and eggs after all. Standing before a long-winded vicar and waiting to say, "I do," wasn't as easy as men had always made it appear. That was probably another reason his father had always told him to put off marriage for as long as he could. Why would a young and healthy man, who had everything he could possibly want, put himself through this?

Only a few people were in attendance, but enough. The children were sitting on the same chairs, in the same place, and looking just as stiff as when he'd first seen them a couple of days ago. An elderly couple and a widow who were neighbors of Miss Hale, the solicitors, and the governess and housekeeper were also present.

Nonetheless, despite feeling a lingering resentment for what he was having to do and why, Wyatt was managing. Yesterday, when papers filled with questions and answers were flying back and forth between Paddleton and the inn where he was staying, he had his doubts the wedding would take place. Luckily, Epworth had already been in touch with Miss Hale's barrister and they both arrived in plenty of time to finalize preparation of all the documents.

It was very businesslike, as he had wanted.

He hadn't seen Miss Hale since he'd let himself out the back door of her house to allow her to deal with Mr. Maywaring however she thought best. It had helped settle some of Wyatt's own misgivings about the hasty wedding when she walked into the drawing room looking more like a beautiful angel with three cherubs flanking her than a nervous, reluctant bride. She wore a long-sleeved simple but elegant ivory dress and carried a small bouquet of dried wildflowers in her hands. More flowers had been woven into her dark-blond hair like a crown.

He couldn't say she looked happy. No doubt, he didn't either. What could he expect? Neither of them wanted to marry, but both were being forced by circumstances beyond their power to change.

Not a situation Wyatt wanted to ever be in again.

Now that the actual ceremony was taking place, he found it incongruous that he was wishing Miss Hale looked a little happier than the restrained expression she maintained. Even so, marrying her wasn't all bad. There were rewards even now. He enjoyed standing close to her, feeling the warmth of her body beside his and looking at the graceful oval shape of her face, narrow bridge of her small nose, and high crest of her cheeks while the vicar spoke.

Wyatt couldn't help but wonder if his father would have given in and married so young if he'd been faced with the same situation. Probably not. Wyatt wouldn't have either if his grandmother hadn't seen fit to want to leave her wealthy property to The London Society of Poetry.

"Your Grace," the vicar said, bringing Wyatt's attention back to the matter before him. "Would you please take the hand of your bride and repeat after me?"

Wyatt placed his gloved hand, palm up, toward her. Her dark velvety lashes fluttered, and she lifted her gaze to his. He saw indecision and trepidation in her beautiful eyes and understood everything she felt. Her chest rose and fell with short, shallow pants. Fear she might back out flooded him. He felt himself willing her to place her hand in his. Not just because there was no time to marry another, but because he wanted *her*.

Time suddenly seemed suspended as he waited.

Unspoken, a battle of wills swirled between them until he felt the barest brush of her fingertips. Relief melted through him. Wyatt gently closed his hand around hers and held firmly. She stiffened, but he also felt a soft, feminine intake of breath shudder over her. A quiver of sensual desire shivered across his lower stomach and settled in his loins.

A hot poker couldn't have heated him more.

He tightened his hold. At first, she resisted by pulling back, but then a calm seemed to come over her and she accepted his grip. Their gazes locked as they repeated words the vicar spoke. During the process, Wyatt felt an intriguing and undefinable emotion surging through him as they stood close together, joined in this pact of holy matrimony.

It was unsettling that she fascinated him so. Being attracted to this lady wasn't part of his plan. He hadn't been prepared to be intoxicated by the fresh womanly scent of her, the hushed sounds of her breathing, or the binding words flowing from their lips. All of it teased his body with masculine thoughts.

"I pronounce you husband and wife."

Wyatt blinked. It was over. The inheritance from his grandmother was safe from the clutches of the London Society of Poetry.

"You may kiss your bride, Your Grace."

Wyatt knew all the traditional reasons for a wedding kiss: to seal the agreement, to make it a legal bond, and, rarely considered anymore, that it would be the first kiss between the happy couple. In this case, that happened to be true.

The room was so quiet he would have sworn to anyone he heard every click of the large clock that stood in the entryway of the house and every intake of breath in the room. He hadn't thought ahead to a kiss.

Slowly, he relaxed his grip on her hand. One finger at a time as if he wasn't sure he wanted to let go of her at all. And for one wild second, he didn't think he did. Her lips were inviting, but the situation wasn't. There were a dozen people in the room, including two little girls and a boy curiously watching them. Not ideal for a first kiss. He bent and brushed his lips so briefly to hers he wasn't sure they'd touched until he heard her startled, innocent breath. Lifting his head, he looked into her eyes. They were starry. It pleased him and a brief smile touched his lips.

He then looked at the vicar with a nod and stepped away.

The children started clapping and his tension eased. He turned toward them and smiled. It was good to see them happy, up out of their chairs and moving about. They should never appear to be soldiers lined up for duty. He wanted to see them playful and full of innocent mischief.

Wyatt would have never thought it possible just a few days ago that he would have a wife and three children to consider as well.

The boy and oldest girl went running up to Miss Ha—the duchess, wrapping their arms around her lovingly and hugging her close. Her neighbors crowded her too. Surprisingly, the youngest girl came over and looked up at him. With her aristocratic little face and ringlets of dark-golden hair, she had the makings of being an exquisite beauty one day.

With a curious frown she asked, "Are you going to be my papa?"

Good Lord.

"No," he responded, after almost swallowing his tongue. "That wouldn't be proper. Your aunt insists that everything be proper."

"She sure does. Elise told me when Mama was married, her husband was my papa."

"Well, yes," he offered, trying to understand her young thought process. "But that was because she was your mama. The duchess is your aunt."

Her expression turned thoughtful for a split second before she beamed. "So, you'll be my uncle?"

Wyatt an uncle? Perhaps he should get used to being a husband before he took on the challenge of being an uncle as well, but he didn't want to disappoint the little girl's excitement. "Yes, I suppose it does," he told the bright-eyed lass.

The new duchess appeared calm and more confident than during the ceremony as she came up beside Bella. Elise was clinging to her aunt by holding on to her waist. Smiling down at Bella, his wife handed her the wedding bouquet.

"As promised, here it is to do with as you wish."

Bella's eyes glowed with awe as she took the blooms and looked from the flowers to her aunt. "I'm going to press them in your favorite book of poetry. That way you'll always have them to remember this day when you read from it."

"That would be lovely, Bella. Talk with Miss Litchfield. I'm sure she will know exactly how you should treat them. She's waiting for you with Charles. You too, Elise," the duchess added, trying to disentangle herself from her older niece.

"I don't want to go," Elise whined, and held on tighter as she gave Wyatt a less than favorable sideways glance. "I want to stay with you, Auntie."

"We had this discussion the other night, remember? I explained to you that I had to marry, but we're going to stay right here at Paddleton. All of us as a family. Just like I promised."

The duchess looked over to Wyatt, as if hoping he could help her in some way.

He remained silent for a moment while he digested what was going on. Fredericka was trying to be compassionate but firm in wanting Elise to obey her.

"Your aunt is right," he offered with a sincere smile, and then did the only thing he knew to do. He reached down and ruffled the top of her head. She shrank back and pierced him with a sharp look from her distrustful blue eyes while she reached up and smoothed down her mussed hair.

Obviously, she needed more reaffirming than a pat on the head.

Wyatt bent toward her and softly said, "I'm not going to take your aunt away from you. You can go with the others. She'll be here when you get back."

Her expression didn't change, but she asked, "You promise?"

He nodded. "I do."

The pout remained on her face, but she let go and reluctantly stepped away.

"All right then, good," his wife said with a sigh of relief and a quick hug to Elise. "I'll see you later in the day. Now off you go to join Miss Litchfield."

Bella looked up at Wyatt with her infectious little-girl smile and said, "Good-bye, Uncle Your Grace." She turned and skipped away, squeezing the mosaic of flowers tightly to her chest. Elise, on the other hand, glanced back several times to scrutinize Wyatt before she disappeared into the corridor with the governess.

Wyatt chuckled, and so did Fredericka. It was the first time he'd heard her actually laugh. He enjoyed hearing the soft sound and liked the way it relaxed her lovely face.

"Thank you for reassuring her. It obviously helped."

"I know from boarding school that it takes some children longer than others to adjust to changes in their lives. I'm sure she'll be all right in time."

"I keep hoping. It's been over a year since her parents died and not much has changed in her fear of being left alone."

An unusual feeling stole over him and settled in his chest. He wasn't sure what it was but felt as if he needed to comfort her in some way. In order to do that, they needed to be alone. "Could we step outside for a few moments before I go?"

"Go?" she asked, a whisper of surprise in her tone as her eyes searched his for answers.

"I have business to attend and must leave within the hour." Members of the Brass Deck Club had a lot of money wagered on the tournament that started tonight. Money the hospital he'd built needed.

"I mean, I knew you had to return to London," she quickly added to qualify her question. "Just not so soon."

He gave her a twitch of a grin. There was no way he could pass on the opening she gave him. It was too perfect. "If you've changed your mind about us having a wedding night, tell me, and I'll be happy to adjust my schedule to take care of—"

"No, no," she hastened to say, interrupting him before he finished while looking around to see if anyone was close enough to hear his comment. "Of course, let's go outside. If there's one thing I've learned about you in this short time, it's that if you say you want to speak to me in private, I should agree without hesitation."

Wyatt smiled to himself as they walked to the front door. She was absolutely lovely when flustered by his teasing remarks. In time, she would get used to them. If they were going to be spending time together, or rather, when they would.

After he helped her settle a brown woolen shawl around her neck and shoulders, they walked outside onto the slate flooring that led three steps down to the gravel entrance. The air was moderately cold and breezy with more of a late wintry feel than early spring. The chill of the wind whipped at his face and blew through his hair as he took in a cleansing breath, feeling quite relieved the ordeal of the ceremony and securing the safety of his inheritance was behind him.

He looked over at his wife and thought to himself that he was damned lucky Epworth knew about her needing a husband. She was beautiful, with a soft countenance and feminine strength that drew him. Thoughts of telling her drifted through his mind, but he held back. There was no need to start something he wasn't ready to finish. Husbandly duties were not in his near future.

"Do you think you'll be warm enough with only your wrap?" he asked as a couple of squawking pheasants flew over the top of the house.

"Yes, thank you." She fitted the shawl tighter around her, tucking the ends around her elbows to secure it. "It's thick and quite cozy, especially with the sun shining so bright. The sky looks like a midsummer day."

Wyatt agreed with a nod, looking out over the front lawn and down the winding lane that led away from the house to the main road. Spring was transforming a brown landscape of baren limbs and bushes to shoots of green leaves and flowering buds. The last of winter was fading from the earth. In its place trees, shrubs, and other plants were sprouting and budding. The grasses were sprigging with their new coats, and a canopy of blue, with sweepy puffs of white clouds, dotted the sky as far as he could see.

Horses and carriages were parked in the drive along the front of the house, making their usual noises of shuddering, nickering, and rattling harnesses. Drivers, grooms, and footmen stood nearby talking, so Wyatt ushered her to the side of the house where they would have privacy from the workers.

After making it around the corner, they continued past the house in silence and kept moving down a well-worn path of uneven rocky ground marked by shallow holes and small ridges. The trail led toward some newly erected wood fencing with an arched iron gate that had been built in the center. Wyatt assumed it led into another garden, a private nook, or perhaps an open pasture, and he headed that way.

The manor of Paddleton sat on top of a small rise. Rolling hillsides merged into a newly greening valley at the back of the house. In the far distance sunshine sparkled off a small pond. On one side of the house, a meadow of early flowers was just beginning to bud and unfurl. To the other, Wyatt saw a walnut orchard and closer to the house were plantings of vegetables, herbs, and more than a few brambles that needed to be cleared before summer. It wasn't a huge property with thousands of acres, but several hundred, he felt sure.

"The house and lands are in good shape," he offered as they strolled. "Charles will do well once he's old enough to manage the estate."

"That's my hope, of course. The trustee sends monthly statements for me to look over and the farmlands are flourishing."

"Really?" That was odd. "He sends you copies to review?"

"I asked for them," she answered without hesitancy. "Why are you looking at me as if you are surprised?"

He shrugged as they continued to walk. "Because I am. It's not normal for a lady to have an interest in such matters."

A soft chuckle blew past her lips as she glanced over at him. "Everything concerning the children is important to me. Of course, at first he didn't feel the need to share them with me and was quite affronted I wanted him to."

Wyatt would have loved to have seen the look on that man's face when a lady wanted to check up behind him.

"It took effort and time, but the trustee and accountant eventually acquiesced to my wishes to be kept informed as to how well the estate was being managed."

Wyatt eyed her carefully and realized he wasn't surprised after all. He was impressed.

"There are some small areas on Paddleton," she continued, "that are mostly impenetrable thickets and others that are marshland; otherwise it's rich arable soil five tenants make good use of."

His eyes met hers and he gave her an amused grin. "It's refreshing to talk to a lady about a subject that is usually reserved for men."

She looked pleased but remained silent.

"On my ride up to the manor I saw paddocks and a large carriage building behind the main house. Are there horses?"

"Only carriage and riding horses. None for breeding, racing, or showing. The tenants take care of the land, crops, and sheep. It's all kept the same as when my sister was alive. I haven't wanted anything changed. I thought it best for the children to leave as much as possible the way it was when their parents were here." She stopped, looked up at him with somber eyes. "I'm sure you don't want to hear about all that. I don't even know why we're walking farther from the house. I didn't mean to delay you from leaving."

Wyatt was enjoying getting to know her now that they were no longer negotiating a contract for marriage. "I want to hear about your life, Miss Ha—Your Grace."

"Please," she said on a casual, breathy note, and glanced out over the field and downlands. "I don't know how formal you want us to be, but I would very much prefer that you use my name."

"I'd prefer that too, Fredericka. Call me Wyatt. I've never been a formal duke. I'm sure you've already noticed."

Turning back to him with a confident lift to her shoulders, she nodded once. "That would be impossible not to notice."

A flock of twittering starlings flew overhead, and he

and Fredericka looked up to watch them pass. The birds soared with little effort and looked so free. A twinge of tightness knotted his chest briefly and he wondered if it was a sign that his freedom was flying away with them. It was up to him to see it didn't.

"I don't know when we might see each other again," he stated, brushing aside the thoughts of disrupted freedom changing his life. "I wanted to make sure you are comfortable sending a message if you need me. I will take care of you and the children. Whatever you desire, let me know and I will handle it."

The breeze fluttered short strands of hair around her face and flushed her cheeks. Since he had to marry, he didn't think he could have picked a more satisfying wife. She was beautiful, strong, and prim enough to be interesting.

"I believe you," she assured him, without a trace of reservation in her tone. "You've done so much already. I can't think of anything else we might need. Having Mr. Franwipple here to read all the documents made the difference in how smoothly everything turned out."

"It was to my benefit to have him here as well. I wanted you to be comfortable."

"I am. It's my hope that now we've married Jane will discontinue her petition to take the children from me. I'll write to her this evening and let her know."

"If she doesn't abandon her quest, get in touch with me. I'll find out who I need to talk to in order to settle the matter."

She expelled a long, soft breath. "Thank you. For everything."

Wyatt didn't know why he was lingering. There was no need now that the vows had been said and the inheritance secured. Maybe it was that he hadn't appeased his curiosity about her. That was dangerous, but he'd never turned away from anything just because there was danger.

He found himself prolonging his departure by asking, "How did Mr. Maywaring take the news of our wedding?"

Fredericka gave him another smile before walking toward the fence again. "I didn't mention you or the possibility of our marriage to him at all."

He fell in step beside her. "Really?"

"Nor any other gentleman. I don't think it would have been appropriate for me to do so."

"What did the two of you do?" he asked with a little more than mere inquisitiveness in his tone.

"We had tea and talked of people we know in common, flowers, and his collection of snuffboxes. Two of which he had brought along in his pockets to show me." She looked down at her shawl and adjusted it once more while saying, "He's quite fond of his assortment."

That news caused a twitch between Wyatt's shoulder blades. Showing his personal belongings to her was a rather intimate thing for Maywaring to do. A rare feeling of jealousy wormed its way through him, but he quickly shook it off. So, the man was into snuff. A lot of gentlemen were. Wyatt had never considered the habit. He had enough vices without adding one more.

The sun suddenly seemed hot on the back of his neck. "So, you entertained him, examined his treasures, but didn't tell him you had already agreed to marry me?"

"It wasn't necessary." She dismissed the event as unimportant.

"That's a matter of opinion," he murmured, not trying to hide his discontent with her handling of the situation.

She stopped and looked at him defensively. "To tell you the truth, at that point, I still wasn't sure it would happen at all. How could I be? You had just walked out the back door, and I was showing Mr. Maywaring into the drawing room. Within the space of half an hour I had become engaged. I—I wasn't going to—" Her words faltered as she looked away.

"Let go of one man until you were absolutely certain about the worthiness of another?" he questioned with a note of devilry in his tone.

"No, not at all," she answered, not meeting his gaze at first, but when she did there was a confident sparkle in her eyes. "That isn't what I was thinking, but now that you mention it, I suppose it's true too. I didn't tell him because it all felt like a dream. I wondered if it had really happened. You have to admit that your arrival and pro-posal was quite sudden and shocking. In many ways, it's the thing that dreams are made of. I'm sure countless young ladies, at one time or another, have thought to themselves, *Wouldn't it be wonderful if a duke arrived at my door and proposed to me?*"

"What's this?" he said good-naturedly. "You had me believing a thought like that had never entered your mind. Are you telling me now it has?"

The breeze rippled her hair again and she gave him a dubious squint as sunshine glinted in her eyes. "Well, if it did, the dukes I envisioned were not nearly as young or handsome as you. Most of the titled gentlemen I've met were much older and—" She cut off her sentence again.

Wyatt liked her honesty. It was as attractive and re-freshing as she was. He had no doubt she was aware of the fascination that was always buzzing between them.

"Plump, perhaps?" he asked, trying not to show amuse-ment in his expression. "Losing their hair and teeth?"

"You said that, not me, and I'll say no more about it." Her mouth curved into a playful smile as she swatted a hovering bee. "And just so you know, I don't mind your lighthearted teasing."

He gave her another grin, amazed at how good that simple admission made him feel. It hadn't been easy to get her to stop being so serious. "I don't mind yours either."

Fredericka seemed to accept that without question and started walking toward the far meadow again. "Anyway, I knew Mr. Maywaring would find out soon enough if you and I actually went through with the ceremony. However, when he asked if he could call on me again, I told him that wouldn't be possible."

"How did he respond?" Wyatt asked, feeling that strange twinge between his shoulders again.

Fredericka moistened her lips as she turned to face Wyatt. "He sniffed and said that perhaps I might change my mind in the future as most ladies are prone to do, and that he'd be in touch to see if I had. Though I don't expect him to call on me after he hears we are married."

He better not.

Wyatt watched her brush a wisp of hair from her cheek. Her movements were natural, graceful, and seductive. Without her being aware of it, they were inviting him to move in closer to her. He accepted and stepped forward. His fascination with her was thriving and heady, but dangerous. He reminded himself he wasn't ready to settle down with a wife and all the trappings that would be expected of him.

Despite these thoughts, he found himself saying, "You are beautiful, Fredericka."

The sunlight caught in her golden-brown eyes again. She huffed a doubtful laugh as a deeper blush tinted her cheeks. Glancing down the uneven path, she swatted at a bee that seemed to be following her. "Truly, Wyatt, I don't need flattery from you."

"None given. I speak the truth and wanted you to know."

She gave him a rather curious but agreeable nod and said, "Thank you."

Wyatt heard the rattle of harnesses in the distance and shouts from one of the drivers. They both looked toward the front of the house. "Some of the horses must be getting restless."

"Perhaps you are too," she offered, stopping at the fence and leaning her back against one of the posts. "You did say you needed to get back to London today."

Yes. He had men counting on him to win the card tournament tonight, and the fencing competition tomorrow. Next week he had his monthly meetings with his accountants to make sure all financial things with his grandmother's will were now settled.

"Remember," he said, "if you need anything, you must let me know."

She nodded and smiled. "I will. You've been most kind already and I expect no more from you."

Kind?

Not exactly the word he wanted to hear on his wedding day. "I'm fair, Fredericka. Reasonable. Usually . . ." He paused. "Right now, I'm not feeling that way."

"Why?" she asked innocently.

"Because there's one more thing I want to do before I go," he answered, giving in to the irresistible pull drawing him to her.

With an inquisitive tilt, she lifted her chin and her gaze centered more squarely on his. "What?"

"This."

Wyatt stepped forward, slid his hands around her waist to her back and caught her up to his chest. Slowly he lowered his lips toward hers, giving her time to push him away, turn her face in rejection or something to give an indication she didn't want this kiss as much as he did. Her hands flattened against his chest, but there was no pressure from her palms to move him back. Understandably, she needed time to think and consider how she felt about what he'd just done and what he wanted to do.

He'd give her all the time she wanted, but he had to satisfy an earnest need to kiss her before he left.

At last, her answer came when he saw her chin rise, her lips parting ever so slightly. Her eyes drifted closed. Wyatt brushed his lips against hers with as much tenderness as he could impart given how much he'd wanted to kiss her.

A fluttering breathlessness filled him. When had such a simple kiss left him breathless? Fredericka must have felt it too. She gasped into his mouth.

Her lips were soft, cool, and enticing. From the first touch he knew he wanted more than the chaste kiss he intended to give her, but Wyatt knew she wasn't a lady to be rushed. While his lips moved tenderly back and forth across hers, with slow, intended strokes, his hands roved up and over her shoulders, down to the sensuous curve of her waist, and farther to the firm flare of her shapely hips and slender thighs.

She felt soft with her breasts pressed against his chest. A hunger for her grew inside him, but he managed to take his time, continued to be gentle and caressing. Right now, he was in no hurry and would kiss her sweetly for as long as she would let him.

When her arms wound around his neck as she leaned fully into his body, a rush of sweet, innocent desire swamped his senses. He tightened her into his embrace. The shawl fell away from her neck and shoulders exposing the inviting scent and warmth of her neck.

Without his knowing how it happened, a masculine moan of anticipation escaped with his breath. Her hands left the collar of his coat and her fingers slid into the back of his hair with gentle ease. Soft murmurs of pleasure floated against his lips, enticing him further. Never expecting her to be so pliant, he longed to deepen their tender kiss, coax her sensual, delectable mouth open, and taste the depths while crushing her lips beneath his. He wanted to tangle his hands in her hair and let his lips explore the column of her neck, chest, and rise of her breasts.

There were many things he wanted to do, but not today.

Perhaps the reason was his honor? His respect for her? Maybe it was the pact they made for a marriage of convenience? It could have been the simple answer of not wanting to frighten her with the intense passion that flared so quickly it left him with thoughts of how good it would feel to lay her down in the early spring grass and cuddle with her under the warmth of the heating sun.

He had to quell his natural instincts to forget who she was, where they were, and act only on how willingly she accepted his kisses and how desperately he wanted to continue what he'd started.

She was his wife after all. He should feel free to be as passionate with her as he wanted. But he didn't. Not now. There would come a time, but it was too soon to settle down with her. It was best he leave things between them as they were. Best he leave her.

By sheer will, he raised his head. Her breaths were as fast and unsteady as his own. In a low, husky voice he said, "Since you are a proper miss, I wanted to give you a proper wedding kiss before I go."

An attractive blush stained her cheeks once more and

she slipped out of his arms. Midday sun sparkled in her eyes again as her gaze held steady on his. "That felt very improper, Your Grace."

He smiled. "It's best I not show you what an improper kiss is."

Yet.

CHAPTER 7

DAISY——BEAUTY AND INNOCENCE
——L. H.

Oh! beautiful upon his sight,
Who bears a heart like mine,
Doth shine the soft unconscious light
Of loveliness like thine.

"That's good to hear, Miss Gladwin," Fredericka told the robust young woman who'd worn the same rigidly drawn smile since she entered the book room of Paddleton and sat down. "I believe in children being well-disciplined with their manners and lessons. But I also want to make sure they are given opportunity to romp outside and enjoy nature on beautiful days."

"Oh, I would do that," the potential new governess answered confidently. "It's important they learn all about the various trees, plants, herbs, and such that grow on this lovely estate while they take in fresh air. I'll make certain of that, Your Grace."

It was exactly what Fredericka wanted to hear. Charles needed to know every inch of the grounds. She had explored parts of the deeper woods with him, but definitely not all of Paddleton's sizable lands. The girls were never eager to be outside stomping around in the forests or marshes, be it winter or summer. The wildflower fields were as far as they wanted to go.

While Fredericka found the explorations a relaxing diversion from everyday life, the girls did not. They were content to remain within the tended grounds where there were stone paths to walk, benches to sit on, and well-tended gardens to look at and play in. It was Miss Litchfield's preference too.

"And poetry?" Fredericka asked Miss Gladwin.

"It's as necessary as the other studies. Poetry can sustain us when nothing else will. I can put it at the top of my list for reading, writing, and reciting if you would like that?"

"That's good to hear. A child needs to know a certain amount to be well-rounded in all things."

"What I don't know myself," Miss Gladwin continued, "I'll find someone who does. The children won't be lacking in their education on any level with me in charge."

Yes, that reference to *in charge* might be the problem with someone as firm-handed as Miss Gladwin appeared to be. Fredericka couldn't bring herself to turn off Miss Litchfield no matter who else she hired. The women would have to learn to work together, even if they had very different approaches to teaching a child. However, Fredericka decided to save that to ponder a different day.

She had been very careful during the interviews to make sure Miss Litchfield was busy with the children. Fredericka didn't want her to know about the possibility of a second governess until the final decision had been made. There had been many people interviewing for various employment opportunities since she became a duchess, so it was unlikely the aging governess suspected Fredericka was looking for an additional one.

"I'll have Master Charles ready for boarding school when the time comes," Miss Gladwin assured her. "There won't be a young man who knows more than he does. The same for the girls, of course. They'll be ready to manage a household as large as this one, or larger, when it comes time for them to make a match."

"That's what I want." Fredericka rose from her chair. "Thank you, Miss Gladwin. You do sound quite capable. It's my hope to decide on someone soon. I appreciate you making the journey out here. I'll be in touch. Mrs. Dryden will show you out."

After seeing the governess into the hands of the housekeeper, Fredericka walked back into the book room but suddenly couldn't bear the thought of sitting behind the desk again to go over her notes on all the women. She had conducted four interviews with prospective governesses earlier in the day and completed three yesterday. She never dreamed there would be so many responses when she'd written to the employment agency in London for their help. Apparently, everyone wanted to work for a duchess. It was good to have several choices to consider, but that made it harder to make up one's mind. They all seemed capable.

But which was best for the children?

Fredericka bypassed the desk and walked over to the window, which looked out over the back lawn. Across the meadow surrounded by trees and dots of woodsy plant growth, it looked as if a storm was brewing in the western sky. Light-gray clouds hovered just above the horizon, and darker ones gathered just above them. They would definitely see rain sometime during the night.

As had happened so often in the four weeks since her marriage, her husband crossed her mind. Why, she didn't know. There was nothing romantic about his proposal or their marriage. Well, almost nothing. There was the second kiss down by the fence. That startlingly tender joining of their lips was impossible to forget.

She must have relived it a thousand times already. That wasn't the problem. The fact that she wanted to relive it in person a thousand times more was. Their kiss had gathered intensity so quickly and easily, Fredericka felt as if she had been waiting for the experience all her life. She had welcomed the deep passionate desires he'd stirred inside her with open arms and mind. To the duke, at the time, her response must have seemed as if she were ready to delve into all the marriage bed had to offer with no boundaries to stop him. Or her.

It was still so unbelievably hard to consider herself married since she hadn't heard one word from the duke since he left Paddleton. But—she hadn't written to him either. One of her fears was that he'd see correspondence from her as a nuisance. He'd made it quite clear he didn't expect her to be a part of his life for a long time to come. She understood. And what could she say other than to thank him for the new staff, the allowance, and other things she'd already thanked him for?

He was by all accounts a scandalous rake of the highest order. More unbelievable was the way she had so quickly and easily melted into his arms like butter on hot toast when he'd caught her to his chest and kissed her as if leaving her was the furthest thing from his mind. He was so daring and she loved it.

She didn't know what had gotten into her. Except for the fact that it felt divine. His languid approach and comforting warmth had seeped through her body and bones, filling something inside her she'd never known was empty. When she'd opened her eyes after the kiss and looked into his, she hadn't expected to see a glow of tenderness and concern for her. It made her feel wanted. Something she hadn't often felt.

The delicious sensations he evoked lingered inside her.

Longing wasn't the feeling she'd expected to be left with, but she was sure that's what it was. Especially since it was clear from the Society pages and scandal sheets she read each week that her husband hadn't given her a minuscule of thought since returning to London with news of his marriage. He was constantly being mentioned for having attended party after party and all without his mysteriously missing bride.

Some of the reasons speculated for her absence were so outrageous she had to laugh at the absurdity of them. One such rumor was that she had suffered a horrific facial burn after the ceremony and now couldn't be seen in public. Though the article failed to mention how said burn might have occurred. Another scandal sheet speculated Fredericka had lost her sanity right after they married and had to be kept in a dark room so she wouldn't harm herself or anyone else. Perhaps the most ridiculous of all was that, unbeknownst to the duke, before the wedding ceremony she had grown a gray beard.

She remembered the duke saying not everything written in the gossip pages was true. He was right!

Shortly after that, she realized she must stop reading the gossip or she would truly go insane. Though not being able to read the pages was a loss. With living at Paddleton and away from Polite Society, the gossip sheets had been an enjoyable pastime. She looked forward to the columns each day, reading every word with relish many times during the week. Upon reflection, she realized she had wanted to believe most of what was written in them was true. Until now. It all changed when she became one of the main topics in the articles.

So, she stuck to her poetry books and writing her verse. She found pleasure there too. Just a different kind.

She turned and looked back to her desk. Underneath all the interviews and notes was one letter from the duke. His proposal about marriage that she hadn't opened until her wedding night. After everyone had gone to bed and the house was quiet. Somehow, reading the few terse words he wrote made her feel that eventually everything was going to be all right. That she would be able to keep the children and bring them up the way Angela would have wanted.

It was truly miraculous, and totally unreasonable, how her life had changed in little more than a month. Sometimes she'd awakened in the middle of the night with her heart pounding and her breath running at a rapid pace, wondering how in the world she'd become a duchess. It had happened so fast. Even the ceremony had appeared far too short while seeming to last forever at the time.

But the changes were a reminder she was indeed a duchess. Dressmakers, milliners, candlemakers, and a host of others were coming to Paddleton daily wanting to know what they could do for her. Mrs. Dryden now had three helpers in the house, not one. So did the gardener and groom. The grounds and house had never been so tidy and splendid.

And Fredericka didn't pay for any of the staff. The duke was taking care of them all.

The sound of voices from the front of the house and the quick stomp of footsteps coming down the corridor broke Fredericka's concentration.

"It matters not to me she's now a duchess. I will see her."

Jane.

Finally, after weeks of silence, she was going to hear from her cousin. Fredericka had wondered why she hadn't received an immediate response from Jane about her marriage to the duke. But then Jane had never been one to answer Fredericka's letters, but was the first to complain if she didn't receive one.

Mrs. Dryden appeared in the doorway, trying her best to keep Jane at bay, but the housekeeper was no match for Fredericka's cousin. She swept through the door with her usual flourish and flair, her eyes shining with what Fredericka could only believe was simmering outrage hidden behind her best fake smile.

Mrs. Jane Tomkin, wife of a viscount's younger brother, was beautiful, petite, and a lady you didn't ever want to cross. As a child, she was selfish, vengeful, and spoiled to the core. If she had been disciplined a little more when growing up, maybe she wouldn't think she was entitled to everything she wanted. Including someone else's children. Years of being married to Nelson, a fairly sedate gentleman who adored her and counted himself the luckiest man in the world for having won her heart, hadn't softened her one bit.

From the first day Fredericka and Angela had gone to live with her cousin's family, Jane had taunted her with slights. She was missing a tooth, too quiet, too skinny, too young, too anything and everything. And most of all, Jane always said Fredericka was in the way—an inconvenience that had come into Jane's life. As they grew older, it had only gotten worse.

Fredericka didn't remember her mother at all and had only vague remembrances of her father, who had died when she was four and Angela twelve. Jane and Angela were the same age. They would talk, giggle, and do things together, always skipping about, and showing their ankles like high-steppers. Never letting Fredericka join in any of their activities even if it was as effortless as sitting in the drawing room reading a book. Because of her sister's and cousin's closeness, Fredericka had felt Jane took Angela away from her. She still felt that way. And now Jane wanted to take her sister's children too.

Yet through it all she and Jane were now the only blood kin the children had left, and Fredericka didn't want to sever that tie. It was best to get the visit over with.

"I tried to stop her, Your Grace," the housekeeper offered with a worried expression.

"It's fine, Mrs. Dryden. Jane is always welcome to come inside the house and find me."

She looked aghast. "But you're a duchess now."

Fredericka smiled at the older woman. "It's still all right. She's family. Please prepare tea."

"No, no. That's most kind of you, Fredericka." Jane walked farther into the room, untying the ribbon of her fashionable black straw bonnet trimmed with red silk roses. "I'm not staying for tea."

"Oh, that's right," Fredericka said, matching her cousin's pleasant tone. "You never stay long enough for a cup when visiting with the children."

"Really, how much visiting could I possibly do with you watching every second I'm with them. Besides, I want to spend all the time I can with the little darlings." She plopped her bonnet onto one of the chairs opposite the desk and started unfastening her short cape. She then paused. . . . "But, please, allow me first to offer my respect." She gave a deep curtsey. "Your Grace, thank you for seeing me on such short notice."

Fredericka didn't mind Jane's insincere tone or false smile. She expected her cousin to be angry that she'd been outmaneuvered. "You know you don't have to stand on formality with me."

Jane smoothed the sides of her dark-brown hair back into place. "No, I don't know that."

"Oh, gooseberries, Jane. We slept in the same bed at times when we were growing up. There was never a thunderstorm when you didn't come running into my room. We can't start being so formal with each other now."

A bright smile eased across Jane's face. "So, I have your permission to continue to speak frankly and treat you as family?"

"Always," she answered, not wanting to put up with her cousin's nonsense. Now that Fredericka was married to the duke, Jane's bark would have no bite. "How will I know what you're thinking if you don't speak forthrightly to me?"

"Indeed," she answered innocently. "Thank you. I was quite hurt you married the Duke of Wyatthaven without so much as a hint to me that you were going to. I'm not surprised you didn't have manners enough to invite me to the ceremony, but not even to write and let me know afterward left me quite hurt. I had to wait until news reached me from friends who came to stay with us."

"What are you talking about? I wrote to you that very evening, and it was posted the next day."

"Yes. To London," Jane chided. "I've been in Kent since Christmastide. I've had more trouble with headaches than usual, which detained us there. The apothecary was trying a new treatment for me. I'm better."

"That's good, but I had no way of knowing," Fredericka defended, while feeling a little sorry for Jane. The headaches had plagued her for years. "You aren't usually there this time of year. You could have sent word that you were staying later so my letter wouldn't have been misdirected."

"And you could have sent an announcement to London and Kent," Jane countered, and then added a tsk of annoyance on top of acting offended.

Fredericka pursed her lips for a moment and remained quiet while she wondered how big of an argument she wanted to have with her cousin. As small as possible, she decided. The more she said, the more Jane would say. Fredericka had been down that road so often she knew every inch of it.

It never served a purpose other than to make Fredericka feel bad after the quarrel was over. Too, she knew pouting about not receiving the letter wasn't the real reason Jane was there. And thankfully marrying the duke had settled that reason.

"Next time I have news, I'll send to both homes. Does that make you feel better?"

"It does." Jane gave her a look that indicated she actually appreciated the concession. "May I?" she asked, pointing to the chair beside the one where she'd placed her bonnet and cape.

"Yes, of course," Fredericka answered, and leaned her backside against the front of the desk.

"I didn't know you and the Duke of Wyatthaven knew each other. You haven't been to London in quite some time that I'm aware of."

Not wanting to say an outright fib, she hedged. "Perhaps you don't remember, but I had a few days of parties my coming-out Season and met many people during those evenings."

"Of course I remember," she answered in a musing tone. "It's still quite perplexing that when the duke could have married any young lady in London, Paris, Vienna, or the world, he chose you."

Fredericka knew how easy it was for Jane to get the upper hand in a conversation and always had to be careful how she handled her cousin. She simply said, "Yes."

"Heaven knows what you must have promised him to get him to do so," Jane added softly.

"Nothing," Fredericka blurted out before she could stop herself. She shouldn't have given Jane the satisfaction of an answer of any kind to such a malicious remark.

Of course, there was *fidelity* the duke had asked for but shouldn't have, and he knew it. That was none of Jane's concern. Fredericka intended to keep it that way.

With an uncompromising stare, she declared, "What would I have to give a duke?"

"Precisely," Jane whispered under her breath. "I'm told everyone in London is talking about your marriage. And I can't blame them. It seems no one believes it's a real marriage. It was so sudden and not even in London surrounded by friends and family. I heard the duke left immediately after the ceremony and didn't even stay for the wedding buffet."

Fredericka tensed, remained silent, and hoped she looked unflappable. Every word Jane threw at her was like a sharp dart. Each one hitting their mark. That the duke hadn't stayed long after the ceremony *was* cause for gossip.

"From all I heard," Jane went on as she touched her hair in seeming indifference as to what she was saying, "he continues to live in London much in the way of the carefree bachelor he's always been."

"My marriage has nothing to do with you. I won't talk about my husband or address any more of your snide comments."

Jane leaned forward and gave her a confident smile.

"If you think marrying a duke such as Wyatthaven in the dead of night is going to change the Lord Chancellor's mind about who will be best guardian for Elise, Charles, and Bella, you are sadly mistaken."

At last, her cousin had revealed her true reason for coming. Fredericka lazily crossed one foot over the other and folded her arms over her chest, not allowing the worry she felt to show. "It wasn't the dead of night." Not even the scandal sheets had said that.

Jane's dark, full eyebrows rose. "There's talk that the two of you didn't even wait the required amount of time before the ceremony."

"Idle gossip," she defended with a wave of her hand, knowing Wyatt had admitted they were cutting it close to finish the ceremony per the law and instructions in his grandmother's will. "We married late morning and every rule was followed appropriately, including the amount of time required after posting the banns."

"We shall see," Jane offered with a flippant tilt of her head. "I'll make sure the matter is looked into quite thoroughly."

"I expect no less, but why would you?"

"Because I don't intend to give up my pursuit of Angela's children and I will use anything at my disposal to do that."

Fredericka felt as if a lead ball had been dropped into her stomach, and she straightened. She'd hoped what the duke had said would be true, marriage to him would make Jane give up the idea of gaining guardianship of the children.

Jane rose from the chair with a sighing breath. "You shouldn't mind that. You have done the same by marrying the duke. I want the children to be mine, and I'm going to see they are."

Old feelings of jealousy Fredericka had always tried so hard to defeat wanted to take root again. "You don't have a leg to stand on."

"Angela always treated me like a sister, and she loved me as much if not more than she loved you," Jane continued in a mock-cheerful tone. "My parents took both of you into our home and treated you like daughters. Angela would want me to care for her children since we were so close. It's a shame no guardians other than my parents were stipulated in her husband's will and they have passed on. Now that you are married, there is no reason you can't have children of your own. That is, if you can get your husband to stay the night with you."

Taking a step forward, Fredericka issued a warning with her eyes. "You are going too far."

Jane held fast to her ground, seeming not the least intimidated by Fredericka's unusual show of aggression. "I haven't gone nearly as far as I'm willing to go."

Fredericka was beginning to believe her and that was terrifying.

"Perhaps you don't remember, but Nelson's brother Viscount Longington has agreed to look into the matter at Chancery, as he has a close friend there. He is willing to put in a good word with the court for us. Nelson and I have had a strong marriage for eight years and have loved the children as our own."

Fredericka couldn't let that stand without a challenge. "Loved them? You've seldom seen them."

"Only since you've been caring for them, my dear. Angela and I visited each other a couple of times a year. Surely you remember." She smiled sweetly and picked up her bonnet and cape. "Now, if you don't mind, I'd like to see the children before I go. I brought confections from London for them."

"Yes, of course," Fredericka said tightly. The sooner Jane saw the children, the sooner she would leave. "They are outside getting fresh air and learning about all the flowers that are sprouting in the garden. I'll have Mrs.—"

"No need to bother anyone," Jane said with a happy lilt to her voice. She nodded toward the desk covered in interview papers. "You look busy. I know the house and grounds well. I'll see myself out to the back lawn."

Watching her walk away, Fredericka was about to sigh with relief when Jane pivoted at the doorway and turned back.

"Oh, not that you asked, but I would have loved to stay for dinner and overnight, but I'll be on my way back to London as soon as I give the children a kiss and a hug and spend a little time with them. . . ." She paused and gave a snobbish glance around the book room. "I couldn't bear the thought of staying in this drafty old house when London is only two hours away and there's plenty of daylight to travel."

Fredericka tensed again. "What do you mean you couldn't stay here? This is the children's home."

"For now. But I'm not opposed to them returning here for a visit after they are mine. I want them to be happy so I'll allow them to visit from time to time."

"Visit?" Fredericka's chest tightened with anger. She thought of how Elise had clung to her after the wedding, fearful she would be left alone and abandoned the way she felt after her mother died.

"Of course. They will have a governess, tutors, servants. Whatever they need, no matter where they are. They are my family, and I intend to make them feel as if they are my own."

"How about love?" Fredericka shot back, the very

real thought of losing them causing a hollow ache in her chest. "They need that as well."

"I'll be sure to give them plenty of that too. I always have. Just as I always loved your sister. Don't worry, Fredericka. Children are adaptable. They settle in wherever they are."

Without saying more, Jane turned and left.

Fredericka walked over to the window again. The children were not studying the flower garden and learning about the various plants and trees that grew on the grounds. Miss Litchfield was sitting on a garden bench with her nose stuck in her own book and paying no attention to the children, as she so often did. Fredericka definitely had to make a decision about an additional governess.

Elise and Charles were throwing a ball to each other, and Bella was twirling around with arms outstretched and holding a doll in each hand. Fredericka smiled as she watched their carefree activities. It gave her such pleasure to watch them play. She knew, at times, she worried too much about how they were behaving instead of simply being happy they were with her, but she wanted to be a good mother to them for Angela.

But right now there was something far more important she had to do. Counter Jane's machinations, and something just flashed through her mind. Though Fredericka would like to take a long time studying over the ramifications of how her idea would affect her or the children, there wasn't time. A decision needed to be made quickly. There was one thing Fredericka was sure of. Jane's impromptu visit to Paddleton hadn't been just to let Fredericka know she was not giving up her desire to take the children. She had been on an expedition to find out more about Fredericka's hasty marriage to the duke. No doubt to use against her in court.

The children stopped playing and ran to meet Jane. She hugged them generously and started dispersing her treats. They had always enjoyed her visits even though they were short. She'd never had to teach them anything, calm them if they got upset, or soothe them when they cried. She'd never had to promise to stay with them when they were frightened to be alone, or discipline them when they misbehaved.

All Jane knew how to do was breeze into Paddleton for an hour or two, lavish gifts and treats on them, and leave. That's what Fredericka's role in their lives used to be too. When her sister was alive.

Fredericka drummed her fingers on her crossed arms. She'd known all along her cousin was serious. When Jane set her mind to something she wanted, she didn't give up. She was going to continue her efforts to do everything possible to take the children away.

"Let her try," Fredericka said aloud. "A duke trumps a viscount and his youngest brother."

There was only one thing Fredericka could do. If the gossips in London didn't believe she had a real marriage with the duke because she wasn't living with him, clinging to his side every day with visits to the parks, attending parties and other social events, she needed to do something to put a stop to that kind of talk.

Fredericka had to go to London, live with the duke, and prove them all wrong.

CHAPTER 8

VERVAIN
——DRAYTON

She night-shade strows to work him ill,
Therewith the vervain and her dill,
That hindereth witches of their will.

Wyatt leaned casually against the doorjamb and looked out over the drawing room in his London town house. He spotted the lovely Miss Priscilla Fenway smiling at him again. He returned her expression with a slight nod as he had throughout the evening. She was radiant in her dove-colored dress with dark-silver embroidered satin banding on the short, capped sleeves and high waist. A narrow crown of pearls and white stones sparkled in her coppery-brown hair.

She was definitely the belle of the evening.

The party was a crush. When a duke invited someone to his house, no matter the reason, they came. If it was a soirée, and not a scolding for an offense, perceived or otherwise, all the better. The room was pleasantly cool, the music lively, and the chatter and laughter full of merriment. A glass of champagne, wine, or other beverage was held in most everyone's hands and the evening had progressed gaily.

His butler, Burns, and staff had managed an excellent job of readying the house in the exclusive section of Mayfair for this special event. The double doors leading from the main corridor into the drawing room where Wyatt now stood, were swung wide, allowing for easy flow to other rooms. All the furniture, except for a few gilt-coated chairs with green velvet cushions, had been moved out to allow enough space for the elegantly clad guests, servants moving about, and musicians with their instruments.

Every candle in the chandeliers and wall sconces had been lit. Fresh flowers of snowdrops, peonies, and jonquils in shades of white, pink, and yellow sat atop the baroque mantelpiece and hand-painted plant stands had been placed in the corners of the large room. A sprinkling of fresh-cut red roses and spikes of greenery were perfectly arranged in every bouquet.

Some guests stood in small intimate gatherings talking quietly while others fluttered about like butterflies on blossoms, sticking their noses into everyone's conversation as they passed.

Wyatt hadn't often hosted a party during the Season, but when he had in years past, it was purely for selfish reasons. He wanted to be one of the first to meet the bevy of young ladies making their official debuts into Polite Society. This year was different. He wasn't looking to meet anyone.

He was only having the party for Priscilla.

"I think this is the first time I've seen you alone all evening," Rick said, coming up to stand on one side of Wyatt while Hurst took the other and extended him a glass of champagne.

"A welcome change," Wyatt answered, and took the drink his friend offered.

"Are you sure?" Rick answered with more than a little

disbelief in his tone. "I saw Mrs. Seymour talking with you for a lengthy time. And later, Mrs. Lovell seemed to have you pinned against the wall. Is anything going on that we need to know about?"

"Only the usual."

A gruff sound of amusement rumbled in Rick's chest. "So, Mrs. Seymour wants you to stop by her house so she can show you how beautiful her garden is in the evenings with all the lanterns lit. And my guess is that Mrs. Lovell wants you to come for tea so she can get your opinion on some thoroughbreds she's contemplating buying."

Wyatt shrugged with indifference. "I think you must have been eavesdropping on our conversations. You are damned near close to being right about both of them."

"But what is it you want?" Hurst asked, looking at Wyatt thoughtfully.

Not the widows who were letting him know they were still available if he was. He knew that for sure, but nothing else seemed as clear to him. However, he wasn't going to bare his soul to his friends, so he remained silent and sipped his drink.

"You have to admit, you invited the widows and other ladies to continue approaching you with solicitations and hints of willingness. You are attending the Season and now giving a party in a young lady's honor without your bride by your side," Hurst pointed out.

"True." Why deny the obvious?

Not too long ago he would have taken both ladies up on their invitations without blinking an eye. The desire to do so was gone. Strange as it was, he'd felt different since returning to London a married man. There had been some changes in his behavior and wants that he never expected.

It was also true that Fredericka was never far from

his mind. He certainly hadn't wanted that. Nor had he done anything about it. Not even a short note to inquire how she was doing. Why should he? He was determined she wouldn't be a part of his life until he was ready to have a son.

His mistake had been in giving his wife the second kiss. The first one was the proper one to seal their arranged marriage. He should have left it at that. No heat. No emotions. No desire. A slight brush of two sets of lips that had left no lingering effects.

Ah, but the *second*.

Memories of that kiss in the cool, fresh air with sun shining so warm and bright upon them had been heavenly to think about these past weeks but had also been a thorn in his side.

If he hadn't been so tempted by her innocent and unintended charm, as well as her acceptance of his advance, he wouldn't know how yielding and deliciously sweet her lips were. He wouldn't know how effortlessly and perfectly she fit into his arms, or how comfortable she felt pressed against his chest. As it was, sometimes he'd awakened at night and thought he heard her soft breaths and murmured sighs so close to his ear he could almost swear she was in the bed beside him.

It was maddening how often she'd been on his mind these past weeks. When he made the decision to marry and fulfill the requirement of his grandmother's will, he hadn't expected to be musing over his wife at all upon returning to London.

But he had.

It didn't take much to remind him of Fredericka. Such simple things as the cool of day, the warmth of the sun, and a bouquet of spring flowers would bring her to mind. It was much easier to push thoughts of her aside when he was in the middle of a heated fencing match, watching horses race, trying to outwit his opponent in a card game, or playing his heart out in a cricket match. But on a night like this, with lovely ladies all around, he found himself wondering how he would feel if Fredericka were by his side giving him intimate little smiles, or inviting sidelong glances and come-hither expressions from across the room.

"Rick says no, Wyatt. What do you think?" Hurst asked.

"Remind me of the question," Wyatt replied with a guilty grin.

"You weren't listening to us," Hurst grumbled. "I thought as much. I asked if you see a young lady here tonight I should consider giving up my bachelorhood for?"

"Any of them and all of them," Wyatt answered, scanning the room filled with belles who were looking to make a match before the Season was over.

"They do get more beautiful each year."

"Bloody hell, Hurst." Rick snorted. "You are getting older each year. If you would get yourself a mistress, as most respectable men do, you wouldn't always be dreaming of finding that true love you're expecting to discover behind every lace fan. Chances are the feeling isn't real anyway. If it is . . ." He paused and downed a good portion of his champagne. "I don't think it will come from among ladies who are promenaded before us during the marriage mart."

Rick looked at Wyatt as if waiting for him to back up his lecture to Hurst. Wyatt hesitated, and Rick must have assumed he knew why.

"You do still have a mistress, don't you?" he asked.

"I haven't seen her lately," he admitted, disinterested in the subject.

A knowing look passed between Hurst and Rick.

"Because you're married?" Rick asked, as if the very idea was a piece of foreign matter to him.

Deceiving his friends had never been easy, but the truth was he didn't know why he hadn't been to see her. It was best to give them an answer that would be hard for them to swallow. "I've been busy."

Hurst chuckled and brushed his pale-blond hair away from his forehead.

Rick sent him a mocking smile of laughter. "Hell, no. Too busy to see a woman for an hour or two of pleasure? What's it been? Five or six weeks since you returned to London? Longer?"

"A month," Wyatt offered.

Rick glanced over to Hurst. "What's the life of a gentleman coming to in England? This?" He pointed at Wyatt with the hand holding his glass. "A man who won't enjoy what God, nature, and mankind gave him?"

Wyatt and Hurst remained silent.

"I don't know what I'm going to do with you two," Rick complained with a scoff. "Both of you are taking women far too seriously."

It was time to change the subject, so Wyatt asked, "How are wagers coming along for the shooting match tomorrow?"

Rick downed the last of the drink in his glass. "Looks as if we'll have a fine day for all festivities. You feeling confident about the card game afterward?"

Wyatt nodded. "I heard Lord Tartanville brought in a marksman from Oxford to enter the match. There's talk the earl insists this man is better than you with pistol and bow."

Rick's brows rose and he smiled confidently. "I hadn't heard but not surprised. Someone is always trying to best me. The stronger the competition, the more bets will be placed. The more bets, the more money we win for the Brass Deck to give away. Unless . . ." Rick paused and shot Wyatt a devilish glance. "If you're worried I'll lose, you can always bet against me."

Wyatt chuckled derisively. "What would you do if I did?"

"What I always do. . . ." Rick paused just long enough to make his point. "Win."

"Don't go further with this conversation," Hurst chimed, quick to keep peace between the two men who didn't always see eye to eye on things even though their brotherly love was never questioned.

"It's just getting interesting," Rick said half-jokingly.

"And I'll end up throttling both of you," Hurst answered. "I would rather not have to stop another duel between my best friends."

"That was years ago," Wyatt reminded him.

"And for a good reason." Rick nodded in agreement. "We were deep in our cups."

"No reason is ever good enough. And neither of us will ever bet against you again be it bow, pistol, blade, or a young lady's attention." Hurst grinned for a second before adding, "The tables are always an exception, Rick. Wyatt has the edge there. A slight one."

"You bloody—"

"Your Graces," Grant Fenway greeted them, walking up and giving them a questioning look. "I hope you don't mind if I interrupt for a moment. I can see each of you another time if you wish."

"No, join us," Wyatt said, and then added under his breath, "before I have to ask Hurst and Rick to step outside so I can remind them who the best pugilist is."

"Ah," Grant said knowingly. "Sounds as if the *best* of the Brass Deck Team are arguing who is *best* again."

They all chuckled.

Grant was relatively short for a man, barrel-chested, soft-spoken, and often wore a timid smile. He wasn't in line for a title, nor did he have a wealthy allowance, but he never made a nuisance of himself about it or anything else. The trio of dukes had always considered him a part of their extended group whenever he was around.

"You were tied up greeting everyone when I arrived. I didn't get the chance to thank you for hosting this party in honor of Priscilla." He looked specifically at Wyatt. "Having a duke show my sister much attention is making all the eligible bachelors take notice of her. I mean, who wouldn't want to be married to a young lady who has a duke for a friend?" He smiled and looked hesitantly at Hurst and Rick. "Three of them in fact. I'm indebted to all of you for showing her such kindness tonight and through the years."

"Nonsense." Wyatt shook his head. "It's her beauty, poise, and sweet nature that has all the gentlemen giving her attention. Her successful debut has nothing to do with who's giving this party or how many dukes are in attendance. I know the Season has just started, but does she have her eye on anyone in particular?"

"Not that she's indicated," her brother said with a worried expression as he scanned the crowded room. "Soon, I hope. Though I will tell you again, she pouted for days after she heard you'd married. I believe she hoped you'd wait for her."

Wyatt chuckled. "There's not a chance in Hades she was pouting about that. She thinks of me as just another brother, and you know I treat her as the sister I never had."

Grant smiled, nodded, and then glanced from Rick to Hurst with interest.

"She's like a sister to me as well," Hurst offered, laying his hand over his heart. "I could never look at her any other way."

"Likewise," Rick added on the heels of Hurst's last word. "If I had a sister, I would never allow her to marry someone like me."

"Nor would I," Wyatt and Hurst said at the same time.

Grant laughed and lifted his glass in a toast to the three dukes.

Wyatt winced silently. Memories flooded to his mind while the others continued to talk.

Beneath Grant's white cotton glove, Wyatt could see the misshapen form of Grant's right hand. The knuckles had been splintered and broken years ago at Eton. The seriousness of the injury was neglected far too long and the bones mended badly. His first three fingers were left with no feeling. Headmaster Buslingthorpe said the damage had come from a fight with other boys and that Grant had hidden the injury until it was too late to set the bones properly.

It was a lie. The damage was inflicted by Buslingthorpe's stick and Wyatt's fault. That morning Wyatt couldn't remember the lines of poetry he was to recite in the classroom. It infuriated the headmaster: *"I can't strike the son of a duke, but perhaps you will make more of an effort to learn your lines for your friend's sake."*

Wyatt still remembered the loud crack of Buslingthorpe's thick birch hitting Grant's hand. The headmaster often carried the wood under his arm while walking around the classroom whispering his favorite refrain, *"Discipline, son, discipline."* Wyatt had hated poetry since that day, and he never missed learning his lines again.

Wyatt had never forgiven himself for not speaking up about Buslingthorpe's abuse, for not telling his father and insisting the man be dismissed from the school. Countless times, Wyatt had wondered how many other boys had been disfigured by the stick the headmaster carried.

Now it was too late to say or do anything. Buslingthorpe had passed on years ago. Wyatt's anger hadn't. Guilt for not doing more when he could have had Wyatt doing things for Grant now, hoping in small ways to make amends for Grant taking the punishment due Wyatt. Buying his drinks, offering to lend him money to gamble, and hosting this party for his sister.

Grant wouldn't accept more from Wyatt and seemed to hold no animosity toward Buslingthorpe. That was all right. Wyatt had plenty for the both of them. And it was renewed every time he saw Grant's hand or remembered the nights he'd heard boys crying in their beds. They weren't all crying because they missed their families. Some were in pain.

"Your Graces," Priscilla said, beaming as she sidled up between Wyatt and her brother, taking the time to smile at each of the four men. "Please forgive me for interrupting, but when I saw all of you together I wanted to come over and ask what you think of Mr. Fergus Altman. He's definitely the most handsome gentleman here tonight. I almost lost my breath when he looked at me."

Wyatt immediately scanned the room. The young man she was referring to watched her, obviously interested. Wyatt only knew enough about him to say the important things. "He knows how to hold his cards and his drink and has a decent reputation in the clubs."

Rick and Hurst immediately nodded.

"I've heard that as well," Grant added.

"His family line can measure up to anyone's," Hurst offered. "Lord Tartanville is his cousin."

"None of that matters," Rick said offhandedly, "nor anything else. If he makes your heart flutter in your breasts, accept his pursuit."

Grant and Hurst cleared their throats uncomfortably.

Priscilla giggled.

"Chest," Rick corrected quickly. "Not brea—never mind." He grimaced. "I should always drink brandy or port. Champagne gives me a damned headache. Grant, don't look at me like that. I swear I meant 'chest.' That's where the heart beats. The chest. Right? Not in the—well."

"We're trying to tell you if the man asks you to go for a ride in the park, we approve."

Rick and Hurst added yeses to Wyatt's sentiments.

Priscilla looked over at the young man before turning back to Wyatt. "I'm glad all of you approve of him." She sighed softly. "It's enchanting to be the center of attention for the evening. To have one duke host a party for me and for two others to attend makes me feel like a princess at a ball."

"It's your night," Wyatt said with a sincere smile.

"Thank you, Your Grace." Priscilla looked directly at Wyatt. "Would you mind doing one more favor and have a short dance with me?"

"Pris, whatever are you doing?" Grant glared at his sister.

"I must ask," she insisted. "Some guests will soon start leaving to attend other parties, and I want to make sure everyone sees me with His Grace."

"Priscilla, please, don't," her brother continued. "You can't ask a gentleman to dance! Nor is it polite to ask the duke to do more for you than he has already done. Show some well-mannered behavior instilled in you and—"

"It's all right, Grant," Wyatt said, hoping to calm his friend. "The three of us were already thinking a dance might be in order to cap off the evening." Wyatt glanced from Rick to Hurst to be sure they would back him in agreeing to something they'd never discussed.

"I'll give you thirty seconds," Hurst said, "and then I'll cut in and take over."

Priscilla's pretty face lit up with delight.

"You will only get twenty seconds from me," Rick answered with a smirk. "I'll finish the dance."

"I knew you would do it!" Priscilla exclaimed, seeming to hum with excitement as she looked at each duke, favoring them with more gleaming smiles. "Well, of course, I mean I was hoping all of you would agree. I couldn't be sure."

"This is most inappropriate, Priscilla," Grant insisted, looking distressed. "I don't want any of you to feel you must accommodate my little sister making a nuisance of herself. She's outrageous and you are encouraging her."

"It's her party," Hurst answered. "Both of you should enjoy it."

"But she's imposed quite enough on our friendships already. She's making a pest of herself," he grumbled.

"Why would we ever feel as if we *had* to dance with a beautiful young lady?" Rick injected. "Besides, I see Mr. Altman continues to give his concentration to your sister. Perhaps it would be good for us to make him think he has competition."

Wyatt hid his amusement and added, "Grant, go tell the musicians to play a waltz."

Priscilla folded her hands together in front of her

and said, "I could kiss all of you for doing this for me."
She gave Grant an engaging smile before adding, "But
I won't, of course. Don't get worried, dear brother. Not
even a sisterly kiss. That would be far too presumptuous
of me."

"As if you haven't already been so," Grant muttered
under his breath before heading toward the ensemble.

Wyatt handed his glass to Hurst and offered an expression that said, *Interrupt the dance whenever you are
ready.* He then proceeded to walk with Priscilla to the
center of the room.

As if realizing what was happening as Wyatt and
Priscilla took a dance position in the center of the room,
the crowd parted and gave them a wide circle to move
around the floor with the sweeping moves the newly
fashionable waltz required.

After they were only a few seconds into the dance
and she had taken a couple of twirls under Wyatt's arm,
he sensed something wasn't right in the room. Looking
over Priscilla's shoulder, he could see no one was watching his partner.

Every guest's head seemed to be turned toward the
double doors that led to the corridor. Must be a new-
comer to the party that had everyone's attention. Curious, Wyatt maneuvered Priscilla so he could see what
the attraction was.

Staring at him in disbelief was his beautiful wife.

CHAPTER 9

WEEPING WILLOW——FORSAKEN
——MRS. JAMIESON

All that it hoped,
My heart believed;
And when most trusting,
Was most deceived.

Wyatt felt as if a thoroughbred's hooves pounded in his chest.

He immediately let go of Priscilla as an inexplicable desire to rush to Fredericka, pull her into his arms, and hug her close sparked through him. He was damn glad to see her.

But . . . the emotion he saw in her eyes for a fleeting moment stopped him from doing what felt so natural. Was it betrayal reflected in their depths? How could it be? He was only dancing. Yet his whole body tensed as if he were being pricked with needles.

On one side of Fredericka stood Bella and Charles. Elise was hugging her aunt's skirts on the other. Fear struck him. His mind raced with the possibility something terrible had happened to bring them to London.

"Fredericka, what are you doing here?" He strode toward her, covering the distance between them as fast as he could.

"Obviously, making a mistake," she answered in a terse tone as Wyatt cleared the threshold of the drawing room and stopped in front of her.

That was an odd thing for her to say.

He glanced down at the children. Bella lifted her smiling, angelic face toward him, clearly glad to see him. Charles looked at him with what appeared to be wide-eyed confusion, and Elise turned her head away from him and locked her arms tighter around Fredericka's waist.

No one was bleeding. None of them looked harmed, sick, or in pain, but something must have happened to bring Fredericka to his door in the middle of the night.

Swallowing past a tight throat, he gave his attention back to Fredericka. His heart started beating even faster. Her eyes were swirling with questions. He had quite a few himself.

"What's wrong?" he asked.

"I'm sorry, Your Grace," Burns hurried to say. "When she said she was Her Grace, I asked that she wait in the entry until I—"

"Not now, Burns," Wyatt said quickly, holding up his hand to halt his butler. "You did fine."

"But it appears I have not." Fredericka's words were icy and her eyes fierce. "It didn't cross my mind that you might be having a party this evening."

Wyatt tried not to let his thoughts get ahead of her explanation, but he couldn't keep his chest from tightening in fear again. "Did you come here straight from Paddleton? Tonight?"

"Yes," she responded coolly as her flush deepened. "We arrived just now."

Wyatt's jaw clenched at the thought of her traveling the lonely, dangerous roads at night. "You shouldn't have come!" he exclaimed.

Fredericka gasped. So did the bewildered elderly governess standing beside her.

Theirs weren't the only gasps. An ocean wave of them roared behind him. He looked back. The music had stopped, the chatter had quieted, and it seemed as if everyone in the drawing room had crowded closer to listen.

Suddenly Wyatt realized how unacceptable *"You shouldn't have come!"* sounded.

"That's quite clear," Fredericka said in a miffed tone as her spine stiffened. "To me and everyone else."

Hellfire! She was taking his words the wrong way.

"Hurst, Rick, keep the partying going," he said in a raspy voice. "Burns, close the doors."

Not waiting for the butler to shut out their audience, Fredericka locked eyes with Wyatt. "However, you are right. I shouldn't have come without proper notice, and I apologize for intruding on your evening."

He matched her stare-for-stare. Anger blossomed in Wyatt's chest. At her for putting herself and the children in danger of highwaymen, coach accidents, or other perils that could happen in the dark of night, and himself for handling her arrival badly.

"You're not interrupting—"

"No? You were dancing!" She might have sounded wounded, but her eyes were throwing imaginary daggers at him with every word she spoke.

"With Priscilla," he answered, having no patience for the accusations she implied. "It's her—"

"Please," she cut him off with the single word. "You don't owe me an explanation about anything."

"Apparently, I do, Fredericka, and on this we will be clear." He heard the doors finally shut behind him and the music start again. "You misunderstood what I was doing and what I said."

"So, this is *my* fault because *I* misunderstood you?"

Tension like he'd never experienced before swirled and sparked between them. She was twisting his words again.

"When I said you shouldn't have come, I only meant you shouldn't have traveled at night. Not that you shouldn't come to my house. What do you mean by such a foolhearted stunt? The roads leading into London from Paddleton are unsafe and riddled with crime at this time of evening."

"I took precautions," she challenged, refusing to back down. "I had the groom come with us."

"A groom?" he barked, and swore under his breath.

"He and my driver are quite efficient with pistols and muskets, and both were well armed. We encountered no trouble. Perhaps the highwaymen took one look at the old carriage and assumed there couldn't be anything of value inside or just maybe a guardian angel traveled with us. Whatever the reason, we are safe."

Wyatt had never known such a headstrong lady. She was stubbornly ignoring his concern for what she'd done.

"You are far too independent for your own good, Fredericka," he retorted. "Whatever the reason you were spared trouble, it doesn't make the danger you put yourself in all right."

"Not according to you," she responded instantly.

"It's just as well you came to London," he said, realizing she'd not only stirred his passions when he'd kissed her at Paddleton, but she'd stirred his need to protect her and the children. He softened his expression and moved closer to her. "You need someone to take care of you."

"I do not, sir. Can't you just be thankful for the miracle you seem to think it was that nothing villainous happened tonight and let it go at that?"

Yes, he could. No matter how she arrived, the truth was he was happy to see her. Wyatt took hold of her upper arms thinking to draw her near and give her a quick hug of welcome but froze when Elise screamed out, "Don't hurt her! Please, please don't hurt her."

"W-what are y-you doing?" Charles shrieked.

Wyatt let go of Fredericka instantly, stepped back, and held up his hands for all to see, wondering what in the hell he had done to cause the children to react so strongly.

"Wait," he said cautiously. "I'm not going to hurt her." Damnation. What was going on?

Fredericka gathered Charles and Bella closer to her, trying to enfold them into the comfort of her arms. "Shh—" she whispered to the children as she kissed the forehead of each one. "Everything is fine, my darlings. There's no trouble," she whispered softly to them.

Unsure what to say or how to restore calm, he offered, "See, I'm not touching her or anyone. Everything is all right. It concerned me to hear about you traveling at night. That's all. Nothing else."

Needing a moment to figure out what had happened, Wyatt kept his gaze on Fredericka's, trying to determine if she really thought he meant to harm her in some way. It was apparent the children did. But why?

A childish sniffle caused him to look down. Bella was holding both hands squeezed tightly over her mouth, her shoulders were shaking, and a tear rolled down her cheek. Elise continued to sob pitifully with her face buried in Fredericka's cloak.

What kind of man was he to make little girls cry?

Their sobs suddenly triggered memories from his past and, unbidden, his thoughts returned to his time at Eton when in the cold dark of night he'd heard quiet whimpers

and deep moans from boys struggling with their fears
and pains as they lay in their beds.

Because Wyatt hadn't understood why the boys were
crying, he hadn't known how to comfort them. He'd just
turned nine when he arrived at the boarding school and
had seldom played with anyone his own age. He didn't
know what to do for them, so he'd stayed in his own
bed and never tried to reassure any of them things were
going to be all right.

Wyatt swallowed the old, tormenting emotions. He
still didn't know how to comfort anyone. Especially little
girls.

But this time he had to try. He wasn't going to be
guilty of hearing a child cry again and not do something
about it. Even if he had no idea how to comfort Bella.

Swallowing the knot of emotion trembling in his
throat, Wyatt bent down on one knee. "Bella," he spoke
softly, and forced a smile through his turbulent feelings
of ineptness and the magnitude of what he was attempt-
ing. "Everything is fine and will stay that way. I promise.
I'm glad to see you. All of you." He made a point to look
up at Charles and Elise before giving his attention back
to Bella. "It's been a while, and I've been wondering how
you are doing."

Bella slowly lifted her head, removed her hands from
her mouth, and whispered, "I dropped Sarah."

"Sarah?" he questioned her.

"Her doll," Fredericka whispered from above him.
"Bella dropped her on the floor."

That he could handle. He searched around his feet
and found the cotton puppet with a painted face. He
glanced from the doll to Bella's damp cheeks and trembly lips.

"Look at her," he soothed. "Sarah is smiling. She

knows everything is going to be all right and you don't have a reason to cry or be frightened." He put the doll's face to his ear and pretended to listen. "She's telling me she wasn't hurt when dropped and wants to go back to you."

He handed Bella the doll and she hugged it to her chest as she rocked back and forth.

To keep his actions from being misconstrued again, he cautiously reached out and wiped each of Bella's wet cheeks gently with his thumb before reaching over to lightly ruffle Charles' hair. "I need you to help me calm your sisters."

Charles hesitated and looked up at Fredericka before asking Wyatt, "W-what d-do you w-want me to do?"

Wyatt wasn't sure what would work, but he had to try something. "Maybe you can say something that will make them laugh. Or make a funny face like this." Wyatt then put his thumbs on his temples and wiggled his fingers while widening his eyes. "Can you do that for me?"

Charles smiled and then stretched out the corners of his mouth with his forefingers and stuck out his tongue. Bella giggled. Elise watched from underneath Fredericka's arm but didn't crack a smile.

"That's a good one, Charles. Thank you for helping me."

Wyatt rose and looked at Fredericka. Her eyes were riveted on him.

"I thought we'd stay here," she said on a broken breath. "I see now that's impossible. We'll go to an inn instead."

"No," he said firmly, giving all his attention to Fredericka. Her eyes were anxious, but so was he. "You are my duchess. No matter the current circumstances. You and the children are staying here."

"You have a party going on," she reminded him, her voice punctuated with urgency. "I have no intentions of troubling you further."

Oh, she troubled him plenty, but not in the way she was thinking.

"Don't be stubborn about this, Fredericka. There are ample rooms in this house. This is your home, and you will stay here." And for the first time, he realized it *was* her home.

"Burns, see to rooms immediately. Have fires lit and trays of food sent up. Make sure there are plenty of sweets on all of them."

"Yes, Your Grace."

Wyatt looked at the governess. "Go with Burns and get the children settled. The duchess will be up shortly."

"I don't want to go with her." Elise sniffled and hugged her aunt tighter. "I want to stay with you, Auntie."

"Elise," Fredericka said softly, as she removed the little girl's arms from around her waist and then held tightly to her hands. "Everything is all right. Stop weeping or you'll upset Bella again. The duke meant it when he said there is no reason for you to be frightened. I'm not going to leave you alone here. Now go with Miss Litchfield."

"You are safe in this house," Wyatt told Elise in the same soft tone he used with Bella. "Your aunt will be up shortly."

"But I—"

"Elise," Fredericka interrupted, giving her a confident smile. "I know this has been a difficult evening for you, but I will be right behind you and we will have a chat about it all."

"You promise?"

Her aunt smiled and touched her cheek affectionately. "I do."

"Come with me, missy," the governess said in a comforting voice as she took hold of the girl's hand and started leading her to the stairs with Bella and Charles. "We can't stand here in the corridor all night. Besides, with a party going on in this house, I know the desserts will be scrumptious. We've already heard His Grace tell the butler to make sure we get a good share of them. I'll let you eat all you want."

As soon as the children were halfway up the stairs, Wyatt said, "We need to talk, Fredericka. Let's go to my book room."

"No," she whispered, shaking her head as she untied her bonnet and took it off. "I'm not up to talking any longer tonight. I need time to think. Something I should have done before I came here."

Wyatt's heart started pounding. She looked as if she was on the verge of tears. That made him feel even more like a monster. "I want to explain. You don't understand about the evening."

"You're wrong," she murmured in a disappointed tone. "Of course I understand. We had an agreement that you could continue to live your life as you please. I've broken that by coming here. I allowed worry to get the best of me today and did something I shouldn't have done."

"What?" he asked, feeling her obvious concern and believing she was finally going to open up and let him know what brought her to London.

"Make a hasty decision. That seems to be something I've been doing ever since I met you. I know better. I should always study on big decisions for a few days and think out all the possibilities before committing to an answer. You were right when you said I shouldn't have come tonight. Please get back to your party."

Fredericka turned away. Wyatt reached for her arm to stop her but caught her hand instead. It was soft but cold. When she turned back to him, he quickly let go. "I don't give a damn—I don't care about the party, Fredericka. I care about whatever it is that brought you here in the middle of the night."

"My cousin, Jane, and it's not something that can be solved tonight. Probably not for some time and maybe not at all. You may not care about your guests, but I care about the children. I've upset them by coming here. Especially as hastily as I did. It's late. I need to be with them and reassure them all is well. Besides . . ." She rubbed her arms as if she were cold.

"Besides what?"

"If you return to the party now, you may be able to quell some of the gossip about us that must be going on right now."

Wyatt scoffed, "It doesn't matter. There will always be gossip about us. I'm not letting you go to bed thinking I was going to hurt you or the children when I took hold of your arms. I only wanted to—" He caught himself and paused. He almost said he wanted to hold her. That was the last thing he needed to say right now. "It's true I was upset you had been on the road so late."

With a steady, serious gaze, she offered, "I never thought you were going to harm me."

"Then why did my action prompt Elise to act as if I was the devil himself? Why did she beg me not to hurt you? You haven't ever been—?"

"Watch what you say, Your Grace." Fredericka inhaled a deep, heavy breath, her eyes flickering in outrage as her shoulders drew up tight in defense.

"I'm trying to understand why they were so frightened."

"You can't do that by offending me."

His gaze held true and unwavering to hers. He had to ask. "No. That wasn't my intention."

She relaxed and looked down at the bonnet in her hand for a moment before lifting her somber gaze to his once more. "I suppose there's no reason I can't tell you. Their father was sometimes harsh . . . with Angela. Not the children, she insisted."

"Bloody blackguard," Wyatt whispered in a low tone.

"I don't think it was often," she said with vague reassurance, and then added, "I always hoped it wasn't. But at times, the children were witness to his anger. More than once, I believe. I don't think Bella remembers much about her parents at all. I assume that when you took hold of my arms, it must have brought back memories for Elise. She's been so fragile since her mother died. I never thought you were going to be rough with me. I wouldn't have married you if I had believed you capable of that kind of behavior."

He nodded with relief. He despised men who used their strength on women or children. "I'll have to make sure Bella, Elise, and Charles know that too."

"They will, in time," she said in a soft whisper. "I'm tired and ready to go up, if you don't mind. The road was bumpy and the carriage cold. I would rather wait until morning when I have a clearer head to carry on this conversation. Go, finish your dance."

He started to snap at her and say again he didn't give a damn about the dance, the party, or anything else, but he could see in her face she was weary and needed to rest. "I'll be waiting for you in my book room in the morning."

She nodded, turned, and started up the stairs.

Wyatt looked back to the closed doors of the drawing

room. The music and hum of chatter had returned, but he had no desire to rejoin the merriment. It was one thing to enjoy the carefree life of bachelorhood when his wife wasn't in the house. When he'd seen her in the doorway, all of it had felt wrong.

What a hellish night doing a simple favor for Grant had turned into.

How could he have ever imagined Fredericka would come to London unexpectedly? Or that the children had been traumatized not only by their parents' deaths but also by their father's ill treatment? Children and women should never feel the strong hand of a man, whether father or headmaster.

Wyatt swore under his breath again and shook his head. He knew a wife was going to be trouble. His father had warned him about it many times over the years.

Now, it appeared he would find out for himself just how much trouble, and if he was up to the challenge.

CHAPTER 10

Seldom was there a reason for anyone to make a hasty decision.

Waking in the duke's house this morning was proof impulsive behavior should be avoided as carefully as the thorn on a rose. Fredericka knew, as in all good judgments, there should be a fair amount of planning and preparation first. She had done neither.

She made her way slowly along the upper corridor toward the stairs holding a candle in one hand and lifting the hem of her apricot-colored dress off the floor with the other. It was daybreak and the house was still relatively dark with no lamps burning and most of the draperies in the house closed.

Once she made it belowstairs, she would have to search for the location of the book room, which she assumed would be toward the back of the house. She didn't expect the duke would be up for quite some time, but she'd become too restless to remain in the bedchamber any longer.

Last night, after getting Miss Litchfield and Elise settled in one room and Charles and Bella in another, Fredericka had closed her eyes to rest, but it hadn't done much good. What little sleep she'd managed was fitful. All the worry had given her a headache behind her eyes. Not even the poetry she read had settled her.

At first light, she decided to dress and go down to wait for the duke to join her. Only Heaven knew what time that would be. Clearly he wasn't ready for the life of a settled married man, but maybe she could persuade him to pretend to be until guardianship of the children was settled.

Her stomach knotted as she remembered him twirling the beautiful young lady under his arm. She felt as if a sledgehammer had been slammed against her chest and knocked all breath from her lungs. Yet, in that moment, she'd realized coming to London was a mistake. Jane and the scandal sheets had warned her the duke's high society evenings hadn't changed at all since their marriage. He was carrying on with his usual life as he'd told her he wanted to do.

When she'd arrived, she'd seen carriages lining the street and the duke's house lit as if it were the Grand Ballroom on opening night of the Season. There were sounds of music and the roar of chatter as she'd walked up the stone pathway to the front door. As she was still immersed in all her worry and frustration and weary from the grumblings of the children about the journey, it hadn't actually sunk in that Wyatt was hosting a party. But what could she have done if it had?

She was already there.

It hadn't been difficult to talk her way past the butler and gain entrance once Fredericka told the man who she was. Perhaps she could have avoided the calamity that happened after if she'd waited in the vestibule as he'd asked. But filled with an alarming amount of worry, she followed the man instead. When she looked into the drawing room where the lovely music was coming from, she'd seemed to freeze in place.

Of all the things she could have imagined happening when meeting the duke again, seeing him dancing with a lady under flickering candlelight with a roomful of people watching wouldn't have been one of them. Neither would the prick of jealousy that spiked through her as quick, forceful, and unexpected as a lightning strike.

Fredericka didn't know why seeing him living his carefree life in the flesh, doing what she already knew he was doing, made her feel as she had so many times when growing up. As if she was in the way and didn't belong. At the time, all she could think was that everything the gossip pages had said about Wyatt's social life was true.

And maybe she did have a gray beard after all!

Though she guessed there had been a small part of her that wanted to believe all the things she'd read about him were false and that marrying her had caused a change in him. Now she knew the fallacy of that.

Morning had arrived; reality had set in. Fredericka was more settled and more prepared to do whatever was needed to clear up the jitters about her husband and outwit Jane. Upon reflection, she was glad she hadn't talked in detail with Wyatt after she arrived. At first, she had been ready to return to Paddleton without so much as a good-bye. Sometime during the long night she'd returned to her sensible self and remembered why she came to London in the first place.

However, her renewed resolve didn't mean she didn't dread the upcoming conversation with the duke.

Fredericka made it to the bottom of the stairs and, deliberately avoiding a glance toward the drawing room, started down the corridor peeping through all the doorways on both sides until she found the book room at the back of the house. With it too dark to see anything other than three tall walls of bookshelves, she walked straight to the desk and placed the candle down so she could open the draperies.

"It's about time you got here."

Startled, Fredericka almost knocked over the candle. She whirled to see Wyatt sitting in a high-back armchair in front of the fireplace, where a bed of embers glowed like a setting sun.

"Jumping gooseberries, Wyatt. You scared me silly. I didn't see you sitting over there."

In response, he rose from the chair and started toward her. An uncommon shiver of excitement wove through her. Heavens! He was a fine-looking man. A heavy swell of anticipation choked her throat. Her heart started pounding like a chunk of iron against an anvil and seemed to reverberate all through her body.

It took a moment to realize why he looked so appealing. He wasn't properly dressed. He wore no coat, waistcoat, or neckcloth and collar. Only a white shirt tucked into the waistband of well-fitted trousers. His hair looked as if his hands, or someone's, had run through it several times, leaving it quite tousled. That, coupled with a night's growth of stubbly beard, left him with a decidedly rakish appearance.

Which was way too attractive for her feminine sensibilities to deal with rationally. Especially so early in the morning. Not only that, she should have been mortified seeing him in such a casual state of undress. With his broad shoulders, tapered waist, and muscular thighs showing so impressively beneath his clothing, he simply looked too magnificent for words.

She really should leave, but he stopped, conveniently or not, between her and the doorway and regarded her intently.

Propriety dictated she at least avert her gaze, but she couldn't do that either. The best she could manage was to say, "I feel I came upon you at an inopportune time. I didn't mean to barge in before you were ready to receive anyone."

"You didn't." His voice was husky and alarmingly sensual as his gaze stayed focused on hers. "I've been waiting for you."

Waiting for her? His face was sober, and his eyes were clear. He knew what he was saying. Had he been up all night? But of course he had. He'd hosted a party.

"But you aren't properly dressed," she responded, hoping her voice didn't give a hint as to how tempting she'd found his current state of attire.

Wyatt snorted a soft laugh and took another couple of steps closer to her. Perhaps too close considering it made her whole body feel as if it turned to liquid.

"We are married, Fredericka. I believe it's all right for you to see me with my coat off."

She wasn't sure. She could see the base of his strong masculine neck and the bulge of his upper chest and arm muscles, and other things she shouldn't be looking at— married or not.

He smiled at her while his sparkling gaze swept over her face. "You, on the other hand, look beautiful, rested, and ready to answer all my questions."

Fredericka didn't know what to say. She'd had a

miserable night. And now finding herself face-to-face with his obvious masculinity wasn't what she'd expected.

"Yes. I suppose you're right," she admitted, powerless to keep a faint rush of heat from creeping up her cheeks as she averted her eyes from his quite astounding body.

It wasn't that she minded his unconcerned attention to his clothing. Far from it. For reasons beyond her comprehension, he looked much more pleasing clothed as he was now than when tucked up to his chin with a pointed collar and neckcloth. But it was best to move on from how he presented himself, or she might find herself trying to also analyze why her body tingled deliciously at the sight of him. Doing that would serve no useful purpose.

She cleared her throat with a cough. "I didn't think you would be up this early."

Wyatt didn't move. He just stared at her with those daring blueish-gray eyes that always appeared as if they wanted to look into her soul. "I never went to bed," he informed her.

Piqued to feel another spike of something that felt very much like jealousy, she flinched and only said, "Oh my."

"As I said, I've been in here waiting for you."

"Here? I would have thought you were tired after such revelry and went straight to your chambers after the last guest left. I heard music until wee hours of the morning."

Seeming slightly amused by her comment, he answered with steady calm, "You must have been hearing music in your dreams, Fredericka. Everyone, including the musicians, had gone on to other parties within a couple of hours after you went up."

"No doubt because they wanted to spread the news of my unexpected arrival."

"Some of them couldn't leave fast enough," he agreed without quibbling.

"I'm sure. Most of them heard you ask what I'm doing here and say that I shouldn't have come."

"Fredericka." He shook his head ruefully. "Those were ill-chosen words not meant the way they were said or heard."

"I know that now." Somewhat. The feeling of being in his way and not being wanted in his life lingered.

"I should have welcomed you properly as my wife and insisted you come join us so I could introduce you to everyone."

"What?" She let out a breathy laugh. "I had on an old traveling dress. And even if I had gone up to change, I have no gowns appropriate for such a gala evening as you were hosting."

Wyatt scowled. "You have an allowance for the purpose of your wardrobe."

She shrugged off his comment and stepped away from him. "I've been considering modistes who have sent me designs to consider, but I haven't settled on anything."

"It's time you did."

The truth was that she had no idea she'd be coming to London so soon. She had no need for fancy gowns in the country. Besides, there was no seamstress near Paddleton with the skills to sew a gown that would compete with the French-designed finery she'd seen last night.

"Tell me," she queried, unable to keep at bay her inquisitiveness about what happened after she went abovestairs. "Were you asked many questions about us when you returned to the party?"

His jaw seemed to harden. "No one would dare question a duke about his wife."

Relief settled through her. "Good. The least said the better. I hope your dance partner wasn't too distraught at being left so abruptly in the middle of the floor."

His brows drew close together. "Not at all," he answered pointedly.

That admission did nothing to make her feel different about the scene she had witnessed. She didn't even know why she'd asked, other than extreme curiosity about the lady who looked so lovely and comfortable in his arms.

"We do need to talk about the party and the dancing," he continued.

Yes.

"But I want to take care of the most important subject first." His expression became more intense. He moved closer again and settled his gaze directly on hers. "Do you really think I could sleep until I heard what was so important it brought you to London well after dark in what you admitted was an unsafe carriage?"

"Oh, that," she acknowledged, thinking it wasn't the most important subject to her. But she was happy to put hers off as long as she could.

"Yes, *that*," he emphasized with the rise of his well-shaped brows. "We haven't spent a lot of time together, Fredericka, but enough for me to know you don't make rash decisions, you don't take things lightly, and you don't run at the first sign of trouble. What happened with Jane that brought you to London when doing so put you and the children at risk?"

Her shoulders tightened at the truth of his words and she glanced away for a moment to collect her thoughts before speaking. Perhaps rushing to London was foolish. No, it definitely had been, but that was neither here nor there now. The deed was done and it couldn't be altered or reversed. They had made it safely. That's what mattered.

"All right, since you want first things first," she said,

squaring her attention on him with unwavering purpose, "I take exception to something you said. I would never knowingly put the children at risk. Second, the carriage is old, but my driver assured me it's not unsafe. Third, the reason I came here is not small, or insignificant. Jane paid me a visit yesterday and told me she's not going to give up her pursuit to gain guardianship of the children as we had hoped when I married you."

His eyes narrowed with concern once again. "And that made you feel you couldn't wait for daylight or possibly have sent a letter by messenger telling me this?"

"A letter!" she scoffed ruefully, remembering the one-sentence missive he'd sent to her weeks ago. "An offer of marriage can't be settled by a simple letter, and neither can this."

Wyatt's expression turned into a full grimace. "Mrs. Tomkin wanted to vex and worry you, and obviously she did."

Fredericka bristled. He could rile her faster than Jane.

"I married you with the belief I wouldn't have to be concerned about her machinations anymore. You and I thought your title would intimidate her into withdrawing her petition. Since that hasn't happened, nor is it likely to, I have an idea that might work and wanted to talk about it in person."

His gaze swept down her face as his expression softened. She wished he wouldn't look at her that way. It caused her stomach to feel jumpy and her breathing to quicken.

"All right. I'm listening. Tell me." He reached over and brushed her hair just above her ear and let his fingers trickle down her cheek to her chin before moving his hand away.

The unexpected touch sent tingles racing across her breasts and quivers knotting her lower abdomen. She was suddenly aware of the warmth radiating from the embers in the fireplace a few feet away, and the heat from Wyatt, who had somehow managed to get within inches of her.

Wanting to settle the tingles caused by his caress, Fredericka pulled in a deep breath and released slowly. His touch had been soft, and almost consoling.

"Since Jane doesn't believe we have a real marriage because we aren't living together in the same house and seen walking arm in arm in the parks, at parties, and other social events during the week, I thought perhaps I could stay here in London with you for a time so that we could attend some affairs together. It would be good for us to be seen in the parks and walking around Town with Elise, Bella, and Charles."

He shook his head immediately. "No, that's not what we agreed on, Fredericka. I have other things to do and cannot accompany you and the children around Town. You will go back to Paddleton as soon as I have arranged for a suitable carriage and guards for your safe travel."

Her chest constricted. For a second or two, she felt as if she were six years old again and Angela and Jane were telling her she was in their way and bothering them. Only now it was her husband telling her she needed to go away. He didn't have time for her and didn't want her around. Taking a deep breath, she forced the unhappy childhood feelings away. She couldn't dwell on the rejection. She had to think about the children and what was best for them.

Fredericka rose above the hurtful memories and stinging words from the duke. Her suggestion was a good one and she wasn't going to let go of it so quickly. There was uncertainty in her voice, but she had to say, "Since I am here, it won't hurt to try."

"It won't help."

"You don't know that. You are being unreasonable," she insisted firmly. "It may quell some of the gossip about us and look good to the Lord Chancellor if we lived together as a properly married couple for a while."

The duke stubbornly shook his head again.

It fueled her to keep talking. "It would prove to Jane and all the gossipmongers they are wrong about us. We will present ourselves as having the same solid and adoring relationship that Jane and Nelson, her husband, have."

"Adoring?" He took a step back and stared at her as if he'd never heard the word before. Certainly not in connection with himself. "We don't have to prove anything to your cousin, Fredericka. I don't see how pretending anything will help in court. Many husbands and wives spend a great deal of time apart and live separately."

Fredericka swallowed hard. "That's true, but many couples aren't trying to gain custody of children."

"Surely Mrs. Tomkin doesn't think our living arrangements will matter in Chancery."

It was as if he wasn't listening to her. "That's the problem, Wyatt. She does, and so far you and I have done nothing to make her believe otherwise. That is why I'm suggesting I stay here and we do things together. Nelson has made claims that his brother Viscount Longington knows the Lord Chancellor well and can persuade him to see things Jane's way."

Wyatt's eyes seemed to study her for a bit too long before he spoke. "There are reasons the two of us and the children doing things together as a family won't work."

She folded her hands across her chest in frustration and stared at his handsome face with determination. "You don't have to remind me it wasn't part of our arrangement."

"Good. I don't have time for walks in the park and rowing on the Serpentine, Fredericka. My training schedule and tournaments for the Brass Deck Club are long, often, and hectic."

"Training?" She had heard of men's sporting clubs where all manner of skills were tested and enormous amounts of money were won or lost on the outcome of the games and matches.

"Billiards, fencing, and cricket as well as others. We take each tournament seriously. Especially this time of year. A great number of wealthy people are in Town for the Season and they want to gamble on their favorite team. It's the opportune time to have tournaments for the men to attend, enjoy, and place their wagers. There are several events already lined up. I have to practice and stay focused in order to make sure I win my games."

"Really, Your Grace!" she exclaimed. "I would think my problem is a little more important than a cricket match or horse race."

His eyes softened and searched hers. "I know, and I'll handle this problem for you, but it won't be by rides in the park."

He seemed to be trying to convince himself more than her that he would get it done. "Today?" she questioned because he seemed hesitant to commit.

Wyatt shrugged, and then gave her a reassuring smile. "I don't see why not. I don't personally know the Lord Chancellor, the Master of the Rolls, or anyone else in Chancery, but I daresay they will listen to me over Viscount Longington and Mr. Tomkin. I have other plans and obligations I must attend to today, but I'll take care of this as well and a carriage so you can be on your way back to Paddleton."

"Plans?" she asked, with an unexpected flare of emotion and frustration that he wouldn't even consider her idea after she'd come all the way to London to present it to him. He was dismissing her as if she were an unwanted fly buzzing about his head. And not for the first time. Blinking rapidly, she held back the threat of tears gathering behind her eyes.

Unreasonably, she asked, "Do those plans also happen to include the young lady you were dancing with?"

Keeping his gaze solidly on hers, he said, "We might as well talk about Priscilla and get it over with."

Priscilla.

It wasn't surprising she had a name as lovely as her face and as graceful as her dancing.

"It's none of my concern. No, I shouldn't have asked. I don't want to hear about her," Fredericka admitted honestly, and glanced away from his tight expression of irritation. She just wanted him to help her keep Angela's children for her own.

"You brought her up," he reminded.

She glanced back at him and matched him gaze-for-gaze. "I changed my mind."

"I don't intend to keep this insignificant matter hanging between us, Fredericka. There's no reason to. I've wanted to tell you about her since you arrived."

"Very well. I suppose I have been curious and I do need to know."

"Miss Priscilla Fenway is the sister of a good friend I've known since my days at Eton. Grant's not a wealthy man but a good man who would like to see his sister marry well. So would I. Since the day of Priscilla's birth fell during her debut Season, I offered to give a party in her honor. I'm sure you know having a duke host an evening for a young lady increases her chances for getting suitable offers and making a good match. Rick and Hurst were involved in the arrangements too. We all wanted to do this for Grant and Priscilla."

His answer sounded reasonable, kind even, but it also brought up the question, "Why didn't you marry her instead of me? That would have settled your problem and hers."

"She's a sister to me and always has been," he answered, his tone becoming less tolerant. "But even if she wasn't, do you really think I'm capable of pursuing a young lady I couldn't possibly marry?"

"No, I guess not," she answered honestly, feeling her own temperature rising.

Wyatt stepped in closer to her once again and put his hands on his hips. "You aren't convincing me, Fredericka."

"You two were the only ones on the floor in what seemed an intimate embrace. The truth is that I have no idea what you've been doing in London these weeks we've been apart other than what has been written in the scandal sheets. And quite frankly, they haven't been flattering to either one of us."

A muscle worked in his jaw and his eyes flared with anger. "The scandalmongers make their money by dreaming up and printing outrageous stories to entertain the ton and anyone else who will read them. You know that. You should also know ruining a proper young lady for my own pleasure isn't something I would ever do. I have a mistress for that."

Stunned by his outrage, by his words, she could only whisper, "You have a mistress?"

"Yes," he answered on a ragged breath. "What do you think a gentleman of twenty-eight—"

"Please, please don't say more." Abruptly, reality closed in on her so fast her head spun. No wonder he didn't want her upsetting his life. An uncomfortable knot rose in her throat, but she managed to say, "I understand completely and no further comment on this subject is necessary."

What was she thinking? Of course he had a mistress. What wealthy young man wouldn't? She had to think rationally about these things. This was the path she'd chosen for her life for the foreseeable future. Fredericka couldn't blame Wyatt for anything she'd agreed to, and she couldn't now start having uncertainties about her arrangement. They agreed to lead separate lives.

She wanted to keep the children and he wanted to keep his freedom. It was that simple.

By indomitable concentration, she kept her emotions in check and continued to look steadily into his eyes as if her will were made of stone. "I really don't want to delve into your private life. Truly. That's not why I came. I don't know why I even mentioned Miss Fenway other than my curiosity and unfortunate tendency to overthink things."

The cadence of Wyatt's breathing altered as he calmed. Regret was strong in his features. "I'm sorry. I didn't mean to get so heated. The truth is I . . ."

He paused, not finishing his sentence. She was glad, feeling quite sure she didn't want to hear any more of his harsh truths right now. But one thing was sure. This conversation settled that they were not going to pretend to live together as a happily married couple. She wasn't welcomed in his life. Her shoulders tightened. Fine. She knew that from the beginning, but it was still hurtful. Years ago, her instinct was to run away and hide in her room when Angela and Jane made it clear they didn't want her with them. Back then, she had no one depending on her. Now she had Elise, Charles, and Bella. They needed her. Fredericka loved them. What would she do without them in her life? She must stay and fight for them.

A calmness settled over her. "We agreed you could continue to live as you always have. I will gladly return to Paddleton, but only as soon as *I* can be assured the children will be left in *my* care as was the stipulation of our marriage. Hopefully you will have that settled by this afternoon."

Wyatt took in a long breath that sounded heavy with derision. For her or himself, Fredericka wasn't sure.

"I will handle this today. Getting you a new carriage and guards might take a day or two longer."

"We can move to an inn."

"You are my responsibility, Fredericka. I will take care of you. In the meantime, you and the children will stay here with me."

Since he was going to talk to the Lord Chancellor today, she could stay the extra time it would take to get a new carriage for the children's safety. But the day it was ready and she had guardianship of the children she would leave, even though, for some reason, the thought of it left a hollow, sinking feeling in her stomach.

"I don't want to force myself on you."

She stared at him, unable to look away from the sudden intensity of his sensual gaze.

Her ears started humming as Wyatt lifted her chin with the tips of his fingers and bent his head down and kissed her lips softly. Once. Twice. Three times before whispering, "Force me?" A gentle laugh fell from his mouth. "You would never have to do that, Fredericka."

CHAPTER 11

POPPY-OBLIVION
——H. K. WHITE

Come, press my lips and lie with me
Beneath the lonely alder-tree,
And we will dream a pleasant sleep,
And not a care shall dare intrude
Upon the marble solitude
So peaceful and so deep.

Wyatt walked through the front door of his town house swinging his black cloak off his shoulders. He chunked it onto a chair with more force than necessary, plopped his hat on top of it with the same intensity, and started stripping the gloves from his fingers.

"I hope you had a good afternoon, Your Grace," Burns said in a low voice, appearing from around the corner.

"I've had better," Wyatt noted tiredly, without bothering to look up from his task. His head was throbbing intensely. Not so much from the brandy—he'd had little throughout the day—but from lack of sleep. He really should have taken a couple of hours to rest before he left the house after having been up all night, and now half of another, but he hadn't been heavy-eyed after his talk with Fredericka that morning. Being with her had invigorated him.

But that was before his well-planned day started falling apart. Now all he wanted was his bed.

"It's unusual for you to be up at this hour," Wyatt groused, throwing his gloves on top of his cloak and hat. "Why haven't you retired?"

Burns laced his fingers together in front of him. "Her Grace is still belowstairs."

Fredericka?

Wyatt whipped his head around to the butler. It was well past midnight. "Where is she?" he asked, taken aback by how swiftly his chest tightened upon hearing she was still belowstairs.

"I believe she walked into your book room some time ago and has remained there. She was in the drawing room most of the evening. Most of the day too. I didn't want to retire in case she needed anything."

"Thank you, Burns. You can go now."

His butler reached for his outerwear things.

"Leave them for tomorrow. I'll see all the lamps are out before I head up to my chambers."

Burns nodded and slipped away as quietly as he'd appeared.

Wyatt wasn't used to having anyone wait up for him. Had something more happened to disquiet Fredericka? Only one way to find out. He strode down the corridor and rounded the polished wooden doorway into the book room without breaking his stride—until he entered the room and stepped onto the deep-red-and-gold-colored rug that covered the oak floorboards.

Blast it!

She stood on a high rung of the library ladder holding

a candle in one hand and a book in the other with her body pressed against the framing to keep from falling.

"Fredericka! What the devil are you doing up there? And holding a light of all things. Get down before you catch your skirts on fire or burn the house down."

"Good evening to you too, Your Grace," she answered, sounding a little perturbed herself as she turned her head to look at him over her shoulder. "I'm not likely to set fire to the house from up here and the flame isn't near my skirts."

"It could be if you drop it when you start down. Now be careful."

"Don't be a fusspot," she answered in an easy voice. "I'm not a bumble-puppy, nor am I prone to accidents."

"Nevertheless, let me have that," he urged in an irritated tone as he made it to the bottom of the ladder and reached up to help.

Frowning, she bent low and handed the candle to him, then rose to her full height once again. She readjusted her footing so she was facing forward and staring down at him.

Wyatt placed the candle on the desk and stretched back for her. "Give me your hand and let me help you."

He was quite sure his voice was persuasive, but Fredericka rebuffed him and made no effort to descend. Instead, she cradled the book she was holding to her chest and held on to the side of the ladder with the other hand.

"I made it up here by myself. I think I can get down without your assistance."

Knowing her, he should have expected such a response. "I have no doubts about your capabilities, Fredericka," he assured her, realizing he must have sounded as if he were ordering her when it wasn't the case at all. Or maybe a little. But too, he didn't want to take any chances she might trip over her hem and fall. "What are you doing up there and why aren't you already in bed?"

Studying him from her seemingly comfortable perch, she gave him a shadow of a smile and calmly asked, "Which question do you want me to answer first?"

"Both," he replied testily, not in a temperament to join her amiable attitude.

Fredericka didn't respond. Except to lift her shoulders, which lifted her breasts, which lifted his spirits. For a moment anyway.

He quickly blew out a sigh of frustration. His head was pounding ferociously, and the backs of his eyes had started throbbing. Thanks to her, his bad day was getting worse. This wasn't the time to have an engaging conversation with a lady who could arouse him without putting out any effort to do so.

Trying to remain composed, he said, "Let's start with what you are doing on the ladder?"

"Good." She gave him another smile. A bigger one, which lifted his spirits even more. "It's always best to go for the easy question first and work up to the difficult ones."

Wyatt's lower body reacted to her sprightly manner. Perhaps she knew his head felt as if it were about to explode off his aching shoulders from lack of sleep, and she wanted to add her own style of delightful torture to his misery.

"I'm doing my best to read the titles of these books." She went on. "The faint yellow glow from the lamp doesn't reach nearly far enough for me to see the writing, so I had to do something about that. I do believe this room could use another lamp or two since it is a reading room."

"Waiting for daylight would have solved that problem for you."

The book room was far more than a reading room. He always came in here when he had important things to think about. It was the place he always felt closest to his father. Some of his earliest memories were of sitting on his father's knee behind the big desk and watching him read and write correspondence.

Wyatt sat in this room each month and critically and accurately assessed every account book. Through all his tutelage growing up, and even more recently, Wyatt had followed his father's example and was never neglectful in his studies or his duty to learn about the vast holdings of the dukedom. Nor anything else. Before his father had died of severe stomach pain eight years ago, he'd told Wyatt to trust and listen to his solicitor, managers, and advisors but go with his gut. That advice had served him well.

He couldn't help but wonder what his father would have done concerning Fredericka. No doubt he would have carried on as usual, and that's exactly what Wyatt intended to do. The Season in London was the busiest time for sporting clubs to make money. He had to stick to his schedule and keep the money coming in for the hospitals.

"Some of the books are very old with thick, textured parchment pages," Fredericka added. "It's marvelous to smell the scent of old paper. Some of the leather bindings have dried, are brittle, and need restorative oil or beeswax."

Wyatt remembered the odor well. His father had loved combing through the old books to see when a section of land had been added to the estates or if a particular person might be related from a long-ago marriage. He had loved books, so maybe he would have liked Fredericka.

"No one ever goes up there," Wyatt grumbled, pushing aside the special reminiscences. "Particularly at night."

"Someone should once in a while." She looked pointedly at him. "It's dusty, and these books are in need of some attention. There are many interesting topics on these shelves that I would like to explore one day— should I ever return to London."

She could really test his patience. And everything else. Of course she would return one day. Later. When he was ready to have a son.

The room was exactly how his grandfather decorated it. His father hadn't seen fit to change anything, and Wyatt didn't either. If it had needed more light for the evenings his grandfather would have put in more lamps. Besides, most men didn't read in the book room at night. It was where friends gathered to have a brandy, a glass of port, and private conversations away from the distractions of servants milling about and cleaning up after dinner.

Wyatt had been drawn to Fredericka since he first looked at her. What he'd felt the afternoon they met had been more than that fleeting spark of intrigue a man can have for a woman who strikes his fancy. He'd thought to get back to London and forget about her, but his desire for her had lingered and now that she was here it was increasing.

Keeping his thoughts away from where they wanted to drift, he argued, "I assumed you were looking for a book to read, Fredericka. There are plenty of them on the lower shelves that you can easily reach. Hundreds. In several different languages. You don't need to be scrambling up the ladder. Day or night. Most of the volumes up there are old journals about the family history and out-of-date account books about the dukedom and its entailed properties."

"I've noticed that." She slipped the book she was holding back into the slot it came from. "But they would be fascinating reading."

Wyatt gripped both sides of the ladder and stared up at her. From this odd vantage point she looked absolutely fetching. She was still dressed in the pale apricot-colored dress she'd worn that morning, though she'd added a matching velvet spencer with a green satin ribbon holding it together at the neckline. Her golden-brown eyes were sparkling as if she were on the verge of doing something devilishly mischievous and knew he would want to be a part of it. She hadn't wilted at all beneath his irritable mood.

That impressed him. Still, she shouldn't have made the climb.

"Why are you not in bed at this hour?"

It was her turn to sigh and she did it so prettily his stomach did a slow roll as she stared down at him. "How could I go to sleep? I was worried about you. I've been expecting you all evening. Where have you been?"

A grunt flew from his throat. Had she really just asked him that? Ah, yes, now he remembered being told that wives always expected their husbands to come home at a respectable hour. That was irritating.

Wyatt straightened and ran a hand through his hair, letting it stop to rest on the back of his neck where tense muscles ached. His eyes felt as if they were pushing out of his head and his temples thumped loudly in his ears.

The devil take it.

Nothing had gone well for him this day. Not his early and unsatisfying meeting with Epworth concerning the Lord Chancellor, the defeat of his final fencing match

of the morning, or the loss of the card tournament tonight. Certainly not the many claps on the back he received throughout the day from men congratulating him
that his wife had finally decided to join him in London.
He had even managed to brush off Hurst and Rick when
he knew they wanted to share a brandy and conversation
about Fredericka after the last game.

As his closest friends for as long as he could remember, they deserved to know a little about his wife's sudden appearance in London. And he would share a word
or two about it with them, but at a more appropriate
time.

Now to top off the evening, his beautiful, stirring wife
was asking him where he had been. He wanted to snap
back that he wasn't used to accounting to anyone for his
comings or goings and he wasn't going to start. But her
gentle manner was so appealing. He had no choice but
to do what any other well-brought-up English gentleman
would. Ignore the question and speak only to her comment. Which was legitimate.

"Worried about me?" He hadn't had anyone worry
about him since he was old enough not to fall down the
stairs.

"Yes," she answered softly. "I assumed you would return earlier."

No matter the drink, the lack of sleep, and the losses,
Wyatt held his eyes steady on hers and what he saw fascinated him. She wasn't condemning him or being intrusive.
She was genuinely concerned about him and had spoken
her true feelings. That was sweet, but annoying too.

"Why?"

"Probably the same reason you waited in here for me
last night. I knew I wouldn't be able to sleep until I heard
what happened at Chancery today."

Wyatt rubbed his neck again and struggled to remember exactly what he'd said to her before he left that morning. His head was so heavy it seemed like days ago rather than hours.

Seeming to understand his hesitancy in responding to her, she continued, "You told me you would speak to the Lord Chancellor or someone at court today about the situation with Jane and get it settled. I thought surely you'd return by midafternoon to tell me all was well and I could return to Paddleton as soon as transportation was arranged. The children waited too, but I finally put them to bed after a late supper."

He grimaced and took in a long intake of breath. "You kept the children up?"

"Don't sound outraged," she answered with a pleasant, almost shy grin, which stirred masculine emotions inside him again. "They didn't mind and enjoyed the extra time for reading. They were eager to know when we would be leaving too."

Wyatt watched the shadowed lighting from the lamp flicker invitingly across her face. Looking at her had him suddenly feeling that if he could just wrap his arms around her, catch her up to his chest, nestle his nose in the warmth of her neck, and close his eyes, his head would stop the incessant pounding.

Then he could kiss her. That's what he really wanted to do.

But it was best he shake those thoughts away for now— if possible. She wasn't inviting him to indulge in the desires his body was craving, but his head was denying.

"I believe I said I would look into it today."

"I'm sure you said '*handled*,' which I took to mean it would be taken care of." Her brows scrunched together determinedly as she moved down a step. "Since you took

so long to return, I assume I can now rest easy that everything is *handled* and I can leave for Paddleton tomorrow
or the next day?"

"No, not yet." His head was fuzzy with tension. "One
reason is that you don't have a carriage, Fredericka." He
never got around to looking into that. Somehow, with
all the other things he had to do that errand had skipped
his mind.

"Well, of course I do." She brushed off his point with
a short laugh. "How do you suppose I got here?"

"I made it clear you aren't going anywhere until I
make arrangements for a new carriage. One that's befit-
ting the wife of a duke and has my family crest on it. I
should have already done so and had it delivered to you,
along with a qualified guard to travel with you and not
just a stable hand."

"And Jane?" she asked without taking her steady
gaze off his.

"It may take a little longer than I anticipated to clear
up the issue with her since she decided not to give up her
pursuit as we'd hoped."

Fredericka's expression morphed into concern. She
moved down another step. "How much longer?"

Pushing the tail of his coat aside, Wyatt rested his
hands on his hips. "I don't know," he admitted, shaking
his head. "A few days. Perhaps a week." *Or longer.* "Rest
assured I will have you on your way to Paddleton as soon
as I can."

"But you were gone all day. What were you doing?"

Wyatt scoffed at her question.

She exhaled loudly. "I'm not understanding the problem. You made it sound as if only a few words from you
to the Lord Chancellor would be all that was needed to
settle this issue with my cousin."

Wyatt grunted a laugh. If only it had been as easy as he'd hoped. "I explained this morning I had other commitments to attend today as well as my promise to you."

"I stand corrected. You did say that, but does that mean you didn't speak to anyone about Jane?"

"Yes. Of course I did."

That's what had been on his mind most of the day. He obviously hadn't had his concentration on his competitions at the tournament. He hadn't lost an important fencing match, a card game, and at the billiards table in the same day in years. That wasn't acceptable to him. By his lack of focus, he had not only let himself down, his club, and his charitable obligation, but he'd disappointed all the other men who were counting on him to win their wagers.

Wyatt was discovering he didn't like letting Fredericka down either.

Figuring honesty was the best way to deal with his intelligent and resourceful wife, he said, "The problem is that when I asked Epworth to arrange an appointment for me to meet with the Lord Chancellor, he reminded me that the Chancellor and I are of different political parties. If I were to speak to him on your behalf right now, he might not be willing to listen to me, so it's best that I wait and not rush this."

"So, what you are saying is that Chancery isn't as easy as walking into the Lord Chancellor's office and declaring you want a certain ruling simply because you are a duke if one is of the Tories persuasion and the other is of the Whigs."

"Yes. Nothing could be settled by me speaking to him today. It's a bit more complicated than I thought because of the politics. This must be handled carefully. There are important issues before Parliament and the two sides are at odds over all of them. If I want the Lord Chancellor to do something for me, I need to be prepared to offer him something he wants."

"This is children we are talking about. Politics shouldn't have anything to do with them."

He understood her indignation, but the Lord Chancellor held a high political appointment and he had a lot of power. "You may not like it, but that's the way it is."

"I see." She studied him closely and took in a deep, steady breath. "Does Jane's brother-in-law, Lord Longington, happen to be of the same political persuasion as the Lord Chancellor?"

There was no need to hide anything from her. "Yes, and quite friendly with him I'm told."

"I don't know much about such things as politics. It's not usually a subject men discuss with ladies, but I've heard men can be very stubborn about their views on certain matters, so that is concerning."

"That's true. There are members of Parliament happy that I stay out of most political discussions and members who are unhappy that I do. Epworth will make some discreet inquiries to see if there is any way I might be useful to the Chancellor. A favor for a favor."

A frustrated sigh passed her lips. He didn't like this any more than she did, but right now there was nothing he could do. The differences in politics hadn't entered his mind when he told her he would take care of Jane's petition.

"In the meantime," he continued, "we will wait. I understand everything in Chancery moves slowly. Some of it due to the Lord Chancellor and some because of the great number of other departments under his control. He not only decides on guardians, but bankrupts, trusts, the mentally infirm, and a host of other issues that need attention.

You should prepare yourself and the children for a longer stay in London."

"I will stay here until I know this matter is settled." She casually descended to the next rung. "It's why I came. But won't that be an even bigger problem for you?"

"In what way?" he asked, thinking more about his desire to kiss her right now than what she was saying.

"My presence might restrict your training sessions and social calendar." She shrugged slightly and gave him another pretty, bedeviling smile before adding, "Parties, dancing, and such. You know, the kinds of things that won't work for us to do together."

Wyatt frowned. She was bent on tantalizing him out of the temper he was in and making him forget the sledgehammer banging against his forehead. And it was working. A warmth of slowly rising passion settled low in his loins. He wanted to kiss her softly. With no reason to hurry. She had strength, charm, and innocence in spades and it was having an arousing effect on him.

He shook his head, knowing his mind was far away from the words he was speaking. "No need to worry about me. I'll carry on as usual with my activities."

"You've given me no reason to doubt that."

"You can use this time to have new dresses and gowns made and anything the children might need."

"I'll do that and other things that need my attention. Nevertheless, I must caution you that Bella and Charles can be disruptive and loud. Elise will join them at times. Children can be upsetting to a quiet household. I'll do my best to keep them quiet."

Was she teasing him again? She had the youngsters acting as if they were afraid to move a muscle unless she told them they could. He couldn't believe she'd ever let them step out of line or that they'd want to for fear her sharp eye would see and banish them to their chairs.

"I enjoy children," he assured her. "Commotion doesn't bother me."

She took another step, finally making it to the next to the last rung on the ladder where he could easily reach her. Perfect. His breaths quickened and a slow throb developed in his loins.

Fredericka folded her arms underneath her breasts, lifting their pillow softness higher. "You don't know how much noise they can make or how fast they can destroy the order of a room."

Wyatt grinned. "Clearly you've never attended recreation day at boarding school with two hundred boys."

And she obviously didn't know how easy it was to tempt a man who hadn't slept for close to thirty hours and yet wanted to feel her softness cuddled in his arms. In one fluid motion, he wrapped both arms around her waist, lifted her off the ladder, and swung her around a couple of times before placing her on her feet.

Fredericka laughed, settled her hands in the crook of his arms, and looked at him. "That was a surprise," she admitted.

For him too. "It appeared you enjoyed it?"

"Yes, it was wonderful." Her gaze stayed on his.

The tension in his head sifted away with the lilting sounds of her soft laughter. His shoulders relaxed as the tiredness seemed to ebb from his body. He locked his fingers together at the small of her back and leaned into her. Simply holding her was a pleasure. She felt good next to him and intoxicatingly familiar beneath his grasp. The warmth, the closeness, and that indefinable knowledge that she was his forever seemed to reverberate through him.

"I haven't been swung around like that since I was a little girl. Probably younger than Bella is now. It's one of my last memories of me and my father together. Thank you for reminding me of such a happy time."

Much as he would have liked for it to be different, for now anyway, he liked the soothing feel of his arms around her. "I'm glad." Wyatt lowered his lids a fraction. "I'll have to do it again sometime."

"Well, n-no, of c-course not," she stammered uncomfortably, but made no effort to step back. "That is child's play."

"And what is wrong with that? If it makes you happy and I enjoy it as well, what does it matter if it's something that is usually reserved for children?"

"I don't think that would be a proper way for us to behave. When I said I liked it, I didn't mean to indicate there should be more swirling around between us."

"I think I would like more of it. And more of this?"

His mouth descended slowly toward hers until their lips tenderly touched. A slight and soft murmur sounded. He wasn't sure if it was an acceptance or a protest at first, but her eyes closed, and she didn't move away as his lips caressed hers with gentleness. Instead, her hands tightened on his arms, her mouth opened, relaxed, and relinquished resistance to the kiss. She gave control of it over to him. Deep, satisfying pleasure washed through him and he added pressure to their kiss.

Sweet, heady sensations filled him as his tongue brushed against hers over and over again. Wyatt absorbed and swallowed the satisfying taste of her while loosening the hold on her back. He let his hands slide up to her shoulders and down as he enjoyed how well she fit into his embrace. Through the fine fabric of her dress, he could tell her waist was small, nicely curved, and as warm as a summer afternoon. The flare of her hips was shapely, smooth, and firm.

Their kisses continued slow, tender, and perhaps more intoxicating for the lack of urgency while he simply relished holding her close, touching her body, and taking comfort in all she was making him feel. Which was heavenly. Her response was equal to his and it fed his desire. Yet he held back and didn't push for advances he didn't know if she was prepared to accept. He would take all she was willing to allow.

Keeping the same leisurely pace, his lips moved to her cheek, then her jaw, and over to the sensitive spot behind her ear before leaving a trail of kisses trickling down the slender column of her neck and back to her lips. She arched toward him. A small involuntary gasp was drawn from her, and he felt her start to tremble. At the hollow of her throat, he stopped to inhale her warm, fragrant skin and allow her scent of summer sunshine to sink into his senses, fill him, and tempt him with desires he had suppressed since he'd met her.

It had been a while since he'd been with a woman. That made him all the more vulnerable to her sweetness and the situation with her even more volatile too. Instinctively, he wanted to sweep her into his arms, carry her to his chamber, and lie with her in the softness of his bed.

With ease, he moved his hand up the shapely rise of her breast to cup, caress, and tease the fullness. It was exciting to explore the shape of her body. His loins tightened achingly until her hand caught his wrist and stopped him.

Wyatt lifted his head and looked into her beautiful eyes. They were filled with the sparkling innocence of wonder. Shivers of wanting raced through him again. He sensed an intimate intensity radiating between them that he knew she felt too. Their breaths were erratic. Nonetheless, she was calling a halt to what they were both so obviously enjoying.

She let go of him, slipped out of his embrace, and stepped back. "Occurrences such as this were not included in our arrangement any more than were outings in the park as a proper family."

Wyatt thought he detected uncertainty in her voice and was tempted to press her on the matter. But then remembered he hadn't planned on passionate kisses with her when he'd asked her to marry him either. Not for quite some time to come, anyway.

If he had carried on with what he wanted tonight, there would be possibilities his life would change. Forever. His carefully laid plans of doing everything as his father had done would be over. If she were with child he would become a father. He wasn't ready to make a commitment like that.

"You're right," he answered, trying to ease his labored breathing and the ache in his loins.

"Why did you kiss me so passionately?" she asked.

"I wanted to. You are very desirable, Fredericka. You are beautiful and strong-minded. Everything about you tempts me." He gave her a little smile when he saw how genuinely curious she was. "Why did you allow me to kiss you?"

"I was curious to see if it would feel the way it had on our wedding day."

Her answer pleased him and he smiled. "Did it?"

"Yes. You are handsome, intriguing, and your kisses are pleasant."

He lifted the corners of his mouth in doubt and narrowed his eyes. "Only pleasant?" He blew out a chuckle. "In that case, I must try again and do better."

Wyatt reached and caught her upper arm. His body reacted again to the mere touch of her, but she slowly pulled away from him, letting her arm glide through his hand.

"I like things that are pleasant."

"But kisses should be thrilling like this." He reached for her again, but she eluded him.

"I think I should go up now," she said with more conviction than her previous words conveyed. "It's late. I'm suddenly feeling weary from the long day. The children are early to rise, and I must be as well."

Wyatt nodded. "Yes." He was exhausted too. But kissing her was a good way to end the evening and he wasn't sorry he had, but he had to be careful. If he'd done what he had wanted, he could find her in the family way and he certainly wasn't ready for anything that serious.

"Good night, Your Grace."

He nodded and watched as she walked toward the door, realizing his head was no longer pounding.

At the entry, Fredericka turned back to him. "I feel certain you must not be aware of it, so I wanted to let you know there are no poetry books or verse of any kind on any of the shelves. That's actually what I was searching for but couldn't find even one."

"I am aware of that."

"Really? I thought for sure in a library this size I would find several dozen. There's not even one on po-ems about flowers. Has someone borrowed them all and failed to return the books?"

"No," he answered. "I burned them."

CHAPTER 12

TO AN AUTUMN ROSE
—CHARLES F. HOFFMAN

The burning story of my love discover;
And if the theme should fail, alas! to move her,
Tell her, when youth's gay summer flowers are past,
Like thee, my love will blossom till the last!

Fredericka closed her book and observed the duke's beautifully appointed drawing room. It was such a peaceful place to sit and read. Four tall windows allowed an abundance of afternoon sunshine to light the room and show off the exquisitely detailed porcelain of vases, bowls, and figurines intricately placed about the room.

Expertly made draperies of a pale rose-colored velvet adorned the room and looked as soft as butter. Over each window, the cornice above the floor-to-ceiling panels was draped with lush swags trimmed with rows of small dark-ivory tassels. Larger ones held the fabric to each side of the window.

A tall, ornately carved gilded mirror hung over the fireplace. The four walls were elegantly and beautifully crowded. There was hardly a space that didn't have a painting of some size covering it. Some were large, with lavish frames and bracketed by a series of smaller ones, while others were of a simple nature. Landscapes were mixed with still lifes and portraits, and garden scenes were paired with dogs, horses, and sheep. But somehow, they all seemed to fit perfectly together.

Fredericka's eyes kept going back to the painting of a garden in full bloom of summer. In the forefront was a white bench with a lady's straw hat and book lying on top of it. It looked to be the perfect place for reading or writing poetry.

She turned away from the art to Bella and Elise sitting on opposite ends of the flower-printed damask-covered settee. Charles occupied the identical one facing them. Miss Litchfield seemed most comfortable in a cozy wingback by the window overlooking a small, beautifully structured knot garden, while Fredericka had taken the stiff-cushioned, straight-back armchair near the doorway.

After a rather hectic morning of helping the governess get the children dressed, fed, and working on their lessons, while simultaneously keeping them as silent as possible, things had settled down to a bit of peacefulness. Now Fredericka was allowing them time to do something they wanted. As long as they were quiet so they wouldn't wake the duke.

Elise was intently studying over her embroidery sample of a pretty rose and leaf pattern. Charles played with his carved horse and man, letting them gallop over his legs, around the arm of the settee, and up the scrolled back. Bella was whispering to her doll and drawing on her chalkboard. Keeping her eyes mostly on the window, Miss Litchfield was busy making strokes with her pencil in a little drawing booklet she carried with her everywhere.

Fredericka seemed to be the only one who wasn't content with what she was doing—reading the only book she'd brought with her to London. And it was no wonder. Wyatt was on her mind.

A place he'd occupied since she'd met him.

Today thoughts of him were especially vivid as she remembered his kisses. They were much more exciting than pleasant as she'd told him. They were thrilling, and it was distressing he knew that. He kissed her with such tender passion her breath left her lungs. Not only that, she wasn't sure she could trust a man who would burn poetry books. At the very least they should have been given away to someone who appreciated verse. It didn't seem the kind of thing a human would do. Only a monster. But he was the best-looking monster she'd ever seen.

She couldn't imagine a reason for such an appalling act. Not that any excuse would be good enough. She probably didn't want to know anyway. All books were a treasure to be cared for properly and shared with others for their enjoyment, enlightenment, or education. By the duke's tone of voice and the intense look in his eyes, there was no doubt he'd spoken the truth. Worse, she didn't think he was sorry for what he'd done.

She remembered good things about him too. He was the man who had saved her from possibly marrying someone who sniffed constantly. And because of the duke's generous allowance, she was close to hiring an additional governess. Now that she was in London, she would find someone to come to Paddleton and help Charles with his stuttering. It wasn't getting worse, but it wasn't getting any better either.

Remembrances of those few minutes in his arms forced their way into her thoughts and crowded out all other contemplations. Which was bad enough, but each time the memories filled her with that uncontrollable feeling called anticipation, making her want to relive them all over again.

If that didn't give her enough to consider, there was the fact that she really didn't know what to think about a man who slept away more than half the day. It was a couple of hours past noon already and he still hadn't come belowstairs. She had even asked Burns just to make sure she hadn't missed him.

Perhaps the best way to get Wyatt off her mind was to have the conversation with the children she had been avoiding all day. She steadied her breath, rose, placed her book in the chair, and walked over to stand between the two settees.

"While I have all of you here together," she started, waiting for the three children to make eye contact with her. "I wanted to let you know that we won't be returning to Paddleton in the next day or two after all."

"But yesterday you said we would be going home soon." Elise immediately reminded Fredericka of her previous words.

"I thought that. However, some important things have come up to keep us here longer than expected. Don't be disheartened. I think you'll like some of them very much."

"I already know I don't like them," Elise complained under her breath, and plopped her embroidery hoop impatiently onto her lap.

"I l-like them," Charles said in his loud, high-pitched boyish voice. "I w-want to stay here."

"Me too," Bella chimed.

"Not too loud, please," Fredericka prompted, putting her forefinger to her lips. "Remember, we don't want to wake the duke and be a bother to him while we are here."

Bella pressed her finger against her lips too and whispered, "Shh, Charles. You must talk in a whisper in this house."

Fredericka smiled. They really were delightful children and she loved them with all her heart. She didn't know what she'd do if Jane took them from her. It was important she nurture them and bring them up in a way that would make Angela proud of her, and them.

"Thank you, Bella. And as for you, Elise and Charles, you don't know what the *things* are yet, so you can't possibly know whether you'll like or dislike them."

Elise rolled her eyes and huffed.

"One of the reasons we must stay longer is because the duke is getting us a new carriage. He's insistent we have one, so we'll bend to his wishes." Some of the time.

"A b-big c-carriage?" Charles asked. "W-with six horses?"

"I'm not sure, but I think six would be too many."

"Five," Bella told her brother.

"W-white. C-can we have w-white horses?"

Fredericka laughed and clasped her hands together in front of her. "We will let the duke pick the number of horses and the color of them, as well as the size of the carriage. I would assume the coach will be larger than the one we have now. So, whenever we return to Paddleton, it won't be as crowded as when we came here. I'm sure it will be well-sprung and more comfortable. Each of you will have your own elbow room."

"I want to go home now," Elise said without looking at Fredericka.

Deciding to ignore her niece, Fredericka continued with the lighthearted conversation. "These few days will be a good time for us to do some things you have never done before. Play in the parks, watch puppet shows, walk downtown, and do some shopping."

Elise whispered, "I don't want to."

"We all need new clothing," Fredericka went on congenially.

"I don't want anything new."

"Bonnets, capes, shoes, and dresses. Shirts and waistcoats for Charles, among other things. I haven't been to a fabric store in such a long time. I will enjoy—"

"I want to go home," Elise interrupted her again.

"I need a new dress too," Bella said, seeing her chance to get into the discussion and have her say. "May I have one with a yellow ribbon and lace around the sleeves, and with a matching bonnet?"

"Of course. I think that would be lovely."

"And one for Sarah? She needs a new dress too."

"That's an excellent idea." Fredericka looked at the doll and smiled. "I'm sure we can find someone who'll make clothing for her that looks just like yours. Would you like that?"

Bella grinned, hugged Sarah tightly, and then stuck the doll up to Fredericka. She took it and gave it not only a squeeze but also a kiss on the cheek. Laughing, she kissed Bella too when she gave the doll back to her.

"I only want to go home." Elise kept her head down but made a noise that sounded very much like a sniffle.

"Elise." Fredericka said her name softly as she walked over and knelt in front of her. "I know it's upsetting to be in a strange place and around different people, but you are with us. We won't leave you alone." She lovingly took hold of Elise's small hands. "You are a part of this family and, if we go to the park or shopping or wherever, you will go with us and participate in whatever we do. And we will all have a wonderful time together as we do at Paddleton."

Clearly upset, Elise pulled her hands out of Fredericka's and started feverishly looking through the embroidery basket.

For months after Angela's death, Fredericka had sympathized with Elise and allowed her much latitude to grieve. She wasn't getting any better at coping. Perhaps a different tactic was needed, but Fredericka wasn't sure what it should be.

Without commenting further, Fredericka rose, turned, and headed back to her chair. On the way, her gaze caught sight of a secretary at the end of the wall near the door. On it were a quill, inkpot, and small sheets of neatly stacked paper. Her spirits lifted. Surely the duke wouldn't mind if she used some of the foolscap.

Instead of rereading her poetry book, she could work on her own verse. She loved to write poems about flowers, trees, and plants of all types. Writing had always been rewarding, but she hadn't packed any of her writing materials.

Fredericka pulled out the chair and sat down. Within moments she was immersed in describing wildflowers, moss-covered trees, and tangled, withered vines.

"Auntie," Elise whispered a few minutes later. "May I talk to you?"

Fredericka looked up and smiled, motioning her forward as she placed the quill in its stand.

Elise stopped in front of her and held up her needlework for inspection.

"This is excellent work, darling," Fredericka praised, but realized Elise hadn't actually completed any more than she had accomplished yesterday or the day before. The stem and all the leaves were beautifully finished in varying shades of green. Her initials were perfectly monogrammed at the bottom, but she hadn't made one stitch on the open rose or the attached bud. "You are doing so well," Fredericka further encouraged. "I think it's time you started on the bloom. What do you think?"

Elise's eyes lowered to the sample and she shook her head. "I can't. I'm not ready."

Sensing something more was wrong than her ability

to make the stitches, Fredericka softly brushed the side of Elise's hair. "Do you need my help to get started?"

She shook her head again. "I can't finish it because I don't have the thread I need."

"With as many colors as there are in the basket, that's odd." Fredericka touched her niece's shoulder. "Should I see if I can find the shade you're looking for? When I last rummaged through the threads there must have been more than twenty colors that would be suitable for a rose."

"But none of them are the color of Mama's favorite rose. I've thought about using one of the shades that's close, but I can't bring myself to use any of them."

Fredericka's chest constricted, and she derided herself for not having more patience with Elise. She didn't know why she was sometimes so short with the children. Of all people, she shouldn't be. Compassion flooded through her. She remembered what it was like being orphaned at a young age, dependent on someone other than your parents to take care of you. Fredericka also knew what it was like to miss the love of a mother and feel unwanted, abandoned. She didn't want to ever make Elise feel that way. Fredericka had wished a thousand times she hadn't suggested Angela go with her husband to London. What Fredericka thought might be a time to have a recommitment of the love they once had for each other had ended in the tragedy of their deaths.

Swallowing past a dry throat, she smiled at Elise and said, "I've heard it said that in London one can buy anything the world has to offer. Why don't we find out tomorrow if that's true? We'll go looking for thread. In every shop in London, if we have to. Between them all, there should be thousands of colors to choose from. Hundreds at least. Anyway, we won't stop looking until we find the color you think is perfect. And when we do, we will buy every inch they have so you'll never run out. How does that sound?"

Elise smiled. "Thank you, Auntie." She reached over and hugged Fredericka and stepped back. "I would like that."

"Good," Fredericka answered, her heart swelling with tenderness. "It shouldn't take us all day to find thread, so perhaps we can mosey over to the fabrics and have a look too."

"I guess so," Elise conceded shyly.

"I want to go," Bella said from behind them.

"M-me too," Charles whispered from his place on the sofa.

"Yes, of course, we'll all go tomorrow."

"A-and n-no lessons," Charles added with a laugh, and a few jumps up and down.

"I don't know about that, young man," Fredericka added with a laugh. "I'm quite sure as early as you rise, Miss Litchfield can manage to get one or two lessons in before the shops open."

The children settled back down. So did Fredericka with working on her poetry. The only sounds she heard were an occasional voice from one of the servants in other areas of the house.

Until she heard whistling and masculine footfalls coming down the stairs. The master of the house was finally up. And obviously in a lighthearted mood.

She strained to listen in order to ascertain in what direction he would go. Directly out the front door or elsewhere in the house? The sounds came nearer. She kept her gaze on the open doorway, her stomach tightening, ridiculous as it was, wondering if he would walk by. He did. Splendidly dressed in a short dark-blue double-breasted coat with tails, buff-colored trousers, and shiny knee boots. Only a stride or two past the doorway, his footsteps halted. Her heart felt as if it skipped a beat. Seconds later, the duke appeared in the doorway, glanced around, and walked inside.

Without prompting, Fredericka, the children, and Miss Litchfield rose, giving the duke the respect his title deserved when entering a room.

He nodded to them all as he stood looking so handsome and debonair. Flashes of how she'd felt wanted last night when he'd held her so intimately flooded over her. She smiled at him with all the warmth she was suddenly feeling.

"Good morning, Uncle Your Grace," Bella greeted with a beaming smile, rocking from her heels to her toes and back again as she continued to hold out her skirt to the side.

"It's afternoon," Charles corrected.

Bella jerked her hands to her waist, pivoted, and gave her brother an evil-eyed glare. "I know that." Just as quickly she twisted back to the duke, popping the same bright-faced, little-girl grin on her lips and cheerfully saying, "Good afternoon, Uncle Your Grace."

Wyatt smiled affectionately at her. "Good afternoon, Bella. And everyone." He looked at Elise and Charles with the same caring expression before his gaze settled on Fredericka. He gave her a curious look and suddenly asked, "What on earth are the children doing in here?"

Fredericka sucked in a surprised breath. Her entire body seemed to go still. Every thought in her brain scattered like autumn leaves blowing around a desolate garden. "Oh, well," she hurried to say, not sure if she was even breathing. "I didn't know you preferred they not be in your drawing room. Where would you like for them to go instead?"

CHAPTER 13

LILACH——FIRST IMPRESSIONS OF LOVE
——MRS. WHITMAN

Oh, early love, too fair thou art,
For earth too beautiful and pure;
Fast fade thy day-dreams from the heart,
But all thy waking woes endure.

"Wait, wait," Wyatt said, looking mystified. "What are you talking about?"

"There's no schoolroom, so I thought to allow them in here for a change of scenery from their rooms, but never mind." She started motioning with her hands for the children to go with Miss Litchfield, who was also signaling them to join her. "It's not a problem that you'd rather they not be in here, Your Grace. We'll go back abovestairs immediately."

"Fredericka." Wyatt grimaced. "That's not what I meant. There's no reason they can't be in the drawing room or anywhere else in the house. I only wanted to know why."

"No, no, you're right." Fredericka dismissed Wyatt's effort to explain. "Now that you're up and about you want your privacy. It's perfectly understandable you don't want us belowstairs to bother you. Come along, children, Miss—"

"Stop, Fredericka." His eyes narrowed, darkened, and zeroed in tightly on hers. "Hold on a minute. All of you, stay where you are. I didn't mean what I said. . . ." He paused and inhaled a sharp breath. "Not the way it sounded to you." He looked at each child. "I only meant you should be outside enjoying the fresh air. Running, skipping, chasing each other, throwing balls. The kinds of things boys and girls do when they are frolicking on a beautiful day."

Fredericka was certain she looked at him as if he had lost his sanity. Perhaps she'd lost hers too for coming to London in the first place. From the day she met him, she knew he needed her to secure his property, but he didn't want her around.

Not wanting to lash out at him in front of the children, she said, "They are very loud when playing outside. They would have awakened you."

"Hell's bells," he murmured irritably while keeping his hot gaze on hers. "Are you telling me you kept them from going out and having an enjoyable time only to sit here like little—"

He hesitantly bit back the rest of what he'd intended to say, which was judicious of him. By now she could imagine what it was going to be. And *that* didn't sit well with her either. Whether or not he said it, he thought it, and that was almost as bad as speaking it out loud. With hot eyes, Fredericka shot another blistering look toward Wyatt.

"I can't believe you wanted them to sit quietly because you were afraid to wake me!" Wyatt rushed on. "What were you thinking?"

"That you were in training and needed your rest. That we don't belong here and are in your way." How else was she to feel when he'd made it perfectly clear he wanted her to leave for Paddleton as soon as transportation was settled?

"In my way?" His shoulders straightened as his head leaned forward. "Exactly what kind of ogre do you think I am that I can't abide a little noise from children for a few days?"

"I was only considering your comfort and the children's proper behavior in your house, which you apparently don't appreciate," she retorted defensively, unable to keep her voice from rising a notch or two. He had some nerve taking her to task when he's the one who said she needed to go back to Paddleton because he had *things* to do.

"I lived in a boarding school for ten years!" he exclaimed. "I can sleep through anything."

"Obviously," she answered in a frosty tone, cutting her eyes around to the elaborately painted porcelain clock displayed on the mantel that showed it was well past noon.

He eyed her with what looked like anger, which was probably the same way she was watching him.

"I like children. All of you," he said, specifically looking at Elise, before settling his eyes on Fredericka. "Now that you are going to be here a few days, you need to enjoy yourselves. And you shouldn't be so prickly about everything I say."

Filled with indignation, she stiffened. Why did *he* always get upset with *her* over impolite things *he* said *to her*? "I'm not prickly," she admonished. "How dare you suggest I am?"

"You are," he argued, not backing down a whiff but standing his ground. "You take offense at almost everything I say."

"Almost everything? What an exaggeration, Your Grace. But if I do, have you ever thought the reason might be because you are always saying the wrong things to me?"

"No," he answered. "It's not what I say but how you take what I say."

"Auntie, are you two arguing?"

The soft voice startled Fredericka back to reality. Her heartbeat surged and her cheeks burned with disappointment in herself. She inhaled slowly. Clearing her throat, she glanced at the children, who, looking scared, had gathered around Miss Litchfield. She knew keen arguments reminded Elise of her parents.

"No, of course not," she answered. "We are having a discussion. A mild one." She looked at Wyatt and implored him to help her. "Isn't that right, Your Grace?"

"Very mild," he added quickly.

What was it about the duke that made her lose all rational reasoning and her good sensibilities and disposition? She had always been even-tempered before she started caring for the children, and a clear-headed person before she met Wyatt.

Calming herself, Fredericka gave Elise a smile. "See, all is fine, dearest. Miss Litchfield, take them upstairs and put on their coats for an outing. I will join you shortly and we'll all play outside."

"Auntie?" Elise said in a trembly voice as she studied Wyatt with childlike concern. "I want to stay with you."

Fredericka's heart constricted. Maybe it would help Elise if she could see that arguments could be settled without hands being raised and no one getting hurt. "Yes, of course. I have more things to discuss with the duke, but there's no reason you can't wait and go out with me."

"Yes, stay," Wyatt replied in a soothing tone. "You have no cause to worry about your aunt when she's with me. We are trying to come to an understanding about something we disagree on."

Elise smiled and ran over to lock her arms around Fredericka, who promptly placed a kiss on top of her head and squeezed her close.

"I'm not worried," Bella said in a cheery voice, smiling at Wyatt.

"I'm n-not either." Charles nodded with a grin. "I-I like to p-play outside."

"Me too," Bella chirped.

Wyatt reached down and cupped Bella's chin for a brief moment. "Good." He then gave a couple of pats to the top of Charles' shoulder.

Wyatt looked at the governess. "Miss Litchfield, before you dress the children for outside, I want you to wait for Burns. I'm going to send him up to help you and the children decide which room will be suitable for your lessons each day. Give him a detailed list of any supplies or books you might need for their instructions. Let the children pick out anything special they might want."

"I like to paint," Bella said.

Wyatt chuckled. "I'm sure paints and brushes can be arranged."

Miss Litchfield seemed reluctant to move and looked at Fredericka for confirmation to do as the duke instructed. Fredericka nodded, and the governess left with Bella and Charles.

"Auntie," Elise said, looking up at her with big blue eyes. "I want to help pick out the classroom. May I go up?"

A prick of hopefulness nicked Fredericka. "Yes, of course. If you're sure you want to."

"I do. Bella and Charles will need my help. It's difficult for them to make up their minds about anything."

She reached up and kissed Fredericka's cheek and off she ran.

Fredericka regarded Wyatt with calm. "I should have never started arguing with you in front of them. I don't even know how it got started."

"It doesn't matter." He gave her a reassuring smile. "A healthy disagreement between people is good from time to time, my father used to say. It helps to clear the air. I think it will benefit the children to know that a man and woman can disagree without the argument ending in someone being abused."

"Yes. They do need to know that."

Wyatt took a patient step closer to her. "This entire incident happened because I didn't stop to think about what the children needed while they are here. I'm going to take care of this now. Burns!" Wyatt called.

Fredericka swallowed a morsel of guilt too. She bore some of the responsibility for their quarrel. She should have asked about a study room yesterday, and probably would have if she hadn't kept thinking the duke was going to talk to the Lord Chancellor and settle the matter with her cousin. Fredericka fully expected to be in a coach on the way to Paddleton today.

"I should have had this done right after we married," Wyatt went on. "I knew the children would be coming to London at some point. I should have prepared for them, and you. I'll get it done."

"Yes, Your Grace," the butler said, quietly coming into the drawing room.

"The children need a room where they can have their lessons each day. Show them all the available areas. And a place to play as well. Talk to Miss Litchfield and get whatever she needs. Pencils, paper, chalk and boards, desks, paints. It doesn't matter. Get all she asks for."

"I'll see to it," the butler said with a nod.

"Miss Litchfield is up with the children waiting for you," Wyatt continued his instructions. "Let them decide which room is best for their needs. I want everything in place and ready for them by tomorrow morning."

"Yes, Your Grace."

The door knocker sounded as Burns started to leave, and he turned back to look at Wyatt as if waiting for direction.

Wyatt nodded. "See who's at the door before you go up."

Fredericka started to leave too. "Not you," he said firmly. "You and I aren't finished."

"Splendid," she answered in the same tone. Fredericka gathered her courage for another round with the duke. "Since arguments are healthy, let's have another one."

Her comment caused a low, husky chuckle in his throat. It was attractive, inviting, and completely disintegrated her building antagonism. The atmosphere around them changed. As if by a magical force, his features softened. She knew he felt the shift in emotion between them too. His expression turned endearing. Slow, comforting heat started covering her body. He flashed a mischievous smile, and she saw the enticing man who had kissed her so passionately and intimately last evening that she'd remember the effects of it for the rest of her life.

Did the dreamy look in his eyes mean he was thinking about their kisses too?

Fredericka heard masculine voices coming from the entryway, and the moment passed.

Wyatt swore under his breath. She took that as a sign he had visitors he needed to see. Good. She'd happily put off another argument.

Burns appeared in the doorway and said, "It's the

Duke of Hurstbourne and the Duke of Stonerick, Your Grace."

Dukes? Heavens!

"Their timing has always been impeccable," Wyatt muttered to himself. "Very well, show them in." He looked at Fredericka. "It's time you met my friends."

She glanced down at her simple sprigged muslin dress. At this time of the afternoon, she had no idea what her hair looked like. Most of it could have fallen from her chignon and be hanging in loose strands all over her head. "I'd rather excuse myself and do that another time. I'm not properly attired for meeting anyone."

"You are beautiful, Fredericka," he said huskily. "That shade of champagne with its spruce-colored trim is becoming on you. I like the way your hair curls along the sides of your face and neck. Believe me, you have no cause to worry about how you look."

He brushed his fingertips through her hair along the crest of her ear. His sudden touch startled her, and she reached up to smooth her hair. Their fingertips touched. Warmth sizzled through her and she quickly let her hand drop to her side.

"Our argument has heightened your cheeks and lips to a tempting shade of pink." He continued to observe her with single-minded intensity as a hint of a smile lifted one side of his mouth. "You couldn't look lovelier than you do right now. I don't want you to go. Stay. I want to introduce you as my wife."

Fredericka smiled. He wasn't pushing her away or asking her to leave. Wonderful sensations of gratitude, acceptance, and desire twirled and spun through her. She opened her mouth to respond but realized she didn't know what to say. *"Thank you"* seemed hardly right. He'd gone from quarrelsome to making her feel as if she were a ray of sunshine in a darkened room, but more importantly, he wanted her there. For now. She knew things would change after the carriage was ready and Jane's petition had been stopped, but for now he wanted her with him.

"The Duke of Hurstbourne and the Duke of Stonerick," Burns announced from the doorway.

Two exceptionally built men strode into the room and immediately caught Fredericka's attention. They wore their titles and privilege as well as they wore their expensively tailored clothing and entered the room as comfortable, seasoned guests. Like Wyatt, they were undeniably good-looking, with wide chests and shoulders, trim waists, and not an ounce of extra flesh on their tall, lithe frames. Both exuded the same masculine sensuality that was so prevalent in Wyatt.

While introductions were made, Fredericka studied the two men she'd read so much about in the scandal sheets and Society pages. There was a time she would have considered she knew a lot about them—if she still believed everything that was printed in the gossip pages.

Now she wasn't so innocent as to be fooled by the writings of people who were making up stories for the benefit of sensationalism and to make money off half-truths and vivid imaginations.

Though the duke's friends were handsome as the day was long, it didn't take more than a glance to notice their personalities were as different as the color of their hair. It was written on their faces.

The Duke of Stonerick looked as curious as a stoat about her. His thick, light-brown locks swept away from his face showing a strong forehead, light-blue eyes, and chiseled features that gave him a rugged, devil-may-care expression would make any lady take a second look. The

Duke of Hurstbourne wore a solicitous smile, and was stunning to look at with classically handsome features that gave him an easygoing, yet strong, expression. She'd never seen a man with such silky-looking light-blond hair. It swept across his forehead so low the ends of it were almost touching his brownish-green eyes.

The Duke of Stonerick stepped forward and received her hand. "Your Grace. I've been looking forward to meeting you."

"Likewise, Your Grace," she answered with an appropriate expression of interest. "I've read much about you."

"Have no doubts about every word of it being true."

Fredericka laughed softly. Obviously, he didn't mind his bad reputation or half truths being written about him.

He chuckled too. "I'd like you to call me Rick, if you'd be agreeable. And you are Fredericka, I believe. A beautiful name for an even more beautiful lady. I now know why Wyatt has been keeping you to himself. You are a jewel among ladies." He bent and politely kissed the back of her palm.

Fredericka gave him an appreciative smile. "Thank you for the compliments."

Hurst nudged Rick out of the way and took her hand with a friendly grin. "It's a pleasure to meet you, Duchess. I would be pleased for you to call me Hurst." He kissed her hand and stepped back.

"Certainly, if that's what you would prefer," Fredericka said to the immensely handsome and charming man.

Both dukes were more gracious than she would have expected *if* she'd expected to meet them today. Most titled men didn't forgo their titles for many people and some not at all for anyone. It simply wasn't an accepted rule of Society to do so. She welcomed their willingness to accept her so readily.

"Don't be bothered by the freshness of either one of them," Wyatt said from over her shoulder. "I'm afraid we have been friends so long that we seldom watch what we say to each or around each other anymore, and are never formal when we're together."

"I don't mind at all," she assured him.

"What's this?" the Duke of Stonerick asked.

Fredericka looked around and saw that he had picked up her poetry from the secretary beside him.

"Nothing," she said, feeling slightly awkward, wondering if he might have read some of her scribblings. Ordinarily she wouldn't mind, but it was verse she'd written off the top of her head and not ready to be scrutinized by anyone. She wanted to take it from his hands but held back and remained calm. "Just idle thoughts I was writing down."

"Blast it, Rick," Wyatt said incredulously, as he strode toward his friend. "Are you reading her private correspondence?"

"No," Rick defended innocently, yet continued to hold the sheets in front of him. "Shocking as it is, I do have more manners than that. Besides, it's not a letter. I wouldn't stoop so low as to read your wife's personal mail. Only yours," he mumbled as if an afterthought.

"Give me that." Wyatt yanked the pages from him and immediately started folding them so his eyes wouldn't be tempted to look down and scan a word or two.

"Don't be upset with him," Fredericka intervened, not wanting Wyatt or anyone to make a scene over her musings. "He's right. It's not a correspondence to anyone, but it is somewhat of a private nature. It's my poetry."

A degree of silence that she'd never experienced before fell over the room, startling her. The dukes looked at one another as if an unwritten secret code passed between them.

Was it the word "poetry" that hushed them and made them go so still? Did all three of the dukes have an aversion to poetry? How could that have happened? Fredericka suddenly felt quite out of her depth in a house surrounded by men where verse wasn't respected with the esteem it rightly deserved. Clearly their education was lacking on something most people deemed important.

Feeling she must defend herself from such troubling and unimaginable beliefs, she went on to say, "I've written poetry since I was a young girl. I have a collection and thought perhaps one day I might put them in a book."

The silence continued.

They looked suspiciously at one another again before returning their attentions to her.

Determined not to be cowed by what was happening between the three friends, she continued, "Most of my poems are about flowers and nature. Of course, I don't expect to ever receive any acclaim for them. I write only for my own enjoyment, but it's nice to think of others receiving pleasure from my writings someday. I've shared various stories and poems with the children on occasions."

"There's nothing wrong with your poetry," Wyatt offered gently, finally breaking the silence. He handed the folded pages to her.

"No, certainly not," Hurst agreed. "I'm sure your efforts are beautiful and would be inspiring to many should you decide to let anyone read them."

"Right, Fredericka," Rick added in the same gentle tone as the other two dukes. "Not just anyone can write verse and make it stir the imagination of one's soul and dreams. You should have read the first letter of proposal Wyatt was going to send to you. I'm sure you would have found favor with it."

That was an odd statement. "I read it." She glanced from Rick to Wyatt.

"Truly?" Rick's brows shot up. "I thought Wyatt decided against sending it and wrote another. Well, it's no wonder you agreed to marry him. I suggested to him a lady would appreciate a proposal filled with poetic lines and romanticisms."

"What?" she asked, knowing all she had received from Wyatt was a terse one-line statement. It seemed there was another.

"That's enough, Rick." Wyatt issued a warning with his tone and tightness around his eyes and mouth.

Fredericka had no idea what exactly was going on, but she was curious.

Could what the Duke of Stonerick said be true? If so, that meant there had to be another proposal letter. Fredericka's interest grew and she turned to Rick. "I think I should have liked that one very much."

"My thoughts too," he answered.

"No, you wouldn't have," Wyatt said firmly, sliding another warning gaze over to Rick. "It was rubbish and completely muddled by all the brandy we'd drunk by the time we finished writing it."

"We?" Fredericka questioned as she straightened instinctively. "You were allowing them to help you write a letter asking me to marry you?"

Hurst mumbled something that sounded much like a swear under his breath. Rick held up his hand as if to proclaim innocence and turned away.

Fredericka cocked her head, shooting Wyatt a sidelong glance, waiting for confirmation, but there was no need for him to confess. Guilt was written on his face.

Wyatt shifted his stance uncomfortably. "There was an overindulgence of brandy consumed by all of us that night."

"We might have been a little carried away with our desire to help our friend and verbose with our wording," Hurst admitted quite innocently as he brushed his overly long hair away from his forehead.

"But rest assured most of the letter was written by Wyatt," Rick added in a less than convincing tone.

Fredericka studied the men. She didn't mind that he'd sought assistance from his friends. Every writer could use a good critique and a suggestion here and there. Whatever was written she never received it, but the dukes seemed quite concerned she might be upset about it. Why not use it to her advantage?

"Oh, I understand completely," Fredericka said with an understanding smile as she stepped closer to Wyatt and settled her gaze intently on his. She added a sweet smile for good measure. "We are supposed to help each other when needs arise. You're so busy with your training, I'm glad you found time to be with your friends and accept their assistance. That's important. To be with people and help them when they need it."

"It was very late in the evening, Fredericka."

His intuitive stare and the quietness of his voice told her he knew where she was heading. Good. She'd carry on.

"Perhaps you'll indulge me and find time for an afternoon ride in the park. I must take Elise shopping for thread tomorrow, but does the day after work for you?"

Wyatt opened his mouth to immediately answer, but

he obviously and smartly thought better of it and waited a moment or two as if to assess his answer.

"We have no tournaments that afternoon." Rick volunteered the information.

Fredericka appreciated his friend's assistance but kept her eyes only on her husband.

Wyatt kept his attention on her. "Perfect," he finally answered with a frown tightening the corners of his mouth just before he gave her a smile of admiration, letting her know she had won that battle.

She nodded and stepped back. "Your Graces," Fredericka said coolly, nodding to Hurst, Rick, and then Wyatt, giving him a satisfied look. "I'll take my leave and join the children so the three of you can retire to the book room to finish your conversations."

CHAPTER 14

THE REMONSTRANCE OF THE
TRANSPLANTED FLOWERS
—EMMA C. EMBURY

Oh, lady, list to the voice of mirth,
By childhood wakened around thy hearth,
And think how lonely thy heart would pine,
Should fortune the ties of affection untwine.

When was he going to learn to just keep his blasted mouth shut?

Wyatt closed the door to his book room and stood there looking at it. Fredericka had definitely won that argument.

"I wouldn't visit a mistress either if I had a wife like her waiting for me at home," Rick said from behind Wyatt.

Wyatt growled and spun to face his friend. "What did you say?"

"Nothing," Hurst answered immediately for Rick. "He didn't say anything."

"Maybe I should teach him how to guard his tongue since he doesn't know how," Wyatt offered with a warning in his tone.

"That won't be necessary." Hurst moved closer to Rick and looked directly into his eyes. "I don't know what's wrong with you today. You are stepping into a pot of hot water, and then fanning the flames underneath it. Are you trying to get burned? You don't have many friends, Rick. I suggest you try to keep the ones you do have."

"All right, all right," he muttered, holding up his hands in surrender and looking at Wyatt in an attitude of repentance. "What I said just now was out of line. I shouldn't have said it."

Wyatt continued to glare, not certain he wasn't going to smash his fist into Rick's face.

"It wasn't my fault Fredericka excused herself and left the room," Rick argued.

"It was," Hurst insisted.

"You were reading her private writings." Wyatt added his accusation with a slight sneer, refusing to give him an inch.

"The paper was lying on the secretary right beside me. When I looked down, I couldn't miss seeing the sheets. Wet ink. Four lines, three verses. I was curious. Anyone would have been. But I didn't read it. Bloody hell, Wyatt, it was poetry. In your house. I was too surprised to read it."

"That's no excuse for you picking it up and bringing it to our attention."

"No, it's not. I wasn't trying to upset her, you, me, or anyone else." Rick sighed loudly and shook his head as if trying to clear his fuzzy brain. "I only mentioned the proposal letter had poetic lines in it, romantic notions, because I thought she would like to know you were capable of such lyrics. I thought it would help smooth things over with the two of you."

"Smooth what things?" Wyatt's shoulders flexed. "What are you talking about?"

"I don't know. Maybe dancing with Priscilla? Leaving

Fredericka at Paddleton all this time rather than bringing her here and taking away the mystery of her."

Wyatt pointed a finger at him. "That is none of your concern! I don't need your help with my wife."

Fredericka was fully aware and accepting of the conditions of their marriage. She was to keep to her life in Paddleton. Not put herself and the children in danger by hightailing it to London without any warning. No one hated her walking into his house and seeing him dancing with Priscilla more than Wyatt. But he wanted to give the party for Priscilla—for Grant. And he wasn't sorry he had.

"You're right," Rick offered, appearing somewhat remorseful. "I shouldn't have said anything to either of you. But everyone could see how upset she was when she saw you dancing. Hurst and I know how you feel about poetry, and we just learned how she feels about it, so the words just came out. You're the one who said the unforgivable '*we*' in connection to the letter. I never mentioned *we* helped you write it. I wasn't going to. You did that to yourself."

"Stop this," Hurst groused, and walked over to the side table behind Wyatt's desk. He lifted the top off a crystal decanter of brandy and splashed a dash of it into each of three glasses. "I've had my fill from both of you. Rick should have never been eyeing papers on a desk in your house, no matter how interesting they looked, or who wrote them. He certainly shouldn't try to help you with your wife. Concerning anything. But how you two feel about each other right now isn't important. Rick should march himself back out there and apologize to her."

"Nonsense," Wyatt scoffed at that idea. "She might

look delicate and soft as a rose petal, but her sensibilities, will, and fortitude are made of iron."

"Good." Hurst blew out a mocking breath. "She's going to need the strength of all of them in order to put up with you for the rest of her life."

"Take my word for it, no mere man will ever frighten her," Wyatt avowed as he took the drink Hurst held out for him.

Over the years Rick and Wyatt's different temperaments sometimes had them coming to blows. Hurst had always known how to step in at the right time and cool them down before irreparable damage was done to their friendship.

"I'm not sure you need any more of this right now." Hurst handed the other glass to Rick. "I think you've already been hitting the bottle hard today. Do you want to tell us the reason?"

Rick took the glass and downed a good bit of it but remained silent.

"I didn't think so. We'll assume it's lack of good judgment."

"A reasonable assumption," Rick answered after a deep, wincing breath.

Giving his attention to Hurst, Wyatt asked, "What are you two doing here anyway? Other than causing me grief."

"We came to find out what was going on and how you were doing," Hurst admitted. "Not to offer advice as Rick was trying to do, but you have to agree Fredericka showing up at the moment you were dancing with Priscilla was quite extraordinary. Not only for you but everyone at the party. The scandal sheets are filled with gossip about it."

"That was to be expected." Wyatt motioned to the high-back brown leather wing chairs set up in front of the fireplace on the back wall, signifying his disagreement with Rick had ended.

Once they were settled, Hurst continued on the same stream of thought. "You were late showing up for your first match yesterday, so we couldn't ask you about her unanticipated arrival."

"I had a meeting with Epworth that took longer than I assumed."

"There was no time for us to talk to you during the day, and by the time everyone had finished settling their wagers last night, you brushed us off like a piece of lint from your coat and left without a word. Is it any wonder we came over today?"

Wyatt sipped his drink before saying, "Fredericka came to London suddenly because she needs my help with her cousin."

Hurst stretched out his legs and crossed his feet at his ankles. "That should be simple enough for you to do."

"One would think, but it's not. Mrs. Tomkin didn't give up her petition to take the children away from Fredericka as I expected. I have Epworth finding out more about the Lord Chancellor, Tomkins, and Longington."

"Is there anything we can do?"

"Not presently. Epworth is making inquiries as to what might be an appropriate way to approach the Lord Chancellor. Apparently, just walking in with a friendly smile and stating my case won't get the job done since we are on opposite sides politically."

"Damnation," Rick whispered. "That's not good."

"It's children. Politics shouldn't matter," Hurst argued.

"Fredericka thought the same, but apparently politics always matters. I have to make sure I have something he wants in exchange for doing this favor for me. And it has to be a damn sight more than whatever it is Viscount

Longington is offering him, as they are hooked at the hip politically."

"That won't be an easy joining to separate. You know you can count on us," Hurst said, looking over to Rick for agreement, which came in the form of a salute with his glass.

Wyatt gave him a flicker of a nod as a high-pitched squeal and the patter of small feet scampering across the floor sounded above them. Hurst and Rick looked at Wyatt.

"One of the children," he said in an offhand manner. "Playing."

No doubt they were wondering if that happened often. Wyatt smiled to himself. Not with Fredericka around. She was probably on her way to give Bella a good dressing down for daring to raise her voice and run inside the house. His wife was the most conscientious person he'd ever met.

"There's a couple of other matters we wanted to discuss with you," Rick said, inserting himself back into the conversation.

Wyatt would readily change the conversation from Fredericka to anything else.

"Lord Tartanville wants to set up a rematch. The expert shooter from Oxford wants to give it another go."

Wyatt smiled. "So, he didn't lose enough money yesterday? I'm sure you'll look forward to going against him a second time."

"He wants more than just a chance to get even," Rick explained, placing his ankle on the top of his other knee. "He's looking to set up a three-day tournament with fencing, horse racing, cards, shooting, and cricket. He'll invite sporting clubs from Oxford, Liverpool, and Southampton—as far away as clubs want to travel. And not just Society or gentry. Any club wishing to participate. Wherever they come from, and as many as want to compete. As long as they are willing to sign up and pay the entry fee."

"It seemed like something our club would be interested in, so we went ahead and agreed even though we didn't know if you would be up to it," Hurst added.

Wyatt shrugged and slipped farther back into his chair. "I think it's a solid idea. Why wouldn't I be for it?"

Rick started to speak, but Hurst held up his hand to quiet him, and took over. "With Fredericka now living with you and our schedules already full with practices and matches because of everyone being in Town for the Season, we didn't know if your plans might have changed."

"Living with you?" That turn of phrase caught Wyatt off guard. But, yes, that's exactly what she was doing. Living in his house. No, *their* house. With him. But not for long, he told himself quickly. Just until things were settled about the carriage and with Jane.

"My plans are what they've always been. Nothing's changed. A large event in Oxford sounds challenging for everyone in our club. I'll train as usual and be ready as I'm sure the other members will. The hospitals can use all the money we can win."

Another shrill screech sounded from above. More than one. Charles had joined Bella and they both seemed to be jumping up and down right over Wyatt's head. He purposefully made no reaction to the noise. It appeared Miss Litchfield and the children had chosen the room directly above the book room for their play area.

Or, he thought suddenly and with a bit of humor, maybe when Fredericka left the drawing room she went to join them and she was the one who suggested they choose that particular room. Thinking their antics would annoy him. If so, she could have saved her steps. It would be a cold day in hell before he complained about children having the opportunity to play.

"It's settled then." Hurst walked over to the decanter and added a splash to his glass. "Now, about the other matter we wanted to discuss. I'm not sure it will be as easy for you to hear."

Wyatt didn't like the sound of that, so he sipped his drink. "Gossip again?" he questioned, knowing there had to be plenty of it making the rounds since so many people were in attendance when Fredericka arrived at his house. Human nature wasn't something most people could do anything about. They simply accepted it, lived with it, and never tried to change it.

"There's plenty of that too," Rick offered, sounding more casual than the sudden fidgeting in his chair indicated. "What we wanted to tell you is a bit more than the common scandalbroth the gossipmongers print."

"Wagers were started at White's this morning," Hurst filled in the rest. "Viscount Longington started the first one, laying down the bet that your wife would lose the children to Mrs. Jane Tomkin."

Hell's teeth!

Wyatt fought to keep his face passive. The man was brother-in-law to Fredericka's nemesis, Cousin Jane. Wyatt knew of the man, but not well. He was older than Wyatt and they lived different lifestyles. Their paths seldom had a reason to cross. But Wyatt knew exactly why he had placed the wager. He was hoping it would aid his sister-in-law's pursuit to take guardianship of the children from Fredericka.

"Involving a man's wife is crossing a line," Wyatt said in a quiet tone as instinct to protect Fredericka rose up inside him.

"There are no lines in the betting books at White's and you know it," Rick reminded. "You would do well to stay quiet and not get riled by this. You know the rules. You can't stop a wager once it's placed. If you involve yourself in any way with what the viscount has done, the stakes will only get larger, spread to other clubs and possibly other towns."

Hurst leaned forward. "Listen to him, Wyatt. If it was only the viscount, you could challenge him to a duel or lay him out flat on his back and settle this slight the proper way. Others are already betting, and you can't take on every one of them. No matter what you do, the wager won't go away. Swallow this and forget it or you will have every gambling hell in the city laying down bets."

"That's not my nature."

"If you do anything, London will sizzle with the gossip of it for weeks. You better be ready for it and prepare your wife for it as well."

Fredericka.

Yes. He had to think about her. Going after Longington would not be good for her pursuit of the children, and the viscount damn well knew it when he placed the bet.

Hurst and Rick were right. Much as he detested the thought of it, he had to buck up or see this grow into a firefall of scandalous wagering. But it was that human trait he was thinking about earlier that made him want to coldcock Longington right between his eyes, challenge him to a duel, and then send a lead ball through his shoulder.

Instead of dwelling on that, he casually asked, "Were there many takers?"

"Not when we left. Hopefully, there will be more gentlemen who feel the way we do than the way Longington does. Wives and children should be off-limits for any bet. Maybe honor will win over purses and most of the members will stay clear of this one."

Staying out of this wouldn't be easy, but he had to for Fredericka. It wouldn't help her for him to end up shooting the viscount.

Bella let out a blood-curdling shriek of delight and Charles chimed in right behind her as laughter pealed again. More drumming of feet too.

"Hellfire." Rick grimaced. "I didn't know little girls had such loud voices. It's way too early in the day to deal with that sound."

"What do you say we head over to White's or the Heirs' Club and get some food in Rick before we meet the others for our cricket practice? I think he had one too many glasses of brandy last night."

"I'm ready to leave whenever the two of you are." Not waiting for an answer, Rick finished off his drink and rose from his chair.

Wyatt hesitated as he continued to hear the children moving around abovestairs. He didn't know why the noise bothered Hurst and Rick. They boarded at Eton too and it was a hell of a lot noisier there.

Another squeal of delight sounded from above. The little devils needed to go outside and run around. There was no reason for her to keep them huddled around her all the time. They probably hadn't been out for a good romp since they left Paddleton.

Wyatt stood up and downed the rest of his drink. He had readily and eagerly agreed to adding another competition to their already hectic Season schedule. One competition for three days and out of Town, but as of yet, he hadn't done much to stop Mrs. Tomkin. Until he could come up with a political favor to offer the Lord Chancellor in exchange for favoring Fredericka over her cousin, Wyatt needed to do something to show Frederica he was helping her. She was right to remind him of his part of their arrangement. She was depending on him as much as the club and its members. If one afternoon ride in the park would make her happy, he'd do it. He was certain the children would love it.

"You two go ahead and I'll catch up with you in a couple of hours. I have some things I want to take care of around here."

"Good luck having the fortitude to do it," Rick grumbled, rubbing his temples with the pads of his fingers as more shrieks rent the air. "I find the intermittent noise is distracting. I couldn't concentrate on a damn thing for wondering when the next squeal would come."

Wyatt laughed. "That's only because you swam in the deep end of a bottle of brandy last night."

"Too true."

"He'll feel better after he's eaten," Hurst said. "What do you want to do about next Thursday?"

Wyatt looked at Hurst, not immediately bringing to mind what he was referring to. "Concerning what?"

Hurst gave Rick a knowing grin and chuckled low under his breath. "Just our every Thursday afternoon card game. It's your week to host the club."

"You know," Rick added with a flicker of amusement in his eyes. "Twelve men at three card tables in the drawing room swearing, drinking, and occasionally arguing. Cribs continuously puffing his pipe, Woolsey lighting one stinking cheroot after the other, and Robertson's ribald humor. You buy only the highest-quality tobacco and cheroots for their smokes. Remember any of that?"

The children and the sometimes-rowdy men from his card club in the same house?

"Oh, damn."

CHAPTER 15

THE VIOLET
—MISS LANDON

Ah! who is there but would be fain
To be a child once more,
If future years could bring again
All that they brought before?

A comfortable coolness had settled into the sunny spring air and the sky was a fair shade of blue. The winds had eased and the sun beamed down bright and warm. As usual, the Season had brought more people to London and mild weather had caused most of them to crowd into Hyde Park for the afternoon. Wyatt's driver maneuvered the horses onto Rotten Row and in line behind a brand-new lacquered barouche with a fancy liveried postillion standing on the side of the carriage.

The sight reminded Wyatt that he still hadn't put in an order for a new coach for Fredericka. Every time he thought about doing it there was always a reason he didn't have the time.

The park was busy with activity. Couples strolled arm in arm while gazing into each other's eyes as they chatted. A few people walked with a striding purpose, as if in a hurry, while others had spread a blanket on the ground and were enjoying refreshments and conversation. There were also plenty of park goers in carriages and on horseback and the usual array of milk and vegetable carts on their way to make deliveries.

It was a good afternoon for a ride down Rotten Row with Fredericka. There were the usual members of the ton out for their daily jaunt to see and be seen by others. Wyatt was constantly nodding and tipping his hat to those he knew as they passed. Fredericka seemed to be enjoying herself, looking around, waving when he would acknowledge someone with the tip of his hat. He'd enjoyed introducing her as his duchess when they stopped to say hello to Lord and Lady Windham and later to Mr. Christopher Belhart and his wife. The introductions seemed to please Fredericka too. At last, he was doing something she approved of.

It would have been a perfect outing if not for the glum expressions on the children's faces.

Elise, Charles, and Bella should have been chatting nonstop as the open landau clipped along through the park, but they hadn't said a word. Wyatt expected them to be pointing and squeaking with oohs and aahs at the magnificent pair of white horses with the fancy riggings they passed, or encouraging the driver to move closer to the shiny black carriage with an intricately designed crest that was just ahead of them. They hadn't cracked a smile to the gray-bearded man on horseback who tipped his hat and nodded as he passed, nor to the gentleman who looked as if he was almost being dragged behind four Irish wolfhounds.

Not one of them took note when Wyatt pointed to the brightly colored kite that sailed on the wind high in the sky. Wyatt didn't know what it would take to gain the three's attention.

Stuck between his sisters, with their wide-brimmed

straw bonnets, Charles should have been elbowing and shoulder-bumping both of them while grunting, smirking, and squirming like a snake slithering through a garden. Wyatt would have never believed a seven-year-old boy could be so still. It wasn't natural.

Girls were supposed to fuss with the bows on their skirts or buttons on their gloves. They should have been constantly jumping up and down, squealing with delight at the sight of someone selling sweet cakes, or begging the driver to stop at a puppet stand so they could watch. And they should have been doing all this while stepping on the toes of his highly-polished boots every time they stood up.

Wyatt was beginning to think the children had never been in an open carriage ride before and had no idea how to act. Everything they passed, from houses, to shops, to carts and kites, should have excited them. But no. They remained prim as always and perfectly still with their hands clasped sweetly together in their laps. Wyatt had a feeling it was because Fredericka had given them detailed instructions on how to properly behave in a carriage before they left the house.

Though there had been little conversation between the two of them since she met Rick and Hurst, it was nice to feel the warmth of her sitting next to him. It helped soothe his concerned thoughts about the children's lack of enthusiasm to be outside.

When Wyatt couldn't take the children's silence any longer, he reached into his pocket and pulled out the small leather ball he'd had since youth. He'd brought it for them to play with once they stopped for a walk and refreshments. It was about the size of a fresh apple and would fit nicely in the palms of the children's hands.

He glanced at Fredericka. She had closed her eyes

and lifted her chin, seeming to be soaking in the warm rays of the sun. She looked beautiful in her reposed state, and he enjoyed looking at her for a few seconds. As he did, an idea too mischievous to resist popped into his mind. While she wasn't looking, he flipped his wrist and pitched the ball right into Charles' resting hands. The lad fumbled it a little but managed to hang on. His eyes rounded in surprise, and he quickly looked at Fredericka as if suspecting a scolding before shifting his gaze to Wyatt. He smiled at Charles. Fredericka hadn't stirred from her relaxed state, but Bella and Elise saw the action. Their eyes had brightened too.

Wyatt motioned with his head for Charles to toss the ball to Elise. Charles studied on the request, grinned, and plopped it right into her hands. She caught it and looked into Wyatt's eyes. He motioned for her to throw it across Charles to Bella, who'd witnessed everything and was patiently waiting her turn with hands cupped together in eagerness. Cautious as always, Elise hesitated. He gave another short jerk of his head toward Bella. Without further ado, Elise sent the ball flying to her sister, who caught it and hugged it to her chest.

Wyatt pointed to himself with his thumb and nodded to Bella. Understanding, she threw it back to him, but much harder than expected, and closer to his face than his hands. He ducked and bobbled the ball to keep it from falling to the floor of the coach. That caught Fredericka's attention.

"What are you doing?" she asked, looking at the ball in his hand.

"Playing," he stated, throwing the ball to Charles again. "Something you don't know enough about, Duchess."

Charles snickered and Bella clasped her hands over her mouth trying to stifle her giggle.

Fredericka tweaked her shoulders and tried to look as if his comment didn't bother her. "Of course I do."

"Then you can prove it right now. Stop the carriage." he called to the driver.

The man maneuvered the conveyance off the road and onto a grassy area. As soon as the wheels rolled to a stop, Wyatt jumped down and reached back into the landau to help Bella and Elise down. Charles jumped off by himself.

"Your turn," Wyatt said, reaching back for Fredericka.

She held out her hand. "I'm not much good at throwing or catching a ball."

"Don't worry." He closed his fingers around hers. "You won't have to be." The moment her feet hit the ground he tapped her on the shoulder and said, "Tag, you're it."

"Come on!" he called to the children, and started running. "Don't let her catch you."

After a few minutes of chasing the youngsters across the budding slopes and swapping tags with them, Wyatt motioned for Fredericka to join him for a rest while the children continued to play. She started walking toward him and, smiling, he strode to meet her.

"It looks as if everyone is having a good time," he offered as they stopped under the shade of a small tree.

"They are," she said after inhaling a deep, calming breath.

"And you are having an extremely good time." Wyatt's gaze stayed on her face. "You're tired from running and your cheeks are flushed, but I've never seen you so relaxed." It was as if the concern and weariness that he usually saw in her eyes was gone. "You look like a new person."

Her smile softened, as it always did when things were

good with the children. "I didn't realize the strain of what's happening showed so distinctly. I admit I wasn't ready for the challenge of children, but now I don't think I could bear losing them." She breathed deeply again.

That protective instinct kicked inside him again. "Nonsense, Fredericka. You're not going to lose them. Don't even think that," he insisted. "I've not met a lady with your courage, resourcefulness, or determination. You've coped very well so far and will continue," he said, then realized she wasn't looking for pats on the back for looking after the children.

She was opening up to him about her feelings, and that caused an affection for her in Wyatt he didn't want to explore. Getting too involved in Fredericka's life would upset his. That was the last thing he wanted. He would indulge her while here, but she would be going back to Paddleton in a few days and that's the way Wyatt wanted it.

"It's good to see Elise enjoying herself as much as the other two," Fredericka explained as she watched them play. "Thank you for agreeing to do this. It's like the old adage of killing two birds with one stone. The children need to play, and we need to be seen doing family things."

"As you said, it won't hurt, and may help. Besides, I needed to do something to make up for what happened the night you arrived and then in the drawing room. I don't want the children to think I'm an ogre or that they aren't welcomed in my home."

Fredericka turned back to him. Her gentle gaze held his. "They certainly don't think that now. They were tremendously excited to pick out their own schoolroom and supplies. Each of them made specific requests to Burns for their own personal supplies."

"I'm glad," he said, feeling much too comfortable with her for his own good, and future.

Bella screamed and Fredericka focused her attention on the little girl who was sprinting faster toward Charles and Elise, who were in the lead.

"Slow down, Charles; let her catch you!" Fredericka called, shielding her eyes from the sun with her hand as she walked toward them.

Bella complained loudly again but didn't let the protest stop her pursuit.

Elise, on the other hand, stopped running, jerked her hands to her hips, and provoked her little sister by singing, "Tag me if you can!"

Bella immediately changed course and took a straight line toward her. Elise squealed with delight and started darting between bushes of peonies, clumps of daisies, and patches of not-yet-blooming lilies that had been planted in the park.

"Watch out for the bushes," Fredericka admonished as Bella barely missed tromping down one of the budding thorny plants. "And don't try to hit Charles. You must play nice."

"Fredericka," Wyatt said, coming up beside her and touching her arm. "Let the children play on their own. Let's you and I take a stroll."

"We can't leave them."

"We won't." He smiled. "They don't need your help to do what comes naturally. They know how to run and chase. Tease and provoke. Let them."

She looked a little stunned by his suggestion and pulled away from his touch. "I wasn't trying to tell them how to play. Just to make sure everything is fair."

"Let them figure it out." He gave her a shrug and another smile. "That's how they grow and learn to take care of themselves. Walk with me. We won't lose sight of them, I promise."

Hesitating, she glanced at the children again but then slowly started walking without looking at him. He fell in step beside her and sucked in a deep breath of cool afternoon air. It smelled and tasted of fresh vegetation. Trees in the full bloom of spring foliage sprinkled the landscape. It reminded him of the lush meadows of Wyatthaven. For a moment, he imagined walking the stone paths that led to the glades. With Fredericka.

"You don't know me very well, Your Grace," Fredericka offered.

He wasn't sure that was true. She had revealed a lot about herself the first day they met. She was extremely cautious. Most ladies would have jumped at the chance of marrying him. He had to entice her into agreeing. Her strength, efficiency, and loyalty were impressive.

"Maybe, but I get to know you a little better every time I talk to you."

"I often enjoy frolicking in the garden at Paddleton with the children." When he didn't make a comment right away, she glanced over at him. "Are you surprised about that?"

"A little. Usually when you're with the children you seem so—" He scrunched his eyes in an exaggerated manner as if he were searching for a suitable word.

"Strict?" she asked, more worriedly than defensively as she stopped and narrowed her eyes too.

He laughed softly and tipped his hat to a gentleman who passed by them. "I'm not going to admit to anything so reckless and find myself in deep water with you again."

She tilted her head back and gave him a comfortable smile. "That's astute of you."

"I'm learning."

"I'm not always stern," she said with conviction.

He gave her a mock look of surprise as his gaze caressed her face. She didn't like to give an inch on anything. He liked that about her. And that wasn't all he liked. There was the sensuous quality to her full lips and the amusing twinkle that often lurked in her eyes. They beckoned him whenever she took issue or teased with him.

Without thinking, and only acting on what he was feeling, he moved far too close to her for being in a public park. She could have easily stepped away but didn't. The frisson of exciting energy that sometimes passed between them so intensely neither of them wanted to miss it held them spellbound. Wyatt wanted nothing more than to untie the pretty ribbon that rested under her chin and kiss her lips for as long as he wanted.

The sound of masculine laughter and an approaching carriage stopped him.

He stepped back and so did she. They started strolling again. It was easy to filter out the park's noise of carriage wheels, distant chatter, and loud bursts of laughter. It was easy to forget others were around when he was with Fredericka.

"It's true," she said, picking up their conversation where they left off. "Because Charles relishes it so much, I have tramped through the forest and into the muddy marshlands below Paddleton with him a few times in the past year. The girls joined us only once and decided they didn't enjoy the tall grasses and soggy ground. They love for me to skip to the meadows with them in the heat of summer and cut wildflowers. We pulverize the blooms and petals to make flower water."

"You make your own perfume?" She was beautiful,

intelligent, and industrious too. He stopped walking and gave her his full attention. "I'm impressed with all you do for the children."

His unexpected praise seemed to cause a wave of shyness to wash over her. Before focusing on him again, she averted her gaze to look toward the children.

"I wouldn't go so far as to call it perfume. It's simply something we take pleasure in accomplishing together."

The girls came running up, talking over each other as they vied for Fredericka's attention. "One at a time please," she calmly said. "I can't listen to both of you together."

Elise grabbed Fredericka around the waist and held tight. "Why were you leaving us?"

"I wasn't, silly girl." Fredericka hugged her close and then caressed Elise's cheek affectionately as she looked into her bright blue eyes. "You know better. We were just moving about."

Bella folded her arms over her chest defiantly, pouted, and declared, "Charles and Elise won't play with me."

"Of course they will," Fredericka insisted, lifting Bella's chin with one hand and running the other over the top of Elise's hair to tame the windblown curls. "You've been playing together half an hour already. Your hair is damp from running and Elise's face is red."

"It's not fair I don't ever get to win, Auntie," Bella grumbled. "I want you to play with me."

"She's upset because she's little and can't catch us," Elise bragged.

"I want to tag them now," Bella huffed out, and then in the blink of an eye transformed her pout into a charming smile, gazing up at Wyatt with adoring eyes. "Will you play chase with me again?"

The girls were having a tiff and Fredericka was

handling it with patience that Wyatt wasn't sure he'd have under the circumstances. He could see that she truly cared and wanted to please them. Wyatt would have told the little ones to go settle their own differences.

Fredericka reached over and started tying the sash on Bella's dress as Charles joined them.

Wyatt looked around and saw they weren't far from the Serpentine, where there was a line of tents and vendors selling their sweets and wares.

Wyatt knelt in front of Elise. Thankfully, she didn't shrink away from him or try to hide behind Fredericka. "Do you know how to count money?"

"Yes," she answered, warily.

"Good. See that refreshment stand over there?" he asked, pulling some coins from his pocket. "The one with the red-striped awning? There are several people waiting in line."

She nodded and let go of Fredericka.

"I noticed them unloading a tray of fruit tarts, sweet cakes, and pies." He picked up Elise's gloved hand and dropped the coins into her palm. "Take your brother and sister and buy whatever you want."

Elise looked at the coins and then quickly to Fredericka, who pursed her lips and considered her answer before finally nodding.

Wyatt gave Elise a light touch on the shoulder as he rose. "Take Charles and Bella and go."

The children took off running.

Fredericka started to follow, but he gently took hold of her arm and stopped her. "Let them go alone."

Her eyes signaled protest before she uttered the words, "I don't think that's a good idea."

"Elise is responsible. She needs to do something without your help. Give her the chance to prove she can manage."

Studying the distance between her and the refreshment stand, Fredericka countered, "But it's too far for them to be away from us."

"We'll walk closer. They won't be out of sight, and we can hear if they call to us. Tell me," he encouraged, eager to change the subject. "What's wrong with Charles?"

She stiffened. "What do you mean?"

Wyatt held up his hands, palms opened in front of him. "Before we get into a disagreement, I'm not being critical. I only want to understand. The first time I heard Charles speak I thought he was just excited. But now I know he has a problem with his speech."

"Do you think it might be because of me?" she asked, concern washing across her face.

"No, Fredericka," Wyatt said calmly, shaking his head and filling his tone and expression with sincerity. "How could you leap to that conclusion?"

She folded her arms tightly across her chest and lowered her lashes over her eyes. "I feel guilty I haven't been able to do more to help him."

"Fredericka," he whispered softly. "I asked because I'm concerned too. At Eton there were boys who stuttered. Some worse than others, but all were mocked and treated harshly. Not only by the headmaster and other teachers but by other boys. I wouldn't want that to happen to Charles."

"I've worried about that," she admitted, looking at the backs of the children marching toward the refreshment stand. "I keep hoping it will stop as quickly as it began and he'll speak normally again. It started shortly after his parents' deaths. There hasn't been improvement."

"So, he hasn't always stuttered?" He stepped closer, wanting to take hold of her hand and offer comfort, but refrained. Any show of affection in public was judged harshly. Even if the couple was married. Wyatt didn't want to add to the gossip already swirling about them.

"No. Miss Litchfield has worked with him and tried to get him to slow down and say every word properly, but she hasn't made notable progress. I've tried a few times, but whenever I mention his speech, it seems to embarrass him and he refuses to say anything to anyone for hours. I'm forced to remain quiet about it."

"What about a tutor?"

"I checked into the possibility when I realized it was lingering past a few months. There was no one near Paddleton who could offer more assistance than what we were already doing. I wrote to an agency in London seeking a teacher who would come to Paddleton. They wrote back that no one qualified in speech treatment had an interest."

"But you are here in London now."

"Yes. Now that we'll be here longer than expected, I'll check with the agency again. Each of the children has had some difficulties since their parents died. I'm sure you've noticed that Elise never wants to be left alone. Though she won't talk about her fears with me, I know she worries I'll be like her mother and leave one day and never return."

"That's understandable," he answered softly.

"Is it truly?" she asked, looking deeply into his eyes as if she wanted to understand how he could possibly know about a little girl's fear of abandonment.

Memories Wyatt didn't want to think about surfaced, but instead of keeping them to himself, he said, "There were boys at Eton who felt they'd been deserted by their families and would never see them again. It was difficult for some to accept living with two hundred other boys. Whether that was from the unhappiness of being away from home, anger, physical or mental pain of being thrust into a whole new life, I didn't know. At the time, I didn't understand what they were going through. If I had, maybe I could have helped."

"I don't imagine you ever felt abandoned."

Her voice was soft, her expression tender, and her intuitive words touched a place deep inside him. She was obviously thinking of when her own parents died and she had to live with Jane's family. Wyatt knew he couldn't begin to comprehend the depths of her feelings, Elise's, or the boys at Eton. He reached up and touched her cheek softly, quickly. It wasn't the hug or kiss of comfort he wanted to give, but he needed her to know he was trying to appreciate what she'd gone through.

"There was no reason for me to feel I had been left alone," Wyatt continued. "I was heir to a dukedom. It never entered my mind that my father wouldn't come back for me. Before I could walk he'd place me in the saddle in front of him and we'd ride over Wyatthaven. He'd sit me on his knee when playing cards and let me watch him. He was a good father. Whenever he left me to go hunting or to do other things, I never feared he wasn't coming back. I want to think that's the reason I didn't understand what some of the boys at Eton were going through until it was much too late to help them."

Her shoulders shifted and she tucked a loose strand of hair underneath her bonnet. "No doubt as a duke's son you were allowed to say or do whatever you wanted when you were in school."

Yes, by most everyone, he was treated differently. Grant's injury stood as a constant reminder that he had to do his best at all times. Wyatt didn't like to revisit those memories. He had debts he could never repay. For today he'd leave them where they were and lighten the tone of their conversation.

He tilted his head, narrowed his eyes as if studying her, and smiled. "You enjoy thinking the worst of me, don't you, Duchess?"

Her eyes brightened and sparkled with humor. "Perhaps I do. You make it so easy for me to—"

A scream rent the air. Wyatt knew instantly it was Bella and so did Fredericka. They looked toward the children. Bella was on the ground trying to raise herself with her elbows. A young lad about Elise's age was running and shoving other people in his haste to get away.

Charles yelled for the youngster to stop.

Fredericka lifted her skirts and took off running. Wyatt passed her quickly. Anger at the footpad and himself for thinking everything would be fine stabbed Wyatt with every stride. By the time he skidded beside the fretting Bella, Elise had helped her to sit up.

"T-there he goes," Charles squeaked, pointing. "H-he p-pushed her d-down."

"Are you hurt, little one?" Wyatt asked softly as he took hold of her small hands while Elise moved out of his way.

"I don't think so," she answered in a whimpering voice.

For a second he closed his eyes in thankfulness, and then glanced toward the boy who was running for all he was worth. Wyatt wanted to catch the kid and throttle him but instead concentrated on Bella as other park goers gathered around.

With caution and gentleness, he moved his hands up and down her arms, feeling for lumps or signs anything that might be injured. "Did you bump your head or hurt your back when you fell? Your knees or ankles?"

"No," she mumbled, then plastered an obstinate expression on her face.

"Good." Wyatt smiled at her. "I knew you were strong and could handle yourself. I wish you'd had time to smack that boy before he ran off."

Bella smiled. "Me too!"

"Oh, my darling." Fredericka rushed up and knelt on the other side of Bella and gathered her into her arms, hugging her tightly. "Are you all right?"

Bella pushed away from her aunt, sniffed defiantly, and declared, "He's not a nice boy. He took my cake."

"He stole the money out of my hand!" Elise exclaimed in a fearful tone. "I didn't know what to do."

"It's all right, Elise," Wyatt said soothingly, looking at her with an easy smile. "It doesn't matter about that. None of you were hurt and this wasn't your fault."

Fredericka looked at Wyatt. Frown lines nestled tightly between her eyes. "I told you we shouldn't let them come over here on their own. We were too far away to stop this."

Wyatt heard accusation in her voice and guilt settled in his gut. Fredericka was right. It was his fault the children were alone when this happened. But she was wrong too. "This could have happened if we'd been standing right beside them. Street urchins often pick on children knowing adults will hesitate to go after them and see to the children first."

"That doesn't excuse our neglect," she quipped fiercely.

"No," he responded, remaining calm. "Sometimes children get knocked down. They must always shake it off and get up. That's how they learn to take care of themselves."

Her golden-brown eyes darkened perceptibly. Her shoulders straightened instinctively. "No, Your Grace. I take care of them. They are my responsibility. I should have never let you talk me into allowing them to get so far away. If Jane hears about this, there's no telling what she might do."

More guilt assailed Wyatt. He glanced at the surrounding crowd and didn't see anyone he knew. "There's no reason she should hear. No one was hurt."

"Aren't you at least going after him?" she asked incredulously.

"I'll let him go."

"Why?" Her disbelief quickly turned to anger. "He's a thief! He pushed a little girl to the ground and could have caused serious injury."

"If he'd hurt her, I wouldn't have stopped until I found him. He's just a runt, Fredericka. No doubt he was hungry and picked the easiest prey for his daily meal."

"That doesn't make it right," she argued earnestly. "If you won't go after him, I will."

Fredericka's display of courage was admirable, but misplaced. She started to rise, but Wyatt put his hand on her upper arm and gave a gentle squeeze, mindful of her, the children's fear he might harm her, and the crowd who watched every movement he made.

"Don't." He spoke softly, wanting to settle her need to apprehend the devilish boy and punish him. "The rascal is probably starving. Stealing is how street scamps survive."

She looked wounded by his answer. "But you didn't even try."

Wyatt looked deeply into her eyes, willing her to understand. He'd never been any good at explaining his intentions, his motivations, or his feelings to anyone. But for Fredericka, he'd try. "The truth is that if I had caught him, I would have probably given him some coins so he wouldn't have to beg or steal for a few days. I'm glad Bella's not hurt, but I can't find it in myself to condemn a hungry boy."

Her eyes searched his and suddenly softened as she brushed her hand down the back of Bella's long hair. "I know, but not doing anything is rewarding wrong behavior. Children need discipline."

A chill froze down Wyatt's back. He'd seen more than enough of it at Eton and wouldn't apologize for wanting to help a forgotten, lonely boy. He was always trying to make up for not doing more when he was at the boarding school, and he wouldn't apologize for that either.

"He was no older than Elise and it's probably not his fault he's living on the streets and having to rob little girls to have enough to eat."

"I didn't know he was hungry," Bella said, softly. "I would have shared with him but didn't want him to take it all."

"I-I'll share m-mine with you," Charles offered, holding his treat out to his sister.

"No need for that." Wyatt reached into his pockets and pulled out more coins. He looked at Elise and smiled as he handed them to her. "Buy enough to share with Miss Litchfield."

Elise glanced at the money with glistening eyes and looked at Wyatt. "You trust me with this after what happened?" she asked timidly.

"It wasn't your fault. You took good care of your sister and helped her sit up before I got here. I'm proud of you."

Wyatt glanced at Fredericka. Her face was drawn with worry. A wave of protective instinct surged inside him. What he'd hoped would be a pleasurable afternoon to help her had gone wrong. He could have made things worse with Jane. Was his father right and there was no pleasing a wife?

Wyatt swallowed hard.

"It's time to get the children home," he told Fredericka softly.

He picked up Bella and secured her in his arms. Looking down at Fredericka, he gave her a reassuring smile. "You stay while Elise gets the sweet cakes so everyone will know she's not alone. I'll get this little one and Charles settled into the landau and have the driver watch out for them while I come back for you."

CHAPTER 16

Of boyhood's thoughtless glee,
When joy from out the daisies grew,
In woodland pastures green,
And summer skies were far more blue
Than since they e'er have been.

Sitting at the secretary in the drawing room, Fredericka looked at the embroidered rose and lightly ran her finger over it. After visiting several shops and looking through what seemed to be thousands of colors of thread, Elise had found the shade she was looking for. It was a deep but bright reddish-pink. Angela's favorite color, according to her daughter. The rose was beautifully and perfectly stitched. Elise had been so careful it had taken her a couple of days to finish the sample.

After framing it, Fredericka was going to ask Elise where she wanted to hang it at Paddleton. In her own room, the drawing room, or maybe there was another special place she wanted it displayed. The problem was that Fredericka didn't know when they would be returning to Paddleton or if the children would be returning at all. She tried not to worry, but did. She wasn't as convinced as the duke that Jane would not win custody of the children.

She hadn't seen the duke since the disastrous incident in the park. Fredericka hadn't even passed Wyatt in the entryway since then. That didn't mean he hadn't been on her mind, along with thoughts of what Jane might be planning now that Fredericka was in London for a few days. She had expected to hear from her cousin before now. Maybe the reason Jane hadn't stopped by the duke's house was because she'd returned to her home in Kent.

As luck would have it, she not only wondered where Jane was; she wondered where the duke was too. It was as if Wyatt were two different people. The man she'd read about, saw dancing with Miss Fenway, and kissed Fredericka so thoroughly she still hadn't managed to forget how the passionate embrace made her feel. And the man who was accepting of her nieces and nephew far better than she could have imagined any gentleman would be. A man who was kind enough to let a young thief get away without punishment for fear he was hungry. Fredericka should have shown kindness too. She liked to think she would have if she hadn't been so worried Jane would use the incident against her in court.

But that wasn't half of her cluttered thoughts concerning Wyatt. She'd often mused about the proposal letter his friend, the Duke of Stonerick, had mentioned. Much as it vexed her, Fredericka was still curious and wished she could have read it. Three handsome rakes putting amorous thoughts together to try to win a lady's hand? The very idea of it made her smile. What in the name of Cupid would they have come up with?

Was it blather, as Wyatt had assured her, or something that would truly make a lady swoon? She had no idea. After all her thinking, studying, and worrying about him, she wasn't any closer to understanding him, but she was more intrigued than ever.

"No," she whispered to herself, carefully laying Elise's lovely embroidery aside on the secretary. "I won't think about it anymore. It's high time I put the duke and his discarded letter to the back of my mind where they belong."

However, her next thought was that she would have loved to have read it anyway. No doubt it would have been more interesting than the terse one-sentence statement she'd received.

She huffed a laugh to herself and thought about joining Miss Litchfield and the children in the classroom to look more closely over all the supplies Burns had delivered over the past few days. But Fredericka had a tendency to take charge whenever she was with the children. In no time she would be telling the governess what lessons to start with, where to place the chalkboards, the papers, and learning books. She would have told her what to use first and what to save for later. Where to move the tables, desks, and chairs for the best possible lighting.

Sweet woman she was, Miss Litchfield wouldn't have uttered a word in opposition. She always agreed with Fredericka. Probably for fear she would upset Fredericka and possibly lose her employment.

Fredericka would never do that to the older woman. So, instead of usurping the governess with all their new materials, she would make a list of things she still wanted to do while in London. She had met with Miss Gladwin again yesterday and was quite sure she would offer the young governess a position once they had a date to return to Paddleton—which shouldn't be too long. She had talked with a woman from the employment agency about tutors for Charles and arranged interviews. After that, she met with the modiste she'd chosen. Measurements were taken, fabrics and designs selected, so the seamstress could get started on new dresses and gowns.

Fredericka trimmed the tip of her quill, dipped it into the inkpot, and started making her list for things to attend to tomorrow. Shoes, clothing, and coats for the girls and Charles. She'd let them skip their lessons to go with her to pick out fabrics, and to the bookshop. That was quite important. While the schoolroom was now well-stocked with appropriate books, the duke's library wasn't. She wanted to read the most recently published poetry. That thought reminded her of her own verse still tucked away in the drawer. She took out the sheets and started reading.

It was really quite good.

"Excuse me, Your Grace," the butler said from the doorway.

"Yes, Burns."

"Mrs. Jane Tomkin is here and wants to know if you are available to see her."

Fredericka's stomach jumped as it always did when she heard Jane's name.

"Of course. She's my cousin and always welcome."

"Yes, Your Grace. Would you like for me to arrange to have tea or other refreshment brought in for you?"

"Thank you, no. She never stays long."

Fredericka opened a drawer on the secretary, slipped the sheets of paper inside, and closed it. No use in taking the chance Jane might accidently see her poetry as the Duke of Stonerick had. While she considered her lines about the beauty of flowers moving, lyrical, and quite good for someone not trained in the art of persuasive and entertaining verse, she had no doubt Jane would consider them old-fashioned, boring, and uninspiring.

Suddenly childhood memories of writing poetry for Jane and Angela flooded Fredericka's mind, bringing unwanted feelings. She was always so proud of what she composed and eager to share it with them. She would write a simple verse and leave it on their pillows, in a drawer for them to find, or by their dinner plates. Sometimes they would mention having read her poetry, but most of the time they never said a word to let her know they'd discovered it.

Fredericka swallowed down the sadness that washed over her. She'd tried everything her young mind could think of to be a part of her older sister's life. Nothing had ever worked. Now she had to do everything possible to keep Jane from taking Angela's children from her.

With a flourish of royal-blue skirts swishing about her legs and a bright pink reticule decorated with exceptionally long fringe hanging from her wrist, her cousin paraded into the drawing room. "Your Grace," she greeted with a rather firmly set smile on her lips while offering a brief bend of her knees. "So good of you to take time for me. I hope I'm not interrupting anything too important."

Taking a steadying breath, she rose from the desk chair and replied, "I always have time to see you."

In a sweeping glance, Jane's eyes scanned the beautiful details of the decor. "A blessing indeed, if only it were true. Really, Fredericka." She sniffed disdainfully as the fake smile evaporated. "Shouldn't I have been the first to know you'd come to London? Why do I always have to be the last to know what's happening in your life? Your lack of doing what is proper never ceases to amaze me."

"Should I take that as a compliment or a complaint?" Fredericka asked, moving away from the secretary and walking to the center of the room to meet her.

"You choose," Jane answered peevishly before fixing the smile on her face once again. "Remember when we were younger? You used to always say I never let you choose what we played, where we could take a walk, or what we should do when the house went quiet and dark after the servants retired for the evening. You always accused me of letting Angela decide everything." She flicked her head to the side and smiled. "It's your turn."

Fredericka remembered their shared childhood quite well and recalled not being included at all. Her sister and cousin's favorite pastime had been to run and hide from Fredericka. The only time she felt truly welcomed to be with them was during thunder and lightning storms. They would always come running to her bed, giggling as they huddled under the covers.

"Would you like to sit down?" Fredericka asked, refusing to be baited.

"Not today. I'm too restless, and besides, I can't stay long." She glanced around the room again. "I have plans I couldn't possibly change, but yes, of course, another day I'd be delighted to have tea with the Duchess of Wyatthaven." She offered another of her practiced smiles that always looked so sincere. "You know how it distresses me when you treat me as if we're not family, so I do appreciate that you want me to visit."

Her cousin was an expert at playing the victim. "It's never my intention to distress you, Jane."

"Nevertheless, it's true. You must have left Paddleton right after I did."

"Probably," she answered cagily, not wanting Jane to guess she was the reason for Fredericka's mad dash to London.

"When we talked, you never mentioned you were coming here. By the saints, Fredericka, wouldn't that have been the polite thing to do?"

"It didn't come up in our conversation. We had other things to discuss and your time was short."

"Don't make this my fault," her cousin griped with

ease. "How long does it take to say, 'I'm coming to London'? Have you noticed that I'm always finding out what you are doing from other people?"

"But I sent a note over to you and to Kent as well the day after I arrived."

"I didn't see it. I've been down with a headache again. You know they sometimes plague me for a week. I didn't receive callers or open any notes. If Nelson hadn't returned from his journey late last night, I still wouldn't know you'd returned. You simply have no idea how hurt I was to hear you were in London. When I didn't answer, you should have checked into why. After our last conversation, you promised you would keep me informed."

"I don't know what more I could have done, Jane," she answered in a level voice, wanting to get the visit over with. "Since you don't have long, I'll get the children now so you can see them, if only for a minute or two."

"Not today." She fiddled with the brim of her bonnet. "I'm not up to a visit with them. I left a basket of tarts with the butler."

Fredericka nodded. "That will please them. They're with Miss Litchfield having their lessons in *their* classroom. The duke arranged for them to have all new supplies."

Jane's brows rose and her eyes narrowed shrewdly. "Really? Does that mean you are staying in London?"

"For now," was all Fredericka would commit to. "That's what husbands and wives do, is it not? Live together."

"Yes, it's just that it surprises me. You have always been adamantly against leaving Paddleton and disrupting the children's lives for anything."

On that, Jane was right, but desperate situations

called for desperate measures to be taken. "True, but there were some things we needed to take care of here. A new carriage, clothing, and embroidery thread," Fredericka replied, thinking quickly.

"Yes, the clothing I understand. You do need to, to . . ." She paused as she looked up and down Fredericka's simple gown with a discerning eye. "Well, needless to say that a change of fashion from your country clothing would be appropriate now that you are a duchess and in London too. You simply must get rid of your old dresses. There are plenty of shelters for women who will take them. I know how you hate to waste anything."

"Yes, of course, I'll donate them."

"Mrs. Parashu is garnering much attention for her designs this Season. She might be persuaded to help you."

Fredericka wished she'd never mentioned clothing to Jane. It appeared she was actually trying to be helpful. "Thank you for your approval of her. She sent sketches of designs to Paddleton after my marriage. We selected fabrics yesterday."

Jane smiled sweetly again. "That's delightful. And I must say you do seem rather chipper for someone in your position."

There was something about her cousin's tone that caused Fredericka's stomach to jump again. "Do you mean my position as the wife of a duke?"

"No, no, my dear." Jane shook her head, mumbled a husky laugh, and slid her fashionable reticule off her wrist and yanked open the drawstring closure. Digging her hand inside, she pulled out several sheets of folded newsprint. "Perhaps you haven't seen them since you've been so busy picking out fabrics and such."

Fredericka's heart felt as if it sank to the bottoms of

her shoes. The scandal sheets, gossip columns, and Society pages. It appeared Jane had a copy of all of them.

Distaste grew inside Fredericka. She was glad she'd stopped reading the pages. After marrying Wyatt, she'd found they weren't good for anything except to put her in an excitable state she'd rather not have to deal with. Jane, the children, and the duke were all she could possibly handle.

It was best to feign ignorance. "What are they?"

"Oh, don't try that old trick." Jane walked closer with the papers outstretched toward Fredericka.

"I don't read them anymore," she replied, lifting her chin a notch.

"You can't fool me. We lived together for too long. But I understand you wanting to try." She quirked her head and shrugged. "If I were you, I wouldn't want to read them either. They are quite revealing of your return to London and your marriage."

Fredericka stiffened. What did Jane mean? Remembering what Wyatt had said to her, she repeated, "Surely, Jane, you know the scandalmongers make their money by printing outrageous stories to entertain the ton. They search the gutters at night looking for something scandalous to say about prominent people."

Jane smiled pleasantly. "What does it matter where they get the information if it's the truth?"

"That's just it," Fredericka shot back. "What they say isn't true but rubbish meant to sully someone's reputation."

"I doubt more harm could be done to the duke's," her cousin responded nonchalantly with a mocking glance at the papers she still held. "On the other hand, my Nelson has always been an exemplary gentleman and everyone in Society knows it. Just as your husband is a disreputable rake of the highest order and it appears marriage hasn't changed that. I even have a copy of this morning's tidbit about your adventure in the park a couple of days ago. Thankfully, none of the children were hurt during the incident." Jane touched her hat again. "Though everyone wondered why he didn't give chase after the thief."

"I'll thank you to keep your thoughts about my husband to yourself," Fredericka responded with a bite to her tone. She wasn't at all surprised someone wrote about what happened. "All the children are perfectly fine."

"Apparently, so is the thief. In this column," Jane said, waving the papers in front of Fredericka as a taunt, "the duke is praised for how expertly he can chase a ball in a game of cricket but couldn't give chase to a young footpad."

A nervous quiver started in Fredericka's chest and quickly spread to her toes. "There were reasons he didn't."

"Yes, I'm sure. Good ones, no doubt. Tell me, is it true you arrived at the duke's house when he was having a party and dancing a very cozy *waltz* with a young lady?"

On that, the gossips were close to the truth, but Fredericka wasn't going to confirm that with Jane.

When Fredericka didn't answer, Jane unfolded one of the sheets and said, "Here it's reported he said, 'You shouldn't have come,' and that he asked, 'What are you doing here?' Did he not know you were coming to London?"

It shocked Fredericka to hear those words were exactly what he'd said.

"Of course he knew," Fredericka found herself saying with only a mild twinge of guilt for the prevarication. Wyatt did know she would come to London at some point. He just didn't know when.

"And I suppose it's not true that the duke grabbed you by the arms and shoved you to the floor while the children were screaming for him not to hurt you?"

Fredericka felt as if steam were suddenly coming out of her ears. "What? Give me that!" She snatched the newsprint from Jane's hands and started looking at the pages. Almost as quickly she realized she couldn't read such trash anymore. With shaking hands, she crumpled the papers into a tight ball. "This is outrageous! That never happened. How dare they print something so vile?"

"I agree, it sounded harsh even for the duke. But, of course, I don't know him well. He could have a quick and violent temperament."

"He doesn't," Fredericka defended, remembering how kindhearted he was to the thief in the park. "He is mild and easygoing with everyone. Especially children."

"Yes, well, I suppose you would know since you've spent so much time with him these past few weeks." She sighed. "But that's neither here nor there. In any case, I don't believe the court would look favorably on me if my husband said and did such things to me where everyone could hear and see it."

"Are you saying it would be fine for a husband to say or do such things if no one could hear or see it?" Fredericka answered back quickly.

"Of course not." Her cousin had the gall to look affronted as she could do so well. "Don't twist my words."

Fredericka glared. "And don't you twist my husband's words or repeat lies about him."

Jane sighed. "Well, of course I wouldn't. He's family now. You know we don't gossip about family matters. I will be the first to defend the duke should the occasion arise. But on to the reason I'm here, because I really must go."

What more could there be? Fredericka held up the wad of newsprint. "This isn't the reason you came to gloat?"

"No, of course not. But I did make sure the Lord Chancellor will receive a copy of the scandal sheets with his morning mail tomorrow."

"Thank you for doing that." Fredericka's stomach pitched, but somehow, she managed a fake smile. "It saves me the trouble."

"Happy to help. I was, of course, distressed to hear a wager concerning us was entered into the betting book at White's. I don't understand a man's need to gamble, but apparently they want to bet on which of us will win custody of the children."

"What?" Fredericka whispered on a raspy breath. "You can't be serious."

"Indeed I am. Men are very serious about their gaming. Man's second-oldest pastime and all that."

"But this involves the children as well." Anger settled through Fredericka. "It's a horrific thing to do and must be stopped."

"That would be impossible, dear cousin. I suppose men assume if women can gossip about the outcome, men can gamble about it. Now I must be on my way. Lady Tewksbury is expecting me for tea. I don't want to be late."

"No, you shouldn't be late," Fredericka answered, struggling to remain calm after hearing the latest news. "I'll show you out."

"Splendid. I would love for you to." She looked down at the wadded newsprint in Fredericka's hands. "And you can keep the copies. I bought them just for you."

"I'll put them in a safe place," she remarked caustically and threw the newsprint into the fireplace. She couldn't get rid of Jane fast enough. She needed to think about what she was going to do. Her cousin seemed to be winning at every turn.

At the open doorway, Jane turned back and said, "Oh, I almost forgot. I had more news today. After my visit with you at Paddleton, I asked Viscount Longington if he might speak to the Lord Chancellor about a hearing date being set as soon as possible. Our little tête-à-tête has gone on for months now, and needs to be settled."

Fredericka remained silent. There was no telling what she might say if she opened her mouth to speak. Nothing good for sure.

"I heard before I came over that a date has been set for the hearing and I wanted to make sure you knew it as well." Jane smiled pleasantly. "Do you think two weeks gives you enough time to quiet the rumors about the duke's bad behavior and your questionable marriage to him?"

CHAPTER 17

THE FLAX-FLOWER
——MARY HOWITT

The farmer hath his fields of wheat,
Much cometh to his share;
We have this little plot of flax,
That we have tilled with care.

Wyatt sat in a corner of the reading room of the private gentlemen's club with a cup of coffee in front of him. He wasn't used to waiting for anyone. Out of respect, he decided not to interrupt the Lord Chancellor and the man he was conversing with, but Wyatt didn't have all morning. He had a cricket match starting in half an hour on the outskirts of town and didn't want to be late.

The club was small, unlike White's, but probably just as exclusive. It was early enough in the day not many gentlemen stirred about. Wyatt wasn't a member, but Hurst was and had gotten him inside before hightailing it to the game to begin the warm-up with the other players.

From a room farther down the corridor Wyatt heard billiard balls smacking together and the muffled clamor of excited voices. A couple of men sat near the door, talking quietly. Otherwise, there was little noise stirring the stale air. As with all clubs, no matter the room you were in or the price of the membership, there were always lingering smells of aged liquor, burned wood, and lamp oils.

Wyatt swirled the coffee in the cup and thought of Fredericka. He smiled. Only a few days in London and already she was fashioning her way into his life. Even with the trouble they'd had getting the children settled into a school room and with the footpad in the park, he enjoyed being with her and the children.

For all her denial to the contrary, she was prickly as a thriving briar patch in the heat of summer when it came to some things he said. It was irritating. He also found it stimulating. Which he wasn't sure he understood. Wanting to take her to his bed and show her all the wonders of intimacy between a man and a woman—that he could understand. That's what he wanted to do. He loved the way she—wait, no, no.

What the hell was he thinking?

He *liked*, not *loved*, the way she felt in his arms. But he had to remind himself where that could lead. It wasn't a path he was prepared to go down right now. He had to keep up his resistance to considering the possibility of Fredericka in his bed and do what he needed to do so she could go back to Paddleton.

Yesterday, he ordered the carriage for her. It would take a few days to add the Wyatthaven Crest, extra padding in the cushions, and other things he'd ordered to make the coach as comfortable as possible for her and the children. The sooner Fredericka could go back to the country the better.

Now that the carriage was on order, he had to keep his promise to her concerning the children. The man keeping him from doing that was less than twenty paces away.

Fredericka was right when she'd indicated he'd received what he wanted from their marriage, but she hadn't. His inheritance from his grandmother was secure. Epworth assured him there would be no further surprises from her will. Wyatt was satisfied. Yet he agreed he hadn't given Fredericka what she rightly deserved pertaining to their wedding agreement. Being a duke, he had always gotten everything he wanted without fanfare or resistance simply because of his position. Now he was up against someone who was, for all legal purposes, more entitled than Wyatt. The Lord Chancellor held a powerful political position and was fourth or fifth in precedence after the royal family.

Wyatt's early morning meeting with Epworth and his investigator had yielded an enlightening tidbit, but not something Wyatt was willing to consider. In trying to find common ground on a political issue, one of Epworth's men had stumbled upon what he called reliable gossip—as if there were such a thing. Whether it was true or not, the Lord Chancellor would not want it to land on the front page of every newspaper in England.

According to Epworth, the Chancellor's wife had a younger brother whom she adored, who had quietly raided the inheritances of his stepchildren to settle personal gambling debts. And not just the children of his first wife, who died in childbirth, but also the children of his second wife too. Gossip, truth, or disgruntled family member, his party wouldn't want the headlines to read that the man they put in charge of all trusts, guardianships, and many other things had allowed his own brother-in-law to drain his stepchildren's inheritances for his own pleasures.

The sordid tale would not only call into question the Lord Chancellor's credibility and his party, but also hurt his wife and children if the story began to circulate. Whether or not it was true. Wyatt wouldn't involve the man's family in this.

He looked up from the cup before him and saw the chap who'd had the Lord Chancellor's attention ever since Wyatt had been in the club was walking away, and the Lord Chancellor held up newsprint in front of him so no one could see his face. A gentleman's way of letting others know he didn't want to be disturbed.

Wyatt had no intentions of standing by that rule today. Epworth's way of finding out what it would take to have the ruling in Chancery favor Fredericka was taking too long. Sometimes direct communications was the best way to go. He rose and walked over to stand before the man. "Lord Chancellor, a word with you, if I may?"

"I'm busy, sir," he said without lowering the paper to see who was talking to him.

Not surprisingly, the man felt his worth. No one made it to his lofty position without a lot of power and money. Apparently they also had a large dose of arrogance, and the unyielding support of many political cohorts. "So am I, but I made time for you."

"You shouldn't have bothered."

Wyatt didn't take the Lord Chancellor's rudeness as an affront. They didn't know each other by voice. They had met, but Wyatt wasn't sure the man would recognize him. However, he would surely know the title.

"I am Wyatthaven."

The newsprint dropped to the side of the chair with a rustle, and he rose quickly. "My apologies, Your Grace," he offered with a stiff nod. "I had no idea to whom I was speaking."

The Lord Chancellor was a tall, slim man with a

headful of gray hair. A pair of spectacles rested on the bridge of his sharp nose, and his thin lips formed more of a grimace than a pleasant greeting. That didn't bother Wyatt either. He motioned with his hand for the man to retake his seat, and then made himself comfortable in the opposite chair.

"I wasn't aware you were a member of this club," the Lord Chancellor offered in a suspicious tone. "I haven't seen you in here before."

"I'm a guest of a friend. I wanted to have a personal word with you and thought it best not to have it in your office."

The Lord Chancellor shrugged in a noncommittal way and remained silent.

"I believe you are aware a case will be coming before you soon that involves my wife and her nieces and nephew. She's been their unofficial guardian for some time now. I'd like to know I can count on you to make sure she keeps them in her care on the date of the hearing."

The Lord Chancellor took his spectacles off and laid them on his knee but once again said nothing. He was shrewd and obviously wasn't going to be caught making promises he didn't know he was going to keep.

"I know Lord Longington has spoken with you about the petition on behalf of his sister-in-law, Mrs. Jane Tomkin."

"I have many cases before me." He rested his elbows on the arms of the chair and pressed his fingertips together. "I've made no promises to anyone, Your Grace. Whatever the case, I hear the arguments of both sides and allow them to stand on their own merit. I judge based on what is best for the child or children involved. Proper care, a respectable home life, and the like."

"That's good to hear. Remaining with the duchess is

best for her nieces and nephew. I'd count it as a favor if you were to grant guardianship to my wife for that reason. After all, she kept them for over a year before Mrs. Tomkin petitioned the court to take them from her."

The Lord Chancellor remained calm and still as a windless day. "As one must in my position, I listen to all sides—family, political, or otherwise. It's my duty to do what's best for the children."

"That's what I'm hoping."

The Lord Chancellor lightly tapped the pads of his fingers together, but his passive face remained resolute. "I'm sure you know it's unlikely a female would ever be named a legal guardian for children who have property or money. It's the husband who would be awarded guardianship."

"We know it would have to be granted in my name," Wyatt assured him.

"It's also unlikely I'd choose a viscount over a duke as guardian unless there were extreme circumstances where I thought the children were in danger."

The incident in the park immediately flashed in Wyatt's mind. Some might consider the children were in danger, but would the Lord Chancellor?

"Ah," the man said, grabbing his spectacles from his knee. "The gentleman I was waiting for has arrived." He rose. "If you'll excuse me, Your Grace."

Wyatt remained seated while the man walked away. Epworth was right. The Lord Chancellor was not an easy man to talk to. There was no reason for him to be easy to deal with. He had the support of a whole damn political system behind him. He made no promises, other than a duke would likely be chosen over a viscount, as Wyatt assumed.

For now, he and Fredericka needed to keep making

appearances together as a happily married couple with a home devoted to the welfare of the children. That meant he had to continue making time for her even if he had to miss some of the upcoming tournaments. For some reason, that thought didn't bother him as much as it once did.

Wyatt watched the pious Lord Chancellor walk out the door. Family, politics, or otherwise, there was no way in hell he was going to let that man take Elise, Charles, and Bella away from Fredericka.

CHAPTER 18

TULIP——DECLARATION OF LOVE
——L. H.

I have a tale for thee; the Tulip's pride
Must tell thee with its rich and varied dyes
My dream of ardent love, for never yet
Have these same lips had power to whisper thee
How warm hath been my passion: take my flower,
And bid me breathe again.

Fredericka headed down the corridor toward the back door. She had wanted to talk to Wyatt after Jane's upsetting visit, but once again he hadn't come home by the time she'd finally drifted off to sleep last night. He might have quietly slipped into the house sometime before dawn, but she didn't think so. She'd spent the entire night in the drawing room waiting for him on the uncomfortable settee and hadn't heard so much as a mouse scampering across the floor.

There had been no sight of him before she'd left to go to her appointments for the day. She'd asked Burns if he were home when she returned. The butler hadn't seen him either. That led her to wonder where the duke was and what he'd been doing the past few days, which caused her to remember he had a mistress. And of course, she then started stewing about that.

She wasn't kind to Wyatt when they last spoke. She was angry, frightened, and worried at the same time. He'd been too blithe about what happened to Elise and Bella in the park. He'd once said she was too prickly. Maybe she was. At times. And possibly she'd been a little too emotional at the park and that had made him want to seek refuge with a woman who had no worries or responsibilities other than to make him happy. That thought did nothing to lift her spirits. It only served to make her feel terrible.

But then making Wyatt happy was never her goal in their marriage anyway. She had accepted that when she married him.

Fredericka had already served her purpose for him, she thought with a stab of sadness and pinch of jealousy. Perhaps that wouldn't have bothered her so much if he'd never kissed her. That was definitely his fault. He should have never awakened her to how earth-shatteringly wonderful it felt to be held so tightly in such strong arms and kissed so passionately she would never forget the feeling.

As she stepped outside and onto the patio, sunlight was fading from the afternoon. Dusk would soon be settling across the skies. Rumbling, turbulent gray clouds were gathering from the east and threatening rain. Fredericka breathed in the heavy air as she fitted her brown woolen shawl around her shoulders.

The prospect of ill weather wasn't going to keep her from seeking the sanctuary of the duke's well-tended garden for a few minutes of solitude. The grounds of his Mayfair home were lush and inviting no matter the weather. Topiary trees and boxwoods had been trimmed to perfection and positioned like sentinels guarding the house. Paths, bedded with finely crushed stones, wound their way around and through beautiful shapes, shades, and heights of greenery sprinkled with colorful budding flowers and shrubs.

With Miss Litchfield and the children enjoying their evening meal, it was the perfect time to get away and think over her conversation with Jane again. Distant thunder sounded as she started down the five steps, heading to the bench at the back of the grounds. It was secluded by a tall hedge of yew on three sides. It reminded her of a secret garden. A small fountain with a fairy blowing a kiss to a bird held in its outstretched hand stood in the middle of the nook. It was the perfect place to be alone with her thoughts. No squeals, screeches, or calling for Auntie to settle an argument or see a painting.

"Fredericka."

Startled, she turned. Wyatt stood in the back doorway looking more handsome that ever. *He was home.* Her stomach rolled and tumbled softly with inviting curls of pleasure at the sight of him.

Wyatt was splendidly dressed in a crisp white shirt, neckcloth beautifully tied, dark red waistcoat, and black coat and trousers. He looked as if he had just washed. The ends of his hair were still damp. An amazing thought flashed sharp, brilliant, and quick as lightning through her mind. What would it feel like to press her lips to Wyatt's cool, razor-fresh cheek and inhale the scent left behind by his shaving soap? Would his skin be as smooth as it looked, or would there be a faint trace of beard stubble to tickle her lips?

"Good evening," she answered, pushing the intimate thoughts away as she looked at him. "I didn't know you were here."

He stepped outside and closed the door behind him.

"I saw you walking down the corridor when I came in. Burns said you were looking for me earlier."

For days, she thought. "Not really," she answered softly, and pulled her shawl higher on the back of her neck.

An attractive chuckle passed his lips. "That means you were."

"You are impossible at times," she replied, a little miffed he seemed to know her so well and could easily stir her senses like the most fragrant of roses. His easy-going tone was helping her relax. "Of course I've been looking for you. Did you once stop to think I might need to talk to you? I haven't seen you in days."

Wyatt tilted his head and grinned at her in a rather mischievous manner that caused his eyes to sparkle invitingly. "You can always ask Burns where I am, or when I'm expected. Only—there may be one problem."

"Ah," she said in a guileless tone, trying to hold on to her frustration despite his endearing approach. "The butler seldom knows where you are or when you will return."

"But he always knows how to get in touch with me. I received no messages from you."

He watched her patiently as if he assumed she would say more, so she obliged him and added, "Just so you know, I didn't care where you were. I just wondered when you would return."

His brow lifted slightly suspiciously. Thunder sounded again as he hurried down the steps and stopped in front of her. "It wasn't my intention to be unavailable to you." He smiled sweetly at her. "The Brass Deck had a tournament this weekend. I should have told you. We've been training and playing. It was easier to stay at my club because we start our practices early. I'll be heading back to the club shortly for card games to finish the competition."

If what he said was true and he was going to his club, it was a shame only a group of men would be seeing how handsome he was. Suddenly she was reminded of when he was so passionate with her in his book room. He had leaned his hard, muscular body into hers and covered her cheek and neck with eager, delicious kisses that even now caused a shiver of delight to course through her. Unsure of all she was feeling and desiring that night, she hadn't returned his forward advances, only enjoyed them. Now he looked so inviting with his fresh-washed appeal, she wished she had tasted his skin too.

"You're looking lovely this evening," he said, gazing warmly into her eyes.

Scattering her errant thoughts and swallowing hard, she sighed, not wanting to be further charmed by him. Her insides always felt tumultuous when he was near and her breathing never seemed to be at a peaceful rate.

"I haven't looked into a mirror since early morning, Your Grace. After shopping and interviews at the employment agency for most of the day, I have no doubt I look like a kitten who's been chased around the neighborhood by a mastiff."

Wyatt chuckled again and shook his head slowly. "You're lovely, Fredericka."

She smiled.

"Now tell me, what are you doing out here?" He looked up at the darkening sky. "Rain can't be far away."

"I know." She tried to focus on their conversation and not the way he was making her feel. Kisses should be off-limits to her brain. He had a mistress for that. But her emotions didn't seem to matter to her brain as she tried to make sense of wanting to be with him. "I came out here to go to the bench in the fairy garden and be alone."

"Then I'll be alone with you," he stated in a calming voice. "Let's go."

The wind kicked up and blew strands of hair about her face and rustled the leaves on the trees and shrubs as they left the shelter of the house. Distant thunder continued to rumble overhead.

"I need to concentrate on what is important while I'm still in London," she said. "I've spent more time getting proper clothing than working on how to defeat Jane. What good will it do to have ordered new clothing for the children if I'm not allowed to keep them?"

"You will keep them, Fredericka."

His statement sounded firm. She wanted to believe him. The darkening clouds and whipping wind matched her erratic mood. She folded her arms across her chest as they continued toward the back of the spacious garden. "You say that but Jane was here while you were away."

"Why did you see her when she always upsets you? You could have turned her away."

"I couldn't do that." She didn't bother to glance his way as she spoke. "No matter how intolerable she is at times, she's family. If for no other reason, I must always receive her out of respect for her parents taking me and my sister into their home. Too, Angela and Jane were close. I know she loved my sister and in her own way she cares for the children. I couldn't turn her away."

Wyatt touched her arm and guided her around the corner of the yew as they entered the nook. After they were seated, he asked sincerely, "What did Mrs. Tomkin have to say?"

Fredericka steeled herself for a moment. "Enough to worry me. She brought copies of the gossip columns."

"You didn't read them, did you?"

"There was no need. She took great relish in telling me about them. Some were very close to the truth of what happened when I arrived at your house."

He scoffed a disgruntled breath.

"Then there was the disgusting wager at White's about which of us would win custody of the children." Fredericka huffed softly. "That didn't seem to bother her at all."

"There was no reason for it to. Her brother-in-law is the one who placed the bet and probably with her blessing."

"That's outrageous even for Jane!" she exclaimed, feeling a moment of extreme anguish. "I should have guessed that was the reason she was so calm about it. She's never stopped at anything to get her way."

"I was hoping you wouldn't hear about the wager."

She stared at him. "Can you stop it?"

Frown lines of worry settled between his eyes. He leaned toward her and laid his hand on the top of her shoulder. It was warm. Intimate. Comforting. But she didn't want comfort. She wanted action. She wanted to know this wager could be ended and Jane's machinations would cease.

"There's nothing I can do about the wager," he insisted earnestly. "I can't cancel another man's bet at White's. If I tried, the possible repercussions would be endless and only hurt your chances."

The damp air seemed to be seeping into her soul, chilling her. Fredericka didn't know why Jane was making such inroads while she was only running into dead-end roads. The possibility of her losing Elise, Charles, and Bella was very real and could happen very soon.

"None of that is the worst of it, Wyatt," she said, weary with worry. "Lord Longington persuaded the Lord Chancellor to set a date to hear her petition. It's in two weeks."

"That soon?" The corners of his mouth tightened.

"Sounds as if the viscount and Lord Chancellor have been busy today."

Fredericka's stomach was tying itself in knots. "I don't know what we can do. It was bad enough with the gossip sheets vilifying us because you weren't the welcoming husband and I wasn't the courtly wife who stayed at Paddleton and left you to your untroubled life of cards and games. Now there is the matter of the wager and your political persuasion too." She sighed softly and wrapped herself tighter in her shawl as she leaned against the back of the bench and stared straight ahead. "Sometimes I think I don't have a chance against Jane."

"Not *you* but *we*, Fredericka," he said softly and confidently as thunder reverberated directly over their heads. Placing his fingertips under her chin, he turned her head to face him. "It may not seem so, but I am working on this. I spoke to the Lord Chancellor this morning."

"You did? Why didn't you tell me this immediately?" Anxious to hear, she scooted to the edge of the bench.

"I came home to tell you but wanted to know about you first. And then what Jane had to say. Besides, I didn't learn much more than he is a man of few words. He wouldn't make any promises but gave me hope that he'd rule in our favor."

"How?" she asked quickly.

"He said under most circumstances he would always consider a duke's wishes over a viscount's unless there were extenuating circumstances. Such as the children being harmed in some way."

"I work very hard to see they are safe at all times." Hope throbbed in her chest but Wyatt didn't seem as joyful as she was feeling. "So then, we are almost assured to win."

"I believe that. I always have. He's a political man

and very careful what he says and how he says it. I still have Epworth working the possibility there might be a matter before parliament where I can be of help to him or his party to reinforce our position but right now they have the majority and there's nothing pressing I can help with."

"So there's nothing we can do to make absolutely sure?"

"Yes, there is. Exactly what we've been doing. Being a family and proving the children are not only safe in your care but happy." Wyatt's fingers lightly caressed down her neck, over the crest of her shoulder, and down to her upper arm with warmth and tenderness. She wanted to reach up and place her hand over his and accept the comfort he was offering. "I'll practice for my club's upcoming matches in the morning. In the afternoon we'll take the children to the park again, let them play—"

Fredericka's brows tightened as she pulled away from his touch again. "That was not a pleasant experience, Your Grace."

"Nonsense," he offered with a smile of amusement.

She gave him an expression of disbelief because sometimes he simply left her speechless. How could they see the same thing so differently? Was she just too prickly about some things as he'd suggested?

"Most of it was anyway," Wyatt added after she remained silent. "The children loved it. Don't worry, we won't leave them to—" He stopped. "Wait, we'll have to go to the park tomorrow morning. My card club is meeting here in the afternoon."

"Here? The children will be in your way. I'll take them with me to see the modiste and to meet with a tutor for Charles."

"The children won't be a bother. They can have their

lessons as usual. You go ahead with whatever you had planned."

"I don't know about that. I really think I should stay here and make sure Miss Litchfield keeps the children upstairs, quiet, and away from gentlemen engaging in their card activities. The girls especially shouldn't witness such adult behavior."

Wyatt touched her cheek again. "It's cards, Fredericka. Keep your appointments as scheduled. The children will be fine. You need to stop worrying so much about them."

Her chin lifted defiantly. He was so exasperating at times. "I fear it is you not worrying enough."

"This falls right in with our plans. It will be good for the men to see me here with the children in the house and you out shopping. The kind of afternoon a real family would be expected to have, and the Lord Chancellor would like to hear this when we stand before him to plead our case."

She pursed her lips as she considered his reasoning.

"That makes sense. Of course, we'll do as you suggest."

"Good." He smiled sweetly as his gaze stayed on hers. "And I want you to go with me to the dance at the Grand Ballroom the day after tomorrow. We need to be seen together just the two of us."

"A dance?" The unexpected invitation caused her breath to flutter in her throat. Her mind raced with possibilities of such a grand evening. "Are you sure me attending with you won't upset your plans?"

His eyes narrowed. "I'm sure the ball will be the perfect time for me to properly introduce you to Society."

"I don't know if a gown can be finished by then," she whispered.

"You could have one finished by tomorrow morning," he insisted lightly. "You are a duchess, Fredericka. Your modiste will work day and night for you if necessary."

"All right. Yes, of course I'll go. I want to do everything possible to keep the children."

"And remember, the children don't have to be quiet all the time."

"It's best they have discipline in their lives."

Wyatt's jaw clinched hard as he sat back on the bench when she said the word "discipline," but she continued, "If not for it they would end up being spoiled, self-centered, demanding attention, and thinking everyone should always agree to their wishes and be just like Jane."

A clap of thunder rumbled and rolled right over their heads. "They need love, attention, understanding, and a fair hand."

"I like to think I give them all that too. Contrary to your opinion of how I manage Elise, Charles, and Bella, my greatest wish is for them to grow into lovely adults who are well-mannered and filled with joys and merriment."

His dark mood seemed to pass as quickly as it came and a twitch of amusement played around the corners of his mouth. "But only at the appropriate time, right?"

"True," she answered in the same easy manner he'd spoken. "You know what is often said about there being a time for every season. A time to plant and a time to reap. A time to play and a time to work. A time for praise and a time for discipline."

He studied her again and touched her cheek with his warm hand. The gentle stroke soothed her. His gaze swept down her face and her gaze lingered on his smooth cheek. She wanted to reach up and caress it.

"I know the verses well, but I like my father's guide to life better."

That intrigued her. "What was it?"

"Eat, sleep, and play. Every day."

Fredericka smiled, fighting the desire to lay her cheek on his shoulder and snuggle deep into his strong and protective embrace.

Instead, she said, "I've admitted I wasn't prepared to take care of my nieces and nephew. I've agonized over it every day since my sister died. At times I feel so guilty it's almost more than I can bear."

"Guilt?" His expression filled with compassion. "You have no reason to feel guilty."

She did but hadn't meant to convey that to him. It was revealing more than she wanted to share with anyone. The responsibility of what she'd done in encouraging Angela to go with her husband to London that fateful day wasn't something she ever talked about, but it never stopped haunting her. Loving the children, being the best aunt she could be was the only way she could atone for her part in Angela's death.

"I have many reasons to feel guilt, but right now fighting Jane is more important than anything. Thank you for asking me to the dance. It's important that we be seen together as often as possible."

Before she could stop herself or think about what she was going to do, she gave the duke a kiss on his cheek. His skin was cool, smooth, and without a stubble of beard. He smelled of fresh-washed skin and a tangy woodsy scent. She let her lips glide slowly down his cheek until they dropped away from his jaw.

The kiss was brief but delicious and long enough to seal the feel, taste, and scent of him into her memory so she could enjoy the experience time and time again.

She settled back onto the bench. That inexplicable, unrelenting attraction between them ignited. Hot as ever and it seemed to be steadily growing instead of diminishing. She knew he was aware of it too.

"That was forward of me."

He brushed his fingertips along her cheek again and leaned in so close there was no getting away from his penetrating stare even if she had wanted to. What he stirred inside her was heavenly. Wyatt's caress was tantalizing and his husky words caused a quiver in her chest and stomach. Her breath felt as if it pooled in her throat until she took in a quick shallow gasp.

His gaze held steady on hers. "No, my dear wife, it wasn't forward. It was an invitation for me to kiss you."

Her breath leaped again. "You misunderstood," she argued without conviction in her voice. "I wanted you to know that even though it might appear I don't appreciate your help and sometimes I feel it's not enough, I do. It was a thank-you."

His chuckle was natural and pleasing. She loved looking at his handsome face in merriment. A loud burst of thunder sounded again and almost as close to her as the duke, but she didn't want to break the spell he'd cast over her.

"You could have just said the words. I think you like kissing me."

"Nonsense—I . . . I'm interested because it's not something I've done many times."

Wyatt's beautiful eyes centered intently on hers. He slipped his hand to the back of her neck and rested his open palm on her nape. The soothing warmth of his touch heated her all the way to her toes. With soothing ease, tension drained from her body and she relaxed.

"It was an invitation," he whispered again, and moved his face closer to hers. "I can't refuse such a tempting one."

A tingling awareness of what was about to happen gripped her as shivers of anticipation ran through her. She wanted these enticing feminine senses awakened again. At the far back reaches of her mind a worry tried to push through this beautiful moment. Wyatt was her husband, but also a privileged, titled rake who married her only for his own personal gain. She wondered if she should give in to his seduction and enjoy it?

Drawing on a thin sliver of strength, she stated with a certainty she wasn't sure she believed, "Kissing is not something we should be thinking about or doing."

His gaze feathered down to her lips and lingered a moment before moving slowly back to her eyes. "You want me to kiss you."

Of course she did! In all of her life she'd never had a feeling, a taste, or an experience as all-consumingly delicious as his kisses. But was it the right thing to do for her?

A twinkle shone in his eyes. "I've been wanting to kiss you again."

Her hesitation was easing. "It's not part of our arrangement."

"No, but I'm not thinking about that now and I don't want you to."

His lips touched hers lightly. Delicate. Sweet. Intoxicating. Her stomach quivered and her heart pounded. Swiftly the kiss turned eager. Wyatt slanted his lips over hers with firm, mounting pressure. He whispered her name with such feeling, it was as if he treasured how she was making him feel.

For a long second, she felt he was ravenous and only the taste of her could satisfy him. The ardor coming from him startled her until she realized she was returning his passion with the same intensity. Matching every gasp he inhaled, every moan he uttered, and every breath he took. What was happening between them was powerful, exhilarating, and impatient.

Exquisite shivers tightened her lower abdomen with spiral after spiral of delectable sensations. Dropping the hold on her shawl, she wound both her arms around his neck, pulling him closer, urging him to kiss her harder and deeper, wanting to feel her breasts press against his hard chest.

She skimmed her hands along the width of his shoulders and down the breadth of his back as she feasted on the stirrings of passion building inside her. As her hands searched, she felt him tremble, causing her arms to curl, locking herself securely into his embrace.

Fredericka kissed his cheek, loving the tang of his skin before returning and melting her lips to the contours of his once more. Their tongues met, swirled, and played, triggering dizzy pleasures that astounded her.

Too caught up in the moment and wanting to explore more, she kissed over his jaw to taste the skin of his neck as far as his collar would allow. Her behavior was shocking. Total madness, and so spellbinding she didn't want to stop.

Yet, slowly, the movement of Wyatt's lips upon hers became more relaxed, less feverish. They were cool, moist, and enticing.

Winded, Wyatt lifted his head and looked into her

eyes. Something wet plopped onto her nose, her cheek and eyes. She blinked.

"It's raining," he whispered.

Fredericka had been so engrossed with kissing the duke she hadn't realized the storm had arrived and they were getting drenched.

CHAPTER 19

HONEY-SUCKLE——SWEETNESS OF DISPOSITION
——LUCY HOOPER

Thy gentle smile hath won me,
Oh, more than beauty's glow
Is the soft radiance of the heart,
Like Heaven upon thy brow.

Whenever the duke's weekly card club met at his house, the furniture in the drawing room was stacked against the walls, clearing the center for three white-linen-draped tables with four chairs at each one. Shouts of laughter, chatter, along with the *thunk* of hands hitting the tables and the occasional clink of glasses had the room buzzing all afternoon. A low-burning fire and generous amounts of brandy kept the twelve gentlemen jovial competitors and pleasantly comfortable in the manner they were used to.

During the course of the afternoon and between hands of cards, Wyatt had made a few discreet inquiries about who might personally know the Lord Chancellor. Wyatt wanted to continue to maneuver the process of guardianship of the children into Fredericka's favor in any way he could. He didn't know he could trust the man so it wouldn't hurt to have reserve help. None of the members of Wyatt's group were any more versed in that area than he was. Most of them were younger than

Wyatt and of the same party. Not a one had ever had
reason to involve themselves in such matters handled in
Chancery Court.

From above, where the children were ensconced,
there had been a few squeals, a scream or two, and what
was a quite lengthy and obviously childish row between
Charles and Elise. The little rascals seemed to be having
a grand time. When Fredericka was away, the children
liked to play. And argue. Thankfully, the drawing room
was far enough away from the classroom that no one
could hear the running and stomping of little feet overhead. That might have sent some of the youngest bucks
in the card club hightailing it to the door.

The blades at the table with him had raised eyebrows
more than once and squirmed in their chairs at the loss
of concentration, but none had been plucky enough to
utter a question or comment about the new sounds in his
house. Occasionally, Wyatt looked over at Hurst's and
Rick's tables. There was restlessness with some of their
players too, but with the usual raucous behavior of the
men no one else noticed.

It was late in the afternoon when he heard the first
youthful snicker come from outside the room. That caused
Wyatt to give more attention to the doorway than the cards
in his hands. Miss Litchfield was supposed to keep the
children busy in their new schoolroom. Something must
have gone wrong. Wyatt had seen Bella and Charles peek
around the corner into the drawing room several times
and Elise had braved a tentative glance or two.

Hurst and Rick had noticed the children's peeks too.

Wyatt considered going out to check on the three
little bumpkins, but they weren't causing a disturbance
to anyone's game, except possibly his own. He didn't
mind their quick wide-eyed glances of curiosity and in-

termittent titters, though he knew Fredericka wouldn't approve of the children snooping on a gentlemen's card club. What she didn't know wouldn't bother her.

The members were behaving rather decently, considering they didn't know they were being watched by a five-, seven-, and nine-year-old. There had been a fair amount of the usual swears, joking, and the customary amount of masculine blustering, baiting, and betting, which sometimes led to loud, friendly outbursts. Whorls of expensive tobacco smoke lingered heavy in the air and swirled about their heads, but nothing happened that Wyatt would deem too offensive for the children's eyes or ears. After all, he'd barely been old enough to hold up his head the first time his father took him to a card table. And he'd hadn't been traumatized by anything he'd seen or heard in all the years that followed.

The children would be fine, though his prim and proper duchess might see things a little differently. That had worried him from time to time throughout the afternoon. However, not enough for him to stop the games, quiet the group, or send the little ones back to the schoolroom.

The men usually played until twilight or later, but after a trio of hours had passed, Wyatt decided to call the end of the game rather than call for the change of partners. A couple of the men grumbled about the time being cut short and not having opportunity to address their losses. Others seemed to understand what he was doing, as did Hurst and Rick, who helped him hurry the men out the door before they left without prolonged good-byes.

When Wyatt had shut the door behind the last man, he stood in the entryway and said, "All right, you can come out of hiding. The coast is clear. All three of you."

Bella was the first to show her little face with its big inquisitive eyes staring at him. "Were we quiet enough?" she asked, and then put her finger to her lips and whispered, "Shh."

He nodded. "Did you have a good time snooping on my card game?" he asked to no one in particular.

Bella giggled. "We sure did."

Charles and Elise hung back a few moments more before finally stepping forward.

Charles shook his head viciously, sending his tousled blond hair flying from side to side. "D-don't tell him that. We'll b-be punished."

"No one will be chastised. Where is Miss Litchfield?"

"She's napping," Bella answered while Elise remained quiet and simply watched Wyatt with the cautious and uncertain glare she usually gave him.

"And we were very quiet so we wouldn't wake her before we made it belowstairs."

So they weren't silent because of his club. They didn't want to disturb the governess and get corralled again. Clever.

The children had been snickering and peeking around the doorway for over an hour. There was no need to bother the woman now that the gentlemen were gone. He'd take care of her charges until she came looking for them.

"Tell me, have you ever made a pillow fort?" Wyatt asked, looking around the room.

"What is it?" Bella asked, her eyes widening with wonder.

"I'll show you. Charles, grab the pillows off the settees along the wall and pile them in the middle of the floor."

Bella started bouncing on her toes. "What can I do, Uncle?"

"Go help him, little one," Wyatt answered, taking

off his coat and throwing it on top of one of the tables, knocking over a glass or two and spilling the contents when it landed. "Elise, don't just stand there. You are the oldest. Help me move the chairs out of the way. Line them up against the other furniture like this." He picked up a chair in each hand and took them over to the wall. "Leave two tables in the center of the room. That will be the roof for our fort. We'll close it in with the pillows once we get inside."

Bella and Charles were already stuffing their arms. Elise didn't move. Wyatt paused.

From boarding school, he knew some boys had more issues and demons to overcome than others. It must be the same for girls. He hadn't known how to comfort the boys all those years ago, but Fredericka's children were teaching him that now he had to try.

"Come on," he said to Elise in a light manner. "There's no slacking in this effort. Every soldier has to work. Start moving chairs."

"Or g-go nap with Miss Litchfield," Charles said, and finished with a hearty laugh.

"Yes, Elise," Bella added with confidence. "If you don't help make the fort, you can't play in it with us."

That prompted her to pick up a chair.

Wyatt and the children scurried around getting the room ready for the fortress.

"Excuse me, Your Grace," Burns said, hurrying to pick up pillows the children dropped onto the floor. "I'll get someone in here immediately."

"No, Burns. Leave the pillows where they are. We're fine. You can clean up after we've finished."

After a slight hesitation, the butler nodded and turned away. Wyatt continued working, seeing that Elise helped him with all the building. They moved the glasses, cards,

and trays of ash off two of the tables and shoved them together. After that was finished, he lined three sides of the
tables with pillows to make an enclosure and laid one of
the linen cloths over the sides, careful to leave an opening.

"Crawl under, soldiers," he ordered, holding up the
cloth. "It's time to plan our battle strategies."

Bella and Charles squealed and scrambled underneath the cloth.

"I don't want to, Uncle," Elise said timidly, holding
her hands together and twisting her fingers nervously. "I
don't like this game."

"I do," Charles piped up from the safety of the fort.

"Me too," Bella echoed in her loud little-girl voice as
she stuck her head out from under the tablecloth.

Wyatt bent down and looked at them. "Good job.
Give me a minute. Don't talk or squeal. You'll alert
the enemy." He straightened and faced Elise, nodding
toward the fort as he struggled to remember what they
said to boys at Eton. He rubbed the back of his neck.
Well, no, he couldn't do that. Calling her a greenhorn or
a scared little baby wouldn't work. Girls needed something gentle.

"It's safe in the fort, Elise. You'll be with your com-
rades and you can trust them. Or you can be the night
watchman and stand guard out here. Alert us if anyone
wants to sneak into our camp."

The wariness eased from her face. Without saying a
word, she ducked her head and crawled under the linen.
Wyatt followed.

It was light enough they could still see one another.
Charles was between the two girls.

"This is what we called a pillow fort when I was at
boarding school," Wyatt explained. "We didn't have a
table; we only had the pillows to hold up the sheets."

"Who was the e-enemy?" Charles asked, his eyes filled with interest.

"The headmaster. Once we got the fort made, we knew we were safe."

"What do we do while we're under here?" Bella asked, twisting her hands together and moving her shoulders.

"We would see who could tell the scariest ghost story."

Elise moved closer to her sister. "I don't like ghost stories."

"I do, Uncle!" Charles yelled, waving his hands excitedly. "I want to hear one."

"Me too!" Bella squeaked again.

"You've never heard a g-ghost story," Charles declared to his little sister. "Auntie won't tell them."

Wyatt could believe that. "Remember this is our fort. We want everyone to feel safe and no one to get frightened. What kind of stories do you like, Elise?"

"Stories about flowers. Auntie reads poetry about flowers to us and talks about beautiful fairies who live and work in gardens to keep everything blooming. They pick up all the petals that fall to the ground."

"And they grind them up and put them back into the earth so they will help more beautiful flowers grow," Bella finished for her.

"I don't like stories about flowers. I want g-ghosts."

Now that he had Elise in the fort with them, Wyatt didn't want to send her flying from underneath with tales of goblins. "We'll have to do the scary stories another time."

Charles cast his eyes downward. "When?"

Wyatt studied over that. He needed to do something for Charles too. He'd be going over account books in his book room tomorrow. "Slip into my library when Miss Litchfield takes her nap tomorrow."

"I will." His grin seemed to reach from ear to ear.

Wyatt had no idea how to make up a story about flowers or fairies. He'd been thinking more along the lines of a headless horseman riding through town at midnight or a ghost coming out of a grave while a young lad was hurrying through a cemetery. He grew up in drafty old mansions with shadowy rooms, creaky doors, floors, and stairs. More than once when he was a small lad he heard strange and unexplained noises in old houses. Many nights he'd hidden his head under the covers when the winds howled fiercely outside.

Wyatt didn't want to upset Elise. She was responding to him and that touched a place deep inside him. The same place Bella touched when she'd cried the first night they arrived in London. Somehow, he knew that however long they were in London, he had to help them.

He just needed a moment to think about a sweet story containing flowers instead of a skeleton with blood dripping out of his eye sockets.

"You start, Elise," he finally said. "Do you have a story you can tell?"

"If she does, I've already heard it," Charles complained.

Wyatt's attention snapped to the boy. Had he just spoken a complete sentence without stuttering? And for the first time since Wyatt had known him.

"I can tell you one," Bella offered happily.

"Let's allow Elise to go first," Wyatt said, making note of the fact that all the children were squirming, constantly moving their arms and legs. Enjoying themselves and acting like children, not—

"Auntie once told us about a fairy named Delfina who got lost in the garden. It was getting dark. She didn't know how to get back home."

"What did she do?" he asked, stretching out his legs and crossing his feet at the ankles.

"She hid under a mushroom," Bella answered for her sister.

"That's Auntie's tale." Elise lifted her chin defiantly. "I'm telling mine. The fairy didn't hide in my story."

Wyatt chuckled. "Sounds like a clever thing to do, but let Elise tell us her story, Bella. You can be next."

"That means I have to listen to two stories about f-flowers and fairies?"

Charles was definitely getting better with his stuttering. "Men have to be patient and wait for ladies to go first, Charles. It's the right thing to do."

"If I have to."

"Go ahead with your story, Elise." Wyatt shifted his weight again, trying to get comfortable on the hard floor.

"Delfina was looking for a certain flower. It was her mother's favorite color. She couldn't find it, so she kept wandering farther away from home."

"Was she frightened?" he asked.

"She—" Bella started answering, but Wyatt looked at her and put his finger to his lips. She smiled and put her finger to her lips too.

Elise nodded. "Delfina was afraid her mother wouldn't find her before darkness covered the garden. Big dragonflies would get close to fairies and knock them with their long wings. She didn't want to meet any of them. She flew to the top of the tallest flower she could find."

"Were you lost in the woods one time?" Wyatt asked softly.

Reluctantly, the young girl nodded. "For a little while. A long time ago when I was little. I thought Mama had left me."

He kept his voice low and tender. "But she hadn't."

Elise shook her head. "She found me before it was too dark to see. But she left again and didn't return."

Wyatt's throat felt tight as he looked at her pretty little face filled with sadness. He wanted to comfort her and say something. But what? He was always saying things the wrong way to Fredericka. What could he say to offer solace to a sad girl?

Suddenly Wyatt remembered his father and smiled. He liked to think his father never left him and was always with him.

"Maybe she does return." He said the first thing that came to his mind.

Elise lifted inquisitive eyes to him. So did Bella and Charles. Wyatt had gotten himself into a pinch here. He had to add something.

"Every time you see a flower in bloom, or maybe her favorite color of dress, I think it's your mother's way of letting you know she's watching over you, and there's no reason to feel you're alone."

A smile like he'd never seen started breaking across Elise's face. Hope surged inside Wyatt's chest. He was getting through to her.

The table linen whipped back and pillows toppled over. Fredericka stared down at Wyatt and the children with her golden-brown eyes.

Everyone jumped as if they'd just seen a ghost.

CHAPTER 20

COWSLIP——ATTRACTIVE GRACE
——L. H.

I would bring to thee a cowslip,
My beautiful, my own,
Such a fair and modest flower
Is like to thee alone.

"What's going on under here?"

The children scrambled out from under the table, scattering pillows everywhere as they scampered to their feet. It took Wyatt longer to uncross his feet and crawl his large frame from the fort to rise. The three siblings stood in a row, straight as boards with their arms held tightly by their sides.

Fredericka locked her wary gaze on Wyatt. She looked gorgeous standing with her hands on her hips and hair ruffled around her face from wearing her bonnet. "What were you doing under there?"

"Telling stories," he answered calmly, feeling quite happy with how he handled the children by himself.

Fredericka remained quiet, suspicious, and surveyed the messy room from one end to the other. Wyatt had a feeling he was in trouble with his wife when he saw what she was eyeing in particular. A table crowded with glasses stacked high and holding varying degrees of leftover port and brandy. Mounds of cards in disarray and small crystal trays filled with half-burned cheroots and pipe tobacco ash. She couldn't fail to miss the lingering scent of stale smoke and liquor in the air.

She continued to look around the room with more angst than he had expected. There was nothing he could do but tell the truth. "We built a pillow fort. It seemed like a good time to do it since most of the furniture was already moved out of the way for the club."

She settled her anxious attention back on Wyatt. "The children didn't come in here while you were gaming, did they?"

"No, no, of course not." He glanced at the golden-haired youngsters. They were all wearing the most innocent expressions he'd ever seen. They looked sweeter than the cherubs painted in Raphael's *The Sistine Madonna*. Wyatt was damned proud of them. They didn't utter a peep. "Fredericka, you know I wouldn't have let them come in here while the men were playing. We made this after they left."

"This room is a disaster. Is this the way it usually looks after one of your meetings? If so, what kind of card games do you play?"

"You think they did this?" Wyatt smiled. "No, we did most of this." He motioned to himself and then to the children.

Her brow grew tighter. Obviously, that wasn't the right thing to say.

"I did most of it," he corrected. "I had to move things out of the way to build the fort." Best he get her off the subject quickly. If possible. "Elise was telling us a story about a fairy who was lost in a garden. She said you often told them stories about flowers." Wyatt looked at the children again, hoping Bella or one of them might speak up and agree they were having a good time, but they were in their wooden soldier stance.

"Miss Elise, Miss Bella, Master Charles?" Miss Litchfield called from the stairway. "Where have the three of you taken off to?"

"In here, Miss Litchfield." Fredericka glanced over to the children and motioned toward the doorway with her head. "All of you go to Miss Litchfield and stay in the schoolroom until I get there."

"M-may w-we wait o-outside instead?"

Wyatt grimaced. Charles' stutter was back in full force.

"Not until we've had a chat about what's been going on. First, I must finish my discussion with the duke. I won't be long."

Bella and Charles gave Wyatt an expression that seemed to say, *You are in big trouble.* Even Elise seemed to have a spark of sympathy for him hidden in her expression as she turned and followed her brother and sister.

Fredericka focused on Wyatt, and after the children were gone she asked, "Did the children see you playing in here with the gentlemen?"

"No." He shook his head decisively. But then wavered by adding, "I don't think so. I mean, probably not, but maybe a glimpse or two."

He watched the frown she wore form into a tight glare.

"I can't believe this. They were to stay with Miss Litchfield in the schoolroom." Fredericka motioned to the topsy-turvy room with pillows scattered about the floor. "What were you thinking to allow them to play in this? This is not the way properly brought up children behave."

"Why not?" He gave his wife an innocent shrug. "They needed a little entertainment and so do you. Come sit in the fort with me."

She blinked rapidly. "What? No."

"Come on." He smiled and reached his hand out to her. "You need to relax more, Fredericka, and not worry so. You've probably never been inside a pillow fortress, and you know you want to see what it's like. Just for a moment or two."

"You are truly unbelievable." She shook her head as she looked at the room again. "I knew you would be drinking and carousing with your friends as you so often are. And I knew we'd be in your way, but I didn't know you would include the children in your behavior. I told you it's not proper for young girls to see grown men at their play."

Her strength to stay the course was commendable, but her unbending spirit irritated the devil out of him. "They weren't in my way. You aren't in my way, Fredericka, and nothing unsavory was going on that would have harmed them. The club wasn't carousing. We were playing cards— laughing, drinking, and some of them smoking. Maybe a swear or two, but the children never came in here. They only saw friends having a good time. Peeking around the corner to glimpse a card game, a formal dinner party, or even a political conversation is all the same to a child. It's what children do."

"No. It's not what Angela's children do. It's my responsibility to protect them and see they do everything right. Spying on adult pastimes is not acceptable. Certainly not for little girls. Whatever you were doing this afternoon was not good for them, and neither are you. I don't know why I thought you might somehow make us seem like a normal, happy family."

He stood staring at her, his feet braced slightly apart. "They were not harmed today any more than Bella was by getting pushed down in the park."

"You don't know that."

"I do. It is all part of growing up. They are curious. I did things like this when I was their ages."

Fredericka threw her hands up and huffed a laugh. "You cannot be considered an example for anyone. You were pampered, coddled, and allowed to do whatever you wished all your life."

Wyatt flinched at the truthful sting of her words. In many ways all she said was true, but his childhood wasn't as ideal as Fredericka seemed to think. The memory of Grant taking Wyatt's punishment because he hadn't known his lines of poetry came rushing back. If he hadn't been a duke's son, he might have been the one with the useless, scarred hand. Wyatt had to live with that.

His childhood was often lonely until he went to Eton. His father would leave him with doting servants and tutors while he went to summer house parties, London, or on a hunt that lasted for weeks. It was part of growing up and Wyatt managed.

Being at Eton with other boys all around had never been a problem for him, and he couldn't understand why some of them cried and were upset. At home, he didn't have brothers, sisters, or neighbors to play with, and no one to talk to other than adults no matter which of his father's homes they were living in at the time. Eton had been a dream come true for Wyatt. There he had more than enough boys to talk to and play with. He never felt alone. That feeling hadn't changed as he grew older. He enjoyed participating in tournaments with his friends, the clubs, and having the camaraderie of people around.

"No, I'm not an example for anyone, but you are being unreasonable, Fredericka," he declared, letting aggravation show in his voice. "They were having a good time."

"I am their aunt and guardian for now. Nothing is more important to me than their upbringing, welfare, and how they behave. I'm reasonable about everything concerning them."

"No, you aren't. You are always so busy trying to make them behave properly and be perfect that you won't allow them time to just be children."

"Of course I do," she argued, seemingly taken aback by his frankness. "I listen to them and try to grant their wishes when possible. I have to be their mother and you are no help when you try to corrupt what I've worked so hard to instill in them. You seem to have forgotten I am in danger of losing them to Jane. I must have them be proper at all times."

Wyatt held his anger in check. He had to. Tension showed around her eyes and the corners of her mouth. Seeing her outraged about a simple time of play tore at his gut. More so since what she said was true. She was worried she would lose the children. He understood that. He could settle the case right now if he was willing to go to the Lord Chancellor with the repugnant story about his brother-in-law. But did he want to do that on the basis of gossip when the man had indicated he would rule for Wyatt?

"I do realize the position you are in, Fredericka. I told you this would take time and I had to be careful or I would end up hurting you more than helping."

"You should have thought about that before you made the promise to me."

She turned and started marching out.

"Don't forget we are going to a ball tomorrow night. You need to be ready by half past eight."

She swung back to face him long enough to say, "I'm not going anywhere with you. You can go on your own."

"I will," he said defiantly to her retreating back as the heat of anger radiated through him. "And just so you know, Charles didn't stutter very often this afternoon. When he was relaxed, playing, and having a good time he spoke normally. And Elise actually opened up and talked to me about her mother for the first time."

When he finished, he realized he was talking to an empty room. She hadn't heard a word he'd said about the children.

Wyatt shook his head and sighed as his annoyance toward her tamped down. The room *was* a disaster and it didn't look or smell like a place young girls should be. Maybe Fredericka was a little wrong and a little right. Without warning, his father crossed his mind, and he wondered what the duke would say about him playing with kids, comforting them, and liking the experience. What would he say if he knew Wyatt actually enjoyed being with his wife even when they were having an argument?

Sure, she was a lot of trouble, but he couldn't help but think she was worth it.

CHAPTER 21

LINES TO A BELLE
—O. W. HOLMES

Thine eye had other forms to see—
Why rest upon his bashful cheek?
With other tones thy heart was stirred—
Why waste on him a gentle word?

Nervous as a cat on the bow of a boat in the middle of the Serpentine, Fredericka handed her wrap to the attendant and looked toward the entranceway of the large, sweeping ballroom of the newly refurbished Grand Ballroom. Glittering light from the brass and crystal chandeliers could be seen from the open doors. Sounds of lively music were almost drowned out by the solid roar of chatter and laughter.

Walking into the ballroom with Wyatt by her side would have been challenging enough, but walking in alone was downright terrifying. Her knees were knocking together and her legs wobbly as she stood in the vestibule trying to summon the courage to enter the festive room to face Wyatt, and everyone else.

It was never easy to admit to oneself, or anyone, that you overreacted and made a mistake. But she had. The children were only playing under a table. Messy tables they'd had no part in making, and there was no one around to see them except her and Wyatt. Jane was not going to come running in and see the children in such a setup as Wyatt had orchestrated. But Fredericka was always fearful. Because of that she was the one showing bad behavior yesterday afternoon by getting so upset.

She had no idea why she said she wouldn't come with him to the ball tonight other than her mounting frustration about the issue with Jane hadn't been settled. In fact, it had gotten worse since she'd come to live in the duke's house. That was her fault. Not his. He hadn't invited her. He hadn't even welcomed her at first.

But he had asked her to come to the dance.

The modiste had accomplished a miracle by creating several extraordinary designs in a short time. Once Fredericka realized she must attend the ball, she settled on a gown with a gold brocade bodice threaded with copper-colored banding that enhanced her hair and eyes. It was cut fashionably low across her shoulders and neckline where the swell of her breasts rose from beneath the expensive fabric. The high-waist skirt was overlaid with a sheer of white flowing silk that rippled and fluttered when she walked. Combs adorned with dark alabaster beads held up her chignon. A golden ribbon secured a large topaz at the hollow of her throat. Given the time restraints she had to dress, she'd done all she could to look as beautiful as possible for Wyatt.

She'd heard every word he said as she left the drawing room in a huff yesterday afternoon. It had taken a while to come to grips with the reality of their meaning. In short, he was getting through to the children in only a few days when she had failed to do so for over a year. Elise was talking to him and Charles had almost stopped stuttering. All because of Wyatt's easy-mannered attention to them. And he'd accomplished more than he knew about. Bella hadn't had an accident in the bed since they'd been in his house.

There was still no doubt in Fredericka's heart that the duke was a rake of the first order. He cared more for his clubs, tournaments, and friends than anything else. On that she was clear, and his actions proved it: not staying for their wedding buffet because he had to get back for games, resisting her appeal to stay in London because she would be in his way. Too, she couldn't forget the times he'd plied her with ravishing kisses that only made her want more of them. But even with all stacked against him, he was making a sizable difference in the children's lives for the better. She couldn't overlook that and not acknowledge it by thanking him.

Attending the ball would be a good start.

After an additional deep, steadying breath she knew the time had come. Prolonging the event wouldn't make it easier. She walked through the open doorway and into the ballroom. Immediately, she was filled with awe at what was before her. It was the most stunning room she'd ever seen.

A silvery glow of light washed the atmosphere and people of the festive event. Large, richly detailed embroideries and tapestries hung on the tall walls, while the ceiling was painted with a classical scene of Venus holding a golden apple against a blue sky. Life-sized statues of cherubs and urns filled with colorful flowers were scattered about the room. Large Corinthian columns had been wrapped in pale blue tulle, clippings of bright green ivy, and strings of beads made to look like pearls.

Ladies extravagantly dressed in colorful silk with crowns of jewels and feathers in their hair mingled with gentlemen wearing black coats with long tails, white shirts, neckcloths, and waistcoats. Everyone wore white gloves. Some of the guests stood alone simply watching the movements in the room while others were cloistered in intimate groups chatting among themselves.

There were only two steps down from the entrance level to the main ballroom floor, but it suddenly felt as far away as Paddleton. Fredericka searched the crowd for Wyatt. He was taller than most men and should have been easy to spot, but a quick glance of the large gathering showed no sign of him. To the far side of the room was a vast dance floor where guests twirled and swayed to the orchestra's sprightly tune. She searched the faces and heads of brown hair. Wyatt didn't seem to be among them.

Tension caused her legs to wobble again as her mind filled with questions she had no time to study over. What if he had decided not to attend after all? She hadn't seen him all day but that wasn't unusual with his practices and training schedule. What if he had gone to one of his clubs tonight or elsewhere? What if he'd decided to spend the evening with his mistress? Her heart swelled, tightening her chest and throat alarmingly. What had made her think Wyatt would be here waiting for her when she'd told him she wouldn't attend?

The thought of fleeing before anyone saw her standing alone suddenly seemed the best thing to do. There was no time to ponder the pluses and minuses of staying or going. She had to make a decision now. Searching the crowd one last time, she spotted Jane standing near the front of the crowd, staring at her with a knowing smile.

Panic erupted inside Fredericka. Was it too late to flee? Her eyes closed tightly for a moment. In a deep cleansing breath, she willed her strength to return. When her lashes rose, she knew she wouldn't give her cousin the satisfaction of watching her run away.

Swiping barbs with Jane was never easy but would

be better than being alone in a sea of strangers who were laughing, talking, and dancing. She would enter the room unaccompanied and handle any questions with grace and—A gasp choked in her throat. Her heart felt as if it stopped beating for a few seconds and then started racing. Dressed in his formal evening attire, Wyatt was walking toward her looking tall, powerful, and more handsome than he ever had.

"Fredericka." Smiling as he bounded up the two steps, his gaze swept down her face with a tender expression of caring as he took hold of her hand. "I'm glad you decided to come," he said, giving her fingers a gentle squeeze.

All she could think for a moment was that he was glad to see her. Relief slowly settled through her as he lifted her hand to his lips for a kiss.

"I hoped that if I left you alone today you would come to this decision."

The thoughtful, sincere words calmed her fears like a ray of sunshine on a dreary day. Her anxiety about the evening melted away. "I had to do it for the children."

"Only the children?" he asked with a quirk of his head and a twitch of an engaging smile. "Never mind the reason. You're here. You are always beautiful, Fredericka, but especially so tonight."

"Thank you," she answered softly, feeling as if she were the belle of the ball. "I'm sorry I overreacted to your game with the children yesterday. It's always been so important to me that they never misbehave or do things that aren't proper."

"They didn't, but none of that is important anymore." He turned and looked at the crowd. "People are waiting to meet you. And just so you know in advance, your cousin and her husband are here too. We've already said our hellos."

She looked over his shoulder to see if she could catch a glimpse of Jane watching them. For the moment, she was nowhere in sight. "I hope it wasn't an awkward meeting for you."

"Not for me. Tomkin seemed more uncomfortable than his wife. He was probably behind his brother making the wager at White's. In any case, he obviously condoned it. Knowing every eye was on the three of us, we were civil and made it through our short conversation without any real daggers being thrown."

Fredericka smiled gratefully. "That's good to hear. I can't promise Jane and I won't aim a few at each other."

Wyatt chuckled. "I expect you'll both be polite. Now that you are here, all the attention will be on you."

He turned and looked behind him. "Grant and Priscilla are standing close by. I'd like to introduce you to them. Priscilla has been pesty about wanting to meet you ever since we married."

Fredericka stiffened at the word "pesty." Certain words triggered hurts from her past and "pesty" was one of them. Jane and Angela often used the word to describe Fredericka when she wanted to play with them. For a moment, she wondered if Wyatt felt that way about her. After all, she had pushed her way into his life when she'd come to London.

"I won't force you if you'd rather not," he said when she failed to answer.

"I don't mind," she answered.

"You look uneasy about it. You don't still think there is anything between me a—"

"No, no," she said sincerely. "Truly, you made that clear and I believe you. I'm happy to meet Miss Fenway and her brother."

"All right," he answered with a nod. "Priscilla can be

forward at times. You may not appreciate how nervy she can be considering you always want everything so proper. She speaks whatever comes to her mind and sometimes it's quite bold. Just know, she means no harm."

Forcing past the old haunts that wanted to rear up and ruin her evening, Fredericka lifted her chin and said, "That's good to know. I remember you are very fond of her."

Wyatt's gaze held fast on Fredericka. "As a sister. Nothing more."

Fredericka didn't know why she'd needed that assurance but was glad he gave it. "I remembered that too." She glanced at the crowded dance floor. "There's one thing I need to tell you."

An uneasy expression settled on his face. "What?"

"I'm not very good at dancing. Passable at best."

He gave her a teasing wink. "I'm glad there's something I can do better than you."

She laughed softly as the Duke of Stonerick and Duke of Hurstbourne joined them on the landing. Both greeted her with sincere smiles and praise.

"It's good to see you, Duchess," Rick offered after formal greetings were complete. "Wyatt hoped you would start feeling better so you could join him for the evening."

Fredericka glanced at Wyatt. He gave her a rakish shrug. She was glad she'd changed her mind too. Turning back to Rick, she said, "It's amazing what a little brandy and honey can do to make one feel better."

"I always highly recommend it," Rick offered with a grin.

"It's almost as beneficial as putting your feet up and reading a few pages of poetry. You should try it sometime."

"Perhaps I will. In another life."

Fredericka and Rick laughed as a gong reverberated three times around the room. The music and dancing stopped. Everyone quieted and looked toward the entrance where they stood. Wyatt held up Fredericka's hand in his and said, "Ladies and gentlemen. I present to you the Duchess of Wyatthaven."

Wyatt then kissed her hand for all to see. At that moment, Fredericka felt as if she were the queen of the ball. But more than that. She sensed he really wanted her to stand by him as his wife.

The music started again and the roar of chatter and laughter resumed. Fredericka glanced at Wyatt with appreciation as he led her down the two steps and into the midst of the crowd.

The formalities of introductions seemed frenzied as they moved about the room meeting couple after couple. After the third or fourth, she was certain it would be difficult to remember all the names and titles but hoped she would recall the faces if they met again.

No one was familiar to her, until she was introduced to Miss Priscilla Fenway and her brother. Fredericka was not likely to forget the lady with coppery-brown hair who had been dancing with Wyatt at his house.

It didn't take long for Miss Fenway to set her attention solely on Fredericka and say, "I have been waiting to meet you, Duchess. It's been unfair of the duke to keep you all to himself for so long. I've asked him several times if I could arrange to meet you."

There was obviously nothing shy about Miss Fenway but nothing pretentious in her manner either. She was confident in the way she spoke and seemed sincere in what she said.

Taking a quick glance at Wyatt, Fredericka saw he was already in deep conversation with Miss Fenway's brother. "There were many things to get settled after we married and when I came to Town."

"Yes, of course, but I've been eager to talk to you. I don't have a sister and Grant has never married. I was hoping we would get along well together and you'd feel as if we were family as Wyatt does."

That was quite a forward statement considering they had just met. Miss Fenway hadn't sounded pushy as if her wishes had been neglected or that she was disappointed. "That's kind of you to say, Miss Fenway."

"It comes from my heart," she said in the sincerest of tones. "You must know already that Wyatt has been like a brother to me for most of my life."

That was even more forward. Not many young ladies would call a duke by his name in a public setting, though it was clear Miss Fenway was comfortable addressing him so informally. Fredericka didn't detect a spark of envy, malice, or fakeness in her words or expression. She sensed the young lady truly felt like family.

"There was a time Wyatt visited Grant often," she continued, carrying the conversation as if they'd been friends for years. "Not as much since he became the duke. More responsibilities, he says, and I'm sure it's true." She looked over at Wyatt and smiled with fondness. "Since he gave the grand party for the day of my birth, I was hoping I could impose on you to help guide me through the rest of the Season."

Fredericka took a step back and shook her head. That was going too far, family or not. "I wouldn't be a good choice, Miss Fenway. My Season was cut short to mere days, and I have no experience in the workings of the marriage mart. I don't see how I can help you with something so important."

Priscilla smiled sweetly and then laughed innocently. "You help me, Duchess, simply by talking to me. But I meant in the ways of recognizing love and romance when it happens. Not in the details of getting from party to party. My aunt is doing that. I know it was love at first sight for you and Wyatt, but most of us are not that fortunate."

Love at first sight?

Where had Miss Fenway gotten an idea like that? Fredericka's first meeting with Wyatt was contentious. And their meetings still were at times.

"It takes longer for most people to fall in love and want to make a match. I fear I am one of those." She paused and sighed wistfully. "There's Mr. Fergus Altman. He's quite handsome. I've experienced a breathless flutter or two in my chest and butterflies in my stomach when I look at him. But there is also Mr.—"

Miss Fenway kept talking, but Fredericka had stopped listening. She knew about breathless flutters and butterflies. She had never denied a strong connection between her and Wyatt from their first meeting. But it wasn't love. Was it? No, of course not. Fredericka looked over at Wyatt. Her heart seemed to lift with happiness at the sight of him. He must have sensed her watching him. He smiled and her skin tingled. Was it love she felt for the duke when she had melted so easily and readily into his arms when he kissed her at Paddleton, in his book room, and in the garden?

No.

Fredericka banished that line of thinking quickly. It couldn't be love. The duke was an undisciplined man-about-town. Except, she thought, for his training and club's tournaments. He was quite serious when it came to preparing for those games so he could win the matches and the wagers he'd placed on them.

"So do you think you could help me if I came for a visit one afternoon this week?"

"Perhaps sometime later in the Season, Miss Fenway. I don't know if Wyatt told you, but I'm responsible for my two nieces and nephew. They are still adjusting to London and need a lot of my attention."

"Yes, I understand," she said, but Fredericka could see that she didn't. The sparkle left her eyes and her smile turned tentative. She expected an invitation to tea, and soon.

Feeling she might have sounded harsh, Fredericka added, "If my schedule changes over the next week or two, I'll send a note over to you."

Miss Fenway's expression brightened. "That would be lovely. I can hold any particular day open for you, if you—"

"Your Grace," Jane said, sweeping from behind Miss Fenway to curtsey before Fredericka. "I'm sorry to interrupt, but I must be leaving soon and wanted to make sure we had time to speak. Since we are family." She looked over to Miss Fenway and smiled. "You don't mind, do you?"

"Not at all," she answered, but made no move to excuse herself. "Please join us."

Fredericka knew that's not what her cousin wanted and wouldn't take kindly to Miss Fenway not respecting the hint to leave.

Jane gave Miss Fenway her practiced smile. "I need a moment alone with my cousin. Walk with me, Fredericka."

Fredericka looked at Wyatt. He was watching her so

she lifted her chin and gave him a confident smile as she and Jane started weaving their way through the crowded room at a slow stroll.

"You look stunning tonight," Jane said without a hint of mockery. "I see Mrs. Parashu was the perfect designer for you."

Praise wasn't something Jane dished out easily or often. She wasn't one to say you looked lovely if you didn't. Sparing someone's feelings had never been something Jane would do. Fredericka took the compliment as intended and felt herself walking a little taller.

"Thank you. I've been pleased with her eye for color and style."

"And I'm sure she appreciated the extra you paid her for working so fast and diligently to see you had an appropriate gown for this evening."

"Quite pleased," Fredericka agreed with no reservation.

"It's nice to see you and the duke working so hard to make everyone believe you are now indeed a happily married couple. Quite impressive how he introduced you tonight—making the showy display of getting everyone's attention with the gong." Jane smiled again. "Only a duke or the king would have the courage to do it. How many times did you have to practice looking so adoringly at each other?"

Did they? Fredericka felt curls of pleasure at the thought of the duke looking at her that way and Jane noticing! Her thoughts magically flew back to the garden with his lips so deliciously pressed against hers, the drops of rain cooling their heated bodies as they kissed and kissed so passionately before escaping into the house. There *was* something between them. She just didn't know what it was.

"Actually, Jane, the way we looked at each other is quite natural and normal. No practice or pretense is needed for either of us." Which was surprising after their heated disagreement about the children yesterday. That was none of her cousin's concern.

"Amazing considering all the gossip. But, in any case, it appears everyone is delighted to see you two finally together at a ball after that calamitous reunion at the duke's house the night you arrived."

It was impossible for Jane to be nice for long. Fredericka raised her brows as if she were unconcerned. "It's easy to talk gossip."

"So true," Jane added as if she were as disinterested as Fredericka.

"Excuse me, ladies."

Fredericka turned to see Wyatt striding up beside her. He lightly placed his hand to her lower back as he stopped.

"I hope you don't mind, Mrs. Tomkin, if I take Fredericka away from you long enough to have a dance."

Fredericka's heartbeat pounded. He'd come to rescue her. Appreciation filled her and she smiled at him.

"No, of course not, Your Grace. I'm going to be leaving soon anyway."

"A shame since Fredericka just arrived."

Jane looked at Fredericka and lifted her chin a notch above normal. "I know," she said, giving her attention back to Wyatt. "I heard your Brass Deck Club has a tournament in Oxford soon. Several gentlemen are traveling up for the event. There seems to be quite the excitement surrounding it. Clever to have such a large event during the Season. It should be rewarding. I'll be cheering for your club now that you are family. You don't mind, do you?"

"I'll look forward to it."

Jane nodded to Fredericka before turning and disappearing into the crowd.

After she was a safe distance away, Fredericka looked softly at Wyatt. "Thank you for joining us. I can't believe we were both so nice to her."

"You know what is said about keeping your enemies close. But, we are not going to think about Jane any more tonight. Come with me to the dance floor. I've asked they play a waltz. I want to feel you in my arms and I want everyone to see you in my arms."

Expectancy shortened Fredericka's breaths. The meaning of his words settled deeply inside.

His eyes looked so dreamily into hers. "Dance with me, Fredericka. I'm happy you came, and I want everyone to know it."

"Yes," she answered softly.

"And, Fredericka," he spoke softly, "tonight isn't for the children. It's for you to be with me."

Dressed as a princess, standing beneath lighted crystal chandeliers with the most handsome man in attendance, holding out his hand for her, Fredericka had never felt more precious in her life. It was a dream come true, and while she was dreaming, maybe she wasn't in his way now that she was living with him in London. And just maybe she'd found a home where she could one day have not only her nieces and nephew but also a true husband to love her and children of her own.

She reached out and took Wyatt's hand.

CHAPTER 22

THE MICHAELMAS DAISY
—ANON.

Thy tender blush, thy simple frame,
Unnoticed have pass'd;
But now thou com'st with softer claim,
The loveliest and the last.

One lone lamp burned in the vestibule when Wyatt and Fredericka entered the house. Though it was near dawn and cold as a deep wintery night, Wyatt immediately swung his cloak off his shoulders and placed it onto a chair. His body was tired from all his hectic training sessions and the long evening, but inside he felt good. The reason was because of the lady standing beside him, quietly watching him remove his gloves while she waited patiently for him to help with her wrap.

It puzzled him that he enjoyed watching her watch him do something so ordinary. That made him smile and want to remove her cape and everything else she was wearing and, well . . . He'd been having fleeting stray thoughts like that all evening. Since he'd known her actually. There was a dazzling innocence about her that kept drawing him even as he tried to continue his life as usual and keep his distance from her. She wasn't supposed to be on his mind. She wasn't even supposed to be living with him. But that thought crossed his mind less than it should.

"I'm amazed at how long we stayed at the ball," Fredericka said, hugging her velvety black cape tightly at the neckline as if to ward off the early morning chill. "I never expected we would be some of the last people to leave."

Wyatt dropped his gloves and scarf on top of his cloak. "I have to admit, I've never stayed so long at a ball."

"I find that astonishing, considering how many you've probably attended. I hope you were having a delightful time and didn't stay just for me."

"Both," he answered honestly. "I had a good time, and stayed just for you. Is anything wrong with me wanting to please you?"

She continued to smile softly at him. "Nothing, since you were enjoying yourself. It was most gratifying to find I wasn't as terrible at dancing as I thought."

Wyatt chuckled. "Perhaps you never had the right partner and I'm the one who made it so easy for you tonight."

By the way her eyes narrowed and sparkled, he knew she hadn't thought of that possibility.

"That's probably true." She hesitated a moment and then, with a childlike wonder in her expression, added, "Thank you, Wyatt. This was the best night of my life."

An instant tightness grabbed his chest. He was touched by the truthfulness in her words and sincerity in her tone. Of all the wild, wicked, and even heroic things he'd done, he'd never had anyone tell him he'd given them the best night of their life.

"I suppose that sounds dramatic to you, but it's true," she added almost shyly, as if suddenly feeling embarrassed she'd let her true feelings escape.

Her words were humbling, and he was at a loss what to say as she continued on.

"You've been to many parties, and with your travels, tournaments, and all your wins, I'm sure there've been many nights you thought were the best of your life."

He couldn't think of any night but the one he'd just had with her.

"Anyway," she sighed. "It's nice to know I wasn't in your way, or in anyone else's way, this evening. I enjoyed every moment."

Her words caused a catch in his throat. He wasn't one to get choked up about anything, but she had him damn close. He moved closer to her. "What are you talking about, Fredericka? In my way?"

"I know you didn't want me here in London with you. You made it clear I would only be in your way."

"No," he said, but knew immediately it wasn't true. "Yes. It was true. At first, maybe, but not now."

"Don't be kind. You've had many things to do and we both know it. You didn't need me adding to your schedule." Her eyes took on a glossy sheen. "I was used to the feeling. It was always that way with Angela and Jane. They were the same age and eight years older than me. They had things in common, and I was too young to realize I was annoying and in their way. I do now, of course. At the time, all I wanted was to be with them. They looked at me as a silly little girl who wouldn't go away and leave them alone."

Wyatt heard a trace of a tremble in her voice and it tightened his chest. "Is that what they told you?"

She looked away for a moment, seeming to search for something that had always eluded her. Finally, she dragged in a rapid breath and whispered, "Many times. And it was true."

Thoughts of Eton and his own life stirred within Wyatt. He knew how some of the older boys treated the younger ones. They could be brutal with words meant to hurt and embarrass. He didn't know girls could be that way. He always thought of them as softer. Kinder. This rejection must have been especially hard on Fredericka because Angela was her sister.

"That was callous of me, and them to make you feel that way."

"It was," she said with a smile that held no malice or offense. Just truth.

Her honest reaction caused his gut to twist. She had every reason to hate him, and he was hating himself for telling her she needed to go back to Paddleton. From somewhere deep inside himself, he must have known she was going to be the one who upset his carefully planned life.

"I never meant to make you feel unwanted. I have no excuses other than my own selfish needs." And the truth was that he'd always believed a wife would be in his way and upset—no, destroy—his carefully laid plans. But it wasn't bothering him that she had.

Fredericka moistened her lips, swallowed, and laughed lightly. "I didn't intend to make you think I'm looking for sympathy. I only wanted you to know that being with you tonight—meeting people you know, dancing with you, and drinking champagne—it was very special."

He wanted to say it was for him too, but sensed she wanted to keep talking, so he didn't interrupt.

"I understood and agreed to our marriage arrangement. At the time, it was best for me as well. I'm most appreciative you changed your mind about letting me stay in London for a time." Her eyes glistened with a sheen again. "I know in my soul I still feel resentment toward

Jane for stealing my sister's affection, and so much of the time with her that should have been mine."

He was beginning to understand Fredericka and Jane better. He moved closer but didn't want to tamper with whatever she was going through. She needed to talk and he just needed to listen.

"Your rivalry with Jane has been going on for a long time?"

"Yes." She looked around the vestibule as if to keep from meeting his eyes. "I don't know that it will ever end. Even if the Lord Chancellor awards permanent guardianship of the children to me and you. Jane and I have been at each other for so long we probably don't know how to stop."

By the look in her eyes Wyatt could see she was reliving something from the past, so he stayed quiet. Her hands relaxed and her arms eased to her sides. He could see memories were swamping her. "The hardest part was that Angela never stood up for me. She never told Jane, *'No, let her stay.'* I was her little sister and she never insisted that I should join them in their talks, giggles, and walks. I was her sister, yet she always sided with Jane. Never me."

"So maybe Angela is the one you are truly angry with and always fighting."

"What?" Fredericka looked stunned. "No, of course not," she said with a breath of nervous laughter. "I don't know what made you say that. It's certainly not true. I loved Angela very much. I've told you it's guilt I carry about Angela's death. I should have never encouraged her to go with her husband that day. Jane never would have." Fredericka looked toward the stairs and started to remove her wrap. "I should go up now."

"Wait, let me help you with this."

Wyatt placed his hands on her shoulders to remove her cape at the same time she reached up. Their fingers tangled together in the velvet. Fredericka turned her head and looked into his eyes. She was the most beautiful woman he had ever seen. The most unselfish woman he'd ever met and, since he'd first seen her, the only woman he'd wanted.

"Perhaps I'll just keep it on until I get to my chambers," she said, holding her gaze on his eyes while slowly letting her fingers slip from his one by one. "It's nippy in the house."

"See if this warms you." He pulled her to him, wrapped his arms around her, and hugged her close.

"Oh, yes," she whispered, and pressed her cheek against his chest and settled comfortably into his embrace. "This should warm me in no time."

"Not too fast, I hope. I'm enjoying holding you. You feel good in my arms, Fredericka. You always have." It's where she belonged.

Wyatt closed his eyes and drew in a deep, heady breath. He kissed the top of her head, and tightened his arms. Guilt had been an unwanted friend of his for years. He was very familiar with it. It could eat at one's insides day and night. He didn't want that for Fredericka. And he sure as hell didn't want her feeling she was in his way.

Lifting her head, Fredericka looked up at him with contentment. "It's wonderful being close to you."

"Do you know how many times I looked at you tonight and wanted to kiss you?"

A smile twitched at the corners of her beautiful mouth. "Did you keep count of the number so you could tell me?"

He whispered a laugh, slid his hands underneath her

cape, circled her waist with his arms, and caught her tightly to his chest once again. "I stopped at a thousand. After that, I kept looking for a secluded corner where I could escape with you and do this."

Without another word, without a pretense of being gentle to her proper sensibilities, Wyatt pressed his lips upon hers and kissed with the hunger he'd felt for her all night. There was no caution in her reaction. Her lips were warm, smooth, and tenderly moist. She accepted and returned each kiss, matching his fervor. His tongue slipped in and out of her mouth with tempting little strokes of pleasure, each one shooting desire through his loins like fireworks into a dark sky. She swallowed small gasps of satisfaction as he explored the depths, letting him know she was as eager as he was.

He shoved his hands up her back and pressed her tighter against him. Their kisses were long and more generous with each second that passed. Rapid breaths, heated sighs, and soft moans of passion mingled easily, becoming one passionate purr the two shared.

When Fredericka lifted her arms and circled his neck, her cape parted and the sides fell to the back of her shoulders. His hands slid around to her breasts and cupped them, pushing more of their fullness from the confines of her low-cut gown. A rush of desire exploded between his legs at the sweet touch of her bare skin.

Fredericka sucked in a deep rapid breath too, letting him know she desired this intimacy with him. The tremble of her body almost drove him to the edge as he caressed her softness, kissed her neck and chest, and pressed his lower body against hers.

He bent his head to taste the—

"Auntie."

Wyatt jerked like the blast of a ball from a pistol. He swirled around, doing his best to shield Fredericka behind him. Bella stood halfway down the darkened stairs.

Hellfire, that was close. He'd forgotten children were in the house. Fredericka could make him forget everything. He'd never breathed so hard and deep, but wanting to give Fredericka time to recover from the near disaster, he managed to ask calmly, "What is it, Bella?"

She rubbed her eyes with her fists. "I had a bad dream."

Bad dreams were not uncommon at Eton. When boys had them, they were told to buck up and go back to sleep. "Snuggle back under the covers and you'll be fine," Wyatt said to Bella. Hearing Fredericka's deep intake of breath as she swept up beside him, he knew that wasn't what should be said to a young girl.

"I'll handle this," she whispered. "Bella isn't prone to bad dreams. I wonder what's wrong?" She started up the stairs. "Perhaps you only need me to sing to you. Do you think that will make you sleepy?" Fredericka bent down to Bella's level and pulled her close. "Tell me what kind of bad dream you had, my darling?"

"The ghost story Uncle Your Grace told me and Charles in his book room this afternoon."

"What?" Fredericka whirled back to Wyatt. "A ghost story? To a five-year-old?"

"No." Wyatt strode to the bottom of the stairs. "I mean yes. I told them a story, but it wasn't about a ghost. Just a shadow. A small one."

"It was following a little boy in a boneyard," Bella whimpered. "He couldn't get away and was afraid it would pull him into the grave and eat him."

Wyatt thought Fredericka's eyes might pop out of her

head as she looked at him with astonishment. The story did sound more horrific coming from a little girl's voice.

"A ghost in a cemetery, and a little boy!" Fredericka exclaimed. "Wyatt, what were you thinking?"

"They were loving the story when I was telling it," he insisted. "It wasn't scary. It was a harmless little shadow. They wanted to hear gory—but didn't. I mean—no—"

"Never mind," she said rigidly as she rose, her arms still wrapped tightly around Bella. "You've said enough, and I will thank you not to be telling any of the children more stories."

Damnation.

Wyatt strode to the book room with fast, heavy stomps. Not bothering to light a lamp, he poured himself a splash of brandy and took a long burning sip that ended with a gasp, a sigh, and a wince. Then he took another and started pacing back and forth in front of the desk.

What had he been thinking earlier? Maybe his father was right after all and a wife couldn't be pleased. Maybe Fredericka had been a bother to him from the moment he'd met her. It appeared he'd done a damn poor job of pleasing her ever since she'd come to London.

But he still wanted her. He enjoyed being with her. Yes, he said and did everything wrong, but the truth was he liked the way she bothered him. She was gorgeous and invigorating when upset, shooting daggers with her eyes that sparkled like dewdrops in sunlight. They twinkled when teasing him. Which she did with great relish and he accepted with ravishing hunger. He even liked it when she got the best of him as she had the afternoon she met Rick and Hurst.

Wyatt shed his evening coat and started pulling at his neckcloth. Once he untied it he threw it aside and sent his collar down on top of it.

There had been a few missteps along their way. Referring to the children as wooden soldiers had upset her after only five minutes in her presence. That was a bad start. It made her livid, he remembered as he unbuttoned his waistcoat.

The pillow fort hadn't been his best idea, nor had what led up to the incident in the park. That could have gone really badly. And no more ghost stories for sure. But there had been deliciously inviting and stimulating times. Kissing in the secluded warmth of his book room late at night when he was deadly tired but heavy with desire to have her beneath him. He'd wanted her so badly it was almost more than he could bear. Being so wrapped up in the joy and passion of kissing her with such uninhibited freedom in the garden that neither of them felt the rain gently sprinkling their hair, faces, and clothing was something he'd never forget.

There was no doubt that what he felt when he held Fredericka was different from what he had felt with any other woman who had ever been in his arms. He kept thinking it was much too soon to be experiencing all the emotions she worked up in him. They crowded into his mind and body when he looked at her and touched her that he had to wonder, was it too soon to want to be with his wife?

He'd always believed he was just like his father. Wyatt had patterned his life after him. If he wanted to be like him so badly, if that was the way his life was supposed to be, why was he still desiring to be with his wife so desperately? It didn't matter that she irritated him sometimes. Their arguments didn't matter when he thought about the way he felt about her. So, why was he waiting to take her to bed and make her his wife in every sense of the word? His father had said he couldn't do anything to make his wife happy, but Wyatt had given Fredericka the best night of her life. That meant something to him.

Wyatt stopped pacing. His heart pounded so loud he heard it vibrating in his chest. He wasn't sure, but maybe he loved Fredericka?

"No, no, no," he whispered, and helped himself to another shot of brandy and downed it quickly. He never expected to even consider the idea of loving his wife. His father never had loved Wyatt's mother.

But if Wyatt loved Fredericka, that was a terrifying thought. And how could that be? There had been women in his life. Probably far too many. None of them had ever touched him or made him feel the way she had.

Was love the reason he couldn't stop thinking about her, couldn't stop wanting her, couldn't stop wanting her to want him no matter the mistakes he'd made along the way, or the promise he hadn't yet kept? If so, could they weather the problems without him ending up feeling the way his father had about his mother?

There was nothing he could do about the past. Not his. Not hers. Not theirs. The only thing he could do was go forward. And, if she was willing, that started tonight.

He plunked the empty brandy glass on his desk and headed toward the stairs. He didn't know what she would do when she found him in her room, but he was about to find out.

CHAPTER 23

THE REMONSTRANCE OF THE
TRANSPLANTED FLOWERS
—EMMA C. EMBURY

Together we drank the morning dew,
And basked in the glances the sunbeams threw,
And together our sweets we were wont to fling
When zephyr swept by on his radiant wing.

A few verses of a lullaby, the brush of a soft hand to
reassure, and covers tucked under her chin for security
could do wonders to comfort a troubled child. Bella fell
back to sleep almost as soon as her head settled onto the
pillow. Still, Fredericka lingered at the bedside, staring
at the child's serene little face and sleep-tousled curls.
Of the three children, Fredericka had always considered
Bella the strongest. In most things she was fearless and
outspoken for one so young.

Obviously, remembrance of a shadow in a boneyard
was too much for her to handle in the dark of night.

Wyatt should have known that, Fredericka thought.
Common sense should have taken over and helped him
see reason, but it hadn't. She smiled a little. She appreciated that he thought Bella was strong enough not to be
bothered by the scary story. More men should believe

girls and women are capable of much more than they allow them to do.

However, Fredericka would wait until morning to contend with the duke. She had come in from the ball feeling exuberant and more wonderful than she could have ever dreamed. It had been a magical night for her with Wyatt by her side the entire evening. She had never felt so wanted and she drank it in. The duke had probably already gone to his chambers anyway. It was best they not talk tonight. She needed time to figure out a few things and to know why she always reacted so defensively to Wyatt and then responded to his kisses with such fervent abandon.

She needed to make a list and study it. That process had always helped her in the past and she would do it tomorrow. Her best decisions came from putting quill to paper. Lists, poetry, thoughts about life and all manner of emotions. When she saw things in the written form and categorized, it helped her focus and think better. She'd begin by looking at the lists she'd already started on the duke and add where necessary. After that was accomplished, maybe she could figure out what about him kept her on edge, kept her wanting to see him, and to be in his arms.

It was maddening. She couldn't look at him without feeling the desire to cuddle against his warm chest and bask in the strength of his arms tightly around her. Every time she thought about the way his kisses made her feel, she was filled to overflowing with delicious, expectant sensations of pleasure deep in her most womanly part.

Most of all, maybe she could figure out if what she was feeling for him was that elusive thing called love. And worse, what would she do if it was? That worried her most. If it was love, how on earth had she managed to fall in love with a man she felt was constantly doing something wrong? A man who planned to send her back to Paddleton to live until he had need of her to give him a son. A man who, at times, made her feel she was in his way and a bother to him so that he couldn't continue his lifestyle, and at other times made her feel he was happy she was a part of his life.

Fredericka rose from Bella's bed. If she kept thinking like that she'd never get to sleep. Clearly there would be no answer forthcoming about her feelings or his now. The children would be up in a couple of hours and looking for her.

After kissing Bella's forehead, she checked on Charles, sleeping soundly in the other bed, before easing quietly into the corridor and down to her room.

The first thing she noticed upon entering was a lamp that had been left burning on her dressing table. Movement on the far side caught her attention. Wyatt was kneeling in front of the fireplace tending a small fire. Seeing him in her room felt so right. But how could that be? He did almost everything wrong. Being in her room without invitation was proof.

He rose slowly and cautiously, which, as she was feeling as she did, was prudent of him. She should ask him to leave but their gazes met across the room and the thought fled. Nature took over and she felt the same way she had the first time she saw him. Every time she saw him. Desirous. Her heartbeat pounded, her breaths quickened, and her disgruntled attitude about him telling Bella a ghost story started to dissolve.

He looked divine, dressed the way he'd been the first morning she was in London and they'd talked in his book room. So disrespectfully casual and inviting. In such a state, he appealed to all her senses and appeared so strong and masculine, clothed only in his trousers and collarless shirt.

She denied herself the yearning to indulge in studying him longer and shook the tempting thought away. Settling a hard glare on him, she whispered, "You have some nerve coming in here," as she closed the door softly behind her.

"I know." His answer was quiet and true.

"I've never been able to predict what you are going to do, or say, or how you will behave."

He remained relaxed in front of the fire. "I'll take it as a good sign that you're not immediately throwing me out."

"I should." She unfastened her cape and tossed it on the edge of the bed as she walked farther inside. "What were you thinking, Wyatt?" she asked, keeping her voice low.

"That you were chilled and I should stoke the fire for you."

It seemed impossible under the circumstances, but she had to bite back a smile at his reply. By some miracle, she managed to huff a frustrated sigh. She untied the bow of her brocade spencer, shrugged out of it, and sent it the way of her cape. "That's not what I meant, and you know it."

He took a few steps toward her but made no move to come around to the side of the bed where she stood. Which was good. She might be tempted to strangle him. Or kiss him.

"I wanted to make sure Bella was all right and no longer frightened."

Fredericka's eyes strayed back to him. She appreciated his caring and walked over to her dressing table to remove her gloves. "She's fine now. Asleep, but really, a ghost story for someone so young?"

"I shouldn't have let her stay when she came into the book room with Charles. I had promised him a story if he would listen to Elise's fairy tale and I didn't want to disappoint him. She seemed to enjoy it as much as her brother."

"Of course she did," Fredericka replied, refusing to look at him lest he see her inner turmoil. It was vast, consuming, and confusing. "You must know she craves any attention from you. She's vulnerable, and you are strong and solicitous toward her." Saying the words, Fredericka suddenly realized she could have been talking about herself instead of her niece.

"You're right about it all," he said earnestly. "But you must know I would never knowingly hurt a child."

His tone and words were sincere, and she did know that. Unbelievably, she was already forgiving him, though a small part of her didn't want to. Not yet. Wasn't it better to continue with umbrage than desire? She stripped off one glove and started on the other.

"I hope the nightmares won't be lasting," he offered in a conciliatory tone.

Fredericka laid the other glove on her dressing table and glanced at him through the mirror again. He looked far too handsome for her overwrought state. Without thought, her gaze strayed to the neckline of his shirt. The V was open, showing a good portion of his bare chest. Her stomach tightened and her cheeks heated at the thought of kissing the very exposed hollow of his throat.

Annoyed at herself for such wayward thinking, and at him for making her feel them rather than the matter at hand, she started unfastening one of her earrings, avoiding another glance his way. For some reason her fingers were trembly. She kept fumbling with the catch.

"I'll make it up to her by telling a story about flowers and fairies."

"What?" Fredericka looked up and saw he was directly behind her. She quickly averted her gaze back to her ear. "You've told her quite enough." Finally conquering the jewelry clasp, she tossed it onto the table with a frustrated drop.

"I'll leave if you want me to, or . . ." He trailed off the last word cautiously.

Their gazes connected in the mirror again and she was more aware of him than ever before. Was that longing she saw in his eyes? Was that the emotion that suddenly filled her too and clawed at her insides so ravenously? Tension between them intensified. "Or what?" she asked.

"I can help you with this." He took one step forward and put his hands to the ribbon at her nape. Fredericka stiffened but didn't shrink away. Wyatt held still as if waiting for an indication to back off or continue. "If you pull the bow the wrong way and make a knot you'll never get it off."

His low and husky voice relaxed her shoulders.

Lightly, as he untied the necklace, his fingertips tickled across her skin. Each feather-like brush, intended or not, tingled and tantalized. At his touch, she shivered from her head to her toes and back again. Fredericka felt warmth and strength radiating from him. Maddening as it was, she wanted to forget her vexation for his lack of understanding Bella's age, sensitivity, and everything else, and lean against him.

"I didn't come just to stoke the fire and check on Bella," he whispered softly across her shoulders, stirring the fine hair at her nape. "I wanted to see you."

Fredericka remained silent. Attraction was growing every second she looked at him. It was difficult fighting irritation and enticement. She didn't know which emotion would win.

Once the ribbon ends were separated, he let the topaz slide down her chest to pool in the valley between her breasts for a few seconds. She shivered, thinking he was going to bend his head and shower the back of her neck and shoulders with little moist kisses that would drive her wildly insane. Instead, he removed the necklace and placed it on top of the gloves.

"There's something else I want to say," he said softly.

"I'm not sure I want to hear it." If she was going to send him away, it had to be now. Remaining with her back to him, she lowered her gaze to the top of her dressing table for a moment, searching for inner strength before she lifted her lashes to him and whispered, "You should go."

His gaze swept over her face, settling on her eyes. She knew he was weighing whether to comply or challenge her. She was contemplating how she would react when he made that decision. When she thought she couldn't take the waiting any longer, he nodded as if to acquiesce and strode over to the door. Crestfallen, she gathered the shreds of her courage to accept his choice.

When he made it to the door, instead of opening it, he turned the key in the lock and walked back over to her.

A tremor ran through her. Fredericka swallowed hard and only then did she know for sure that was exactly what she'd wanted him to do.

"There's something I need to say. I'm not going until I do." He remained resolute. "I don't want you thinking I kissed you earlier tonight only to make up for all the things I've done wrong."

Fredericka blinked rapidly, still facing him in the mirror. Had he said what she thought he had? Did he actually think she would let any man kiss her the way she had him simply to make amends? Seconds ticked by before she turned to him and said, "How dare you think that? You, sir, are a rake and an ace among men at saying the wrong thing."

A firm grimace formed on his features. "I thought you'd want to know I kissed you because I desire you more than any other woman. Ever since you arrived I've been having one hell of a time keeping my thoughts and my hands off you."

"You think I don't know that?" she whispered, exasperated, finding it difficult to keep her voice low. "Our attraction has always been real and intoxicating from the moment we met. How dare you think I thought you would kiss me out of pity."

"Hold on just a minute." His eyes and mouth tightened with intensity. "I never said pity. You are misinterpreting what I said the way you always do."

"That's because you never say what you mean."

"I do," he insisted, in a rough yet gentle voice, firming his stance by jerking his hands to his hips. His eyes widened with annoyance. "I keep asking myself when in hellfire am I going to learn to keep my mouth shut and just—"

"Kiss me," she whispered.

Fredericka lunged at Wyatt, throwing him off-balance and knocking him backward as her arms circled his neck. His arms closed tightly around her as he sucked in a grunt of surprise and caught his footing. She pressed her lips to his with daring and confidence she'd never known she possessed.

Their kisses and caresses were passionate, urgent, and unforgiving in their wanting. Her fingers tangled in his hair, his shirt, and his trousers. His hands caressed her breasts and buttocks at will, and he pressed her securely against the hard bulge beneath his trousers.

For how long they stood there and kissed she had no idea. Time didn't matter. Only what they were feeling was important.

With ease and a puzzling grin, he picked her up, swirled her around two, three, four times before landing on the bed with her on her back and him rising above her.

"That made me dizzy," she whispered in between their kisses, as the bed spun.

He cupped the side of her face with a loving hand and looked into her eyes. "Then we're on even footing now. I've been reeling since we met. I wanted to make sure you felt the same way and are dizzy for me."

"I am."

Wyatt brushed her hair across her forehead, removing the combs and throwing them aside. He looked tenderly into her eyes and whispered, "I want you with me, Fredericka. Like this."

No other words could have pleased her more than "I want you with me." She didn't know how much she'd needed to hear them until he spoke them. It was as if a deep, longing emotion inside her had finally been satisfied. She smiled and lifted her lips to his. There was no need for more words. Only mounting feelings, sensations, and more of being enchanted and delighted with each other. The scent, taste, and touch of Wyatt was familiar and welcoming to all her senses. Their embrace was pursuing and savoring as they clung together and encouraged each other to higher depths of pleasure with each breath they took.

Through every caress Fredericka's body trembled with expectancy and anticipation as Wyatt patiently showed her the intimate ways between a man and woman. He revered her while teaching her how to enjoy every moment they were sharing.

He was confident, commanding, and masterful without force or cajoling. He knew where to touch and how long to stroke to create feelings she could never have imagined existed. Somehow, he knew exactly when to rush ahead and when to slow the building ardor and fervency she was experiencing. With skill and tenderness, they came together as husband and wife. Their bodies joined as intimately and sensuously as possible.

When delights she hadn't known were gifted to mankind erupted inside them both, the only thing left from either of them was gasping breaths and contented sighs. She was also left with the hope that what had just happened wasn't a once in a lifetime experience.

Fredericka didn't know how long it took to realize she didn't have on any clothes. Wyatt was naked too. In the frenzied leisure of their lovemaking, they had somehow removed all their clothing. She reached across the bed for her gown or shift, something to cover herself, and touched her black velvet cape. That would do nicely, so she dragged it over her body.

The movement must have disturbed Wyatt. He rose up on his elbow and said, "I should have realized you are cold."

"Just not wanting to feel so bare."

"You're lovely without a stitch on," he said huskily, as he helped fit the velvet over her breasts and around her legs. "Better?"

Fredericka nodded, but her attention was on his broad shoulders, wide chest, and the planes of his lean-muscled hips and legs. "You have bruises."

"Cricket can be a rough sport."

"I don't like that you get hurt," she said, brushing her fingertips over one of the reddish-brown marks on his upper shoulder.

"They don't hurt for long."

"You are a beautiful man, and it's a joy to look at you."

Wyatt chuckled as he reached over and kissed her tenderly. "Does this mean you are no longer peeved with me?" he asked, caressing her cheek.

Forcing her gaze away from his body, she looked into his eyes. "I have reason to be," she admitted honestly, but then smiled. "Of course not. You are very good with the children. Most of the time."

Amusement twitched his lips attractively. "And you are prickly sometimes."

She accepted his good humor. "I'm trying to get better about that."

"As I am trying not to say the right thing the wrong way."

Fredericka reached over and brushed her fingertips across his muscled chest. "Your endless training shows."

He tilted his head and gave her a quick nod to let her know he appreciated she noticed. "It's necessary. I have an important tournament in Oxford coming up soon."

A tingle of concern nipped her. "That seems a long way to go."

"It's a large gathering of clubs competing. I'll be gone a few days."

"That long? The hearing before the Lord Chancellor is coming up soon as well."

"I promise I'll be back for that. The games are important, but you are more important." He brushed her cheek with the back of his fingers and placed another tender kiss on her lips.

A lump formed in her throat and she found she couldn't respond to his unbelievable statement that she meant more to him than his sporting club.

"There's something else I've wanted to clear up since

shortly after you arrived in London. I told you I had a mistress and—"

"No, please," she said, pushing the cape away and trying to shake her legs free of it so she could rise. "I can assure you I don't want to hear this, and even if I did, this is not the time to bring up your mistress and quite frankly I can't think of a time that would be right."

He stayed her again with his hand. "I haven't been to see her since I met you."

Fredericka stilled. Could that be true? He might not say everything the way she wanted to hear it but she hadn't known of him telling her something that wasn't true. "I don't know what to say to that."

"Nothing." He gave her a smile and a shrug. "It was just something I wanted you to know. I didn't like the way we left this subject when it came up before. I've not been with anyone. I don't want anyone but you."

Fredericka's pulse pounded, and she suddenly knew without doubt it *was* love she felt for the duke. She didn't need to make lists to study and ponder after all. Looking into his eyes, filled with so much emotion, she knew for sure. Her heart, her life, and her soul were his. Though he talked only of wanting her, for now that was enough. She knew how special she was to him. She felt it in every touch and saw it in every glance.

"Thank you," she said softly. "You're right. I needed to know, and it was the perfect time to tell me after all."

He placed his fingertips under her chin, kissed her warmly on the lips, kindling those beautiful feelings of desire within her once again.

When her lashes fluttered up and she looked at him, humor glinted in his eyes. "Do I remember you calling me an ace among men?"

She teased him by wrinkling her forehead as if in

deep thought. "I seem to remember I called you a rake among men and that's what you are."

The grin stayed on his face. "You said I made you dizzy."

She reached over and pressed a kiss against the center of his hard chest. "You were dizzy first," she murmured softly.

Wyatt chuckled. "I still am," he whispered, cupping the back of her head in his hand. "Kiss me in the same spot."

She kissed his chest again.

"Now a little to the left." She did as he asked.

He breathed in heavily. "Not quite there. Maybe over to the right will be the right spot. Try there."

Fredericka laughed and pushed at him. "You are a monster."

Wyatt wrapped her in his arms and laid her back against the bed. "And you are the most beautiful and exciting person who has ever been in my life, Fredericka. I'm so glad you are mine."

She was glad too. At that moment, a slice of sunlight streaked through a slit in the drapery panels. "The sun is up. You should go to your room. I'd rather the children not know about—" She suddenly felt shy.

"I'll listen and know when they are up and about. I'll slip out. Right now I want to do this."

Wyatt slanted his lips over hers. Fredericka twined her arms around his neck as he settled his body onto hers.

CHAPTER 24

PRIMROSE——THE SAME——MICKLE
——MRS. HEMANS

Say, gentle lady of the bower,
For thou, though young, art wise;
And known to thee is every flower
Beneath our milder skies.

It was a beautiful day as Fredericka and Wyatt walked along the pavement in Mayfair leading to their house at the end of the street. The late spring air had lost its chill. No cape, pelisse, or shawl was needed. Only a parasol to keep the sun out of her eyes. Overhead, an expanse of blue sky was breathtaking with tufts of white clouds scattered as far as she could see. Every lawn and trellis they passed was filled with bright green shrubs, blooming flowers, and tended to immaculate condition. Carriages rolled by with horses clipping along at a leisurely pace. Fredericka and Wyatt greeted everyone they passed with smiles.

Before they'd begun their walk, Fredericka had written some lines of poetry about the joy in her heart and life since she and Wyatt had become husband and wife. For real. Words had failed her. For the first time, she truly understood why some poets were gifted with the talent of verse and why some, like her, only dabbled in it.

Every word she'd read about the eager excitement and beautiful contentment love could make one feel was true. Her heart had overflowed with happiness these past few days, even though some things hadn't changed.

Though Wyatt continued to assure her there was little chance the Tomkins would win guardianship of the children, Fredericka worried. Wyatt still trained long hours for his tournaments while she helped Miss Litchfield with the children's endless fittings for their new wardrobes, settling the usual sibling squabbles, and making sure there was no nap time for the governess. At least until the new addition arrived. She had spoken with Miss Gladwin and the young lady would start next week.

Since their first night together, Wyatt had made a difference in not only her life and happiness but he continued to make strides with the children's too. He'd been to the park with them to play with balls, fly kites, and watch puppet shows several times. They had even taken a boat out on the Serpentine, and he had given Charles his first cricket lesson. Fredericka was thrilled with the changes in Charles' speech. He only stuttered when he was excited, and Elise was no longer constantly clinging to her.

Thrice, Wyatt had been with Fredericka to the extraordinary Vauxhall Gardens in the evenings to enjoy conversation with Hurst, Rick, and others while watching the festive entertainment of jugglers, tightrope walkers, and a man who appeared to swallow a sword. For once it seemed as if everything was going her way. She and Wyatt were showing London they were the perfect newly married couple. There would be no reason for the Lord Chancellor to choose a viscount over a duke and rule for Jane and Nelson in the guardian petition.

"I know you're eager to join your friends and begin

the journey to Oxford today, but I'm glad you took a few minutes for a walk with me before leaving."

Wyatt glanced her way with a subdued smile. "I'm glad it's the last big tournament of the Season."

"Are you really?" she asked, an expression of doubt in her tone.

He chuckled. "You find my comment suspect?"

"I do," she answered honestly, even as she enjoyed the amusement dancing in his eyes. "Your dedication to your sporting club has been unparalleled."

He touched her arm and they stopped walking. His gaze fluttered sensually down her face as he picked up her gloved hand and kissed it. "I know you are worried but I promise I will not miss the hearing in Chancery Court. I will be back in time to be there with you."

She moistened her lips and lifted her chin before giving him a longing sigh. "I know you will. Since the guardianship has to be awarded in your name and not mine, I'm sure there will be questions for you."

"I'll make sure the man has no doubts we are the better guardians."

They started walking again, and after a short time he said, "While you are waiting for my return, perhaps you can explain to the children that you are now sleeping in my chambers instead of your own. After this trip, I won't be getting up early for practices, and I'm going to want you to linger by my side in the mornings."

"That sounds tempting, Your Grace. Perhaps by the time you return—" Fredericka cut off her words as she noticed a carriage stopping in front of their house. "Jane," she whispered.

Wyatt looked down the street. "Did she make plans to visit today?"

"No. She would never consider doing that. She always

arrives unexpectedly. I hope she's not here to deliver news I don't want to hear."

"What could it be?" he asked with no concern at all as they continued walking. "The gossip about us has been unpredictably good this week."

"I hope you are right," Fredericka said softly, a shiver of apprehension washing over her. "I don't trust Jane. I never have a good feeling when she arrives."

"She's not an ogre, but to make sure she has nothing up that lace sleeve of hers, I'll stay with you until she leaves."

A protective warmth settled over Fredericka and she looked lovingly at Wyatt. "I appreciate that you would delay your departure even longer knowing Hurst and Rick are waiting for you. I know your journey to Oxford is a long one."

"I thought I made it clear to you that you are more important than my tournaments, Fredericka. I'm staying with you until she is gone."

Fredericka wanted to throw her arms around him and kiss him, but of course that would cause a scandal as Jane would be sure to see it so she merely enjoyed how wonderful his words made her feel.

A few moments later, they greeted her cousin and entered the house together.

"So when I realized I hadn't seen the children in almost two weeks," Jane said, placing her bonnet and gloves on the entryway table beside Fredericka's, "I decided to come today. You're sure you don't mind, Your Graces?" she asked with a smile that was as pleasant as the morning.

It amazed Fredericka how perfectly normal Jane could seem at times. Giving her typical answer, Fredericka answered, "You are always welcome."

"Join us in the drawing room," Wyatt said.

"So kind of you, but I only came to see the children, and I have only a short time."

Excellent. She wasn't staying long. Fredericka returned Jane's congenial smile. "Yes, of course. They should be in their schoolroom. I'll have Burns get them for us."

"No need for that. I'd love to see where they are tutored."

Sharp cackles of laughter suddenly erupted from Charles and Bella. The merriment didn't come from abovestairs.

"That seemed to come from the book room," Fredericka noted, slightly bemused. She'd never known of Miss Litchfield taking the children there.

"Why do you suppose Miss Litchfield has them in there?" Wyatt asked, appearing as puzzled as Fredericka.

Unease skittered up Fredericka's back. It was never a good sign for the children to be somewhere they shouldn't. She had a bad feeling they had escaped Miss Litchfield's attention. It seemed they had become experts at slipping away from her.

"Why don't you two go on up to the schoolroom," Fredericka suggested. "I'll go find them and we'll join you."

"Nonsense," Jane replied as cheerfully as any delighted guest would be. "Perhaps they are having a lesson about the importance of reading. We can visit in there. Besides, I'd enjoy seeing the duke's library collection." She smiled affably at him. "You don't mind, do you?"

"Of course not. Allow me to lead the way."

The uneasy feeling stayed with Fredericka as she followed Wyatt down the corridor. From the giggles that continued, the children were definitely having a good time. Not lessons. If Miss Litchfield wasn't with them, they could have destroyed the entire room and all the books in it by now. She whispered a silent prayer she wouldn't see Charles standing on the top rung of the ladder or, worse, find him swinging from it.

When Wyatt reached the door, it was closed. He gave Fredericka a curious glance before opening it and immediately stepped aside to allow Fredericka and Jane to enter first.

The room spun before Fredericka as she entered and beheld the sight in front of her. A roar filled her ears and she couldn't catch her breath. Surely what she was seeing couldn't be true. She must be having a fit of vapors or some kind of demented episode.

Elise sat in the chair behind Wyatt's desk holding what appeared to be a cheroot between her fingers. Stacks of cards were strewn before her. Bella and Charles were seated in the two big wing chairs in front of the desk. A pipe dangled from Charles' mouth. Spilled tobacco littered the front of his white shirt. And Bella, dear angelic Bella, had a cheroot pressed between her rosebud lips.

"What are you doing?" Fredericka whispered as her legs went weak.

All three children went stiff as wood.

"By all the saints!" Jane exclaimed. "I think I might faint."

"What's in those glasses?" Wyatt exclaimed, rushing over and picking up the crystal sitting beside Bella. He smelled it. "Brandy." He glared at Charles. "What the devil are you allowing your sisters to do?" he said gruffly. "Give me that!" He yanked the cheroot from Bella's lips and the pipe from Charles' mouth.

"They all have filled glasses sitting by them!" Jane stared at Fredericka as if she were seeing a monster. "You've been letting them drink and smoke!"

"No, of course not!" Fredericka managed to gasp out as she stared transfixed at the front of Bella's dress. It was wet from what had to be brandy.

Fredericka realized she might faint too. "You, you didn't drink that, did you?" she asked the little one.

"Charles, Elise?" Wyatt demanded as he picked up all three glasses and moved them away from the children. "Don't sit there mute. One of you answer your aunt."

"No, we didn't drink it," Bella said. "It tasted too bad."

"So they did drink from the glasses!" Jane huffed in disgust. "I've never seen or heard anything so disturbing, Fredericka."

Wyatt fastened his gaze on Charles. "Don't ever do anything like this again. Boys are to take care of girls. They don't lead them astray."

Charles' eyes widened in fear as he nodded.

"I don't think you have to worry about that again," Jane said tightly. "I believe we all now know the children aren't safe in this house."

Fredericka turned rigidly toward Jane. "What do you mean? They are perfectly safe here. I don't know where Miss Litchfield is presently, but will find out. The children might occasionally slip away from her and do things they shouldn't. I don't know what led to this or how it could have happened but I'll get to the bottom of it and sort it all out. The only thing I can imagine is that they are going through an adjustment."

"An adjustment?"

"It wasn't easy for them making the move to London," Fredericka defended.

Jane looked at her as if she'd lost her sanity. "What

poppycock. They've obviously seen this behavior before and had reason to feel it was all right to mimic it. Probably every night given the duke's reputation. How else would they know how to do this? Children copy the people they live with." She looked directly at Wyatt. "Cards, drinking, and smoking is not something they'd learn in church."

Wyatt's eyes narrowed dangerously as he stared at Jane. "I won't let you think we'd encourage or allow this kind of behavior, Mrs. Tomkin."

"We were just having a card party," Bella said softly. "We didn't want to make anyone angry."

Wyatt walked to the door and called, "Burns!" He pointed to each of the three children one at a time. "All of you get over here."

"Auntie, my stomach doesn't feel good," Bella said, hopping off the chair and grabbing Fredericka around her legs and holding tight.

"I want to stay with you, Auntie," Elise whispered, and clasped her hands around Fredericka's waist. Fredericka's heart melted. She wrapped her arms around both girls. They might misbehave from time to time, but they loved her even when she was cross with them and she loved them all the more because of it.

"So this is how you have been caring for Angela's children. This," Jane said, sweeping out her hand as if to encompass the room. "And not a governess in sight."

"No, it isn't," Wyatt said, gruffly. "If there is blame it falls on me."

"I assumed so," Jane said as calmly as if she'd been talking about the spring day. "However, I believe you both live in this house now. As a proper family. Right? One is as guilty as the other."

"It's time for you to go, Mrs. Tomkin. Fredericka needs to see to the children."

"Yes, by all means. I will. No doubt if Bella is feeling sick, the others will be quite soon."

"This will never happen again, Jane," Fredericka felt compelled to say. "I have another governess coming next week."

"Oh, I believe you. And I'm quite sure it won't happen again." She flashed a triumphant smile and with a swoosh of her skirts left the room.

CHAPTER 25

ILLUSTRATION OF THE PLATE
FRINGED PINK—DISDAIN
—L. H.

Thy words are weighed with costly art,
They come not wildly free—
Oh! Never hath my spirit part
With one I deem like thee.

After seeing the children were washed, changed, and given tea and scones to settle their stomachs, Fredericka had a difficult conversation with Miss Litchfield about her lack of supervision for the children. Miss Litchfield took the scolding and the news of a new and younger governess coming next week well. There was little else she could do and seemed appreciative she was going to be allowed to stay on in a diminished capacity for a year. That would give her plenty of time to decide if she wanted to find another post with a different family or settle into an easier life. It would also be easier on the children.

Weary from it all, Fredericka then went to her chambers and was surprised to see Wyatt standing at the window waiting for her.

"How are the children?" he asked upon her entering.

"They are quiet but fine and back in the schoolroom,"

she answered tightly, still troubled about what happened. "I thought you would have left for your tournament by now."

"I had to wait and make sure you were all right. I know how upset you were." Wyatt walked over to stand beside her.

"'Upset' seems such a mild word for what I'm feeling. I'm livid and disappointed with myself, you, Jane, Miss Litchfield, and the children too. I'm feeling quite infuriated at the world right now."

He reached for her, but she stepped away. She couldn't bear his comfort right now. She didn't want to fall apart in his arms. That wouldn't solve anything.

"Don't you realize if Jane tells the Lord Chancellor what she saw he will consider us unfit and won't allow us to keep the children?"

"This incident doesn't make either of us unfit. Jane knows exactly what to say to worry you. Stop letting her hold that over your head. At some time in their lives, all children copy what adults do."

Fredericka rounded on him in disbelief. "Bella is five and tasted brandy, chewed on tobacco, and was acting like a worldly man."

"She didn't like the drink or the smoke and will probably never try either again."

How could he be so cavalier about this and not see the gravity of what happened? Wyatt reached out to take hold of her arm, but she shrank away from him again. She wanted to be comforted, but he was the man who had caused this problem in the first place.

"I admit it was a shock to see," he continued in his calm, soothing tone. "Jane knows Bella couldn't have ingested enough brandy to hurt her. None of them could have. It stings like hell. Bella was probably the only one who had the courage to even put her tongue in it."

Why was he looking at her as if she was the unreasonable one? "If they never try it again is that supposed to make me feel better about what happened?"

He inhaled deeply and implored her with his penetrating blueish-gray eyes. "I'm not trying to make light of how serious this was, but it's not as bad as you think."

She shook her head in amazed anguish. He was unbelievable. He always had been when it came to the children. "You told me they didn't see you carousing with your card club."

"I told you they never came into the room while the men were here. All they saw was twelve men having a good time. They had a peek and might have heard a few words. They're curious. That's normal."

"Normal?" Fredericka stiffened more. "Maybe for a duke's son, but not for my sister's children."

"Then maybe it should be," he said, his voice rising. "They need a chance to grow up and experience things without always having to be so damned proper."

She gasped in outrage. "I beg your pardon, Your Grace. That is the way they are supposed to be."

"You're stifling them."

An ache started at the back of her neck. "You know nothing about children."

Wyatt ran his hands through his hair and scoffed frustratedly. "You know I lived with them at boarding school for years, Fredericka."

She did know, but sound reasoning wasn't what she needed right now. Squaring her shoulders, she held her ground. "Children need to be disciplined and to know how to act properly at all times, whether or not an adult is monitoring them."

His eyes narrowed and his lips set in a firm line for a second before he spoke in a hushed, determined voice. "'Discipline' is not a word I want used in this house."

"What?" Fredericka's back bowed. That astounded her. "Now you're banning words as well as poetry books."

"I have good reasons," he insisted without a hint of backing down.

"There aren't any," she answered back just as firmly.

"In this house, I don't want Charles, Bella, and Elise treated as if they were in a military school."

Fredericka was speechless for a moment before she could breathe. "That is unfair."

"Sometimes it seems true." His gaze softened as if he was earnestly trying to get her to understand what he was saying. "Often, the firmer you treat children, the more they rebel when given a chance at freedom. I take responsibility for what happened today, but you don't have to treat them as if this is the end of their innocence. Angela wanted you to love her children."

Fredericka gasped again and set angry eyes on him. "You don't think I love the children?"

He held his hands up in the air. "That's not what I'm saying."

Trying to keep her voice calm, she whispered, "It's what you said."

"I meant your *focus* should be on loving them and not trying to make them perfect." Wyatt shook his head again and pushed his coat aside. "You're taking everything I'm saying wrong again."

She edged toward him. "Maybe that's because everything you are saying *is* wrong." Anger punctuated every word. "If I don't make them mind and be proper in all things, they'll grow up selfish, self-centered, and caring for no one but themselves and being the same kind of person Jane is."

"But Angela loved Jane. She loved the person you don't want her children to be like."

Tears shot to Fredericka's eyes so fast there was no time to stop it from happening. "You have no right to say that."

"I don't," he said earnestly. "I shouldn't have, but I'm only repeating what you told me."

Fredericka felt as if a weight were pressing on her chest. Tears clogged her eyes, but she held them by blinking and whispering intensely, "Angela loved me. I know she loved me. I was her sister."

"Of course she did." Wyatt's features softened. "But she loved Jane too. Have you ever considered that Jane is the way she is because you are the way you are?"

Her heart throbbed slow, hard, and she heard every beat in her ears. "I suggest you clarify yourself, Your Grace."

"You've both been so filled with jealousy over each other that neither of you have been able to love and enjoy Angela's children."

"That's not true," she insisted even as she wondered if there was truth in his words. "You aren't helping." She turned away from him but swung back quickly. "You haven't helped me from the moment we married. I had to force you to allow me to stay here."

Anger lit in his eyes. "You couldn't force me to do anything, Fredericka." He looked at her almost desperately. "I was reluctant at first, but now I want you here. For me."

How could she believe him after all he'd said to her? "You have always been more interested in your training, clubs, and tournaments."

He tried to take hold of her arm once again, but she sidestepped away from him again.

"Not anymore," he answered softly. "I'm going to—"

"Don't say another word to me. Your friends are waiting for you. Go to your games and your important tournament. Being a duke, I would think you already have enough money and don't need to constantly practice and worry about games and winning wagers all the time!"

"Me?" He took a step closer to her and patted his chest with an open hand. "You think the money I win is for me?" He grunted a laugh and nodded. "You actually think I do all the gaming for me?" He grunted again. "Yes, Fredericka, I believe I will take my leave of you and go back to my carefree life before you came into it. It had far less trials than the ones you have brought me."

He started out of the room but at the door turned back to her. "You and I are more alike and have more in common than you think. We are both wayward souls that can't find peace. I am searching for redemption and you are looking for validation. You are still blaming Jane for Angela's transgressions, and I am still condemning my youth for mine. Neither of us have exorcised our ghosts from the past. There may be no hope for either of us until we do. Maybe settling guardianship once and for all with Jane next week will do that for you, and perhaps one day I'll feel I've paid my debt and settle mine."

Fredericka closed her eyes against the truth of his words and didn't open them again until she heard the front door close behind her husband. She clasped her hands together and hugged them to her chest and silently wept.

Wyatt was right. Ghosts, memories, whatever they were called, still haunted her. And because of them, she may never have happiness with the children, or Wyatt.

CHAPTER 26

AMARANTH-UNFADING LOVE
——M. J. JEWSBURY

A common loss might tears bewail,
But not a loss like thine,
And words might soothe Love's fancied tale,
But not a love like mine.

It hadn't been an easy day as Fredericka worked through all that had happened concerning the children. Wyatt leaving with so much anger between them left her heartbroken. She spent some time alone in her room to pull herself together. After that she went into Wyatt's book room. No signs remained of the children's venture into the world of adults. The usual smells of aged parchment from all the books and burned wood from the fireplace were the only scents that remained.

Making lists to study always calmed her and helped put important things in perspective. She sat down in the big chair behind Wyatt's desk and started with the reasons she was so strict with the children and then listed why she wasn't. From there, she moved to the possibilities of why Wyatt had been right concerning her feelings about Jane and her sister and why his observations couldn't possibly be true. She even listed why she and Wyatt should win guardianship of the children and why the Tomkins might win. Except, of course, she couldn't think of a reason Jane should get the children.

By the time she finished her multitude of lists it was late in the afternoon. Since the children loved to be outside, she spread a blanket on the back lawn and gathered them around her. Elise and Bella settled on either side of her with Charles facing them. The sky was gray but not threatening rain. Many of the flowers in the garden had bloomed and there was a beautiful array of colors to take pleasure in all the way down to the back gate. A slight breeze signaled the evening air would be chilly but Fredericka would have them back inside long before darkness fell.

The children must have known what she wanted talk about. They were sitting very still. Maybe Wyatt was right and they did look a little like wooden soldiers at attention. There was no twitching, wriggling, or even a stray fidget. They were being perfect like she'd taught them. Now she wanted to see them moving about as if they had ants in their unmentionables.

Fredericka smiled. "You don't have to be so stiff. This isn't a punishment. I only want to talk about what happened today."

"I know already," Bella said. "What we did was bad."

Charles' eyes widened and Elise gave Bella a stern stare as if she shouldn't have admitted they had done something wrong.

"Yes, it was. It doesn't matter who had the idea first. But I thought it might help if we talked about the reasons you used something that belonged to someone else without permission and when you know brandy and tobacco are not acceptable for children."

"I don't know why," Bella said, holding her hands out in front of her to make her point.

Fredericka looked from Charles, who had started twisting his hands together in his lap, to Elise, who took her time but finally spoke. "I wanted to feel the way the men were acting."

"Feel?" That word surprised Fredericka. "What do you mean by that?"

"Happy," she answered innocently. "They were talking, laughing, and enjoying themselves just by being together."

A spasm tightened Fredericka's chest. "But aren't we happy when we're together?"

"At the p-park," Charles said quickly.

"And when Uncle throws the ball to us," Bella injected right behind him.

Elise lowered her head, picked up the ends of her blue ribbon sash and held them tightly in her hands. "The men were having a jovial good time, and I wanted to feel as happy as they were. I'm the one who told Charles we should find the cards and tobacco and see if we could have as much fun as the men had."

"B-but we didn't," Charles added.

"We tried laughing loud like they did," Bella admitted. "It didn't work either."

"I'm sorry, Auntie," Elise said sincerely, looking at Fredericka again. "I was wrong and I won't ever do anything like that again."

Bella and Charles followed with their softly spoken apologies.

Fredericka's heart squeezed and softened at their honesty and what their words revealed. They needed more happiness, teasing, and laughing. She hadn't allowed them to have enough free time in their lives to be happy. Charles was generous when he said they had fun in the park. Wyatt had tried to make her see that. Fredericka couldn't see it for wanting them to play perfectly for Angela, but her sister probably only wanted them to be joyful.

"I think I understand now," Fredericka whispered. "We could all use more amusement in our lives. I'm glad you now realize that some things that are normal for adults are not for children to copy or participate in."

"Like ghost stories," Bella said.

Fredericka smiled. "That's a good example."

"I hope Uncle's not so angry he's going to make us leave," Bella said softly. "I like it here at his house."

"S-so do I, and I want to b-be strong like him one day."

Fredericka thought back to her conversation with the duke. A throb started at her temples. She didn't think she and Wyatt could reconcile. He had said as much before leaving. He was busy with that part of his life that didn't include her. When they first arrived he was eager for her to return to Paddleton. Though the thought made her eyes glisten with tears, she was certain he'd be happy if she was gone by the time he returned.

"I like it here now too, Auntie," Elise said. "I enjoyed going in all the shops with you when we bought the embroidery thread, and I was glad Uncle trusted me to hold the money when we went for sweet cakes in the park."

"That was good of him," Fredericka managed to say with a smile. "He wants you to have responsibilities so you can learn to be a strong and capable young lady and not fearful." Fredericka had to learn some things too. Including how to give them more time and freedom to be children. She was to start right now.

"Come here," she said with a laugh, pulling all three of them into her embrace, but stopped and looked around when she heard the back door of the house open behind her.

"I'm sorry to disturb you, Your Grace," Burns said, walking down the back steps toward her.

Jane, and a man and woman Fredericka didn't recognize, walked out the door behind the butler. The children squealed, jumped up, and ran to Jane, hugging her with laughter.

Fredericka rose from the blanket. "It's all right, Burns. Thank you for bringing them out here."

The butler nodded and turned away. Fredericka didn't recognize the tall, rotund man with thinning brown hair, or the younger, simply dressed woman standing beside Jane, but she walked over to join them.

"Aunt Jane, what did you bring us today?" Bella asked excitedly.

"It's in my carriage," she said with a bright smile. "And you are going to love it. My spaniel, Rosebud, had puppies not long ago, and today I brought one for you to see and hold." The children squealed with youthful delight. Jane looked at Fredericka. "My maid will take them to the carriage to see the puppy. You don't mind, do you?"

How could she? Elise, Bella, and Charles were thrilled at the prospect of seeing and touching a warm and precious little puppy. "No, of course not." She looked from the maid to the man who hadn't spoken a word. "No need to go back through the house. There's a gate to the left side that will take you to the front street."

"I'll s-show you," Charles said and took off running.

His sisters and the maid followed close behind him. Jane seemed to always know what to do to make the children happy as chirping larks. As soon as they rounded the corner Jane's smile faded. Fredericka looked from her cousin to the stranger. Her skin prickled. Something didn't feel right.

"Your Grace, may I introduce Constable Hartford," Jane said in an unusually somber voice as the man bowed. "He's here on official business at the behest of the Lord Chancellor."

A foreboding shiver crept slowly up Fredericka's spine. Her breath hitched with apprehension. "I don't understand. What official business does he have here?"

Jane clasped her hands together in front of her. "After I returned home this morning and talked with Nelson about what I'd witnessed, we both agreed we should have his brother solicit the Lord Chancellor."

Fredericka felt as if her stomach was sinking to her feet, but she forced herself to remain calm. "What did you have the viscount talk to him about?"

"The incident involving the children this morning, of course," Jane remarked impatiently.

"Why? The official hearing is next week."

"I didn't feel we should wait, and after everything was explained to the Lord Chancellor, he agreed it's in the best interest of the children if they come live with me immediately. The constable and his men are here to see that's accomplished."

A chill shook Fredericka. "His men?"

"Yes. They were told to wait on the street until the children were in my carriage to see the puppy. I didn't want them to come with the constable for fear of frightening Bella, Charles, and Elise."

Frederick looked toward the side of the house leading to the gate. Two men appeared, blocking her path to the children. Her hands clutched into tight fists at her sides. She swung toward the constable. "You can't do this. My husband, the duke, isn't home, but he'll talk to you about this as soon as he returns."

"It's not up to me, Your Grace. I'm carrying out instructions from the Lord Chancellor. I was told the children were in danger. I'm here to see they go with Mrs. Tomkin."

"Danger? No," Fredericka insisted. "They were play acting."

The man remained stone-faced. "I'm following orders, Your Grace. Your argument isn't with me."

"Jane, they were never in danger." Wyatt's words came rushing back to Fredericka. "They were only doing what normal children do when imitating adults."

"You can make this easy or difficult, Fredericka." Jane gave the constable a nod.

"The children will have to come with us, Your Grace."

"No, they will not," Fredericka said defiantly. "They will remain here. The duke will be home soon and confirm there was no harm done to the children. Tell him, Jane."

"Bella was sick," she answered with a huffing breath. "You heard her say as much. We have no idea how much brandy she ingested. It had been spilled down the front of her dress."

"She told us she didn't drink it."

Jane held up her hand to stop Fredericka from saying more. "You were as horrified by what we saw as I was, if not more so."

"Yes, of course I was, but I've talked to the children and they are fine. They know what they did was wrong and apologized." Fredericka turned to the constable. "I'm sorry your afternoon was interrupted, but as I said, the duke isn't here. I'm going to have to ask you and your men to leave." She then turned to Jane. "I must ask you to leave too."

"Yes, I am, and the children with me. Though you've

never thought I knew anything about children, I know everyone loves a puppy and that would get them in the carriage with no fear. When I join them, I'll explain we are going to my house to see the rest of the puppies. They will be delighted. I trust you'll have their clothing packed and sent over later."

"What? No, Jane, you can't do this!"

"I know it's heartbreaking, but under the circumstances I can't leave them in this house another night. There is no telling what they might get into next."

"Nothing," Fredericka insisted earnestly.

"This isn't easy for me, Fredericka." She spoke softly, reassuringly. "The men will remain with you until I'm gone. It's best for the children that you don't put up a fight in front of them."

"You are trying to take them away from me," she said fiercely. "You think I'm not going to put up a fight?" Fredericka glanced at the side of the house where the men were standing and then picked up her skirts and rushed for the back door. One of the men was fast and caught her by the arm on the first step.

"Let me go!" She tried pulling away but was no match for his strength and the other man quickly took hold of her other arm and held it behind her back.

Her heart was beating so fast she could hardly speak. "They belong with me."

"I do hate to see you so upset, Fredericka. I never wanted to win this way. I would have done something like this months ago if I had. We are family. I had no choice when I saw the children in peril."

"No, not peril," she pleaded. "It wasn't."

"I must ask you again not to create a scene for the children's sake. And for mine too. I feel one of my headaches coming on and I really must get home and drink a tonic."

Fredericka sucked in a deep breath and struggled against the strong men again. Jane's headaches put her in bed for days. That would frighten Bella for sure and probably the other two.

"Jane, wait. I'll go to the carriage with you and explain what's happening and why we must do this. Tell the men to let me go."

Her cousin looked at her for a long moment. She wasn't gloating, or even triumphant. Just serious. Fredericka thought she might relent.

"They love me, you know," Jane said. "You've never believed it, Fredericka, but they do. I'm not a stranger taking them away forever. You can visit. Often, if you wish." She turned to the constable. "You can let her go after you hear my carriage drive away." Jane hurried past them and out the gate.

Fredericka felt as if the world was crushing in on her. What would she do not seeing Bella's sweet face first thing in the morning? Not hearing Charles taunt his sisters? Not having Elise rush up to her with a tight hug? What was she going to do now that her worst fear had come true? Jane had taken Angela's children and Wyatt hadn't been there to stop her.

When the officials finally let go of her, Fredericka swung the gate wide and rushed out.

Jane's carriage was nowhere to be seen.

CHAPTER 27

DAISY——BEAUTY AND INNOCENCE
——L. H.

A wearied man seeks not the smiles
That brightly beam on all,
For dearer are thy simple wiles
That only one enthrall.

Travel to Oxford yesterday had been long, hot, and uncomfortable. Wyatt usually enjoyed the coach ride whenever he, Hurst, and Rick went out of town together for their tournaments. He wasn't up for their usual drinking, jokes, jousting, and reliving wild times they'd had through the years. His friends knew something was wrong but had done their best to carry on with tradition.

Wyatt hadn't wanted to go. Leaving Fredericka with such rancor between them hadn't been easy, even though she'd wanted him to leave. The coach had hardly made it to the outskirts of London when he knew Oxford was the last place he wanted to be. His life was now with his wife. Not his friends and clubs.

Wyatt had won all the fencing matches of the day. Handily. With the pent-up frustration and anger against himself it had been easy. The Brass Deck had won the cricket competition too. Every player had bruises to prove it. The gentry and Oxford players were never easy on Polite Society. Neither group would have it any other way. Tough wins always made the wager payoffs sweeter.

Wyatt was seated in a private dining room beside a noisy taproom at the inn where he was staying, waiting for Hurst and Rick to join him. Later in the evening, the card tournaments with double elimination rounds would begin and go on all night. It was Wyatt's best event and where he made the most money.

Ordinarily, he would be ecstatic at how well the members of the sporting club were performing, but he was brooding. A feeling that wasn't common to him. He didn't like the way he left things with Fredericka.

Instead of telling her what he felt her problem was with the children, Jane, and her sister and adding he might go back to his old life without her, why hadn't he'd said, "*I love you*"? He should have told her the first time they made love. And the second and third. Every time he touched her, he should have told her. That was only one of the many mistakes he'd made with Fredericka. He should have been sensitive to the fact that she was already reeling from the incident with the children and Jane being witness to it.

Why hadn't he told her why he hated poetry and the word "discipline"? Why hadn't he asked her to help him slay his own demons rather than point hers out? He'd been such a damned bloody blackguard, he didn't know if she could ever forgive him.

She had every right to be outraged. He'd been upset too, but his displeasure hadn't affected the way he felt about her. It took a while to realize that. He was in love with her and should have told her that together they would make sure everything turned out all right. A talk with the children to make sure they understood what they'd done was wrong would have been a good idea too.

It was his fault things got so heated between them before he left. And he had to make it right.

Soul-searching was a damned hard thing to do, especially since he'd never done much of it. The process ate at his inner being little by little as he tried to figure out where he went wrong and how he could repair his relationship with Fredericka.

Life was filled with decisions. Some more difficult than others. He'd had responsibilities to his friends, the club, and the hospital since he'd funded it almost ten years ago. That had always come first. Fredericka was supposed to have been a convenience. Nothing more. She had become a necessity. Now she was his life and it was time she came first.

His father was right about wives. They were a lot of trouble. Wyatt smiled. But the difference was that Fredericka was worth every minute of trouble she gave him and he had no doubts about changing his lifestyle for her. Forever.

"Perhaps you should start thinking about giving that brandy in your glass a try if you are going to get your head out of your heart and into the game tonight?" Rick said as a round of laughter came from the taproom on the other side of the wall.

Wyatt looked from Hurst to Rick as they joined him at the table. So, they'd been talking about him. He expected no less.

"Tell us what's going on." Hurst picked up the bottle of fine spirits and poured a splash in each of their glasses.

"Perhaps he needs us to help him write another romantic letter to Fredericka. And this time we'll see he actually delivers it."

"Rick," Hurst cautioned, "I don't think he is in a temper for your humor."

"He is a blackguard," Wyatt mumbled.

"True." Rick pushed back from the table and leaned his chair on the back two legs as Hurst handed him the drink. "I'm grateful you continue to be my friend despite my wicked tongue and occasional attempt at amusing you. I don't know much about wives, but tell us what's wrong. Perhaps we can help."

Wyatt picked up his brandy and swirled it in his glass. He'd never forget the image of the brandy glasses sitting in front of the children. Not just a splash in the crystal as Wyatt, Rick, and Hurst poured. No, they had filled the glasses to the top and emptied the entire bottle of the most expensive brandy money could buy. Kids didn't do anything halfway. And the cheroots. He was throwing every blasted one of them away when he returned. All the expensive pipes and tobacco too. That was probably a bit drastic, but he was going to do it anyway.

I should have never left.

"Fredericka and I had an argument concerning the children." He replaced his glass on the table after taking a sip.

"Is that all?" Rick quipped, as if it were the most banal statement he'd ever heard.

Hurst shrugged. "Don't mind him. Arguments are normal between husbands and wives. Between friends, siblings, or with someone who accidently bumps you on the street."

Wyatt had tried to convince Fredericka what the children had done was normal. That hadn't worked. Maybe she was right and he *was* wrong.

"As long as she's been in London, I'm surprised it's the first quarrel you two have had."

Wyatt remained quiet.

"I see," Rick added. "It wasn't the first."

Nor the second or third. "The others were manageable," Wyatt admitted.

"That's good to hear." Hurst relaxed back into the chair with his drink. "Though you never said, we assumed she was upset about the incident in the park with the footpad."

Wyatt nodded. "And several other things."

"The children are all right, aren't they?"

"Everyone is fine."

"So that's half the battle," Hurst added, toasting his glass toward Wyatt. "No one's hurt."

"Just Fredericka. I said things I shouldn't have."

Hurst whistled under his breath and shot a glance toward Rick as he murmured, "That's not good."

"No doubt she did too," Rick was quick to answer. "That's usually what arguments are about. Throwing words around that you don't really mean."

Yes, but he deserved everything she'd said about him. She didn't deserve what he'd said to her.

"It happens," Hurst added. "Forgive, forget, and go on to a new day. She'll be ready to make up by the time you return."

Right now he wasn't so sure. "I saw the children imitating my behavior. It was like a mirror of my life reflected to me when I saw them. Things that are fine for me aren't for them. Fredericka is the first person to make me want to change my life."

"That's deep, Wyatt. Almost poetic."

Wyatt scoffed at Rick's comment, but it was too true for him to argue with his friend about it. Wyatt's father had always said marriage was a struggle and a necessary evil. For the first time, Wyatt wondered if the reason for his father's belittling attitude about wives and marriage lay with him and not Wyatt's mother.

Fredericka had good reason to complain about him. He was probably too lenient with the children and she a little too strict. There had to be a middle somewhere they could compromise.

And a way to bury their demons. He understood how she felt about her past, Jane, and Angela too. Some things just never went away, no matter how much time passed.

Knowing how desperate she was about Jane, he should have done more. He'd start by not giving her his opinion on Jane and her sister when she wasn't asking for one.

Wyatt had to put to bed some memories about his father as well. The duke had been a good father but was wrong about wives. Wyatt didn't know why. Maybe he would have known if his mother had lived and he'd had the chance to know her. That had been denied him. It had taken Fredericka to help him understand he didn't need to be like his father and he didn't want to be like him. Wyatt wanted to love and cherish his wife.

A roar of laughter from the taproom disturbed Wyatt's thoughts.

"The reason I wanted to meet you in private rather than with the others was to tell you this is my last tournament. I'll let the rest of the club know when everyone gets back to London."

Hurst's eyes narrowed and he gave a quick glance to Rick before saying, "You sound serious."

Wyatt nodded, feeling relief and good about his decision to quit the club he helped start ten years ago.

"I've been thinking about it for a couple of weeks now."

"It was bound to come to an end for one of us sooner or later," Hurst replied. "We aren't getting any younger and the bucks we have to face are getting harder to beat."

"I'll continue to help fund the hospital," Rick said without equivocating. "You don't even have to ask about that."

"We both will," Hurst added.

Wyatt stood up. "I know, but I have something different in mind. I'll explain it all later. Right now, I'm going to do something I've never done before." He picked up his glass and downed the brandy. "I'm leaving before a tournament is finished."

Hurst rolled his shoulders and looked at Rick but remained silent.

"You are a gentleman, Wyatt," Rick said with no condemnation as the front legs of his chair hit the floor with a thud. "The club and everyone who has wagered are counting on you to play your card games and finish the tournament with a total win."

Fredericka was counting on him too, and it was past time he did what he'd promised her before they married. He'd left her in anger yesterday. That would never happen again. He would stay until they worked out their differences.

"I won my fencing match and we won the cricket game. I'm not leaving you completely without having helped. You two will have to step in and finish for me with the card games." Wyatt smiled at Rick. "You always said you were as good as I am with a deck. Now's the time to prove it."

"I'll be happy to," Rick said with a grunt.

"Say whatever excuses you like for my absence. I'm going back to London tonight to make amends with my wife."

CHAPTER 28

A CLUMP OF DAISIES

—RICHARD DANA

Ye daisies gay,
This fresh spring day,
Close gathered here together,
To play in the light,
To sleep all night,
To abide through the sullen weather.

The overnight journey back to London was arduous. Not only did Wyatt have wind and rain to contend with, the horse he'd borrowed was skittish at times and sluggish at others. He would have probably made it home faster and in much better spirits if he'd just taken the coach as his friends had urged him to do.

He walked through the front door, whipping off his drenched cloak, and stumbled over baggage in the entryway. Who the hell had come to visit, and why had Burns left the satchels in the middle of the floor?

Irritated, Wyatt looked around as he stripped off his saturated hat and gloves. Something didn't feel right. He'd grown up in this house and knew it like the back of his hand. The early hour of morning had nothing to do with the quietness that surrounded him.

He looked at the bags again. The damp hair on the

back of his neck stirred as Burns quietly appeared in the entryway.

"Where's the duchess?"

"In your book room, Your Grace. Said she needed to do something in there before she left."

Left?

Where was she going this time of day? Forgetting about his soggy boots and wet coat, Wyatt strode down the corridor with only one purpose in mind: to make up with Fredericka.

She was standing in front of the window holding sheets of foolscap in her hands. Sunlight had broken through the rain clouds and shimmered in her hair the way it had on their wedding day when they'd walked to the fence at the back of Paddleton. Their kiss in the fresh, crisp air flooded his memory with sweet feelings of how warm and right she'd felt in his arms the first time he held her close.

Yet, he sensed something wasn't as it should be. Something more than remnants of the argument they'd had before he left. His breathing felt fast and pitchy. "Fredericka?"

"You're home early." She turned to face him. "I thought to be gone before you returned."

Her rigid movements caused him to tense more. She had every right to be upset and disappointed in him too. He understood, but not the quietness of her tone and disposition. "Where are you going?"

"That's none of your concern anymore."

Not his concern? Everything about her mattered to him. His damp collar and neckcloth did nothing to lower the hot flame of irritation that flashed through him at her comment, but remembering why he rode most of the night to get home to her, he tamped down his irritation.

He wanted to make things right between them. Not to keep their argument going. But he'd never run from an opponent. He wasn't going to start with his wife. If she wanted another quarrel before they made up, he'd give it to her so they could settle their differences.

"I beg your pardon, Duchess. What you do *is* my concern."

"Not any longer."

She was too calm for her emphatic words. The blush was gone from her cheeks, and the sparkle had left her eyes. That worried him. Maybe their argument had been worse than he thought.

"I am your husband," he stated with no equivocating.

"But you are not my master or jailer," she said confidently. "I am leaving unless you are going to go back on your word and force me to stay with you."

"Fredericka." He whispered her name, walking closer to her. She sounded far too serious. "I stand by my word. I'll never force you to do anything." He inhaled short and tight, trying to control the uneasiness spreading over him. "Do you want to go to Paddleton? I have no objection."

"I don't have time to talk about this right now. I must go. Let's leave it at we married for convenience. That's no longer a relevant situation for either of us."

She was far from just serious. She was resolute. The silence in the house bothered him again. No noise, no running of little feet from the schoolroom directly above where they were standing. His stomach tightened. "Where are the children?"

"With Jane."

His stomach clenched. "For the day?"

"Forever."

His gut wrenched. "What happened?"

"It doesn't matter."

"Hell, yes it does," he snapped back at her, tension getting the best of him. "What are they doing with your cousin?"

After inhaling a deep breath and slowly letting it out, she said, "Jane came with the constable. She'd told Nelson and her brother-in-law what she'd witnessed in the book room. They talked to the Lord Chancellor and he agreed the children would be safer in Jane's care."

"You let her take the children?"

"Let her!" Fredericka exclaimed passionately. "How dare you think I *let* her?"

In a flash, she drew back her hand and slapped him across the face. His head snapped back. The sting was sharp. His ears rang as the crack of sound reverberated around the silent room. He didn't know which of them was more shocked by what she'd done, but no doubt he deserved it.

"Two men had to hold me back while Jane took them away," she whispered on a broken breath.

Rage lit inside Wyatt like a brush fire. "Someone dared to touched you?"

"They were officials from the court," she said in a softer voice, shaking as she struggled to gain control and stay strong.

"I don't care if they were saints from heaven! No one puts their hands on you."

"Then you should have been here," she shot back quickly.

The truth of her words was vivid and hit harder than her slap. "You're right. I should have. I know you wouldn't let her take them without a fight." Damn his insensitive way of speaking. His fist tightened with anger at himself for not being there, and anger at Jane for her callous disregard of Fredericka's feelings.

In that moment, Wyatt knew what he must do. First, he had to find a way to comfort Fredericka.

"It's over now." She cleared her throat.

"No, hell, it's not."

"I've had time to ponder and consider my options. It's always good to make lists. Keeps things in perspective. This morning I knew what I had to do. Not expecting you to be here, I put my intentions in a letter. No need to discuss it. You can read it later. Our marriage of convenience is no longer necessary. You don't need me and I no longer need you."

"That's not true," he whispered, shaking his head, realizing he wasn't getting through to her. There wasn't a damn good reason she should believe him. "I need you more than I ever have. I love you, Fredericka," he answered as sincerely as he knew how.

"We are simply too different to live together with any happiness. Every fiber of my being was telling me not to marry you, but you wooed me with your handsomeness, your gifts of trusts for the children, and that spark of attraction between us that wouldn't go away and leave me alone."

"That was love, and it's still there."

She straightened her shoulders. "I want you to know you were right. I do obsess over the children's behavior. I've always wanted them to be perfect." A soft, sad laugh passed her lips. "I wanted my sister to look down from Heaven and see what fine ladies and gentleman her children had grown into, and be proud of *me* so she would finally love and forgive me for encouraging her to go to London with her husband."

Remorse for all he'd said to her about Jane and her sister rushed through him. "You did nothing wrong by urging her to make the journey. You couldn't have known what would happen."

"It's hard to forgive oneself," she whispered.

Wyatt exhaled a tired sigh. "I know better than most, Fredericka."

"I miss Elise, Charles, and Bella so much. I don't think I knew how much I loved them."

"I knew." He moved closer to her. "I will be right here beside you helping to see that Angela's children grow up happy."

"No, Wyatt." She gave him a sad smile. "Your friends will always come first. I know how important your clubs and tournaments are. I gave you your inheritance, and now it's time I give you back your freedom."

"You didn't take my freedom. I gave it. I didn't finish the tournament in Oxford. I left in the middle of it. Something I've never done before, but I knew my place was here with you. I told Hurst and Rick I'm resigning from the club. No more sporting games or matches with the Brass Deck."

She still didn't believe him, but her lashes fluttered and hope stirred inside him again.

Wyatt stared into her beautiful golden-brown eyes. "You were on my mind almost every minute I was away, Fredericka. I remembered everything about you. The arguments, the laughing, the loving, hurting you with my callous words, and kissing you in the rain. I knew there were many things special about you the moment we met. I just didn't know it was love."

"Wyatt, I can't think about this or about us right now. The children are up early and Jane sleeps late. And with any luck, after yesterday, she'll be staying in bed all day with one of her headaches but I can't count on that. In any case, I intend to go visit the children. She said I could, and while I am there I will find a way to slip out the house and take them with me. I know of a place where we can go and be safe."

He smiled. It didn't surprise him she had a plan and was going after them. "I have a plan to get them too, but let me finish saying this first."

"Hurry," she murmured. "I don't know how much time I have before Jane is up and about."

Wyatt felt as if he could hardly breathe. Making her believe him right now was the most important thing he'd ever done and he wasn't sure he could hurry it. "I'm sorry I wasn't here for you when Jane came, and that I didn't do more sooner. It's easy to take things for granted when you're a duke, and I shouldn't have where you and the children are concerned. I'm sorry I let you down. It's taken me too long to realize how deep my feelings are for you. I'm sorry for the things I didn't say when I held you close and lay with you and for all the things I said that didn't turn out right. I'm sorry I made you cry."

She looked at him as if she loved him too but remained quiet. If she'd given him the slightest hint, he would have pulled her into his arms.

"Before I left, I should have told you that I've never kept a halfpenny of the money our club wins on the wagers at our games. Neither do Rick and Hurst. All our winnings go to the hospital I opened after I inherited the title almost ten years ago. We continue to support it."

"Hospital?"

"Mostly for men who were wounded fighting against Napoleon and his forces. Men who continue to have problems with wounds they'd received years ago and the military no longer supports them."

Her expression filled with kindness. "I didn't know."

"No one but the three of us know that we do this. Now you. It's not necessary anyone know what we do. I do it because of the ghosts in my past. I didn't do anything to help the lonely, hurting boys when I was at Eton. I blame it on the fact I was young and didn't understand their pain. Now I do. This way I can help men who are in pain. Some of them attended Eton as boys."

"Then no," she said, quite adamant. "You can't give up your efforts. I feel terrible for thinking all this time you were simply being callous toward my concerns. You must continue with the Brass Deck. Your cause is too important."

He shook his head. "I'm not going to stop supporting the hospital or the one my father supported. I've just found an easier way to do it. I'm going to give the hospital all the income I receive from my grandmother's estate. She obviously wanted her inheritance to go to a charity, but I couldn't let it go to an organization I had no respect for. One of the headmasters at Eton was Mr. Percival Buslingthorpe, and he was also a member of The London Poetry Society. He had an obsession with verse. In every class he carried a thick birch stick and walked around the classroom whispering, 'Discipline, son, discipline.' He'd crack his stick on the knuckles of the boys who stuttered or were so nervous they couldn't remember their poetry lines. Grant Fenway was one of them, but not for anything he did."

Her breathing grew rapid again. "Is that what's wrong with his hand?"

Wyatt nodded. "One day I hadn't learned all of my lines. Buslingthorpe said he couldn't punish me, but he'd punish one of my friends instead. So his stick came down hard on Grant. I live with the regret that he took the punishment from Buslingthorpe that should have been mine."

"What a deplorable man," she whispered.

"I have no idea how many boys he might have injured over the years he taught there. So no, Fredericka, I don't like poetry and make no apologies. I don't like the word 'discipline' and make no apologies for that either. I should have explained this to you earlier but it's never been easy to talk about."

Compassion showed in her eyes and expression. "I'm glad you told me."

"There's something else you need to understand. I love you. I need you, and I don't want to live one day without you in my life." He reached over and ran his finger across her soft cheek. "I won't stop you from leaving me or even from leaving the house right now to go get the children, but I have an easier way to get them. Your way is temporary. My way we will make sure we keep them until they are ready to make lives of their own. I'm not coming back until I have them with me where they belong and settle this for good. I hope you'll be here when I return."

Wyatt turned and headed for the door. With no promise from her, each step was a struggle. At the threshold, he heard his name and turned.

"I love you," she said, and bounded into his arms.

He circled her waist and caught her to his chest, pressing his face into the curve of her neck feeling as if he'd been given a new chance at life. "I love you so much," he whispered as his fingers curled into the folds of her clothing.

"I'm so glad you came back. I've been lost. I need you and love you more—"

His lips came down on hers before she finished the sentence. They kissed with such tender passion it stole Wyatt's breath. "I was beginning to believe you were going to let me walk away without saying a word."

"I'm not letting you leave without me," she answered, clinging to him as if she meant to never let him go. "I'm going with you to get the children."

The trust in her eyes made his heartbeat pound. He may not deserve her but he was glad she was his. He placed his hands on the sides of her face and looked into her eyes. "You need to stay here. What I have to say to him is something that needs to be said man-to-man."

"No," she replied with a smile. "You can tell me all about it on the way. We are a family, Wyatt. We are going to do this together."

CHAPTER 29

THE PASSION FLOWER
—BARTON

We roam the seas—give new-found isles
Some King's or Conqueror's name;
We rear on earth triumphal piles,
As meeds of earthly fame.

The butler at the Lord Chancellor's house had been trained well and was good at his job. He used several stalling tactics in hopes Wyatt and Fredericka would get tired and leave. The longer they waited in straight back chairs in the vestibule, the more determined they became to spend the entire day and night waiting for the man if they had to.

Finally, they were invited into the Lord Chancellor's book room. The man stood and bowed when Wyatt and Fredericka entered, but wore his displeasure on his lean, wrinkled face.

"Please, sit down, Your Graces," he offered, though he never bothered to look at Fredericka. Most men felt ladies had no place in matters of business.

"We'll stand," Wyatt said. "This won't take long."

"I am glad to hear it. My days are busy and long. I don't usually receive anyone at home or my office this early in the day. I do this out of respect to your titles. If you say it's urgent, I take you at your word it is."

"We appreciate your concession."

"Let's get to it, shall we? What can I do for you?"

Wyatt and Fredericka walked in tandem closer to the desk. Wyatt took an imposing stance. He didn't want there to be any misunderstanding about how important this was to him. "Mrs. Nelson Tomkin has my wife's children. I want them back."

"The matter has been handled." He waved his hand dismissively. "I was told the children were neglected to the point they were put in harm's way. When Mrs. Tomkin entered the room there was no adult present. A decision was needed immediately for their safety. I'll make the official ruling next week and award her husband, Mr. Tomkin, guardianship of the children."

Wyatt felt Fredericka start to move forward to confront the man but he stayed her by putting his hand out in front of her. The Lord Chancellor's flippant attitude infuriated Wyatt as much as it did Fredericka, but staying calm was necessary. "You might want to listen to what I have to say before you do that."

"I don't," he said, this time including Fredericka in his glance. "I believe I told you when we met, Your Grace, I rule on what is best for the child if he is in danger." He looked down at his desk as if he couldn't be more uninterested. "However, if you insist, go ahead, and I'll listen."

The Lord Chancellor was making it easy for Wyatt to do what he had to do. "I've tried to handle this matter between my wife and her cousin honorably. But you have allowed yourself to be used by your friendship with Viscount Longington and perhaps my political leanings as well to punish my wife."

"I've done no such thing." He looked at Fredericka as if she was the one who had done this to him. "I don't know what you've heard, but you do me a discredit, Your Grace. I was told the children were in serious danger by ingesting unknown amounts of spirits and tobacco. I acted only in their best interest."

He was making this too easy for Wyatt. "I'm glad you mentioned a child's best interest, but perhaps you are selective about that. When you indicated you sometimes grant political favors, I think one of them was to save your own political power. I hadn't wanted to say anything about your wife's only brother, whom she adores."

The Lord Chancellor went still. His eyes seemed to want to burn holes into Wyatt. "Now see here, Your Grace, I will not discuss my family with you."

"But you are more than happy to discuss mine or anyone else's," Fredericka said in haste.

"It is my sworn duty to do so."

Wyatt stepped closer to the desk, keeping his gaze pointedly on the man's ashen face. "I don't like discussing my family with you either. The truth is that I could have told the story about your brother-in-law when I learned of it, but you see, I have always considered wives and children off-limits to gossip, scandal, and people who are self-serving. Something that you, Viscount Longington, and the Tomkins don't seem to have a problem with. I didn't want to hurt or punish your wife and her family with gossip that might or might not be true. However, you leave me no choice but to reveal it because you have so ruthlessly wounded mine."

"Are you threatening me, Your Grace?" His stare was unyielding.

"I'm making you a promise." Wyatt put his hands on the desk and leaned toward the Chancellor.

Fredericka put her hand on Wyatt's arm. "Allow me to say this, Your Grace."

Wyatt straightened and Fredericka leaned on the desk in his place. She looked directly into the man's eyes. "You either bring the children to us before we leave this house today, or we are going straight to *The Times* and telling them all we know about your wife's brother, both his marriages, and the children's inheritances. What would the head of your party think if it was suspected the man who is in charge of trusts, wills, and guardianships for all children has allowed his own brother-in-law to pilfer and raid his stepchildren's inheritances?"

"All lies," the Lord Chancellor said, his head tremoring. "That was gossip started by a disgruntled family member."

"As was what you heard from a *disgruntled family member* about our children," Fredericka said without blinking a lash. "Gossip hurts whether or not it's true."

"And not just the children of your brother-in-law's first wife," Wyatt reminded him for emphasis, "but also his second wife's children, so he could keep his gambling habits and debts a secret. What do you think your party will do about a man who would allow something like that to happen?"

The man's lean frame shook with fury.

"So tell us, Chancellor," Wyatt continued. "Should we sit down and wait for the children to arrive so we can take them with us, or should we walk out the door?"

EPILOGUE

A wearied man seeks not the smiles
That brightly beam on all,
For dearer are thy simple wiles
That only one enthrall.

"Be patient, Bella," Fredericka instructed as she stood in front of the window in the drawing room, trying to make a small loop in a length of thread. "It will feel better if we can get it out."

"But it hurts," the little girl who had just celebrated her sixth birthday whimpered. "I need a different color of thread. Blue hurts."

Fredericka huffed and smiled. "Don't be silly. The color doesn't matter. Neither red nor yellow thread will make a difference in how it feels when the tooth comes out."

"No, I don't want to lose it. It's mine."

"You're being a baby," Charles spouted from close by, insisting he wanted to watch.

"I'm not a baby. You are a poo-poo bird."

"Don't call her a baby," Elise demanded, looking up from her reading to defend her little sister. "It hurts and you know it. You cried when yours came out."

"I did not." Charles squealed and ran around the room singing, "Bella's being a baby."

Elise threw her book down, quickly caught up with him, and belted him on the back of the shoulder with the palm of her hand. "She's not a baby."

"You better not do that again or I'll forget Uncle Your Grace told me not to hit girls."

Fredericka started to tell them all to be quiet and sit down but remembered how happy she was to have them back home with her. With thanks to Wyatt, she'd made a promise to herself that she would love them more and discipline them less. She was learning to put up with a little disorder and confrontation between siblings by letting them work out their own issues between themselves.

"What's going on in here?" Wyatt asked, walking into the drawing room, looking as handsome as the day she married him.

Warmth from the glow in his eyes settled over her. Fredericka smiled. That was only one of the million reasons she loved him. "Bella's tooth is hurting again. I think it's ready to come out, but she's not cooperating with me."

"Let me see," he said, bending down on one knee to Bella's level. "It looks to me as if your aunt is using the wrong color of thread. What do you think?"

Bella nodded and sniffled. "I tried to tell her."

Wyatt glanced up at Fredericka and winked. "Sometimes you don't need thread at all. Can you open wider and let me have a look?"

She nodded.

Cautiously, Wyatt put his thumb and forefinger in her mouth, and almost as quickly as his fingers went in, they came out holding her tooth.

She gave him a snaggletoothed grin. "Here, take it and go wash up."

"Let me hold it for you so you won't drop it," Charles said.

"I want to see it," Elise said, rushing over.

"All of you, go up and help her take care of the tooth," Wyatt said. "I need a few minutes with Fredericka."

The children ran out squealing while Wyatt slipped his arms around Fredericka's waist and kissed her sweetly on the lips.

"You do have a good way with the children," she told him. "I don't know why I can't be more patient."

He pressed her close and kissed her briefly again. "You have your strengths and I have mine. It evens out. Now, there's something we need to talk about."

Fredericka hesitated, removing her arms from around his neck. "I'm not sure I like the seriousness I see in your face."

"You may not like what I've done, but I felt I had to do this. Stay right there." He walked over to the doorway and motioned for someone to come forward.

Her curiosity plunged as Jane walked into the room with all the confident aplomb she always managed. Her skirts swirled and her fringed reticule bounced against her summer-blue pelisse.

Startled to see her cousin, Fredericka couldn't say or do anything. Her whole body went rigid. She hadn't seen Jane since the day she took the children away more than a month ago.

"Silence isn't what I expected between the two of you," Wyatt said, giving his attention to his wife. "It took me more than a couple of visits with Jane to convince her to come over."

"What for?" Fredericka asked tightly.

"It's time you two made peace for the good of Charles, Bella, and Elise. She's made the first step in agreeing to see you."

"Peace?" Jane asked in her usual pleasant way. "We're not at war. As you can see, we're not even speaking."

Fredericka remained quiet. She only wanted Jane to leave. Her cousin had never brought her anything but heartache.

"I want that to change between you," Wyatt said. "You both need to put the past behind you."

That wasn't going to happen. Fredericka cleared her throat and breathed in deeply.

"You are family," Wyatt continued. "The children ask about Jane and want to see her. It's time to mend your fences, once and for all."

"I don't know if I can," Fredericka replied, remembering the afternoon Jane and the constable took the children away.

"I understand completely," Jane said, walking closer to Fredericka. "I'm not here because the duke asked me to come today, and I'm not asking for anything from you. I agreed to come because I have something to give you."

Fredericka looked at Wyatt. He shrugged and lightly shook his head. He had no idea what it was. Fredericka remained stiff and wary.

Jane opened her reticule and pulled out a multitude of scraps of parchment, foolscap, and vellum and extended the handful toward Fredericka.

Remembering the last time Jane pulled that stunt, Fredericka scoffed, "I am not interested in old gossip sheets. It's time for you to leave."

To Fredericka's surprise, Jane walked closer and gave

her one of her prettiest smiles. "It's poetry, my dear. Yours."

Fredericka's gaze flew to Wyatt. "Poetry" wasn't a word they said in this house. He shrugged again, indicating he didn't know what was going on, but he nodded for her to take the papers.

Still, she hesitated. "Mine?" Fredericka asked, wondering what mischief her cousin might be up to.

"It's the gibberish you wrote when you were a little girl." Jane cleared her throat and lifted her chin in a toffee-nosed way before continuing. "Poetry you used to write and give to me and Angela as a way to get our attention. Most of it has our names on it, so you'll know which was for me, which I'm sure you'll want to throw away, and what you wrote to your sister. Perhaps, you'll keep those."

Fredericka couldn't move. Her cousin, who had reviled her as an annoying little girl and a nuisance, had kept her poetry? Wyatt walked over, took the pages from Jane, and handed them to Fredericka. She looked down at them. Her heart felt as if it might beat out of her chest. Jane was right. It was Fredericka's poetry. She recognized the flowers, hearts, and curlicues she'd drawn at the bottom of the pages, and her very fancy F to begin her name.

"Where did you, how did you, get them?"

"Well, from you, of course. You gave them to us two and three times a week during the dead of winter when there was nothing much to do. After we read them, we'd throw them into a box. We didn't read them again that I remember, but you were our sister, and we didn't want to throw them away. I left the box at my parents' home when I married and came across them when I was sorting through other things. I should have given them to you then. But you know me. I never found the time to bring them to you. Perhaps you'll only want to burn them anyway. They weren't very good."

It was so like Jane to get in that last remark. Fredericka could never destroy her own childhood. She would treasure each one. This was the best peace offering Jane could have brought her. She loved having this remembrance of her childhood to read again, savor, and keep with her forever.

She looked at Jane, standing as tall, proud, and confident as always. "I don't know what to say."

"Nothing, of course," she answered. "That's always best. Perhaps this will make up to you for the way Angela and I always ran away from you when we were nothing but silly girls ourselves. Just older."

Yes. It did. "I can't believe you kept them when you hated me."

"Hated you?" Her eyes held steady on Fredericka's. "What an awful word. You should know I'm not capable of hating anyone. Especially not family."

Fredericka was astounded by her comment.

"You were *our* little sister. I always claimed you, even when it made Angela mad. We both loved you, Fredericka. We may not have wanted you around, listening to our conversations, and being obnoxious with your shrill little voice and demanding ways, but we loved you. Don't be ridiculous."

Fredericka couldn't believe how truthful Jane sounded.

"Angela and I had adult things to talk about and you were just a child. We wanted to discuss the boys we'd see when we went into the village, getting old enough to go to dances, having lace on our unmentionables, and the girls we didn't like. You couldn't understand any of that.

You weren't old enough. But we loved you. Do you think we would have rushed to jump in the bed with you during storms when you were so little if we hated you? We didn't want you to feel alone and frightened even though you never acted as if you were."

Tears rushed to Fredericka's eyes and she fought to hold them in. She'd always thought they'd come to her room because they were frightened—not her. Wyatt came up behind her and lightly touched her waist.

"We read every poem you wrote us because *you* gave them to us."

"You never told me you read them. Why didn't you let me know?"

Jane sighed heavily and looked around the room. "Perhaps we didn't have the time." Her expression softened and her eyes looked dewy too. "I always told you Angela loved me best because I was so jealous you had a sister and I didn't. Many times I wished Angela was my sister, not yours. As ugly and selfish as it is, that's the truth of it. I suppose that, and my barren state, is why I wanted her children."

Fredericka didn't understand that kind of love, but Jane seemed more sincere than she'd ever been. And for the first time, Fredericka was feeling Angela must have loved her, just not in the way Fredericka felt she was entitled.

"I have one more thing before I go," Jane continued. "I am sorry, Fredericka. I hope one day you can forgive me for taking the children from you. For wanting to. I don't mean this harshly, but it will sound that way. Someone who has no reason to doubt they can be a mother has no way of knowing the extreme agony and heartbreak of a woman who knows she will never have a child of her own. No excuse, but the truth. Just because I can't have children of my own doesn't mean I can have Angela's. They are rightly yours."

"Thank you for that, Jane."

"Don't feel sorry for me. I see it in your eyes. I'm still upset I didn't get my way. I don't know what made the Lord Chancellor change his mind. The headache I had from his decision put me in bed for over a week. It's probably best we didn't get the children. Nelson and I are busy. Constantly having them underfoot would be a nuisance. Much like you were to me and Angela."

Jane's reminder pricked, but not as much as it used to. She was learning to forgive and forget the past.

"Life becomes much easier when you accept you are never going to get what you really wanted. Nelson and I will never have children."

"You don't know that, Jane," she said, finding herself sensing her cousin's sadness.

"It's been eight years now. Nelson said it didn't matter to him. It always mattered to me. I won't try again to take them from you. But I'd like to see them." She looked at Wyatt. "If the duke will allow it."

"I have no objections, Mrs. Tomkin," Wyatt said softly. "But it's up to Fredericka."

"Bella lost her first tooth today," Fredericka said, making an attempt to mend their relationship. "Would you like to go up and see her?"

"Not today. I don't have time."

Fredericka smiled and nodded. Jane was back to her old self.

"There's one other thing though," Jane said. "If, God forbid, anything should happen to the two of you, Nelson and I would like to be listed as guardians for the children."

"With Fredericka's permission, I'll see it's done."

"We are family, Jane. I'd like to keep it that way, but I need to think on this before I answer."

Jane smiled. "Of course. I'll be around soon to see the children. Don't bother seeing me out. I know my way."

With a swoosh of skirts, she was gone. Fredericka's limbs suddenly felt weak. She didn't know what to make of everything Jane said. She didn't know if she could trust her cousin. It would take time.

Wyatt slipped the old poems from Fredericka's hands and laid them on the desk. "Do you know what I think?" he asked, as he circled her waist with his arms.

Fredericka looked into his eyes and nodded.

"I think she truly thought for a time the children were in danger. We were all disturbed seeing the cheroot between Bella's lips and the full glasses of brandy beside them. I believe she loves you in her own way and the children."

"I'm not sure she loves me at all," Fredericka answered, still trying to understand all Jane had said. "It was nice to hear her say she was sorry and ask forgiveness."

"Saying 'I'm sorry' is never out of line for anyone and it is one of the hardest things to say. She owed you that. I also believed her when she said your sister loved you. She and Jane just had a different way of showing it." He reached down and kissed the top of her head. "I like the way you show love better."

Fredericka laughed softly. "Are you just trying to make me feel better because I've been jealous of her relationship with my sister all my life?"

"No. I don't think she was either. She wasn't forced to come. I don't think anyone could make Jane say something she didn't want to say. Maybe she simply missed arguing with you." Wyatt kissed her lips briefly, softly.

"Just leave it at she's different from you and sometimes we have to realize and accept those differences. I was told all my life that I was just like my father. It took you coming into my life for me to realize I'm not like my father."

Her brows rose. "Does that mean you don't want us to wait until you are forty to have our first child?" she said with a curious smile.

"When it happens, it happens. All I want to do is love my beautiful wife forever as deeply as I do right now and to enjoy your body just the way it is."

"I like you doing that too."

"I have a surprise for you," he said. "Wait right here."

"I'm not sure I can handle another surprise today."

"You'll like this one." He was gone only seconds and came back in the drawing room holding his hands behind his back. When he brought them around, it was a book with a white ribbon wrapped around it.

"Do you know what the color white represents?" he asked, giving it to her.

"Purity."

"Ah, yes, but something else too. A truce. You can have poetry in the house and fill the book room with it if you want to. Here is your first copy."

"Wyatt," she whispered, her chest swelling with love. Her eyes searched his as her hands clutched the book tightly. "Are you sure?"

He smiled. "I thought it was time for me to put my ghosts to rest."

Fredericka untied the white ribbon. She fingered the soft leather as she read: *The Lady's Book of Flowers and Poetry.*

"The book is a compilation of poetry written about flowers by ladies, and some gentlemen," Wyatt told her.

"Like you, they are poets who wanted to put their talents together in a book so they could enjoy each other's poetry. I thought you could read this and, perhaps, one day publish your own book." He nodded to her childish poems on the desk.

Fredericka looked at her verses too. "Probably not those." She smiled. "Thank you for relenting on your oath to never have poetry in the house. This is so beautiful. I'm thrilled and can't wait to read the first one." She kissed him tenderly.

"Perhaps one day you can read some of your poetry to me."

He wanted to read some of her poetry? Her heart lifted and she smiled. "Would you really like that?"

"Elise loves your poetry. Charles . . . ?" Wyatt shook his head.

Fredericka laughed. "I'm so grateful you changed your mind, but I think you have something wrong."

His eyes narrowed. "What do you mean?"

"A truce means we have a treaty. We aren't going to fight anymore. A white ribbon means surrender."

He nodded and pulled her up to his chest. "It does, and I surrender my heart, my love, and my life to you, Fredericka."

Her eyes closed and she breathed in deeply. "I love you, Wyatt."

"And I love you, my darling."

Wyatt placed his lips on hers and Fredericka thrilled to her husband's touch.

AUTHOR'S NOTE

Dear Readers,

I hope you enjoyed the first book of my new series. A marriage of convenience story has always been one of my favorites to read, and they are a joy to write. Fredericka and Wyatt's tale of how they reached their happily-ever-after was so special to me because I loved watching their love grow around and involve the children.

There was no lack of discipline in boys' schools during the Regency, and cruel corporal punishment is well-documented. At times it was unfair and inhumane, but it is a part of our history. The referenced character of Mr. Buslingthorpe was loosely based on a man named John Keate, who was a headmaster at Eton from 1809 until 1834. Though he was a strict disciplinarian and known for using his birch stick often and without mercy, he was also known for making much-needed changes in how boys were taught. Though it may be hard for us to believe today, Mr. Keate remained a well-respected man in Regency London throughout his life.

All the beautiful lines of poetry at the beginning of each chapter come from *The Lady's Book of Flowers and Poetry*, published in 1859 by Derby & Jackson and edited by Lucy Hooper. I have an original copy I used.

The poets in the book were happy to share their poetry with others. The name of each author, the wording, and punctuation of the poetry is listed in my story as it's printed in the book. I hope you found the old poems of yesteryear as enjoyable as I do.

Please watch for the next two books in my Say I Do series, *Sincerely, The Duke* and *Love, The Duke.*

Hearing from readers is always a pleasure. You can email me at ameliagreyauthor@gmail.com, follow me on Facebook at Facebook.com/AmeliaGreyBooks, or visit my website at ameliagrey.com.

Happy reading!

Amelia Grey